P

CW01522143

'It may end up 1
My Brother Jack as one of the great Australian ...
melodramas of love, war and divided allegiance.'
—**AUSTRALIAN BOOK REVIEW**

'If you start this book be sure to have a few free hours ahead
—it is not to be put down.'
—**AUSTRALIAN BOOKSELLER AND PUBLISHER**

'tightly plotted and gripping love story ... emotionally
engaging, morally challenging and historically confronting.'
—**COURIER-MAIL**

'An authentic and action-packed evocation of an era when
life was turned on its head and no one quite knew what the
morning skies would bring.'
—**HERALD SUN**

'Woven of tantalising snippets and packed with adventure.'
—**SUNDAY AGE**

'a captivating ... moving, story about charting territory and
desiring a fixed place in a world where every point of the
compass has shifted.'
—**SYDNEY MORNING HERALD**

'Disher has written a persistently exciting book ... with a
spritely and compelling confidence.'
—**BULLETIN**

GARRY DISHER lives on the Mornington Peninsula in Victoria. His novels, many of which have been published overseas, include *The Divine Wind*, winner of the NSW Premier's Ethel Turner Award, *Kickback*, winner of the German Crime Fiction Prize 2000, *The Bamboo Flute*, regarded as a classic of Australian children's literature, and *The Sunken Road*, nominated for the Booker Prize.

PAST *the* HEADLANDS

GARRY DISHER

ALLEN&UNWIN

This edition published in 2002
First published in 2001

Allen & Unwin
83 Alexander Street
Crows Nest NSW 2065
Australia
Phone: (61 2) 8425 0100
Fax: (61 2) 9906 2218
Email: info@allenandunwin.com
Web: www.allenandunwin.com

National Library of Australia
Cataloguing-in-Publication entry:

Disher, Garry, 1949–.
  Past the headlands.

  ISBN 1 86508 827 7.

  1. Ranches — Western Australia — Kimberley — Fiction
  2. Man–woman relationships — Fiction. 3. Singapore — History —
  Japanese occupation, 1942–1945 — Fiction. I. Title.

A823.3

Set in 12/14 pt Bembo by Asset Typesetting Pty Ltd
Printed by McPherson's Print Group

10 9 8 7 6 5 4 3 2 1

For Tim Healey

Table of Contents

Acknowledgements

The writing of this novel was assisted by the Commonwealth Government through the Australia Council, its arts funding and advisory body.

Portions of the novel first appeared in the following publications: *Overland, Island* and Caro Llewellyn (ed.), *My One True Love* (Sydney, 1999).

My thanks to Lucy Healey, Liam Davison and Carl Harrison-Ford for their perceptive readings of the novel while it was in manuscript form.

As a novel of Malaya, Singapore, Sumatra and north-western Australia between December 1941 and April 1942, *Past the Headlands* combines actual and imagined events, the latter faithful to the spirit of time and place. I drew upon a number of published and unpublished sources for background: see 'A Note on the Sources' at the end of the book.

Exultation is the going
Of an inland soul to sea,
Past the houses—past the headlands—
Into deep Eternity—

Bred as we, among the mountains,
Can the sailor understand
The divine intoxication
Of the first league out from land?

—Emily Dickinson, 'Exultation is the Going'

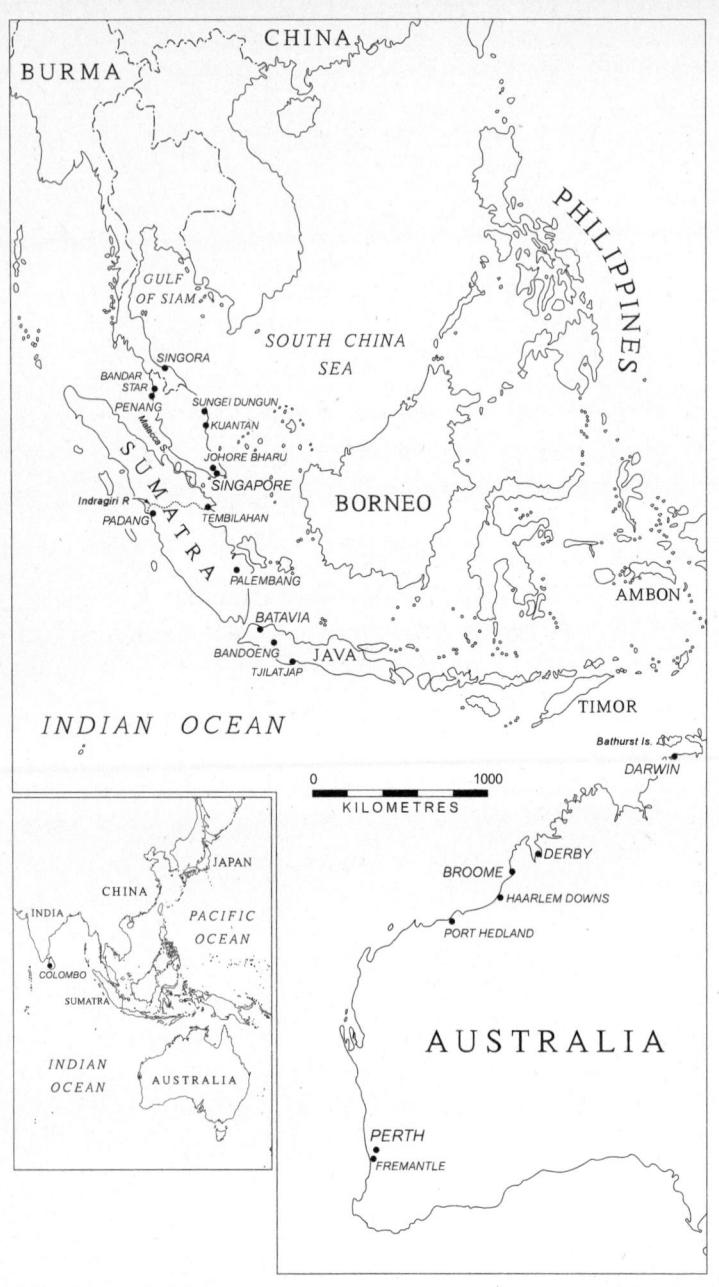

Prologue

*Haarlem Downs Station,
Kimberley coast, north-west
Australia, 1934*

Machine Dreams

In the days and nights of his reckoning with the heat, the dust and his wrong-footed ways, the boy has this: the hushed bite of his tyres along the sheep pads before the world awakens. He freewheels over the packed dirt in a smooth, irresistible dash, occasionally backpedalling for a root or stone-reef kink in the trail. In the east, the basalt escarpment is a static line of pink, a long wave breaching. Soon it will turn, brushed fully red by the sun. In the west, not so far away, the Indian Ocean is breaking along the Eighty Mile Beach. The sheep pads give out at the dunes. You must lean forward and high-step up their flanks, your machine balanced on one shoulder, to reach the downslope and the hard sand at the edge of the water. There might be a pearling fleet on the horizon, or even a Dutch guilder washed up on to the sand after three hundred years of motion and encrustation on the bed of the sea. Neil Quiller has these things, too. Otherwise there is only his numbness.

But then, as he coasts along the sheep pads in the elongated shadows of the rising sun, he registers two faint wheel-thumps in the cork handgrips. He wobbles, risking a backward glance, and sees a snake rear up, hunting him before it flicks away into the grass. Of what use against snakes are puttees, thorn-proof tyres and the sections of rope he'd mounted between the forks to scrape away the burrs? Uncle Leonard's blacksmith hadn't prepared him for snakes.

He begins to tremble. His elbow joints can't sustain his weight, nor his knee joints drive the pedals. He dismounts and ploughs along the bed of a dry watercourse until he's clear of tricky grass shadows and living things, then sits on the ground, breathing in and out, listening to the blood jolt in his temples. Presently, his wits restored, he stretches out on the accommodating sand. If the sand were a February snowfall in the north of England, he'd mark it with an angel.

Strange to think that time here is ten hours ahead of time there. If it's dawn here then a long twilight must be settling there, along the River Tyne. In his old life he would be resisting sleep about now, protesting to his mother that it was too light outside for sleep to come. He might even slip through the back lane to watch for owls nesting in Jesmond Dene, where, in the breezeless shadows, hot voices murmur, waistbands snap, fabrics scrape against thighs, coal eyes flare, and raw smoke drifts. On still nights you can hear the riveters at work in the shipyards. Then darkness and a new day. Perhaps not a school day but one spent with his mother, a day kind to her wasted chest, when she might rally and take him by train to Durham or the Roman wall in one direction, or the priory sacked by the Danes in the other, where three ancient kings lie buried on the headland, together with lives more recently lost to the sea, old age or the experience of childbirth.

And so Neil Quiller brings his mind to his mother's grave, which is hard against the wall that divides the cemetery from the school where he'd had a measure of happiness.

The light had seemed shallower in Newcastle, with tree canopies, lamp posts and chimneytops always crowding the margins of sight. He'd never had cause to gaze up and name the colour of the sky.

As he does here, on the other side of the world.

He opens his eyes. The sky is limitless above him, and he can't bear it.

•   •   •

Perhaps his mother had felt the sky pressing down upon her, too. She'd bolted from it in the end.

In 1917, after a sea voyage of sixteen weeks, she was posted with other nurses to an army hospital south of London. It wasn't duty calling, but adventure, for Hazel had always inclined toward risks and opportunities.

All those sweet fellows passing through her ministering hands. She saw many of them die of wounds, scoured lungs and hopelessness.

Then the war ended and she set out for Aberdeen. She couldn't go back to the north-west of Australia, only forward to somewhere else. 'I thought Scotland would be as good a place as any. But as we crossed the Tyne Bridge you were kicking so much inside me, and I was so taken with the river, the ships and the castle, that I got off the train there and then.'

She was full of stories like that, and full of secrets. Neil listened, put two and two together, and conjured up who his father might have been: an English officer, no, an Australian, no, a Canadian, a soldier with a hard, flat, tobaccoey chest for cushioning a son's love-starved little spine. A man who always wore a grin; lights always danced in his eyes. A man who later died, or went home.

But Neil's mother would say, 'Oh, your dad could be anywhere now, son. Not to worry. We have each other.'

Newcastle was an end to the bolting. There was a son to raise, and plenty of work for a nurse in a city of furnaces and molten metal. She settled in Jesmond, just a twenty-minute walk from the Royal Infirmary and the centre of the city. When, thirteen years later, her lungs gave in to the prevailing dampness, Neil wondered if they'd failed in sympathy with the lungs of her soldiers and shipwrights. She hid nothing from him; it was her way of preparing him for her death, and soon he was so immersed in her dying that it was like a condition of her life.

But she wouldn't confirm or deny that his father was a Canadian soldier.

'Auntie Crystal and Uncle Len will take you, dear,' she said. 'Be brave for me now.'

• • •

Neil, his steamer trunk and his bicycle were at sea for fourteen weeks. In Fremantle the agent for the line met him, hurrying him along the wharf, saying, 'We don't have much time.' Apparently Neil was to board another ship, the monthly Fremantle to Singapore steamer, which would drop him at Broome. For the next six days he stood at the rail, in vegetably currents of air, as crates of fresh provisions for the northern ports rotted around him.

Crystal, his mother's sister, met him at the other end, holding a scented handkerchief to her nose. She was as stiff and plaited as a length of rope, with the rawboned look of a disappointed woman in a drying climate—not a bit like his mother, who'd been round and soft until just before she died, and always shrewd and humorous. As Neil walked beside her down the long jetty in Roebuck Bay, the bicycle ticking against his hip, a Koepanger behind them carrying the steamer trunk, his aunt didn't once ask after him, or speculate, or mention Hazel's death. It was as if she couldn't get her head around England, a sea voyage or the needs and grief of a thirteen-year-old boy. Neil observed the line of her lips and was reminded of a day toward the end, a letter crushed in his mother's claw:

'My sister has never mentioned you, acknowledged that I'm sick, or offered to come and be with me, even though Leonard would have paid for her ticket. I was always the favoured older sister, with the looks, brains and luck, and apparently I'm still the favoured one, even on my deathbed.'

His mother had paused then, looking down the years. 'Leonard was in love with me, you know.'

Feeling that he was another raw deal in the life of his aunt, Neil walked mutely to the end of the jetty, where a dusty touring car waited under a tree. Haarlem Downs, Crystal told him, was six hours away, dirt road all the way.

That first evening, his cousin Cameron had said: 'Neil, say "home".'

'Hawm.'

'Hah! Say "stand".'

Neil obliged. 'Stund.'

The Dunns grinned at him around the dining-room table.

The gleam in Crystal's eyes was like a nail in Hazel's coffin; Uncle Leonard's pipe sucked wetly; Cameron watched beneath his lazy lids. Neil pulled his familiar numbness around himself and sawed at his slab of goat. He was in a solid room in a house on a frontier. The dining chairs were upholstered in buffalo hide, rifles sat on wooden pegs above the sideboard, there was a chipped piano, and porcelain dishes and shepherd girls gathered dust on the shelves. He knew at once that he'd never be able to take on the Dunns' colouring, or make their stories his own, even if he'd wanted to.

'Say "lass",' Cameron said.

'Luss.'

Leonard removed his pipe from his teeth. 'Cam, leave your cousin alone.'

Neil glanced at his uncle in gratitude, and saw the man's pain. *You're the spitting image of your mother:* the first thing Uncle Leonard had said to him.

Neil climbs to his feet, brushing off the sand. The half-light is the time for a thumping heart: curses snarled after him at dusk in Jesmond Dene, snakes in the early-morning dirt beside the Indian Ocean, bad memories.

He remounts and pedals across the flat. He's been on Haarlem Downs for a year now; he's mapped its ruptures and corrugations, been mired in mud and bulldust, splashed across claypans, and traversed wastes of tiny red abraded stone chips—red as though giants had passed by, trailing blood spots. He's even woven the S of American dollar signs around the parallel bars of his old tyre marks, and last month he tracked the leper patrol, the crisp outlines of horseshoes and the softer depressions of bare feet where Trooper Dalvean and his mounted native constables had walked half-a-dozen blacks chained together at the neck.

Neil rides to be solitary, and to encourage the past— sometimes even to banish it—but a part of him is always alert to the singing of his bicycle. Every run is a test run, the wheels, saddle, pedals and handlebars transmitters of information: the chain is working loose; a thread is worn; he's lost a nut in the dust behind him; a welded joint is fatigued.

This time it's the saddle. It begins to tip forward, and wrenches left and right with the motion of his inner thighs. He dismounts: a nut is missing.

He walks the bicycle home.

This is a country where men, women and children flow into their horses, assuming fluid new configurations. As Neil passes the stallion paddock and heads toward the workshop, one hand on the loose saddle, Cameron appears, cantering across the main yard on a mare, his body whipping lazily.

Too late—Cameron has seen him. 'Who's this on a pushbike? A shearer? A ratbag from the union?' He strikes his head with the heel of his hand: 'Wait a minute, it's the lud.'

Cameron canters away again. Neil tracks him past the gins' hut and the cook's quarters and on to the flatland at the edge of Haarlem Downs, where the black stockmen are slopping white paint along a roundstone border and raking and picking clean the new surface. Soon Cameron is no more than a dusty wraith and Neil, watching in his mind's eye, sees him dismount at a distant stand of acacias, where a horse is tethered, and call: 'Jeannie, Jeannie.'

Forget the pair of them. Neil enters the workshop, a vast, cool, dim wooden shed with a sump-oiled dirt floor. It's filled with the odours of hammered metal, hot manifolds, welded pipes, patched inner tubes, and needle valves and dampers soaking in bowls of oily petrol. Tools hang from a wall of stencilled shapes above the main workbench—heaven help those who borrow and fail to rehang them. Neil stops in the shaft of light at the open door and scans the crowded interior, finally locating the blacksmith in a far corner, crouched at a pump. There's an eight-cylinder engine waiting for attention in an angle-iron cradle nearby, together with a tumbled stack of crooked artesian pipes and a broken mangle from the laundry. Wally Webb is irreplaceable. He can stitch a torn chair, carve a table leg or plait a stockwhip.

'The lud himself,' Wally says.

It's a friendly mutter. The blacksmith is absorbed with packing ball bearings in grease, and doesn't have enough fingers for the task. His bony chin juts downward into the guts of the pump. 'Neil, would you hold this for me, please?'

Their foreheads touch. Before he met the blacksmith, Neil's hands hadn't been good for anything but holding a spoon or wiping his arse. From the very start Wally had refused to repair the bicycle from England. Instead he'd demonstrated how it might be done, extolling the simple beauty of logical thought. Presently Neil developed nimble fingers and a knack for plotting the stages of a mechanical task before he performed it, and soon he could think his way into the secret motions of an engine or a gear assembly, or the stresses and strains of a chassis, as others are born to assume horses.

'All done,' Wally says.

They stand, wiping their fingers with scraps of cotton sheet. 'Your saddle's offline, son.'

'I lost a nut.'

'Have a gander under the bench.'

Neil crouches at a crate of mismatched bolts, nuts and washers. Behind him the blacksmith's boots scuff softly across the dirt floor. Wally is often drawn to the open door. He likes to lean on the doorframe and woolgather for a minute or two, his eyes fixed on the indeterminate line between the sand and the sky.

He coughs. 'Cameron was in here a minute ago. Said the boss radioed from Wyndham. We can expect him within the hour.'

Neil finds a replacement nut and joins the blacksmith. Together they gaze out at the landing strip. The hands have finished raking and painting. There's a windsock at one end but no wind, and no hangar yet. A month ago there hadn't even been an airstrip.

'Pull a long face and carry on.'

Neil knows what the blacksmith is thinking. He's thinking about the extra work that an aeroplane will bring: an unfamiliar engine, dust, dirty fuel, bent struts, tears in the fabric.

Wally returns to the comforting shadows, leaving Neil to watch as two figures materialise from the heat shimmers on the flat beyond the border of stones. Jeannie Verco must have been off with her sketchbook again, and Cam is fetching her back to wait for Leonard's arrival. They walk their horses as though they have all the time in the world, but eventually step over the white stone border and pick their way delicately across the landing strip toward the workshop. When Jeannie spots Neil she stands in the saddle, waving, grinning enough to turn his heart over. Are they special or indiscriminate, these smiles of hers? Is she being charitable? Where Cameron has proximity and history on his side, horse sense and carelessness, Neil is no more than the poor, pale cousin from a buttoned-down, penny-pinching land. Ah, well, Jeannie won't be here next week. She'll be down south again, in a pleated uniform, attending chapel, playing hockey, reading Wordsworth with her inky fingers, waiting for the May holidays to roll around.

Neil steps away from the workshop and helps her to dismount. Dismounting is something she's done since she could walk, but she thanks him from a well of affection and good humour. At that moment they both stiffen, hearing the faraway drone, and look up. Now Wally's at their shoulders, tilting an ear at the sky. Finally Cameron shades his eyes against the slanting sun, registering more their expectation than the beat of the approaching aeroplane. As Wally often mutters in the protected corners of the workshop, Cameron Dunn wouldn't know a piston from a pipewrench.

Neil locates the speck in the sky. Uncle Leonard has been away for a month, over on the east coast, taking delivery of a Percival Gull from the agent and receiving instruction from a Sydney Aero Club pilot. There's a sales brochure up at the big house: *A low-wing cabin monoplane of streamlined appearance and superior performance, capable of speeds of 165 m.p.h. with a 160 horsepower Napier Javelin motor.* In the course of Leonard's first pass over the homestead and steeply banked turn above the killing pen and night paddock, the Gull templated against the sun, Neil begins to fuse with the natty wheel cowlings, the neat snout, the ribbed airframe beneath the silvery skin, and his heart shifts, his toes lift from the ground, and his destination is altered forever.

Part 1

RETREAT

7–10 December 1941

Angels

At 0600, the unvarying hour of the tropical dawn this close to the equator, the ground fell away and Neil Quiller trimmed the Buffalo for a north-easterly climb toward the cumulus formation that had massed over the Gulf of Siam. At Angels 18 ice began to form on the wings, chips and chunks of it breaking away and whipping past the cockpit, and when he levelled out at Angels 20 the world beneath him was blanketed with cloud from horizon to horizon. This was virtual blindness for Quiller, who was the eye of the dawn.

He signalled the aerodrome at Bandar Star to say that he was dropping to Angels 5. Here, five thousand feet above the water, he was at times under the cloud mass, at times slipping down a canyon of it, walled in by roiling white-and-grey vapour. Beneath him the Gulf was empty and serene, but he knew that the wind would begin to rise, the sea begin to run. That was the daily pattern: brief opportunities for reconnaissance before the sky turned dirty, full of violent squalls and solid rain fronts that sat high and heavy and stretched farther over the sea than the range of a simple aeroplane. There was nothing to see in those conditions, no news of Japanese convoys that Quiller could bring back with him to Bandar Star.

The canyon closed in on him then and he was properly blind.

A moment later, and between 0642 hours and the time it took him to steady the Buffalo and operate the shutter release, the clarity held, revealing a light cruiser and three transport ships on a bearing of 0900 degrees and a course of 270 degrees. As he signalled Bandar Star with the details, still working the camera, the cruiser apparently opened fire; there were puffs of smoke at the guns, and he felt his insides clench with fear and exhilaration. If war had been declared against Japan, then he was the last to know of it.

He sideslipped away, thankful for the lowering clouds and the rain, which was sheeting past him suddenly.

After that he held to the survey area, vectoring and quartering to the limit of his fuel endurance, but didn't spot the convoy again, or any other shipping. He turned back, one eye on the airspeed indicator. He'd been in the air for over two hours now and had the south-west Gulf and the neck of Malaya to cross—hopping from cloud to cloud amid intermittent squalls and sunlight—before he reached Bandar Star, between the Andaman Sea and the Strait of Malacca. If a floatplane had been catapulted from the cruiser to intercept him, then he'd need eyes in the back of his head.

He emerged from the clouds and crossed the coast of Malaya in clear conditions, passing quite rapidly over a stretch of dirty sand fringed by the coconut palms of a fishing kampong. Then paddy fields, jungle, and finally terraced hill slopes with dirt roads like brown cracks in the variegated green. He kept low, hoping that if he were being hunted then he'd not be seen through the obscuring clouds above him. As his fear dissipated it left only exhilaration. Malaya was as remarkable and intricate as England had been to him fifteen months earlier, when he'd seen the Home Counties from the cockpit of an RAF trainer and put his long sojourn in the empty north of Australia behind him at last. His eyes lit on the jungle with relief. He watched the unfolding—of palm fronds into hen-scratched dirt into the bony, tail-flicked spines of village cows. Children swarmed and ran and tiny goats trembled, full of nerve endings and the zipping howl of the engine in their soft ears. Later, as he swung south for his final approach into Bandar Star, he surprised a company of Punjabi troops in a line of open trucks on the Jitra Road.

When the aerodrome came into view he put his flaps down

and throttled back until he was just above stalling speed, then dropped from the humped back of Elephant Hill and levelled out, sideslipping against a wind that was bending the coconut palms. He crossed the little river, the perimeter fence and the Blenheim bombers in their earthen pens, meeting the main strip at a shallow angle. Even so the wind pushed him down and across, and he found himself snared in the spongy grass verge. Before he bogged to the axles he opened the throttle and powered back on to the metalled strip, arousing ironical cheers from the ground crew detail which spent its days digging the little fuel tankers and the tractors that towed them from out of the binding mud.

He swung left and into the shelter of a hangar, where Whitney and his mechanics were outfitting a bomber. He switched off, leaned over the side of the cockpit and yelled above the wind and engine howl that still lived in his ears: 'Any holes in her?'

The warrant officer cocked his big head. 'Should there be?'

Quiller jumped down. 'The buggers shot at me, Whit.'

'They did? Are you sure? What a lark.'

They walked together down one side of the fuselage, around the tailplane and along the other side. The skin, painted the pale blue-green of the sky, was tight over the airframe; there were no tears, no holes pursing. The twenty-inch camera was intact in the camera well. Whitney crouched to peer at the underside, touching a finger to a streaked and fumy patch of moisture. 'Lovely.'

Fuel often ran down the overflow pipes and along the fuselage, passing under the cockpit. Whitney and Quiller were certain it would ignite one day. They were philosophical about it. The Buffalo didn't repay much tinkering. It was an obsolete aeroplane, unsuitable for just about everything, and all a man could do was fold his arms and not be surprised.

Quiller retrieved the film magazine from the Buffalo while Whitney continued to crane his head toward the undercarriage without expectation or interest. Whitney was a tall, large-boned man who relied on props for swinging about his machines: a wheelstrut for his toes, a bomb-bay rim for his stomach, a lever for one of his hands. He was placid in the face of the rust, the mould, the careless young untried bomber pilots and the shortage of magnetos, tyres, armaments, manuals and most of the other things a squadron needs.

A staff car swung in and parked, and Whitney muttered behind a wheel cowling, 'Damn and blast, it's Janeway.'

'It's me he wants,' Quiller said.

Whitney swung out and dusted off his hands. 'Or both of us.'

The passenger got out and approached them. 'Neil. Mr Whitney.'

'Captain,' they said.

Janeway wore an army uniform and campaign ribbons of the 16th Punjabi Regiment, for he'd at one time fought the Pathans in the North-West Frontier territory of India. Now he was attached to the Air Intelligence Liaison Unit and was Quiller's and Whitney's shadow, always at their elbows or peering over their shoulders. He had the face and manner for it, sharp, keen and forever inquisitive, sidling and on the lookout. This alertness was sometimes attractive, especially when the light of sudden knowledge lit up his eyes and his teeth gleamed with secrets and connections, but at other times he simply repelled Quiller. Janeway would never accept a straight answer but looked for qualifications, always hovering and persistent, even when Quiller was fatigued or late for a deadline.

Janeway turned to Whitney. 'Whit, when I'm finished with Flight Lieutenant Quiller, I want a tour of the field.'

'Nothing much has changed since yesterday,' Whitney said.

'Since yesterday we have had a great deal more rain and wind,' Janeway replied. 'Ergo, are we fully operational? The bombers are parked in water; scraps of tin and wood have been flying about all night; the grass strips are sticky; what do we do if all four refuelling wagons get bogged?'

Whitney shrugged. 'You're the boss.'

Then Janeway took Quiller aside, shielding and intimate. 'Neil, I want the dope on your adventure this morning.'

The questions piled one on to the other. How many ships? What bearing, exactly? Was he sure they fired on him? Had he perhaps mistaken a training exercise for a hostile act? For how long was the convoy visible? Was he sure of his identification?

Then: Did he have a clear field for his camera? Did he have faith in the Buffalo? What were his particular gripes? Was he effective, did he think? Were they pleased with his work at the Combined Ops Room down in Singapore?

And: Just suppose for the moment that Quiller were the enemy—how would *he* paralyse operations at Bandar Star?

Some of these were old questions, as though Janeway expected Quiller to have been sitting on them for the past few days and weeks; others had little to do with Quiller's work. Quiller tried to answer, sometimes pausing to frame his replies, but Janeway always leapt into the breach, piling on the questions, leaving him exhausted. Janeway smelt of soap and shaving cream and clearly hadn't been obliged to rise at dawn and swelter in a cockpit, but he was also full of friendly curiosity, and so Quiller— tired, hungry, anxious for the lavatory—responded as courteously as he could, finally waggling the film magazine and saying, 'Mike, I must deliver these, then debrief.'

'Are you free later?'

Quiller glanced at the tossing sky. 'Yes.'

'We'll drive down to Penang.'

Penang was thirty minutes away. Janeway had a White Russian woman there. He had a Malay woman in the kampong across the river from the aerodrome and a grass widow from Buckinghamshire in Tanah Rata, at the highest level of the Cameron Highlands. Sometimes, when he'd been drinking, he would describe one of these women. 'Dora's twat is like a big old blowsy rose—I expect from years of saddlerub.' He also knew where to eat in all of the little alleyways of Penang.

'Mike, I have to be up at dawn for another sortie.'

Janeway shrugged agreeably. 'All righty, we'll go somewhere local. How about the Lulu Club in Bandar Star?'

'Fine.'

Janeway turned and climbed into the passenger seat of the staff car. Whitney stared after him, eventually calling, 'Sir, I thought you wanted a tour of the aerodrome?'

'Later. Must dash.'

Janeway's driver whined through the gears of the staff car, leaving a trace of exhaust smoke that was soon whipped away in the wind. Whitney shook his head. 'The bugger's always racing around somewhere.'

Quiller joined him and together they watched the car drive out of the main gate and onto the bridge and across the river. 'He's got a woman in the kampong.'

Whitney nodded. 'I tell you, Quill, I wouldn't touch the quim out here even if you paid me.'

But the car didn't turn into the kampong. It headed north, toward Jitra. Whitney said, 'Ten days ago he had one of the drivers take him up as far as the border. Spent the day on side roads photographing bridges and culverts.'

Quiller nodded. 'Last week he had me taking aerial shots. Roads and waterways. He says we're primed for an attack from the air, but what if it came from the ground?'

The adjutant to the Squadron Commander appeared. 'Quill, Freddy wants you.'

Quiller followed, threading between the hangars and the bowser sheds and behind the alert hut to the operations room. He was debriefed for an hour, adamant that he'd been fired upon by a light cruiser. It was information that troubled the men who interrogated him. Quiller could see that it would be picked up by the corners and passed about gingerly and head-scratched over for the remainder of the day before someone informed Singapore.

When they let him go it was close to noon. He set out to trace the inside of the perimeter fence, his habit after a mission. Quiller didn't look in at the aerodrome but out, in the manner of a prisoner hungry for the possibilities of the world. He lingered along the northern fenceline, which offered him the Lipis River, the kampong and the coast road that led up to the border with Siam. Janeway's kampong woman lived in a small hut at the river's edge, above a shallow reach where the kampong men relieved themselves each morning, their skinny hindquarters aimed at the mud. Just west of the road was Elephant Hill, and in line with it was a building he knew well, the Government Rest House, between the river and the road to Bandar Star. Quiller had spent a week there in October until accommodation had become free on the aerodrome. There had been a thick, dampish visitors' book on a teak halltable outside the reception desk, and Quiller, flicking idly through it one evening, had come upon an entry for May 1930. Amy Johnson. He knew all about that flight. She'd flown a de Haviland Moth from Croydon to Darwin in nineteen days.

He continued to skirt the perimeter fence, listening to a stand of bamboo clacking and creaking as the wind gusted around him. He sniffed: eddying in an air current laden with the odours of aviation fuel, the stormfront and the rottenness of human and animal habitation, was a hint of spices, fish and chicken spitting in hot oil. Hunger drew him away from the fence and at a diagonal across the aerodrome. He bounced on each of the grass runways as he went. They were saturated, as spongy as mattresses, and poorly drained. Nothing was satisfactory—not the Punjabi guards and their paltry gun positions, the rudimentary control tower, the level of serviceability for the bombers and his Buffalo, the confusion over fuel octanes that he encountered now and then. There was no fighter cover, no radar, and everything declined into boredom, rust and mould. He'd said many of these things to Michael Janeway, hoping that someone in Singapore might one day sit up and take notice.

Quiller walked through the main gate and on to the road to Bandar Star. After some time he came to a ferry landing, where he joined four Chinese men waiting with bicycles, a jeep and driver of the 2/16th Punjabis, and a Malay man wheeling a cart loaded with banana leaves. As he watched, the fraying iron cable lifted out of the sluggish brown water and the ferry began to cross toward them, groaning, shuddering, the cable taut now, jewels of water springing from it as if shot through with electricity.

In the kampong on the other side Quiller was swamped by children who saluted, called 'Hello, Joe' and stuck two fingers in the air for Victory. They swarmed about him, tugging at his hands and plucking at the cotton pasted to his perspiring flesh. 'You want cigarette, Joe? You want soap? Apple, twenty sen.'

Quiller paid the child and pocketed a soft, brown nugget of apple. When he walked on, half of the children walked with him, but he was striding out, a mad Englishman in the heat, and they fell back after a while, calling *selamat jalan*, pleasant journey.

He found the food vendor at the seaward edge of the kampong, where howitzers had been mounted behind sandbags among flame-of-the-forest trees and pawpaws heavy with yellow gourds. The old man saw him and hurried away from the Indian gunners, his wicker baskets bouncing on a dented tin tray mounted over the front wheel of his tricycle. Quiller paid for rice balls in banana leaves and a thick steak of dry spiced fish. The old man's eyes were moist, the whites muddy-looking. Sparse hair sprang back in surprise from his seamed forehead. He was stringy and very old and sometimes carried with him a monkey he'd trained to climb for coconuts. The monkey was permanently outraged and bared its teeth at the world.

Quiller wandered back among the bamboo huts, the villagers gazing after him from their steps. They knew that he bought commerce to their various households—a snack here, a haircut or needles and thread there—but they were otherwise uninterested in him or the possibility of war. They were unlike the Chinese people Quiller had met in Bandar Star. He wondered how well liked he'd be if he hadn't small change in his pocket and a few halting phrases of greetings and benedictions on his tongue.

A small, shy, vividly smiling girl approached him hauling two open petrol cans of well water suspended from a sturdy stick across her shoulders. He couldn't see that she had the strength for it. Her eyes never left his face and her burden propelled her along; she could not stop, her bare feet softly exploding in the powdery dirt and dodging nimbly among heedless darting baby goats and almost-featherless hens. There was a cow nearby, and Quiller wondered why the child didn't simply hang her pole over its powerful hump and slap her hand on its tough hide or tug its long ears to and from the source of her water.

Any exertion at all encouraged perspiration. Quiller tossed his bruised apple to a goat and loosened a shirt button. He gauged the temperature to be close to ninety degrees, despite the lurking storms. The humidity was always high and the men he served with were full of complaint. As for himself, Quiller had been in Broome and Darwin during the wet season, and knew all about humidity. Broome and Darwin had also given him a taste for the spicy dishes from a spitting wok. He tried to walk close to the huts, seeking shade, now and then wiping his forehead. He loosened another button of his heavy, unsuitable uniform and looked enviously at the shirts and sarongs drying softly on the poles that poked from the shutters—he wondered if in Whitehall they'd always see the world in terms of the Northern Hemisphere.

He stepped under a landline that ran down to the gun positions on the beachhead. They had tried radios but the static had defeated them, the wattage seeping away with the ever-present wetness of the ground, the coconut palms, the huge jungle leaves that hung like swords and shields all about. At the landing he glanced downriver to a slow bend, where the nutrients of the earth had accumulated over time and now supported paddy fields. There was a water buffalo standing face-on in the mud, apparently focused on him, its horns swept back along its neck. Then it tossed the insects from its running eyes and flicked its tail and the illusion of malign intent vanished.

Quiller crossed the river with a despatch rider from the 6th Rajput Rifles and a haji, wearing a white cap to show that he'd made the pilgrimage to Mecca. Above them a Blenheim bomber came in too fast over Elephant Hill and Quiller listened as it aborted the landing and came around again. The next approach was slow and timorous.

Quiller's room was in a long, drab hut of ten similar rooms. He showered, swallowed one of his daily atabrine tablets to prevent malaria, and attempted to sleep, but the wind rose and then there was rain. The bamboo walls around him began to flex, the palm fronds unknitted above his head, and his iron cot rode the impressions of the wind as it channelled and howled around the cement blocks that kept the mess hut clear of the damp earth. He lay with his eyes open. There were no mosquitoes this early in the day and in such squalling weather, but he had his net closed around his cot to suggest the night and encourage sleep. He sweated in the muggy air. Small gusts of wind, concentrated by narrow apertures in the outside wall, tugged and poked at the net. He heard a creak of bedsprings in the next room, bare heels hitting the floor, the throaty, fuggy groan of a man who has slept badly and had never slept in the daytime before he was posted to this hell-on-earth. The afternoon passed. Then outside Quiller's window there was a burst of laughter as a knot of young pilots made for the canteen, Michael Janeway tapped at his door, and in the mosque beyond the aerodrome holy men were calling the evening prayer.

Janeway led him to one of the staff cars. 'You drive.'

Quiller got behind the wheel. 'Where did you go today?'

Janeway gestured at the border country to the north. 'Oh, people and places to see. There's always some damn thing or other.'

Quiller slowed for the main gate, then accelerated on to the road to Bandar Star. Janeway sat half turned in the passenger seat, his arm along the seat back, his fingers beating a rhythm behind Quiller's neck. At the entrance to the narrow streets of the old town, Quiller braked for a bottleneck of Chinese men and women on bicycles. He edged forward. Deep ditches ran alongside the open ground-floor verandahs of grimy whitewashed shops. Signs in Chinese ran down the fretting pillars, while newer signs, on packing-case lids and scrap tin, announced: Tommy Digger Steak and Egg Cafe, or, English Australian Cafe Fish and Chip Served. They passed a cinema that Quiller had attended half-a-dozen times, mostly by himself. He was as fond as the Malay and Chinese patrons of the gangster films it showed, and reflected that nothing was more calculated to undermine European prestige than a gangster film, where European men broke the law and their women bared their shoulders. The locals were rapturous, apt to express shock and delight, and would eye Quiller as they filed out afterward, marking this roundeye down a peg or two.

Quiller leaned his elbow on the window ledge of the car and shifted his sticky spine away from the leather seat back. Janeway drummed his fingers. 'Tell me, Neil, do you hold with the view that the Jap suffers from night blindness?'

Quiller shrugged. 'They say it's true.'

Janeway looked out at the mass of cyclists, their black heads bobbing above their white shirts. 'How would *you* improve things at Bandar Star?'

'We've been over this, Mike.'

'Humour me. What are the pilots saying to one another? I shan't quote you.'

Quiller turned to him. All of his frustrations erupted. 'We don't have enough codebooks, maps and instruments to go around, so it's every man for himself in the ops room before a flight. The aeroplanes are poorly dispersed around the field, the mud walls of the pens will be useless if we're ever bombed. We have no fighter cover, servicing is a nightmare.' He looked away. 'You know all this. Do something.'

Janeway's palms rasped together. 'All in good time. Weapon loads? Adequate, would you say?'

Quiller gestured. 'Speak to the armourer.'

'I will,' Janeway said. 'What about the smoke curtain installation. Will it work? Have you seen it working?'

'Mike,' Quiller said, 'that's still hush-hush. Speak to Freddy about it.'

'Yes, of course,' Janeway said. Then: 'The Australians have a Buffalo fighter squadron at Kota Bharu. How would you rate the Buffalo as a fighter?'

Quiller shrugged. 'Slow. Takes me thirty minutes to reach ceiling height. A lot can happen in thirty minutes.'

'There's a good-guts rumour we're getting Hurricanes.'

'A rumour,' Quiller said, and moved abruptly, shifting into first gear and accelerating as the street cleared ahead. Then the traffic banked up again. They were among the inevitable homebound cyclists, and behind a line of dusty touring cars, which slowly turned into the gates of a large bungalow set back from the street. It was a club for the local Europeans: plantation owners, tin-mine managers, public servants, shipping agents and army and RAF officers. There were several lounges and a dance floor now, but ten years ago only men had belonged, their women limited to a room called the Cowshed. The sign was still on the door.

A shift was occurring in Quiller. He'd spent his years of exile in Australia hanging on to the notion that he was English and did not belong there. Then, in England, his broadened vowels had been detected and he'd never quite been admitted to the company of Englishmen. Now, in Malaya, his displacement was complete. He thought the English civilians futile, beyond recall with their dependence on their clubs and long drinks in cane chairs at sundown, their love of tinned fruit when the local fruit was so much better, their trappings of class and the niceties of dress and dinner, and their obsession with the heat and the servant problem. The officers in Quiller's mess were little better: that single, controlling sensibility again, concerning his vowels and his clumsiness with rugby ball and cricket bat; his sympathetic local knowledge and his curiosity and adaptability. Quiller didn't need to retire to a club after hours. He didn't need relief from the strain of dealing with alien outlooks or maintaining face.

They passed the club and further down the street came to the Lulu Club, which offered a cabaret, a bar, a dance floor and whisky-and-soda for forty-five cents. Quiller parked in the next side street and they walked back and edged through a knot of Australian and Indian servicemen who were milling at the door. Janeway parted with him immediately, pushing through the dancing couples with his sharp, scything elbows to a hostess seated on a stool at the bar. Quiller watched for a while through the smoke haze as Janeway danced with her. It was a dance full of flourishes and insinuations, Janeway biting the woman's neck and seeking the cleft of her buttocks with his right hand. Quiller turned toward the bar and shouted above the din for a glass of beer. Sometime later he saw Janeway seated with an Indian lieutenant. The Indian officer was bent close over the little table between them, gliding a tobacco tin across a slick of spilt beer, listening intently to Janeway, who was speaking into his ear. At one point both men examined their watches for several seconds, as though to count down the hours to an event of some significance to them. Quiller had met the lieutenant several times before in the Lulu Club and in the mess. Although Janeway liked to invoke a conjunction between the three of them, based on their uneasy tenure in the service of the King—'None of us quite fits, you know. Ravi, you want a liberated India; Quill, you say yourself you're neither one thing nor the other; and I grew up in the Far East'—Quiller never felt trusted by either of the men.

But now, feeling adrift and loveless in the smoke, the shouts and the thick odour of slopped beer, Quiller made for their table. He wanted someone to clap him about the shoulders and draw him into a warming centre. Before he could reach them, however, the Indian lieutenant spotted him and pressed Janeway's forearm briefly, causing Janeway to straighten in his chair and watch Quiller with an air of guardedness and rapidly formulated stratagems, almost of fury.

'Neil, we're busy here.'

Quiller retreated at once, and later in the evening found himself at another corner table, where he was appreciated. Whitney was drunk, and Taffy, one of the staff car drivers, was close to it. They were in the mood to hear about Janeway.

'He's a rum cove, all right,' Taffy said.

'Taff's got a story,' Whitney said. 'Tell him, Taff.'

'This afternoon I took the bugger across the border,' Taffy said. He was a balding, sardonic Welshman with the jittery manner of a man forced to stay alert for potholes, wobbling bicycles, sudden rickshaws and cows on blind corners.

'And?' Whitney prompted.

'It wasn't the first time, squire. There's a Dutchman he goes to see up there, on a plantation. It's always the same: I wait in the car while his captainship goes inside the Dutchman's bungalow for an hour or two, then we drive back. Intelligence gathering, he calls it.'

'A Dutchman?' Quiller said.

'So he says, your grace.'

Their closeness, the wall of sound and the pressing bodies all around them warmed Quiller and loosened his tongue. 'Sometimes I'll put down at another field and discover he's been there that day, buttonholing the ground crew about serviceability, weapon loads, fighter cover, warning systems, you name it.'

They fell silent, then Taffy said, 'The bloke's not top drawer.'

'How do you mean?'

'Take Freddy. A real gentleman, never talks down to me. Janeway's just a jumped-up corporal, but he treats me like dirt.'

'Careful, he's watching.'

They all looked. Janeway was now standing alone at the bar, and probably had been for some time. He was handsome in a derisive, glowering way, and coldly returned Quiller's gaze. Then his eyes took in Whitney and Taffy. To the case against Janeway, Quiller mentally added private charges that could not be proven or measured: his dirty nudging; his face. Quite simply, owing to some configuration of appearance, smell and texture, Janeway's face and body repelled Quiller. He looked away to think about this. He liked to be fair. Had he always been repelled and not acknowledged it, or had his feelings been encouraged by this conversation with Whitney and Taffy?

Then Janeway was standing beside them, not speaking. They stared down at the table.

'Did you and Taff drive here, Whit?'

'Cadged a lift, sir.'

Janeway looked at his watch. 'Mr Quiller and I have the Alvis. Taff will drive us all back in it, won't you, Taff?'

'Yes, sir.'

They rode in silence, smacking at mosquitoes. Taffy let them out at the mess hut and put the car away. Their bladders were full and the three men stood apart and splashed the ground. Then Whitney wandered off. Yawning and stretching, Quiller asked, 'Who's this Dutchman of yours, Mike?'

Janeway grew still. Quiller saw an over-wakeful, penetrating alertness in the man's face. 'You know I can't tell you that.'

The Energy for Showy Disasters

In her room in the visitors' quarters on Haarlem Downs, Jeannie awoke to a raised voice in the yard outside: Crystal. There was another voice, a man's low rumble: Wally? Harry Horsetalk? The roof above her groaned and cracked as the iron sheets expanded in the early sun and pressed against nails and beams. Jeannie kicked off the sheet, swung her feet to the floor and sat like that for a time, then showered and dressed.

She stepped out into a greasy kind of heat. It was always a steam bath during the early days of the Wet, the sun beating through dense, moist air. Rain clouds hung in the west, frogs gulped, and mosquitoes bred in the pockets of rainwater trapped here and there about the homestead, in cast-off tyres, empty soup tins, the enamel bowls in which the stockmen sluiced away the day's grime. Jeannie hadn't the energy for showy disasters this morning, but there was Crystal, her hands on her hips, standing over Wally Webb, who was scratching a square outline into the dirt with a pick while Harry Horsetalk stood by patiently with a shovel.

As Jeannie crossed the pitted lawn toward them, Crystal swung around. She did what she always did and eyed Jeannie from head to toe, as though looking for the stains of unspeakable night practices. 'It's time we built that air-raid shelter.'

The nearest building was a hundred yards away. There was an overhang of trees. The big house lay in an unbroken line from the site. It was a good spot for an air-raid shelter and Crystal would have chosen it. She could think when she had to.

Wally and Harry wore shirts in deference to Crystal, but looked hot and damp. When Wally straightened to forearm the sweat from his face and smile at Jeannie, he did it in creaky stages. The old blacksmith had spent his life bent over engine bays and bench vises; his spine ratcheted open like one of his tools now. 'Morning, gorgeous.'

'Morning, Wally. Morning, Harry.'

Harry was grey and bent, his eyes seared by sandy blight and the rays of the sun. He touched the rim of his felt hat but wouldn't look at her, just stared at the shape scratched into the ground as if to fix it in his head. 'Missus Jeannie.'

Wally was the only white man left on the place, too old to enlist, and Harry the only black. The stockmen and the gins had gone walkabout to their ceremonial grounds for the duration of the Wet and wouldn't be back until the April mustering. Harry, the head stockman, had been raised on a Pallotine mission on the coast between Broome and Derby. He never went walkabout. Haarlem Downs wasn't his country and the station blacks weren't his people.

Crystal looked fevered and alert. 'First a nice deep pit with steps going down, then we'll cut that old iron tank behind the night paddock in half and use it as a roof, and finally a layer of dirt.'

Wally began to swing the pick. When he'd loosened a square yard of topsoil, Harry Horsetalk shovelled it to one side.

'It's still packed hard underneath, Mrs Dunn,' Wally said. 'Pity we're not at the end of the Wet.'

'Take your time.'

With each fall of the pick, Wally grunted. He had broad palms, thick fingers, and forearms like hanks of the shipyard rope that Jeannie had seen in Broome. Grey and white threads showed in the tuft of hair at his throat, and his face was seamed and creased from a lifetime with the Dunns, their engines, pumps, horseshoes and strife. He always had a wink and a grin for

Jeannie. Neil Quiller had been the only other one he'd had time for.

Jeannie cleared her throat. 'Shall I bring out cups of tea for everybody?'

Crystal was intent on the pit again. 'And rock-buns.'

Jeannie walked to the big house. While the tea brewed, she slipped off her sandals and ran silently down the creaking hallway to Crystal's bedroom. She tugged at the top drawer of the gloomy bureau, where Crystal kept her correspondence, but it was locked.

She returned to the kitchen. It didn't help that she and Crystal waited for news from, and loved, the same man. They were so close, so cooped up and so bound to a life of marking time that they had little to say to one another. Whenever they met in a corridor or a doorway, or in the gap between the kitchen table and the cup rack or the always-steaming kettle, they would sidle past wordlessly, their stomachs and elbows tucked in, their noses tipped back. If Crystal Dunn was hard to love, then Jeannie Verco was not about to cringe or bow, and so they waited through the days and weeks in an atmosphere of pain and hate.

Jeannie delivered the tea and rock-buns to the deepening chamber of the air-raid shelter then turned guiltily toward the visitors' quarters.

'Where on earth are you off to now?'

'I won't be long, Mrs Dunn.'

'But what will you be doing?'

'I thought I'd write to Cameron.'

Crystal shook her head in bitter wonder. 'If it's not letter writing it's skulking about with your sketchbook. You cut me off and cut me off—'

'That's not fair,' Jeannie retorted. 'He's my husband. I can write to him if I want to.'

'This isn't a holiday camp, Jeannie.'

'I won't be long, Mrs Dunn,' Jeannie said. 'What's on for today?' She rubbed her palms together brightly. 'I know my shoes need a good clean and I could do yours while I'm about it. The dusting. The silver needs polishing.'

'Please don't take that tone.'

'What tone?'

'Trivialising everything. Mocking me.'

'Honestly, I wasn't.'

Crystal shaded her eyes and seemed to gauge the condition of the sky, the wind, and her inner resources. Thunderheads were building above the ocean again and the windsock on the airstrip stood stiff as a teat in the snapping westerly. She fished the nurses' watch from the pocket of her dress and made up her mind: 'All right, write your blarmy letter. I'll help Wally and Harry. But please don't oblige us to fetch you when it's lunchtime.'

Wally, just behind Crystal's left shoulder, dared to flash Jeannie a wink. She turned away, fighting down a grin, and made for her room in the visitors' quarters.

Her writing table was an up-ended tea-chest, her chair a crude reproduction of the dining-room chairs in the big house—buffalo hide over axed hardwood arms and legs—and her bed a horsehair mattress beneath a mosquito net. She said, 'Your mother's imposs-ible,' as though Cameron reclined there on the mattress, propped on his elbow, watching her, perhaps watching her as she dressed, his groin damp and his penis lolling, wet commas slicked in his belly hair, the sheen of her on his bare thighs.

Crystal had always known. She'd known from the very first time, when Jeannie and Cameron were barely eighteen, and she'd tackled Jeannie about it, not her son. Where have you been? You look flustered, my girl—have you been running? What's that on your sleeve? But Jeannie wasn't about to be pinned down so easily: it had been her father's custom to snap the steel tip of his belt at her bare legs not only for the naughtiness he'd witnessed but the naughtiness he suspected and anticipated, so she knew how to deflect and evade. She could conjure excuses and explan-ations so elaborate and baffling that her inquisitors soon gave up on her, as Crystal had, and she and Cameron continued to make love under his mother's nose.

Jeannie brushed dust from the chair, pulled it closer to the tea-chest, and unfolded Cameron's letter. 12 October 1941. It had taken almost two months to reach her. She began to read, and understood, despite the censor's heavy hand, that Cameron's battalion had been posted with other Australian Army battalions from Birdwood Camp on Singapore Island to Batu Pahat, on the west coast of Malaya. He didn't say what he thought about that, or when it would happen, or even what his wider hopes and fears were. He'd been in Singapore since August and in that time had written to her twice; she had written to him *twice a week*. She read quickly. He'd miss Singapore. Walking past the street vendors and their little charcoal cooking fires reminded him powerfully of the odours in the back alleys of Broome. The beer was cheap. A Chinaman called Joe had been his regular rickshaw driver. But he supposed that Batu Pahat would be 'a good place to hide from the Income Tax Collector.' Then he signed off. He liked to call her 'old girl': *Chin up, old girl.*

Crystal, on the other hand, had received six letters, and made it a competition between them. Jeannie hated herself for playing, for feeling competitive with such a tedious and stupid woman. She tried to take the long view—that Crystal was Cam's mother, after all, a widow, and most probably lonely.

Jeannie took up her pen, wrote 'My Dearest Cam', and stopped. She brushed at the page with the edge of her hand. She couldn't see the grit on the page but it was there, in sound and sensation. Making a couple of exploratory circles in the air above the page, she went on: 'I try to picture you, my darling, toiling in the heat.' She stopped, stared at the wall, and added: 'The Wet has started—lots of frogs, lots of humidity and always the threat of more weather to come, so I suppose we're not so very far removed from the conditions in which you find yourself.'

She was trying to make a connection, but it was one that might irritate him if his life there in fact bore no relation to hers. She hated it when she over-reached. Cameron frightened her a little. She glanced at the bed. She'd practically grown up with Cameron, ever since his father, part-owner of a fleet of pearling luggers in Broome, had befriended her father, the Inspector of Pearl Fisheries. After that she'd begun to spend every school holiday with the Dunns, and not even her father's new posting to Albany had been an impediment to these visits and the unspoken understanding that she'd developed with Cameron. She'd fallen in love with him; he'd needed her comfort, for Crystal and Leonard offered little of it.

And then, at eighteen, she'd slept with him.

In part, she hadn't been able to wait, and it was going to happen sooner or later anyway, and she was curious, and he'd just had the most blazing row with Leonard. She'd also thought it

31

might change her, round out her sense of order and completeness. Instead, Cameron's rooting her—as he called it—caused him to change toward her. Suddenly all the old ways disappeared. They stopped being knockabout equals, kids on horseback. Cameron persuaded her that she wasn't complete, and began to challenge everything she knew and believed, and tell her who she was and why she thought and acted the way she did. It was as if he wanted to do to her what had been done to him—and to all of the animals on the place: catch her young and break her in before reason and estimation could set in. The more doubting and irresolute she became, the more he promised to be the only remedy for it, and this hold over her, by so powerful and vulnerable a man, kept her permanently disarmed.

For a long while he'd even pretended that nothing existed between them.

Why couldn't he simply love and admire her? Why couldn't he hold some illusions about her?

She wrote: 'We could have a proper honeymoon when you come home on leave.'

Did he hate it that she knew how vulnerable he was? She wanted to catch him and make things better before—pop!—he was out of range. He couldn't control his temper sometimes. The world hemmed him in. He was impatient. He'd never been able to please Leonard and had stopped trying to. Take the Gull: as soon as he'd learnt to fly it, he stopped being interested in it. He was always saying to Leonard, in effect, 'See if I care.'

'What else can I tell you? Your last letter came via the Reverend Dr Sandilands and his little gospelling plane. He thinks we should evacuate if the war news worsens. Trooper Dalvean came through on patrol, looking for lepers and runaways. None here, of course. He'll be back again at the end of the wet season.'

Jeannie stared at the wall. She sometimes thought that she was at the centre of contesting wills and opinions. The war would play itself out, Cam would return, Crystal would wear him down, and there wasn't a soul in the world that she could tell these things to. Not her mother, who could never simply listen but would want to step in and act, and certainly not her father.

Neil Quiller? He'd have listened and understood. But why had he popped into her head? Because he loved the Gull so much and had been the one to fly it? Because he seemed to read the undercurrents in his uncle's house?

'Your mother wants me to move out of the visitors' quarters and in with her, but I don't know …'

Jeannie had been fooled for a long time. Because Crystal Dunn always expressed her views with conviction and irritation, Jeannie had taken this as evidence of a complete and coherent personality, but, bit by bit, she'd discovered that Crystal's views were borrowed, unexamined and full of contradictions, and her manner the result of long disappointments and failures which she believed were outside of her control, as though she'd never exercised choice in her life. It was clear that she should never have married Leonard, for Leonard didn't see *her*, he saw Hazel, Neil's mother, the sister who had died in the north of England. And so Crystal mistrusted and disavowed passion. Whenever she saw Jeannie slip her arms around Cam's neck or waist, or glue her hip hard against his, she'd snap, 'Oh, get your hands off him, for goodness' sake.'

'We're building an air-raid shelter finally and after that your mother wants Wally and Harry to dig a couple of zigzag slit trenches. Of course, this reminds us terribly of you and where you are and what might be happening to you. Oh, I wish you were here.'

Jeannie sat back. She'd found a natural end point, and could sign off now. Often she couldn't finish a letter until she'd stamped about for some time, composing and then discarding sentences in her head, looking for the one that contained her passion, with no sense of contrivance.

Then Wally murmured outside her window, 'You there, gorgeous? It's lunchtime.'

'Oh, hell, thanks, Wal.'

Jeannie returned to the main house. Crystal had set the kitchen table with cold sliced goat meat, tomatoes split open by their time in the sun, bread and pickles. She was in a dark fury, sawing away at the food on her plate. Jeannie glanced at the old wall clock: midday. She switched on the mantel radio and, as the set began to hum and the green tuning eye to glow, it wasn't the newsreader's voice building in that hot room but the Prime Minister's. He told them what had happened only hours earlier, and Jeannie looked into Crystal's face at last and saw that Crystal was looking into hers.

A Rising Moon

Quiller was woken at 4 a.m. by the cough and snarl of aircraft engines. The Blenheim bombers were being scrambled. He went to his window and tracked them as one by one they trundled down the metalled strip and climbed into clearing weather and a rising moon. Or had voices, tense and avid, alerted him first? He was aware of them now, and showered and shaved, swallowed another atabrine tablet and pulled on his kit, before hurrying to the alert hut. 'The Japs have landed at Kota Bharu,' Janeway said, taking him by the arm and stabbing the wall chart with a forefinger.

Kota Bharu was a fishing village on the South China Sea and in a straight line east of Bandar Star. The frontier lay a short distance to the north of it.

'When?'

'Just after midnight.' Janeway was lifting on his toes. They all were—the pilots, intelligence officers and senior ground staff; the blood was pumping in them. 'Destroyers and cruisers, providing cover for transport ships and barges.'

Quiller peered at a tracery of black lines which reached inland and south of Kota Bharu—the rivers and streams that drained into the sea there. The largest was the Kelantan River, a useful course of water if you were floating an army and its supplies into the interior. An aerodrome lay near the village: Australian Hudson and Buffalo squadrons were stationed there. He glanced at his wrist-watch: they would be tired and ragged men by now.

He described a circle over the Gulf with his forefinger. 'The convoy I spotted yesterday must have been part of the invasion fleet.'

Janeway was watching him closely. 'Are you up to another sortie?'

'Of course.'

'Good show. But you're bound to strike fighter resistance this time.'

Quiller shrugged.

Janeway had a strip of paper in his hands, a signal from the Combined Operations Room. 'We need to know the situation north of Singora. At first light you're to make a sortie over the Lakon Roads.'

Quiller read the signal for himself. If they were fearful of Japanese landings in Siam, then this was a major push. First light was over an hour away. He assumed that the Blenheim bombers were attacking the landing craft at Kota Bharu, in the clear light of the moon, but he'd need better than moonlight for his photographs. He was trembling to be away, though, and made for the Buffalo, which was parked in an earthen pen on sodden ground behind the ammunition dump. He worked down the checklist by torchlight: camera, fuel gauges, rudder, flaps, sundry instruments, anything that moved or registered, and for the sake of filling in time, he repeated the check, when something caught his eye. There was no excuse for grit at the lip of the fuel tank.

Sand? Quiller rubbed at it with the rim of his torch and heard and felt the granules crushing.

Sugar.

By half-past six he and Whitney had the tank drained and flushed and the filters removed, washed for good measure and replaced. A tanker was begged from refuelling the returning Blenheims and by seven o'clock Quiller was ready to take off. Not all of the Blenheims had returned, and those that had were badly shot up. They crouched like crippled birds in the early sun. Whitney patted Quiller shyly on the back. 'Good luck, old son.'

Quiller was moved to think that his safety mattered to

Whitney. The fighting hadn't begun for either of them and yet Quiller wanted them to survive it together. They hadn't met one another before this, and wouldn't meet again after it, but for now they were friends. Quiller understood all of these things in the time that it took for him to say a simple thank you.

Once in the air he swung around on a north-easterly bearing and then trimmed the Buffalo for a steep climb before levelling out at fifteen thousand feet. Engine temperature and oil pressure were normal. He could see curtains of rain far out to sea but conditions were clear over the neck of Malaya. The terrain below was rich and intricate and his eyes drank it in.

Fifteen months earlier, Quiller had been as avid for hedgerows, moorland, thatched cottages and cricket pavilions. He'd taken the train to Heston aerodrome, west of London, and there he'd looped, hedge-hopped, stalled and recovered from stalling for almost forty minutes in the Royal Air Force trainer, ignoring the protests crackling in his headset, before touching down with a flourish, a quick, cramped landing that brought the instructor clambering out after him in a fury. 'This is not the outback, Mr Quiller.'

'It certainly isn't,' Quiller said, and nothing could wipe the smile from his face.

Then he was taken to a wooden hut, where two RAF officers were reading his application. Eventually one of them looked up. 'Everyone wants to be a fighter pilot.'

Quiller said nothing.

'Young chaps like you are flocking from the colonies by the boatload.'

Quiller said, 'I was born in England. Newcastle.'

'Quite.'

The minutes passed.

'You have seven hundred hours up?'

'Yes, sir.'

'You obtained your A and B flying licences from an aero club?'

'That's right, sir.'

'You say here that you published a guide for pilots. Please explain what you mean by that.'

Quiller's kitbag still bore a patina of Kimberley dust. It sat beside his new boots and trouser cuffs like an overworked sheep dog of the dry country. He rummaged inside it and handed over a small, jacketed book with an uncracked spine. 'This,' he said.

One day in the Dry of 1938, when he was barely eighteen, Quiller had been about to take off from Derby with mail and spare parts for Vansittart Downs station when he'd experienced an inexplicable draining of confidence and know-how. Vansittart Downs lay at the end of the Meda River and east of Windjana Gorge. Was he to pass to the left or the right of Mount Behn? And wasn't it tricky magnetic country, apt to send compass readings haywire? He'd sat for some time in the cockpit of the Kimberley Air Services Puss Moth, swallowing, his heart fluttering, the sun beating against the cockpit.

Then he remembered that the doctor at the leprosarium sometimes flew to the inland stations. He got out, crossed to the tin hut at the edge of the landing strip, and asked to use the telephone.

The doctor was in. 'You pass Mount Behn on the right,' he said, 'then follow the river to Mount Broome.'

'Thank you.'

The doctor seemed to sense Quiller's blankness and fear. He said kindly, 'Make a note of it for next time.'

Quiller did. He began to fill a logbook with notes, collecting and ordering seat-of-the-pants information from mail pilots, station managers, drovers, bore sinkers, surveyors of the Vacuum Oil Company, mounted troopers and Pallotine missionaries on the coast. He explored by car and truck, coastal steamer and launch, horse and bicycle. He compiled lists of telephone numbers, pedal wireless frequencies, and road and air-mile distances. Finally he took low-altitude photographs which he pasted into his log-book, annotating them with black ink.

His observations were home-grown and first-hand. Where magnetic interference made for unreliable compass readings, for example, he suggested alternatives: *The woolshed at Mistake Springs has an east–west alignment.* He pointed out that the Wyndham aerodrome was a heat-generating saltpan, the Derby pub stopped serving evening meals at half-past six, and it was advisable to carry a scrap of chamois to filter the fuel at Vansittart Hill. *In fact, you might strike dodgy fuel at any of the stations.* He described the terrain: *Twenty minutes and forty-five miles north-east of Halls Creek the red stony surface becomes corrugated, rather like a static surface chop in an ocean. Hence the name, 'Bay of Biscay Hills'.* He warned that the sugar grass on Missiessy Station was often high enough to hide a man on a horse, and that there was no windsock on Hartog Hill: *Radio ahead and ask them to build a smoky fire.* Finally, he rated landing approaches: *Lambadina Mission may be reached from a southerly, landward approach, or from Cygnet Bay, Cape Levêque or the ocean, depending upon the wind. The Cygnet Bay approach affords a rewarding view of King Sound, while a north-easterly climb on takeoff will take you over Buccaneer Archipelago.*

There was nothing shaped or formal about his notes, but they were serious. They fixed the landscape and, once or twice, had saved him from doing a perish.

Eventually word got out. Other pilots began to ask for his advice or demand to see his logbook. Some of these men and women glanced at him doubtfully, as though to say that a man so young, and from the north of England, had a poor claim on the country. Quiller shut down in the face of their doubt. It was not an insufficiency of language but of fellow-feeling. Finally he did the only thing possible and paid a printer to produce two hundred copies of the logbook. He titled it *A Pilots Guide to the North-West.* The guides sold for twelve shillings and sixpence a copy and by 1940, when Quiller sailed for England, only fifty copies remained unsold. It had been Jeannie Verco who pointed out the missing apostrophe in the title. She meant it kindly, but it just about summed up Quiller's few years in the north-west, and he'd jerked away from her roughly—though not before she caught the pain and fury in his eyes and, mortified, had tried to snatch at his sleeve to comfort him.

Quiller said none of these things to the RAF recruiting officers. He waited while they leafed through his guidebook. Finally the senior officer stabbed his finger upon Quiller's shot of Haarlem Downs homestead and airstrip. It was a well-composed photograph, sharp and free of distorting shadows. 'I think we may have a position for you, Mr Quiller.'

• • •

Now, as Quiller crossed the frontier and followed the Jitra to Singora railway line, he thought that Malaya was as determinate as England. There was no need for him to identify particularities in an endless sameness, as he'd been obliged to do in the Kimberley district. Nothing below his little aeroplane defeated his vocabulary. He didn't need words when he had eyes in his head, and a nose, ears and fingers. In all of his seven years' exile from England, he'd not once felt a sense of hereness. The Kimberley was a place of exile; he'd felt only the elsewhereness of the world beyond the Indian Ocean. If not for his logbook, he'd have been as blind as a pilot flying into the face of the sun.

He caught the Japanese unprepared. He made one pass over the seafront at Singora, and a broad, arcing sweep to seaward before they sent fighters up and brought the ack-ack guns to bear. He worked the camera as he went and signalled Bandar Star with his findings: transport ships in heavy concentrations offshore; troops massing on the beaches; military aircraft parked wingtip to wingtip on the aerodrome; and a large convoy of escort ships out to sea. One thing struck him: the Japanese knew the Air Recognition Code of the day, the letter K, and flashed it at him as if to say, 'Don't mind us, we're with you.'

After his initial pass over the coastline and the water, Quiller flew in erratic and defensive circles, shooting photographs, avoiding ground fire and the fighters that were climbing toward him from the airfield. There were flying boats on the lake, at least forty ships in the harbour, and movement on the main road down into Malaya. He banked steeply, slipped down to barely more than treetop height and, easing back on the yoke, wondered what sort of war this was becoming, for there were horsemen on the beach, and making their way south along the road he saw tiny one-man tanks and soldiers on bicycles, riding six abreast. They didn't stop or weave or glance up at him in apprehension but sped south in waves, intent on business.

Tracers whipped past his wings. He twisted his head to see a Japanese Navy fighter closing in. When the wing cannons flashed, he pulled to his left in a tight turn, but the Japanese pilot anticipated him and, as the initial tracers spent themselves harmlessly above Quiller's head, the second burst raked the fuselage and the Buffalo shuddered as though he'd struck a scudding wind. Quiller hadn't felt the motions of fear until this. His uncertainty at Derby aerodrome in 1938 was a terrible blankness but he hadn't attached it to anything outside of himself. Today he was alone and unarmed amid strangers who meant to kill him. He began to sweat copiously. His body was a loose and self-abasing shell around him. He trembled, cold suddenly, and yet still sweating, streams of it running down his eyes. He seemed to be choking on his heart, and wanted desperately to swallow and wrap himself for warmth. His legs were out of control, jumping ungovernably on the pedals. Then he began to converse with himself, his other self close and confiding behind his shoulder, directing his moves and reflecting on his wretchedness and haste: 'Oh Christ, I'm cold. Watch him, watch for smoke from his cannons. Watch out, pull up, trees, trees, trees. Don't flame out on that fucking hill. Don't let him get you. Left, left, hard left. Watch that hillside. Control your legs. He'll get you, he'll get you, pull out, pull out. No, you're too smart to let him get you, he's nothing but ricepaper stretched over a bamboo frame, he's shortsighted, he's wearing glasses as thick as beer bottles. Too close, too close! He's coming around. Dive, dive, dive!'

There was a pattern to the chase. The sky was crowded with the red roundels of the Japanese fighters but only one pilot had him marked for destruction and he and Quiller were repeating their moves over and over again: Quiller would watch for the smoking guns on his tail, then slam tightly into a turn, on full throttle, the motor sweet from Whitney's attention. The memory of the sugar in his fuel tank came to him and the cold fear changed shape inside him, reconfigured into something purposeful. His heart steadied, his legs tightened, and he could think again. He dived, straightened out and flew low along a valley to the frontier with Malaya, putting the Japanese behind him. This was what he knew best—ground-hugging, moulding himself to the contours where other pilots were afraid to go. Like this he raced home across the neck of Malaya, the wind whistling in the torn skin of the Buffalo.

As he came in over Elephant Hill, Quiller scanned the field. The earthen pens were empty, meaning that the bombers were on another sortie against the landing craft at Kota Bharu. He splashed down, the wheels a little treacherous on the slick surface, and he thought what a cruel irony it would be to die of poor airfield drainage rather than a bullet. Whitney emerged from the open hangar, eyes narrowed to assess the damage, and waved him toward an apron of hard ground, where mechanics were swarming over the shot-up tailplane of a Blenheim bomber.

'Janeway wants a word.'

'He'll have to wait.'

Quiller's stomach felt loose suddenly. His knees threatened to give out. He stumbled to the latrine and, in his relief, sat for some time, shaking and taking stock of his body. He tried to roll a cigarette but his hands were unreliable, and so he formed them into neat fists and rested them on his knees. In time, his ears stopped ringing, and he realised that other men were perched in there, too—ground staff, smoking, snatching a moment of rest. It was almost 1100 hours and they had been patching up aeroplanes all morning, or refuelling and rearming them, or running signals between one hut and another. Quiller reached for lavatory paper and realised with a groan that there was none.

He continued to sit. The man on his left said: 'Did I tell you she's taking in lodgers?'

Another man, on Quiller's right, replied, 'Your missus is?'

'That's right.'

'What kind of lodgers?'

'You tell me,' the first man said bitterly. 'The kind who skips with the family silver, what there is of it? The kind who gets his leg over while the man of the house is away? You tell me.'

There was the soft rattle and flap of paper. The man was reading a letter. He went on: 'It weighs on the mind, I can tell you.'

The second man said, 'Is there someone who can pop round for you?'

'Ah, they're all nosy parkers back home.'

'Well …'

They fell silent on either side of Quiller. He realised that both men were reading letters. Had the mail come, in the midst of battle? The second man said, 'My son's crawling now, I think I told you.'

'You did.'

They were re-reading old letters. Quiller said, 'Either of you chaps spare some bog paper?'

There was silence, then a harsh laugh. 'Chum, why do you think we brought our mail into the jakes with us?'

'That's right. A good bog, a last good read, a good arse wipe, then back into the fray.'

'That way we can shit all over the wife.'

'Rub her face in it.'

These two were jokers. Quiller said, and immediately regretted it, 'At least you get mail.'

'Oh, you poor bastard. Here, want a read? The wife's telling me about her new pink nightie.'

A small leaf from a handwritten letter began to slide under the wall of the cubicle. 'No, I couldn't,' Quiller said, self-conscious and forsaken.

'Go on, chum, take it.'

The tone was dangerous now.

'I might have something in my pocket that I can use,' Quiller said, searching for his handkerchief.

'A chap offers up the last loving words of his missus, the least you can do is take it. Go on, wipe your filthy arse on the only love letter I've had in two months.'

Quiller found the signal from the Operations Room in Singapore in his top pocket. It was hours out of date by now, and he tore it into three small, barely adequate sheets, and used them one by one before hurrying outside, the men behind him muttering, 'Lousy cove.'

He found Janeway leaning, arms folded, on the fuselage of the Buffalo, watching as Whitney tested the tailplane and another man patched the holes with doped cotton sheeting. Janeway straightened immediately and caught Quiller by the upper arm. 'Quill, what did you see up there?'

Quiller ignored him. He retrieved the film magazine from the camera and set off for the alert hut, Janeway trailing closely behind him. 'Neil, this is important.'

'Later.'

He was debriefed quickly. Janeway was waiting for him. 'Now, Quill, about this morn—'

They were interrupted by the uneven beat of twin aero engines and they looked up. A Blenheim bomber was approaching, one engine trailing smoke, and there was something odd about the cockpit, the glass palely black, as though smeared with oil. Quiller continued to watch, expecting the undercarriage to appear, but soon understood that the pilot intended to make a belly landing. The speed dropped, the propellers were feathered, and the battered fuselage suddenly flopped onto the ground and slithered slowly, the snout nosing this way and that, reminding Quiller of a big, baffled fish caught by the tail.

He turned to Janeway, but the Intelligence Officer was gone, threading his way past the barracks and the fuel dump, heading for the front gate, glancing at his watch. Quiller looked up again. The north-eastern sector of the sky was dotted with Blenheims limping back to base. They would be patched and rearmed and sent up again.

He walked across to the mess. It was deserted. Nothing had been cooked, but bread, cans of bully beef and huge steel teapots in tea-cosies sat on a trestle table. He poured tea into a tin cup, spread bully beef onto a slab of bread, and sat on a bench to eat.

The navigator and pilot of the crashed Blenheim came in. They looked bone-weary and frightened, their hands shaking as they poured the tea. Quiller glanced at his own hands.

'Quill,' one man said, turning and noticing him there, 'your kite got shot up, I gather.'

'Had a Navy Zero on my tail,' Quiller said.

Outside, the air was full of sound. The Blenheims were landing only seconds apart. Quiller went to the window and watched as fitters and riggers swarmed over each of the bombers, checking, refuelling and rearming. Men from Whitney's detail were checking for damage and trolleyloads of bombs were being loaded into the bomb bays.

The air-raid siren was late by almost half a minute. Quiller and the crew of the crashed Blenheim had already tracked the sound and identified and counted the twenty-seven Army Type-97 bombers coming in from the north—from Singora?—at about thirteen thousand feet, and were running for the slit trench when the siren sounded. They slithered into mud and water and heard the bombs howling down. Suddenly Quiller felt a searing pain in his hand: he was still holding his tea and he'd scalded himself. A laugh burst out of him, lost in the long crumping sounds of the explosions.

He tossed the tea away and placed the mug on the lip of the trench, then thought better of it and twisted it into the mud, where it would be safe. By now there were other men sharing the trench. They all snatched glances at the bombing. The explosions were small and contained, the work of light fragmentation and anti-personnel bombs. The Japs intend to use this airfield, Quiller thought. Anything heavier and they'd risk putting craters in the landing strips.

After the wave had passed, smaller formations of fighters and bombers returned, peeling off at five thousand feet, diving to strafe the aerodrome at treetop height, first concentrating on the ack-ack positions and then on the buildings and any aeroplane still intact. Quiller saw three Blenheims struggle into the sky. Two were shot down; the third picked up speed and flew low into a mountain pass to the north of Elephant Hill.

When it was quiet, someone said, 'Impeccable timing.'

Quiller climbed out of the trench and made for his Buffalo. It was undamaged, and he stared at it, shaking his head.

'Quill.'

It was Taffy, kneeling on the ground with a man's head in his lap. He looked beseechingly up at Quiller, his hands on each side of the man's head, which looked misshapen to Quiller, lumpish and bloody.

'It's Whitney, skip, it's Whitney.'

Quiller kneeled with Taffy.

'His brains won't stay in, Quill.'

Quiller found himself doing what Taffy was doing, moulding his hands to the remembered shape of Whitney's skull and cramming the leaking matter back into spaces that seemed too small for it. 'Hold him, Taff. I'll get something to strap around his head.'

There was a first-aid kit in the Buffalo. He took out a field dressing and lifted Whitney's skull and began to wrap it tightly. Little Taffy peered into Whitney's face and laughed shakily. 'Congratulations, your eminence, you've got yourself a lucky wound.'

Quiller continued to bind Whitney in entranced anguish. His hands were slick, and blood seeped into the cotton. Then Janeway was there. 'Have you jokers taken leave of your senses? The man's dead.'

Quiller and Taffy cocked their heads and looked. It dawned on Quiller that Janeway was right. He said, 'We're making him comfortable.'

Janeway shook his head. 'Talk about timing. We were sitting ducks.'

Quiller stood and shouted, 'So much for your intelligence gathering.'

Janeway backed up. 'I say, steady on.'

'And someone tried to sabotage my plane.'

'Quiller, that same someone holed several fuel drums. Now, pull yourself together, man.'

Quiller laughed. He thought of Whitney and legions of men tossed into the sky, spinning in tight orbits, pieces of their bodies breaking away.

For the next couple of hours, Quiller helped to douse fires and strip the badly damaged Blenheims of serviceable parts. He seemed to work at half pace, all of his senses dampened. Sounds hissed in his ears, smoke closed around his eyes, fumes thickened in his nose and on his tongue, and his hands—a paste of ash and Whitney's blood on them now—might have been metal pliers, hooks or hammers at the ends of his arms. For a short time he scarcely registered the presence of the other men, but then their concerns became his. His movements grew hurried, he glanced repeatedly at the sky for raiders, and he skirted well clear of the wounded and the dying, just as they did. A dressing station had been set up behind the mess, wounded and dying men laid out in rows on blankets and scraps of tarpaulin, and Quiller and the others were spooked by the noise and the blood. A pilot called for his mother; a despatch rider rocked on his haunches, cradling his arm stub in his lap. 'It's not right,' Quiller said. They all said it.

Quiller began to wonder about his own survival. Did he owe it to something he'd done, or something he'd failed to do? Where did the luck lie? If he'd left the mug of tea behind in the mess when the raid began, would he have been killed? He searched his clothing and body for good-luck charms. He wore his mother's ring on a leather cord around his neck. It nestled with his dogtags in the hairs at his throat. Inside the band his father, the Canadian, had inscribed: *To Hazel, from one who loves her.* Why hadn't he named himself? If he had, would I have died today? Quiller wondered. Or is it the ring that saved me? Why had Whitney's luck run out?

The adjutant found him. 'Freddy wants you, Quill.'

Quiller paused when he reached the alert hut. One wall and the roof were badly holed. He glanced down. Gouges and more holes were spaced across the wooden floor, desks and filing cabinets.

He saw Freddy in the corner with a broom, and saluted. 'You wanted me, sir?'

The station commander had a long, mournful face with a dusting of ginger whiskers on his upper lip. His eyes sat deep and fatigued in dark sockets above the stretched skin and sharp cheek bones of his face. He had none of the clipped, lazy, sportive mannerisms of the other officers but was undramatic, unhurried, full of stalled silences and reticence. He gestured to Quiller to wait, and turned to the adjutant. 'Look here, I seem to be missing the situation reports and the list of cyphers for 11 Division. Have you seen them?'

Quiller waited while both men searched the desk and the filing cabinets. Finally Freddy coughed to get the attention of the other men in the room. 'I wonder,' he said, as though it pained him, 'whether or not in the turmoil any of you perhaps came across some papers and stacked them with other papers?'

The clerks, signals officers and repair technicians glanced at each other. Someone said, 'Captain Janeway said he needed the reconnaissance photos of Singora.'

'Yes, well, Captain Janeway ought to have approached me about that. Now, Quill, are you fit?'

'Yes, sir.'

'Good man. We need a situation report for the Kelantan River. We're badly stretched, there's no-one else I can send. You're airworthy?'

It seemed significant to Quiller that he was always tied so closely to his aeroplane. No-one ever asked the bomber or fighter pilots if they were airworthy. Quiller's Buffalo was seen as an extension of his eyes. If damaged, then Quiller was as good as blinded. 'Yes, sir,' he said.

• • •

But moments after he was in the air and climbing he discovered that the undercarriage had locked in the down position and nothing, not even the manual release device, would retract it. Then, at Angels 18, he lost fuel pressure. He worked the hand pump, one eye on the gauge, and dropped altitude. The locked wheels and the loss of fuel pressure were old, intermittent problems, things that on any other day Quiller would have taken in his stride; but speed and altitude mattered today, and he felt heavy, defenceless and graceless in the sky. It meant nothing that poor Whitney's ground crew had stripped away the Very tubes, parachute flare bins, cockpit heaters and extraneous external fittings to reduce loading and wind drag if the wheels wouldn't retract, or that the wing cannons had been removed.

Quiller picked up the Kelantan River near Kuala Krai, about forty miles south of Kota Bharu, and followed it downstream in the thick of a monsoon squall. The river made a dogleg right at Pasir Mas, and here, ten miles upstream of the mouth, he spotted a tug with a barge in tow. He made a rapid pass, banked steeply and came back, seeing troops behind the gunwales. Then he saw the machine-guns, mounted on turrets just forward of amidships, saw the gunners track him and begin to fire. Tracer shells followed him, wide, low, as he climbed away.

At Kota Bharu a ship was burning in an oil slick one mile offshore. Through the sheeting rain he counted dozens of armoured barges pushing toward the beach or tossing as the waves broke on the sand, and three transports disembarking troops at the river mouth. The ground fire against him was immediate and intense. The Buffalo shuddered. He held steady, took a photograph, then peeled away, signalling his findings to Bandar Star.

The return signal frightened him: they'd been bombed again, with heavy damage to aircraft on the ground, and were evacuating. He should head south for Singapore for fear that other northern aerodromes were under attack.

He flew inland of the coast, and was halfway down the peninsula when a Zero overshot him, its wing cannons flashing. He watched it climb away on his left side, bank, and dive. He couldn't outrun it, not in a Buffalo, so he rammed the throttle forward, hauled back on the shuddering yoke and stepped hard on the rudder pedals, standing the Buffalo on its wing, turning tightly, the engine missing a beat before picking up again. The Zero fired, wasting a burst. Quiller's legs were like jelly on the pedals as he banked to find the Zero and flipped over again, but this time he was hit badly, pieces of the starboard wing breaking away. When oily smoke wrapped around the cockpit he told himself to bail out. The air snatched him, up and out, his parachute whupping open as he pulled the ripcord, and he began to float gently in the whispering sky, far from the howls of the engines. The Buffalo was a cartwheeling speck beneath him, trailing smoke. He lost her behind the flank of a mountain, and then the Zero was back to kill him.

Funny how he'd felt secure behind his perspex cockpit canopy, strapped inside a fragile shell. Here, dangling at the end of his parachute, he had only his flying suit and canvas rigging for protection. The Zero passed within feet of him, the pilot no different from an English pilot with his goggles and black leather skull. Quiller wanted to shrug good naturedly.

The Zero banked, levelled out, and the wing cannons began to spit. Quiller collapsed the parachute, shrinking his outline in the sky, then let it fill with air again. Twice more he did that, the Zero returning to fire short bursts, and each time he dropped like a stone. The ground was coming up. Air was precious. Quiller collapsed and filled the canopy a final time—to hell with the Zero—and drifted down among the mangroves on the bank of a river.

A Gradual, Solitary Whine

'I won't be long,' Jeannie said, the next morning. 'That's what you say. But someone always has to go out in the heat and fetch you.'

'Just half an hour.'

'It's the secrecy that gets my goat.'

Crystal meant secretiveness, Jeannie's general condition. 'Nothing to hide, see? Pad, pencils, watercolour paints.'

'Don't get smart. Any other girl would want to sit with me at a time like this.'

Sit with you and natter and plan and be bossed and bullied about. 'I won't be long, I promise.'

Crystal gestured at the sketchbook and seemed, fleetingly, to envy Jeannie. They were at war with Japan now, the Prime Minister said, which meant that Cameron might die, and she had nothing to take her mind off that. 'What good does drawing do anybody?'

In your empty years it could have done you the power of good, Jeannie thought. 'It's just something I've always done. It's just a hobby. A habit.'

'This isn't ...' Crystal finished helplessly, 'a drawing kind of life.'

Jeannie touched the tips of her fingers to Crystal's stringy arm. 'I won't be long. I promise.'

'It'll be lunch soon, and I'm not fetching you.'

Jeannie shouldered open the flyscreen door and left the house, stepping into stillness and a wall of heat. It was the season for winds and rain and the breathless interludes between them. Today, even the dirt held its breath. She padded past the cook's quarters in her rope sandals and sleeveless dress, past the petrol bowser and the blacksmith's shop, before slipping between the gins' hut and the gardening shed. No-one was about.

On the other side of the airstrip she came to a stand of acacias on a slight rise. Her backside had worn a dusty depression at the base of one of the trees, her backbone a spine of polished bark on the trunk. She settled in the dust and propped her sketchbook open across her knees, turning to a faint, pencilled enlargement of a tiny Box Brownie photograph. It was something she did at night, in the privacy of the visitors' quarters. By day she would snatch half an hour here and there to elaborate upon the sketches with watercolour paints. Leonard on horseback—the day he was killed, in fact. Black stockmen branding a calf. Wally Webb with a horse's hoof between his knees, horseshoes hooked to his belt and a fan of horseshoe nails between his teeth. Neil Quiller in the cockpit of the Gull, shy and self-conscious; Cameron draped against the fuselage, grinning, legs crossed at the ankle. Dr Sandilands' Desoutter parked beside the hangar, roped down in a cyclonic wind. The leper patrol in the distance like an old-time desert caravan. The bore-sinkers' Ford buckboard. The cook skinning a goat.

None of Crystal.

And these days there was nothing occurring here in the plain air to give credence to the photographs.

Jeannie turned to a sketch of Leonard crossing the yard, drawn from memory, not a photograph. When she was fifteen an inspector from the Bureau of Agriculture had visited Haarlem Downs and pointed out to Leonard that his heavy, ravenous, disease-ridden cattle were turning the little gullies and hollows of Haarlem Downs into ravines, broad red gashes that couldn't sustain life or be restored. Leonard had been incensed, but, as Cameron liked to say of his father, short-term profit was the name of the game. The soil wasn't the only thing to suffer; now when the stockmen made for their ceremonial sites during the wet season layoff they relied on Haarlem Downs to provide them with rations, for there were no kangaroos, goannas or yams for them in the cattle-torn bush. And even after twenty-five years Leonard still hadn't understood that when he looked for cattle during a muster, the stockmen looked for *cattle tracks*. To Leonard's mind, the blacks were like poorly disciplined, undiscerning children in need of a firm, controlling hand rather than kindness, which could so easily be construed as weakness. Then eighteen months ago he'd been fatally gored by a steer. Cameron had talked his mother into switching to sheep after that. Then the war had come.

Jeannie held the sketch at arm's length. On this particular occasion, three of the stockmen had been mimicking his sloping, hunted walk. He hadn't noticed them there, but he knew all about their cheekiness in general. Two hours manacled to a sheet of iron in the direct sun would soon put a stop to it.

She turned to another sketch, Leonard in the saddle, leaning over the pummel, Harry Horsetalk showing him a freshly picked cucumber. She added the browns and reds and pinks rapidly, and heard Harry say, behind her shoulder, his voice shocked:

'Him all about died, missus.'

'Oh, you startled me, Harry.'

'Boss Leonard, he dead.'

'I know. It's sad.'

Harry said stubbornly, 'Boss Leonard, he pass away, missus.'

'Yes, I know, Harry. I'm doing this to remember him.'

Harry shook his head as if he were caught in a hollow space in time and stepped agitatedly from one foot to the other. Then Jeannie remembered the dog. About three years ago she'd spent a few days following some old bush blacks about on Haarlem Downs. They were marking the start of the Wet with a brief ritual walkabout to a ceremonial place, and had showed her how to dig for yams, read the soil and paint her face. They would camp by a fire at night and tell stories, or sing and dance, clacking sticks together. One old woman owned a dusty white dog, which Cameron characterised as a typical blackfella's mongrel, more grass seeds than dog. One day a snake got it, but Jeannie hadn't known that until much later, when the old woman saw that Jeannie had placed the little dog in the corner of one of her paintings. She'd looked distressed. 'Him dead, missus.' She made a rubbing motion above the painting with her fingers. 'You makem go, orright?' Jeannie had hurriedly spread a dusty wash of paint over the white dog until the old woman nodded with satisfaction. 'This fella pitcher orright now,' she said, and wandered away. After that the station blacks had always gathered at her shoulder and made corrections: 'Him wear a red shirt, missus, not green.'

Jeannie put the pad and paints aside and turned interrogatively to Harry. 'Did Mrs Dunn send you to fetch me?'

The old stockman nodded. 'Him say you pick tomatoes for sauce and chutney please.'

Jeannie returned to the house and fetched a cane basket. There had been rain during the night. Harry's tomatoes looked renewed, the dust washed from the leaves and ripening skins. She knelt and with an old pair of scissors began to cut through the stalks.

She heard the mutter of an approaching car and looked up to see a black Wolseley creep around the parched lawn and stop at the main house. The car belonged to the Pearces, from Somme Brae, two hours north of Haarlem Downs. She continued to pick and stack the tomatoes until the basket was full, then walked toward the house.

The Wolseley was parked in the driveway, weighed to the springs with suitcases, hatboxes and steamer trunks. Jeannie stepped onto the running board, then down again, trailing her fingers along the dusty flank of the car, mingling her mark with the brushmarks of driveway shrubs and roadside grasses. According to the labels pasted to their lids, the steamer trunks had sailed through the Suez Canal, and from Naples to Portsmouth.

As she'd supposed, Crystal had set morning tea on the verandah. Jeannie mounted the wooden steps in time to hear Dulcie Pearce say, 'That blarmy trooper came through again, looking for lepers. Every three months he shows up.'

'It's his job, Dulce. And you've had lepers in your mob in the past.'

'Even so—'

Jeannie stepped on to the verandah. Crystal was standing, her rump propped against the verandah rail. Dulcie Pearce sat, small, damp and heat-exhausted, on the edge of a stiff cane chair, her heels together, her bony legs at a graceful slant, her cup and saucer trembling minutely in her lap.

'There you are, Jeannie. Out in this heat, I don't know.'

'I noticed your car, Mrs Pearce. Are you evacuating?'

There was a catch in Dulcie's voice. 'Yes. Frank says it's not safe anymore. I popped in to say goodbye. I saw Dr Sandilands yesterday. He agrees it's the best thing.'

Jeannie didn't know which part of the delivery to answer first. 'I think he'd like us to evacuate as well. Isn't Frank with you?'

Dulcie shook her head. 'It's just me and the boys. Frank's staying on. Someone has to. You can't just walk off.'

'Where will you go? Port Hedland?'

Dulcie shrugged. She wouldn't look up.

'Hedland's likely to be a target,' Jeannie said, 'like any town along the coast.'

Dulcie settled her cup and saucer down on the wooden traymobile. Her right hand sought her left, the fingers bunching on the worn gold of her engagement and wedding rings.

'That's what decided me. I thought I'd just drive and drive until we got to Perth.'

'I wouldn't delay. The barometer's falling.'

Tears splashed onto Dulcie's cheeks. 'I'm so afraid. There was a spotter plane yesterday, *one of theirs*. Frank said that could mean they intend to come back and bomb us. Won't you come with me?' She turned to Crystal. 'Crystal? Won't you come? I'll make room for you in the back.'

Jeannie glanced at Crystal, then looked again, more closely this time. It can be difficult to read tension and agitation in big-boned, powerful people. Crystal's lounging seemed to be a counterfeit of indifference. 'Mrs Dunn? Are you all right?'

There was a strained silence. Finally, Dulcie Pearce beamed and said, 'Oh, by the way, I had a letter from Rollo.'

Her son, a shy awkward boy as Jeannie remembered him. He'd been sent to New Guinea, a Vickers gunner. 'That's wonderful,' Jeannie said, glancing uneasily at Crystal.

'Read it if you like. Some hugs and kisses at the end, nothing to be ashamed of.'

Dulcie fished inside her dress and handed Jeannie an envelope. Jeannie withdrew the letter, which was warm and limp from

Dulcie's breast, the paper wrinkled and friable. The hand-writing was mostly illegible and whole words had washed into inky ponds here and there across the page. It was as though her son had been writing by lightning flash beneath a dripping palm tree or tent flap. Or had Rollo been crying? Jeannie scanned quickly: '... two days' leave ... malaria tablets ... playing a waiting game ...'

'For God's sake, you two,' Crystal said. 'I've got a son in the thick of it too, you know.'

Jeannie thrust the letter back at Dulcie, who looked away, hunted and hurt. 'I just thought ...'

Crystal gestured impatiently and clicked her tongue. 'It's all right, forget it, Dulcie. You weren't to know. I shouldn't have snapped at you.'

Dulcie lifted her suffering face. 'You poor thing. The strain of waiting. It must be intolerable.' She glanced hastily at Jeannie. 'You too, dear.' She coughed, to change the subject. 'I see you're digging an air-raid shelter.'

With an effort, Crystal muttered, 'For what it's worth.' She was fed up with Dulcie Pearce.

Jeannie felt teary. She turned away, leaned her forearms on the top verandah rail and gazed through the tangled vine at the roof of the Wolseley, gazed down the weeks and the months, wondering if anticipation of loss could be as debilitating as loss itself. Behind her, Dulcie Pearce said a little desperately into the silence:

'Bad news travels quickly and good news travels slowly. The bookkeeper at Tabba Tabba Plains got a letter from his son in Greece six weeks after a telegram saying he'd been killed in action.'

'Mercy's sake, Dulcie, will you leave it alone?'

The other woman sniffed. 'I'm so afraid.'

More gently, Crystal said, 'Once you're on the road and away from here, you'll feel better.'

The wind was rising on the other side of the vine. The sky was closing in. Jeannie felt the need to check the barometer.

She stiffened. 'Those wretched boys of yours, Mrs Pearce.'

'Oh dear, what are they up to now?'

'Chasing Harry with sticks.'

Dulcie rolled with mirth. 'Little blighters.'

Jeannie darted down the verandah steps, shouting, 'Quit that, the pair of you.'

In their hunger and concentration, the Pearce boys resembled camp dogs. The shirts and shorts on their bony frames were like dusty pelts, and the scent of the prey was in their nostrils. Harry Horsetalk, trapped against the storeroom wall, was marking time in the dust, one shoulder raised to fend them off, his teeth bared at them in a desperate, obliging smile. They were darting at him with their sticks, crying out:

'Funny, is it, eh?'

'Going to welcome the Japs are you, eh?'

Jeannie was reminded instantly of Frank Pearce, their father. Pearce was a bit of a buttonholer. He wanted the north-west to secede and form a new state with the Northern Territory. He scoffed at the yabber-men who called for the subdivision of grazing leases. 'They want a garden here?' he'd ask, outraged. 'A race of sturdy yeomanry?' He'd scowl at the threat of strike action at the Wyndham meatworks, and had had a bellyful of rising transport costs, over-regulation and armchair critics. 'Tax relief, tariffs and less interference, that's what we need up here,' he'd say. 'And now the buggers want me to increase wages. Don't they know I support whole families of hangers-on as well?'

Jeannie waded among the Pearce boys, silent and wrathful, her quick hands stinging. The children yelped. They were shocked, then resentful, and retreated like cowed pups across the yard to the Wolseley, where Dulcie gathered them to her poor, washed-out knees.

Jeannie turned back to the old stockman. 'Sorry, Harry. They're very bad boys.'

Harry was trembling. 'No good, missus.'

'They're leaving now. They won't bother you again.'

'Boss Len, he tan their hides.'

'He would have, yes,' Jeannie said.

Harry slipped away between the workshop and the bulk store. Jeannie returned to the car, where she found Crystal at the driver's door and Dulcie Pearce behind the wooden steering wheel, bending her thumb hard against the starter button set into the walnut fascia. Her sons sat next to her, their dusty faces streaked with tears. The starter motor ground uselessly; the old car wallowed on its springs.

Dulcie rested her forehead on the wheel. 'I can't cope.'

'Yes you can. Try again.'

This time the engine fired, settling into a surging idle.

Crystal and Jeannie stepped back from the car. 'Have a safe trip.'

'I don't even know the condition of the track.'

'Take it slowly.'

'I'm so afraid.'

'Dulcie, the barometer's been falling. Push straight through or you'll be stranded in the middle of nowhere.'

'Come with me? Please?'

They listened, tracking the Wolseley as it disappeared down the driveway. Dulcie slowed for the gate, then accelerated, a gradual, solitary whine along the open road. Crystal was more choked with feeling than Jeannie had imagined, for she burst out, 'It's as if we're the only ones left.'

Too late, Jeannie remembered her letter to Cameron. Dulcie could have posted it for her.

The Fishtrap

Quiller folded his parachute and from the shelter of the mangroves watched the Zero circle a couple of times before swinging away to the north. He judged that he was two days' walk from the coastal town of Sungei Dungun—one day, if he could steal a bicycle, less than an hour if he could intercept a motorist or military convoy. There was a small aerodrome on the northern edge of the town, manned mostly by Australian aircrew and ground staff attached to a couple of Hudson bomber squadrons, with a small detachment of RAF pilots flying Vildebeeste torpedo bombers.

Taking stock of his equipment—revolver, knife, water bottle, ammunition, atabrine tablets and a tin of emergency rations—he set out, pushing between the mangroves into thicker jungle. It was like walking into a hothouse; the perspiration streamed from his scalp and soaked his shirt and groin. But no hothouse was ever this dark, or damp, or steamy; this dense and undivided. He stumbled over the erupted roots of banyans with massive ridged trunks and edged among palms as tall, naked and slender as pencil shafts, trees everywhere hedging him in and leaking water into the leaf mould, so that his boots squelched and were soaked to the ankles, and every step released the odours of dampness and rottenness and the buzz and snap of angry insects. He began to hate the silence.

The drip drip of the water and his soft footfalls seemed to intensify it. If a twig cracked he had no way of knowing where, or why. A mangy tiger, a sladang, a Sakai with a blowpipe and poisoned darts, a forward scout of the Japanese—they might just as well show themselves for all the resistance he could muster.

There was a leech on his wrist. He flipped at it, revolted and badly panicked, all of his good order evaporating. He felt as hateful and teary as a child, and whimpered before he had the sense to fish for his cigarette lighter and scorch the creature until it plopped away, leaving a smear of blood inside a coin of tormented skin. He was close to panic again when the mosquitoes found him, swarming heavily, indifferently, into his eyelashes.

Now and then Quiller found a clearing and would stop simply to express his true size in the meagre hollows of the jungle. He'd look up and see what constituted the canopy of hell: palm fronds, flat, broad leaves, needle leaves, tangled vines, all cutting the light of heaven. He grew aware of the creep of life. In addition to leeches and mosquitoes, he co-existed with pythons, hornets, spiders, scorpions, butterflies as broad as his hands, birds as vivid as watered silk and splashed paint, while monkeys migrated over his head and the silently hanging tropical flowers released heavy perfumes from their waxy folds.

It was no good—Quiller was fearful, taut, ready to windmill his arms and shriek if anything touched him. He found a clearing and stopped, his boots glued deep in a carpet of oozing matter. If only he could see. If only he could find a track and make better time than a few hundred yards an hour, travel with no hesitations or need of caution, no rotten logs, leeches, tangling vines or unseen jaws and poisons. If only he'd been better prepared for this. He'd like to take them by their shirtfronts in Whitehall and say, 'Malaya is not open fields, not desert. You didn't teach us how to listen and creep. Nothing is a rifle shot away but very close. The heat saps us, our spirits are low and to hell with the King, Amen.'

Quiller examined his compass. Could he rely on it? Nothing else worked in this place of swamping humidity. Shoe-leather sprouted mould overnight and field radios leaked their signals away along the wet ground. A compass should work, logically, but the jungle destroyed logic. But the compass was Quiller's only friend, and so he unglued his boots from the leaf mould and set out again.

Just then his eyes were drawn to a corridor. He entered it, and after some distance realised from the compacted ground surface and old, macheted scars on the tree trunks and ferns that people used it as a passageway. A moment later they were there, ahead of and behind him, four native men. They were Sakais, shorter than the kampong Malays, with golden brown skin and black wavy hair, and shyer but less forgiving in the eye. Three of the men were shoeless and dressed in sarongs; the fourth wore an Australian Army slouch hat, vast khaki Bombay bloomers scrinched around his puny waist with a plaited cord of jungle creeper, and laceless army boots. Each man carried a knicked and rust-pitted parang— not menacingly or defensively, but with the potential for either. Quiller immediately halted, shot his hands into the air and stammered, 'Selamat datang.'

The man in the cast-off khakis beckoned, turned and walked off along the track, expecting Quiller to follow. There was a gentle push in Quiller's back, a soft instruction, and so he complied, wondering if he were heading into or away from death. He was struck by the silence of the Sakais. He trod where they did and side-stepped when they did, but was noisy where they were noiseless.

After an hour of trekking they veered off the track, the lead man hacking at the creepers and glossy leaves to clear a path. They were climbing steeply now. Quiller checked his compass: the bearing was still east, toward the coast. They came to the top of a ridgeline, and here, above the lowland jungle, the monsoon winds tore at the tops of the trees, moaning and whistling like wind anywhere, but behind the racket a more constant note could be discerned, shrill and sobbing, and the Sakais stopped to listen. Satisfied, they veered a little to the north and came to a whistle in the form of a short length of open bamboo on the end of a slender pole, mounted to catch the passing winds. The Sakais conferred, pointing along the ridge. Twenty minutes later they came upon another whistle, with a longer shaft this time, the signal deeper. Quiller glanced at his watch. Three in the afternoon. He'd been on the ground for almost four hours now.

There were more of the woodwinds after that. Like signposts they guided the Sakais down to a small clearing on a steep slope crisscrossed with charred logs and tree trunks. The Sakais were midden farmers, slashing and burning to prepare small fields of rice, maize and tapioca. Beyond the clearing the ground levelled abruptly, and on the bank of a tidal stream sat a bamboo long-house accommodating half-a-dozen families. Quiller stopped feeling afraid. Several men, women and children had gathered shyly to watch him arrive, and the man in the army shorts gestured for him to sit on a mat beneath an *atap* shade, the palm fronds freshly cut and densely interlaced. An old woman with a goitre brought him coconut milk in a stubby bamboo cup, a green banana, rice, tapioca, a bowl of what he realised was salt, and two skewered cubes of charred fish. He drained the milk, dipped the fish pieces in the salt, and ate, cramming his mouth.

Bamboo seemed to answer every need of the little com-munity. Their huts, cups and bowls; the whistles that guided them through the upper reaches of the jungle; the blowpipes leaning against the longhouse. For all Quiller knew, the darts were fashioned from bamboo splinters and poisoned with essence of bamboo. A couple of light bamboo rafts had been pulled clear of the river, and in one of the longhouse compartments Quiller could see an old man lying on a charpoy, a mattress woven from coconut husk rope and suspended from bamboo posts.

Why, then, did the Sakais own a collection of haversacks and ammunition cases of the Australian Infantry Forces, and where had they got them? Quiller couldn't reconcile that with the men, women and children who were eating with him so compan-ionably, bringing tiny nuggets of salt neatly to their mouths and smiling and nodding encouragingly at him if he met their gaze.

It had just occurred to him that the Sakai wearing the slouch hat had vanished when half-a-dozen soldiers pushed into the clearing. His first thought was to run. He up-ended his bowl and scrabbled away in a half crouch for the shelter of the jungle, then stopped. The soldiers were European, not Japanese, Australians of the AIF, scratched, grimy-looking, unshaven, but watchful and contained.

Then one man, a sergeant, grinned, his teeth vivid against his beard and browned skin. 'RAF? You're a long way from home, chum.'

Quiller began to tremble. He staggered, and the sergeant promptly put an arm around him. The man stank, perspiration, woodsmoke and insecticide gusting sharply, giddyingly from the neck of his army shirt. Quiller nodded gratefully and found his legs. He'd felt himself lost and loveless, and now this. 'Thank you. Delayed shock, I suppose. I was shot down.'

'What do you mean, shot down?'

Quiller stopped to think. He felt that he'd been at war for days. This man's war hadn't yet begun. 'The Japs landed at Kota Bharu just after midnight.'

The sergeant frowned. 'Dinkum?'

'In fact,' Quiller said, 'I was shot at even earlier than that, flying reconnaissance early yesterday morning.'

The others tried to take it in. 'It's the flaming radio,' one of them said.

'We'll have to get back.'

'Are you on patrol?' Quiller asked.

The sergeant shook his head. 'The Sakais are showing us how to live off the land.'

More food was brought out. The Australians were ravenous. Quiller ate another piece of fish and drained another cup of coconut milk. 'Perhaps I should come with you.'

'Can't be done.'

'Why?'

'You'd slow us down.'

'But I can't stay here.'

'Sungei Dungun's just south of here. There's a direct road.'

Quiller nodded. He hated the jungle. He felt swallowed up in it. He'd be all right if he could rest his eyes on the South China Sea.

There hadn't been a signal that Quiller could see, but the Australians stood as one and gathered their equipment. He supposed that it came from living in each other's pockets for days and weeks at a time. He stood, too, waiting uncertainly.

The sergeant said, 'The Sakais will look after you here, but you'll have to find your own way to the coast—they're suspicious of the lowlanders.'

'What a coincidence, running into you chaps,' Quiller said, as they shook hands, and then he wondered if it was a coincidence. The country was small; there were not so many Europeans; men were bound to run into one another as the war picked them up and shuffled and scattered them around.

Quiller felt bereft as he watched the Sakai in the Bombay bloomers lead the Australians back toward the hills and the deepest jungle. Everything today had happened much too quickly, and was configured like a dream, and, like a dream remembered, was unreal and less than satisfactory.

When the tide turned in the river the Sakais put Quiller aboard a raft, armed him with a bamboo pole and a woven sack of food, and pushed him away, pointing east toward the river mouth and flinging words like bullets after him. He thought sourly: You could take me part of the way.

After a while he managed to stand with the pole and guide the raft through curves and bends and away from sandbars and the knobbly, half-submerged spines and skulls of crocodiles, until eventually the river opened into a larger one and he saw the breakers of the South China Sea a few hundred yards downstream. He glanced upstream, to a road bridge across the river and the swampland, but, before he could turn the raft, the rushing tide began to carry him away. He poled desperately for the bank, a false bank, he realised, an islet where half-a-dozen tributaries drained into the river mouth. Up along one of the tributaries, an inlet into a mangrove swamp, was a long fish trap with a bamboo and *atap* hut at the end of it. Quiller looked at his watch; the hour was late and the tide strong. Better to shelter overnight and make for the road at first light.

Apart from a bamboo stool, which lay wedged into a corner, some rusting fishhooks in a tobacco tin, and a dirty seine net draped over the rafters, the hut was bare. The floor and walls were soft and water-blackened, the air sharp with the odours of reeds and rotting fish. Quiller discovered a leech above his ankle and burned it off. He seemed to be draining away into the country's rivers and jungles, helpless against the cycles of existence and decay.

When the tide woke him, seeping up through the bamboo floor, he'd been asleep on his back and dreaming of wet sheets and of his mother peeling away his pyjamas to pat and powder him dry. He cursed, rolled on to his knees and stood, swaying, lost for a moment. He glanced out. There was a patchy moon, conditions clear before the typical monsoon shroud of dawn, and in it Quiller saw the river—fat, full and devouring. The water was rising rapidly. He stood there for thirty minutes like a flood-tide marker, ticking off the stages—heel, ankle, shins—then climbed onto the window ledge and reached up and dragged himself over the rim of the roof. There was little to support him and little for him to hold. He didn't trust the centre beam or the palm thatch, so he perched on the edge and watched as the water reached his boots.

Perhaps his helplessness was tainting the water or drifting on the air like spores, or he was like a staked goat etched against the moon, for a crocodile brushed against him, and then there were three of the creatures. Quiller's heart leapt. He scooted back from the edge, lifting his feet clear of the water.

They were not the large crocodiles of the main stream, but large enough to drag him into the water. They circled the hut. The river sat heavy, black and still around him, yet there was also the murmur of its inland push in his ears, and once or twice he saw leaves sailing by on the surface, proof that there was a tide—but how many hours before it turned again? He watched the crocodiles. They had all the time in the world.

After a while he began to hate their dim, patient, instinctive circling. He wanted them to show some individual spirit—playfulness, boredom, rage, anything. They were thick, heavy, sullen and stupid, and he hated them. He called insults above their loggish heads. 'Come on, have a go. Climb up and get me. I dare you.' Then one of them yawned past showing its jaws and teeth, and whipped back for another pass in the oily water. Quiller whimpered involuntarily and apologised.

Around, and around, and around. Quiller's fingers ached. Mosquitoes had found him but his arms and legs were locked tight to support his body and he dared not brush them away. He longed for a mattress and sleep.

Some time before dawn the tide turned. As the water sucked and drained through the mangroves and around the supports of the fish trap, the crocodiles vanished. But Quiller wasn't leaving yet. He knew that if he swung down onto the platform a tail might knock his feet out from under him or powerful fore-quarters rise up and snatch him.

And so he dozed, letting the roof take the strain. If this was dawn on 9 December, then the Japanese invasion was thirty hours old, not a lifetime. Quiller found that hard to credit. The invasion changed everything. This time when he flew photo-reconnaissance sorties the photographs would mean something.

A thought popped into his head, an echo of the schoolyard: It takes one to know one.

Quiller had always been a shadow and a spy. His mother's love letters, for example, stored in a shoebox in her bureau in their house across from Jesmond Dene. He had sneaked them out on heavy coalsmoke afternoons as she lay coughing and dying, hoping they'd tell him who he was: the son of a Canadian soldier? Someone better or worse than that? All he'd learnt was that he'd sprung from a deep, mutual longing. A year later, on Haarlem Downs, he'd mapped and measured the tiny disturbances of the air around Jeannie Verco and his cousin, Cameron Dunn. He'd slipped unnoticed from tree to ant hill as they made for the tin hut on the hilltop overlooking the Indian Ocean; but the hut had shut them off from him, the sounds they'd made had told him only part of the story.

Making maps was a form of prying, too. Spying to survive. Forewarned was forearmed. Knowledge was power. Quiller muttered these things like a mantra while the fisherman's hut shifted minutely beneath him and the water ebbed into the South China Sea.

And one day, a few months before the start of the war in Europe and just after he'd been hired by a small airline that was owned by an English trading company with branches throughout the Pacific, an English spy had recruited him.

Quiller's job for the airline was to fly a DH87 in a long round trip beginning in Darwin and stopping at Dili, Jakarta, Singapore, Brunei, Manila and Port Moresby. He liked flying across open stretches of water; he no longer had to strain to find landmarks, only land masses. By the third week he'd begun to recognise the regular passengers. He was in the saloon bar of a hotel in Port Moresby when one of them eased onto a stool next to his and said, 'A toast. Long may you continue to find your way across the water.'

The accent was Home Counties. Quiller said, 'It makes you nervous?'

The man thought about it. 'Disconnected. There's nothing to relate to.'

Quiller nodded. He knew the feeling.

'You're English,' the passenger said. 'Somewhere up north?'

'Newcastle, a long time ago.'

They downed their drinks. The passenger was perspiring and wore a grimy white cotton suit and highly polished shoes. Quiller watched the workings of the man's throat and wanted to say, 'Take your coat and tie off.'

'Another dram?'

'Let me buy this one,' Quiller said.

'That wouldn't be right,' the man said. 'I am, in effect, your boss,' and he explained that his name was William Landy, and he was an agent for the trading company that owned the airline.

Quiller took in Landy's ramrod posture, cropped moustache and clipped speech and thought: ex-military. Landy's eyes were widely spaced under a high, damp, domed forehead and his gaze was restless, touching on Quiller, the mirror behind the barman, the other drinkers. He was about forty, and told Quiller that he bought and sold things—'All kinds of things,' he said, dropping his voice.

That was all he offered at that first meeting. He began to question Quiller, and Quiller, relaxed and thankful to have the company of a man who listened and didn't hide behind the permanent, careless jokiness of the Australian airline pilots, began to talk. He spoke of his mother, Newcastle and his unremitting years at Haarlem Downs. He was full of yearning, loss and patriotism for England. At that meeting, and the others that followed a week later in Dili and Singapore, Landy threw hooks to Quiller, played him like a fish, and finally reeled him in.

'You'll report to me in person, never in writing. We'll meet as we are now, we'll chat, you'll go away and glean things for me, we'll meet again for a chat.'

There was no mention of payment. This was Quiller's duty, for the Empire. 'Listen, observe, report back to me,' Landy said.

For example, there were American business interests

throughout the Pacific and especially in the Philippines. 'The *Irish* Americans concern us the most,' Landy said.

A fortnight later, Quiller reported that a Daniel Finemore, once of New York and now a resident of Penang, was shipping rubber to Japan. 'Is that the kind of thing you want to know?'

'My word it is,' Landy said. 'My lords and masters are obliged to you, Mr Quiller.'

Later Quiller reported that the Japanese were active wherever he flew. 'You don't actually notice until you look, but they have fingers in everything.'

'That they do. Anything specific?'

Quiller replied that he was speaking in general terms.

'We need hard information, there's a good chap,' Landy said, mopping his big forehead with a handkerchief. 'Don't be afraid to nose around and strike up conversations. Remember, where British and local interests clash in the Far East, the good of the Empire should prevail.'

Quiller trembled to have this secret other life. In his mind, Australia became less familiar, less a near image of Britain, and Darwin a tricky, scheming outpost of the Empire. There were Irish Americans in Darwin who had links to Irish Americans throughout the Pacific, the workers on the Darwin waterfront were communistic, and Japanese business interests there were as pervasive as anywhere in the region. He saw a secret, malign web at work, and was proud to serve against it. He felt curiously uplifted the day he happened to see Landy, dressed in his dishev-elled cotton suit, being saluted by a Royal Navy commodore in Singapore, for it reinforced his notion of operating under cover for the King.

Spying was dreaming, too. It was like floating in clouds and shadows where there were no colours and the ground was unstable, where he could be several selves at once, all of them shoulder to shoulder, watching and evaluating, and none of them the Quiller he remembered but only a slice of him.

When war broke out in Europe, Landy simply disappeared. Quiller continued to gather information and impressions, but no-one collected it from him anymore, and so it burned in his head. For relief he sailed to England and told them that he could fly, and although he'd felt faintly excluded and let down ever since, at least he was simply and indivisibly a pilot called Quiller again.

Now with the rapid light of dawn staining the sky, he swung down onto the bamboo platform and freed the raft, which was entangled with the fish trap. The current was strong. He poled hard against the tide, toward the bridge, thinking that it took a spy to know a spy, and only with the aid of a spy could the Japanese have struck so hard and so accurately against the airfields in the north of Malaya.

The Water Seemed to
Bleed Into the Sky

There were two hidden corners on Haarlem Downs that Jeannie and Cameron liked to call 'our place', meaning they'd made love there—a cave and an abandoned hut. The hut was the closer. Jeannie slipped away from the house and all of its miserable distractions and made for the hill on which it sat.

Just as she was stepping onto the airstrip, a willy-willy flicked stingingly at her bare legs. But it was gone in an eyeblink, a small, whipping funnel of dust and grit that lost itself upon a patch of sticky mud—almost as though she'd imagined it, and so, after a moment's hesitation, she set out again, crossing the airstrip at an angle. The hangar was at one end, the windsock, several ant hills and boab trees at the other. The Gull sat inside the hangar gathering dust—coincident, she supposed, with her heart.

And so she ran, across to the other side, before skirting the shallow lake that formed only in the wet season. The water exhaled as she passed. It lapped at the trunks of dead trees and rolled like oil among the reeds, the breeding ground of frogs, mosquitoes and slow, rolling gases.

Swiping her hat at the pandanus palms and turkey bush, she broke through to higher ground. The ocean was green and choppy beyond the Eighty Mile Beach. Behind her were the foreshortened buildings, airstrip and stockyards of Haarlem Downs, then a tracery of sheep and cattle pads across the red dirt, and finally the Broome to Port Hedland road, at the edge of the limitless basalt.

She turned her back on the view and pushed on to a stone-and-tin shed erected by a Dunn at the turn of the century. Its roof was turreted with rocks against the lifting ocean winds. The door's leading edge tended to stick during the Wet and so she lifted the latch and booted the door open in two practised motions, then crossed the threshhold into dim, granular light. The window was uncurtained, but the glass had been scored by wind-borne grit for forty years. The stockman's bunk bed under the scratched window was no more than a horsehair mattress and a Black Watch blanket stretched out on fence pickets nailed to a wooden frame. She kept a straw broom in the corner and used it now to whisk away the dust before stretching out on the bed.

Our place. She tried to conjure up the times she'd made love on the Black Watch blanket, but Cameron was stubborn—he wouldn't take form—and unaccountably then she thought of his cousin, Neil, and the way he'd lurk about sometimes, following them.

Neil had come to Haarlem Downs in 1933. He'd been shy, downcast, numb to everything but his blessed bicycle and the hours he spent with Wally Webb. Then, in October, Kingsford Smith had reached Wyndham in a Percival Gull, breaking the England to Australia record, and Leonard, as excited as a child, had eventually taken delivery of his own Gull. Almost at once, Neil had stopped looking at the ground. Soon uncle and nephew could talk about nothing but aeroplanes and record-breaking flights: a British pilot flies from England to Australia in under three days; Jimmy Melrose touches down at Broome and Hedland in his circumnavigation of Australia in a Puss Moth; P. G. Taylor flies Smithy's Gull from Java to Sydney in two days; Jean Batten flies a Gull from England to Australia in under six days.

Neil had once shown her the route he would take if he were a record-breaker: Croydon, then Brindisi, Aleppo, Basra, Karachi, Calcutta, Rangoon, Bandar Star, Singapore, Surabaya, Koepang and finally Wyndham or Darwin. Wyndham was the favoured destination, for it represented the shortest distance from Koepang, but strong winds were a problem there, the fuel was known to need filtering, and the aerodrome—a saltpan three miles long—generated tricky thermals. He knew those sorts of things. His enthusiasm was touching.

As for Cameron, he'd shrugged at the Gull—because it was his father's and his father was a hard man—but, God, how she'd grown to love it. Streamlined, perfectly formed, like a bird poised for flight, and clean, almost free of the clutter of wires and struts and the general air of flimsiness of the biplanes.

Leonard had waited until they turned seventeen before he taught them how to fly the Gull. It was during the Dry, when there was less risk of crosswinds and waterlogging; but where she and Neil had taken to flying like ducks to water, Cameron was often clumsy and peevish at the controls, and preferred the passenger seat.

A year later the three of them were making trips without Leonard. Then in August 1938, just before Neil joined a freight and mail airline based in Darwin, Leonard gave them permission to circumnavigate the continent. They broke no records—they were away for thirty-nine days—but God, the occasional exhilarations and dangers more than made up for the long, numbing hours when nothing happened.

The first thing was a blocked fuel line after Broome. They stopped at Hedland to have it blown out. They made Roebourne and Geraldton in good time, but if it was the Dry in the northwest then it was the Wet down south, with sleety cold rains and high winds that buffeted and retarded the Gull, forcing them to put down in a paddock near New Norcia on the dregs of the fuel tank.

The next morning, as they waited for a lorry to arrive with a drum of fuel, Neil pointed to a tiny split in the propeller. 'We'd better watch that.'

Watch a chunk break away later and flip back with a slap against the windshield, cracking the perspex. At once the Gull began to shudder, the engine revolutions too great for the unbalanced blades, and Neil reduced airspeed. They lost altitude. He increased speed to grab back a safe margin, then throttled back and they dropped again. In this way they limped into Perth and stayed there for five days in separate rooms in a pilots' watering hole near the airport while a new prop was flown across from Sydney and the bearings were replaced. Neil spent every spare hour working on the Gull, while Cam hired a motor car and took her to see the jarrah and kauri forests. That hadn't been the thing to do, she thought now. They should have stayed with Neil.

They took off on a Sunday, about two o'clock in the afternoon. Neil wasn't infallible. In Kalgoorlie they were advised not to fly further east with darkness coming on, but he'd put his trust in the new propeller and bearings and not enough in their maps and compass, and by dusk they were off-course over stony ground. Jeannie remembered the darkness whipping past the side window of the cockpit and her spectral reflection as she stared out at it.

It was a solitary road to a solitary homestead that saved them. Neil buzzed around the house until porchlight spilled onto the dusty yard and people emerged. 'Can't you see what we want?' he'd said aloud, flying around and around the house.

Presently a car and a buckboard backed out of a shed and made for the road, headlights probing weakly in the gathering dusk. 'No powdery stuff,' Neil said, willing commonsense on the homesteaders.

Finally a landing strip half a mile long had been pinpointed at either end, the stretch in the middle practically in darkness. Neil smothered the airspeed until the Gull was close to stalling and touched down with scarcely a bounce, stone chips pinging around them.

The thing about Cam was, he'd packed the gramophone and a dozen discs of Gilbert and Sullivan and American big band music. Once on an earlier trip in the north-west, the three of them had been obliged to put down for a snap repair on a beach, against a creeping tide. As the gramophone scratched away weakly in the breeze and Neil bent over the Gull with tools and a greasy rag, she and Cameron had danced on the sand with a lot of mad flourishes. That hadn't been the thing to do either, but Neil hadn't seemed to mind, a shy, ducking smile on his face as he worked on the engine.

And so they'd stayed the night at the homestead, dined on mutton and sat around the gramophone afterward. They seemed to host the occupants of the house rather than the other way around. Gaunt, mesmerised, inarticulate people, slow to move and speak, as though visited by raucous gods.

Across to Forrest after breakfast, then a slight south-easterly adjustment that took them along the breakers of the Great Australian Bight to Ceduna, with a landing from seaward over Nuyts Archipelago.

You could hardly call them pioneers but word had got out and next day a flight of Moths from the South Australian Aero Club guided them toward Parafield aerodrome.

Jeannie remembered the way Neil had suddenly peered out and demanded, 'What's that bloke doing?'

Cameron had been at the controls at the time. If he had a fault as a pilot other than indifference it was lack of aeroplane sense. He could take off, fly and land satisfactorily, navigate after a fashion, and read the gauges, but he seemed to tense against the machine instead of fitting it around him like an old familiar coat or a second skin. A Leopard Moth had drifted too close to their starboard wing. Neil could feel it there, so could she, but Cam was blind to it. 'Who? Where?' he said, flustered.

'Bank to port!' Neil shouted.

Cameron confused port and starboard. The other plane clipped them. At once Neil took over the controls, communicating a sense of calm, and sideslipped away. Jeannie could see a tear in their wingtip, the fabric flapping like a pillowcase and the hole gaping. Meanwhile the Leopard was heading toward the ground, sluggish and rocky in the air. Neil followed it down cautiously, remarking, 'The front spar on his lower wing, we almost cut through it. See, the wires are sagging. Let's hope his wing holds.'

She peered and saw that Neil was right. He'd worked back from the motions of the Moth, interpreting its language in the air in order to identify the damage done to it. As she watched, the Moth seemed to break in two just above the ground, dip, and crumple. Neil overshot the wreck and touched down on the other side of it. When they were finally at rest she opened her door and looked back. The Moth's pilot was standing clear of the wreck, stretching a spasm in his neck.

Another week before they could fly on. Their journey up

the east coast—Melbourne, Wangaratta, Goulburn, Sydney, Newcastle, Coffs Harbour, Brisbane—was uneventful but for delays owing to winter gales. Sometimes the coldness seeped in through the seals and gripped them to the bone. What would be the perfect life? Summers in the south, winters in the north-west.

Charleville, Longreach and a faulty throttle, Cloncurry, Camooweal, where they presented prizes to the Belle and Beau of the high school ball, Daly Waters, then a long hop to Darwin, where the plugs needed cleaning. By now Cameron was dangerously bored. He wouldn't keep still and was given to unnerving playfulness in the cockpit, secret erotic attacks where he slipped his hand between her shirt buttons, trailed his fingers between her legs, tugged to ease his straining fly.

They found a couple of rooms in a hotel near the harbour. She didn't see Neil for two days. He came back oddly excited. 'I've a job.'

'Flying?'

He nodded. 'Mail and freight, mostly between Broome and Darwin and along the Fitzroy River to Halls Creek, and the occasional hop across the Timor Sea.'

'When?'

'As soon as we get home.'

It was evening. Cam was in a strange, languid mood, fitting his body against hers and she could picture the lazy, challenging smile he was giving to Neil Quiller.

'Whenever you fly into Broome, you'll come and see us, won't you?' she said.

'Do, old son,' Cameron said. His breath had been warm on her neck.

Neil couldn't look at them. His face darkened a little. 'I'll try,' he said. Then coughed. 'Big day tomorrow.'

They hugged the coast, heading south-west over barren islands, coastal gorges, mangrove belts and desert. At one point Neil made Jeannie traverse Queen's Channel for the experience of flying over water, and the experience unnerved her. The water seemed to bleed into the sky and, mesmerised, she allowed the Gull to sink to within feet of the surface. Neil yanked on the stick. 'See? That's what I wanted you to know.'

At Wyndham he had another test for her. Pouring a cupful of

petrol from one of the refuelling depot's four-gallon tins into a glass jar, he'd made her hold it to the light.

There were tiny flecks of rust, even of grass, and a hint of dust suspensions. 'The fuel can be dicey out here,' he said. 'Always filter when refuelling.'

Only one man was on duty at the aerodrome. 'We need a chamois,' Neil told him.

The man looked slowly, sleepily about the tin shed that stood for an office, and scratched his head. 'Buggered if I know. Had one the other day.'

In the end they used one of Jeannie's gloves, holding it like a teated udder, the fuel streaming raggedly into the tank, reminding her more of a woman pissing than a cow being milked.

The next stop was Ord River Station, two hundred miles to the south. At the mouth of the Ord River they saw crocodiles, but the dangers were not on the ground but in how the ground transfigured the air. Strange updrafts and vacuums bumped them about and the compass went haywire over the ironstone ranges. They wanted Halls Creek but none of the landmarks made sense to Neil and so he scribbled a note and dropped it to a horseman droving cattle, who pointed to a spot forty-five degrees west of their imagined route.

They blew a tyre at Halls Creek, tipping forward onto the prop briefly, then heeling over onto one wing. Repairs took two days, and they took off with the propeller blades shortened by three inches. Then to Broome, Jeannie flying the final stages, falling into sleep now that she was so close to home, and safe, and warm in the north-western sun.

Now she climbed off the little bed, crossed to the stone doorframe and stared at the sky, which was pale blue over the plains, feathered with wisps of distant cloud.

Where was he?

Englishmen Going About
Their Business

The road itself was narrow, with jungle encroach-ing on both sides. Quiller set out, heading south, and around the first bend saw the jungle dwindle away to rubber trees standing in stiff black mud, facing off the uncultivated interior. Ahead of him was another bend, and he could see smoke, smell spices cooking in hot oil, and hear, above the barely audible pull of the river, the chatter of migrating monkeys, a crying rooster and bursts of conversation. He stopped, confused. Clearly there was a village ahead of him, beyond the plantation, but the voices were coming from behind him. They were not speaking Malay or Chinese and were closing rapidly.

He leapt over the monsoon drain and concealed himself behind a nipa palm. Six Japanese soldiers on bicycles appeared, riding three abreast with long, bayoneted rifles slung across their backs. Palm fronds bobbed like over-sized garlands from their tin helmets as they cried out to each other and restlessly scanned the verges of the road. Four of the men wore black-rimmed spectacles, the lenses flashing, and to Quiller they were the dangerous ones—hardened not diminished by their spectacles. His heart hammered. Where had they landed? Were they advance scouts? Stragglers?

What now? If he went inland then he'd be swallowed up by the jungle. The shoreline promised coconut palms, fine sand and the warm green sea—but nowhere to hide. That left the road itself—north into the face of the landing parties, or south at the heels of the six men and who knew how many others, whispering down the peninsula on their bicycles.

Quiller decided to follow, keeping to the narrow rim of the monsoon drain, prepared to duck among the trees. When the village appeared he sought cover and watched for some time. The Japanese had dismounted and while two of them distributed leaflets, the others stood by uneasily, presenting their rifles. A few minutes later, they rode on, exchanging grins with the children who chased and shouted after them in the sunlight.

Quiller gave it ten minutes. The villagers watched as he crossed the clearing at the centre of the village. One or two of them stiffened and motioned toward him, and one man shouted, but Quiller passed by as if to say that the road carried the tides of war now, there would be others like him in the days to come, and they'd better get used to it.

One mile south of the village he stole a bicycle. It lay concealed behind a fallen rubber tree at the far edge of the plantation and he wouldn't have found it if he himself hadn't been intent on concealment. He supposed it belonged to a rubber tapper, but the plantation was deserted, white beads of latex silently bleeding down the trunks of the tapped trees into ceramic jars. So he dragged it out onto the road, mounted it and began to pedal, feeling obscurely released from his life of skulking and scurrying. The scented breeze passed over his nostrils. After a while, his legs began to cramp. Whoever owned this bicycle was a shortarse. He glanced at the crossbar. The bicycle was a Raleigh. The tyres were Dunlops. He was riding a very English bicycle in a hot, dangerous country far from England. The world was forever delivering this paradox to him. He didn't suppose the world was shrinking but that he was expanding.

He came to a wooden mileage peg at the side of the road. Sungei Dungun, five miles. Had the aerodrome and the town been taken? Or was he squeezing the six men ahead of him into a narrowing gap?

The road was fast and straight; he made good time, the pegs

counting down the miles. He was two miles from the town when an aero engine bellowed and a Vildebeeste appeared, climbing at a shallow angle as if from out of the palm trees ahead of him. He stopped and watched as it droned slowly, like a bush jalopy of the skies, northward to the invasion sites.

So the Allies still held the aerodrome. Quiller dismounted. The six Japanese couldn't have passed the perimeter fence unseen by the Sikh sentries, and he doubted they were behind him. He stepped over the monsoon drain with the bicycle, lay it in the grass and slipped among the palm trees. He still couldn't see the aerodrome but could hear it now: engines, muffled shouts and whistles, and faint music yawing on the wind as though some pilot or cook's offsider had set a gramophone needle onto a buckled record. The ordinariness of that notion brought tears of longing to Quiller's eyes.

He heard a cough and stopped to scan the thickets, not thinking to look up until he heard a second cough, when he noticed a man stretched out on a branch. At first he thought the figure was asleep, but it was an unlikely resting place and a broad leather strap held the man to the branch. Then Quiller took in the rifle, resting across a smaller branch, the drab uniform, the webbing, the dusty little pack and the tin helmet, and froze.

Six men against an aerodrome?

Unlikely, but Quiller thought how unnerving a sniper would be. There you are, refuelling a Vildebeeste or stretching tired limbs outside the door of the mess, when you hear a distant crack and a bullet howls past your ear.

He searched for the other snipers. They were not visible. Thoroughly spooked now, he returned to the bicycle feeling that deathdealers had him marked, had the small of his back in their sights. He swung onto the saddle and pushed off, riding low and fast toward the aerodrome. He came to the perimeter fence, then the gates; there inside were huts, friendly old warplanes and Englishmen going about their business, and he stood up on the pedals, shouting, 'Japs, Japs.'

He raced through the checkpoint, past the bewildered Sikh sentries. 'Jap snipers, over there in the plantation.'

Why was no-one listening to him? He pushed on, deeper into the camp, between hangars, sheds, huts and the trenchline in view of the beachside palm trees, until an officer stepped into his path and yanked him off the bicycle. 'What Japs? Who the bloody hell are you?'

Quiller told him. The officer, an Australian flight lieutenant, listened with his head cocked disbelievingly, his cap pushed back from his brow, his hands on his hips. 'Pull the other one.'

'It's true.'

Quiller repeated his story. More men appeared, some British pilots and ground crew among them, including a man who announced that he was Hume, the station commander. 'Snipers, sir, there beyond the fence.'

Hume stared at him, then jerked his head. 'Come with me.'

Quiller was taken to the alert hut, where Hume folded his arms and said, 'Now, what's the dope?'

Over sugared black tea in a chipped enamel cup, Quiller told his story again. Hume listened, then began to test him. Who is the station commander at Bandar Star? What is the stalling speed of the Brewster Buffalo? Who is 'Our Glad'? Describe conditions at Bandar Star, Kota Bharu and Sungei Patani aerodromes.

Hume was pleasant and patient, a Londoner with sandy receding hair, a reddish moustache, nicotine stains on his fingers and heat rash where he'd shaved his neck. But he had a drooping eyelid, and it seemed to spell doubt and dismissal, so Quiller focused on it, hoping to see it register surprise and alarm. It never did.

After a time they fell silent. Hume lit a cigarette and leaned back to watch Quiller. He said, 'Earlier this morning our freshwater pipeline was sabotaged, blown to smithereens. We arrested a local Malay fellow.'

Quiller began to tell him about the sabotage at Bandar Star but was silenced by a Vildebeeste coming in to land. He tracked it, his ears cocked, hearing the crippled beat of the engine as it made a pass at treetop height over the field before touching down. Then others followed, landing one by one. When it was silent again, Hume said heavily, 'Six. Eight went out.'

'Sir, the next thirty minutes are crucial.'

Hume picked a flake of tobacco from his lip. 'How so?'

'Yesterday they struck Bandar Star when the Blenheims were all on the ground, refuelling. They seem to know everything in advance.'

'Do they?'

'Have you been visited by a liaison officer called Janeway recently?'

Hume went very still. 'I don't like this, your turning up out of the blue.' He reached for the cracked and grimy bakelite handset of his telephone, but there was a snarl above their heads, a chatter of wing cannons, and the closer slap of shells striking and fragmenting. A man screamed in fright or pain. Hume dropped the handset. 'This is what you were talking about.'

'Yes, sir.'

Quiller followed him outside. Two Zeros, their initial pass completed, were peeling away at the end of the field, banking, and coming in again at the level of the rubber trees beyond the perimeter fence. Quiller saw the muzzle flashes, washed-out red scarcely registering against the weak monsoonal sun. Shells zipped and danced across the parking bays and punched a mechanic as he ran toward the slit trench. The Indian gunners were firing back now, but too late, failing to anticipate, spending their shots at empty vectors of sky.

All around Quiller, men were shouting and running half-crouched for shelter. He flung himself into a trench behind the mess hut and kneeled in the sluggish air, slapping at mosquitoes, as a flight of RAAF Buffalo fighters emerged from their pens and raced, their tails lifting, along the metalled strip and away from the ground. He watched them flatten out and chase the Zeros eastward toward the open sea.

The men around him were getting to their feet. One shouted and waved his fist. 'Give the buggers what-for. Send them to kingdom come.'

Quiller was reluctant to leave the trench, even when Hume sought him out to apologise. 'It seems you were right, lad.'

Quiller gazed at the sky. 'Sir, I don't like it.'

Hume evidently didn't understand. 'They're on the run now. You may come out of there with your dignity intact.'

'Sir—'

'You'll note how quickly we mustered our fighters. Those chaps have been strapped in their cockpits all morning on standby. Like an inferno, perspiration running down, the metal too hot to touch, but they did it without complaint. Just as well I took the precaution, wouldn't you say? You look foolish down there, if I may say so, Flight Lieutenant Quiller.'

Misplaced confidence, Quiller thought, climbing out of the trench. 'I think it's a ruse, sir. You've let them lure your fighters away.'

He saw the notion strike home. Hume glanced around in dismay at his aerodrome, which lay wide open to the sky. His men were cleaning up and counting the damage, and peace was settling, but now there was a new, unanticipated threat. He stood irresolutely at the lip of the trench, moaned and glanced up. The weak sun was striking on glass, on propeller blades, on metal, five thousand feet above their heads.

'Bombers, sir,' Quiller said.

The siren sounded. Now the sun was striking dully on a stick of tumbling bombs.

Quiller and Hume dived back into the slit trench as the bombs straddled the cookhouse, a hangar and a pair of RAAF Hudsons. For a long moment, punctuated by a sense of breaths drawn and held, nothing happened. Quiller started to shout, 'Delayed-action bombs!' when the first explosion blew out the walls and roof of the cookhouse. The other explosions followed rapidly, stamping across the aerodrome like a tightly focused storm, a series of drumming ruptures that filled the air with gouts of oily smoke, clods of dirt and wheeling timber stakes. Two of the Hudsons and a hangar began to crackle and burn.

Hume stood as the bombers climbed away. 'Do you think that's it?'

Quiller shaded his eyes. There were nine bombers, and he saw them bank, descend and level out, skimming the trees inland of Sungei Dungun. 'They're going to strafe us now.'

Hume ducked with him. Quiller felt the man's arm brush against his; there was need and helplessness in the whole length of the station commander's body. The nine Japanese bombers began to rake the airfield with cannon fire. Quiller trembled. He couldn't give comfort to Hume; he could only repel Hume's fear, fear that seemed to heat the man, releasing the rawhide odour of Hume's holster and lanyard. Metal fragments hummed above their heads like hornets and slammed and rattled against jeeps, refuelling tractors, tin walls, wing struts and boxed pistons and axles. The men huddled, shaking to their bones.

The air filled with metal, shrieking, zipping, apt to cut them down.

When the defensive guns opened on the raiders, too late to do any good, Quiller got back his nerve. He looked out over the rim of the trench at the perimeter gun posts, where the Sikhs were firing Thomson submachine-guns, rifles and Bren-guns at the disappearing tails of the bombers. He glanced around the airfield, counting the damage: the cookhouse, a hangar, three Hudsons and a Vildebeeste, a stack of empty fuel drums, the station workshop and crates of squadron supplies. There were small fires, splintered holes, but no major damage. The petrol, oil, bomb-fusing and torpedo stores were intact.

'Sir, things aren't so bad.'

'They're not exactly tickety-boo, mister.'

Hume stalked off toward the operations room. Quiller hurried after him. 'There's a rainfront coming in,' he said. 'It'll extinguish the fires and keep the Japs away.'

'And when it clears?'

They stopped. Dirt erupted at their feet. Something howled past Quiller's head. The metal siding of a nearby storeroom clanged like a cracked bell and a bullet ricocheted away. Quiller grabbed Hume by the sleeve. He'd forgotten all about the snipers. 'Sir, your insignia, they're targeting you.'

He ran swerving with Hume across a short expanse of open ground and they flattened themselves against a bogged Austin truck. Hume removed his officers' cap and stared wonderingly at the mark of rank on his uniform. 'A ground attack, too. We're hardly prepared for that.'

'A handful of snipers,' Quiller said. 'That's all. They want to rattle us.'

'It's working,' Hume said. 'How can you be sure it's a handful? All this adds up to a full-scale, carefully co-ordinated attack.'

Hume was moving again. Quiller followed him into the operations room. The British Vildebeeste squadron leader was there, conferring with an Australian squadron leader. 'I can put six Hudsons up,' the Australian said.

The British officer placed the palms of his hands against his cheeks and pulled downward. He looked deeply fatigued. 'I have three serviceable Vildebeeste, two on fire, and two unaccounted for.'

'We were sitting ducks,' the Australian said.

He turned as Hume came in. He said accusingly, 'They caught us napping, sir.'

Hume ignored him, going to one of three telephones on his desk. The RAF officer said, 'Andy, that's the Green Line.'

'That's right.'

'You're calling HQ in Sime Road?'

'That's right.'

The Australian said, 'Do you want us to leave the room?'

'Not if you don't want to.'

Both looked at Quiller. 'Do you want this chap to leave?'

'He stays.'

They looked doubtful. The Green Line was a secret telephone link to Singapore. They all stood by as Hume dialled, and listened as he reported the raid. 'And we're under fire from a ground force,' Hume said.

The Australian turned to Quiller. 'A ground force? Here? The Japs are here already?'

The man looked done in, strain exaggerating the long lines of his gaunt face. He leaned his head toward Quiller. 'Is that what the old man's saying?'

Quiller turned away. Apprehension, sweat and coffee were pungent on the Australian. 'Snipers, that's all.'

'Snipers? You don't have snipers without an army nearby, for fuck's sake.'

Hume got off the line. He looked at them with an air of diffidence and vague foreboding. 'I *think* what they're saying is, all serviceable aircraft make for Singapore immediately.'

'An evacuation,' the Australian said.

'The fellow didn't quite say that. He said—'

The Australian cut in, knowing and intransigent. 'Andy, of course that's what they're saying. An air raid wipes us out, Jap troops are on our doorstep, what else could it mean?'

Hume said, 'They don't want to lose any more aeroplanes, I suppose.'

The British officer said, 'With respect, sir, there's a difference between that and continuing to operate as a base. The aeroplanes can still come back when it's safe to do so.'

The Australian turned on him in irritation. 'We can sort that out later. Let's get the aeroplanes away first.'

The British officer nodded. 'I suppose you're right.'

Paying no further attention to Hume, they left the hut. Quiller said, 'Sir, what about the ground staff?'

'What about them?'

'When they see the aircraft pulling out they'll wonder why they're being left behind.'

Hume began to flap. 'I can't do two things at once. I suggest you find a corner and keep your head down, or better still, hitch a ride to Singapore.'

Quiller wandered outside. There was desultory rifle fire from the snipers. The pilots, the maintenance staff, the Sikh gunners, all looked badly rattled. Someone shouted, 'The Japs are inside the fence,' and others took up the cry, passing it contagiously to one another. Then their attention was drawn to the Hudson bombers, where bombs and equipment were being jettisoned to make way for pilots and crew. Quiller counted seventeen men climbing into the cramped spaces aboard the bombers. The man next to him said, 'Are they pulling out?'

'Yes.'

The Hudsons began to taxi and wait for take-off. Some of the Australian ground crew drifted toward Quiller, somehow sensing that he understood what was happening. 'What about us? Friggin' cunts, leaving us in the lurch.'

Quiller looked around. Where was Hume? Still in the operations room instead of out here, propping up morale?

The Australians seemed to want guidance. Quiller was the only officer they could see. 'Mate, what about us? How do we get away?'

By now, Quiller himself was caught up in the notion of a full evacuation. He looked about. Why wasn't Hume giving orders to destroy the bomb and fuel stocks and blow holes in the runways? Where was the man?

He said, 'We can't leave until we deny the Japs of all our stores.'

'Bugger that for a joke. There are Japs inside the perimeter. There's no time.'

'A few snipers,' Quiller said, '*outside* the perimeter.'

'What the fuck would you know?' the Australians said.

They wandered away, bony exhausted men full of grievances, their shirts and brown arms and legs streaked with oil and grease and smudged with smoke. Quiller shouted after them, 'Why don't you get everyone to assemble at the main gate?'

One man waved in acknowledgement, none looked back. Quiller made for the barracks, hoping to find a senior British officer. There were kitbags, cameras and books scattered about on the bunks. A mug of tea steamed on a bedside chest of drawers. One of the men had abandoned a half-completed letter and an uncapped fountain pen. A bottle of ink lay on its side on a bamboo table beneath a pin-up of Rita Hayworth.

He returned to the operations room. 'Sir, they're panicking out there.'

Hume was sitting on his hands at his desk, rocking gently. 'You're an officer, Flight Lieutenant.' He pulled one hand free and reached for the Green Line, thought better of it and sat on his hand again.

'Sir, the bombing barely dented us, and if we send an army patrol to flush out the snipers, we're in business.'

Hume's mind seemed to be racing. 'Vehicles. Do we have vehicles?' He reached for a telephone.

Quiller left Hume there and joined the Australians at the main gate. A rain squall swept briefly over the aerodrome and it seemed to steam muggily in the press of bodies, heated by friction and fear. Someone shoved Quiller; he rebounded and was spun around and shunted to the sidelines.

One of the aerodrome's lorries wheezed through to the outside and onto the main road with men clinging to the running boards and tray. Later, an Indian merchant pulled up outside the gates in a rusted buckboard, prepared to sell goods to the airmen, but he was flung aside by a Hudson mechanic, who climbed into the driver's seat and was already driving away as others pulled themselves aboard. When a pair of ancient Morris taxis from the village crept toward the gates, several men broke away and swarmed around them, shouting at the Chinese drivers, who got out, their hands clasped beneath their chins placatingly, bobbing as they retreated. Quiller shouted, 'Where's everyone going?'

He said it several times. The Australians were wound as tight as springs, squashed tightly together, craning their necks to search for a truck or a car in the road beyond the men in front of them. One man, shorter than the others, fell back with Quiller. He was trembling and out of breath. 'The railhead at Jerantut,' he said.

Jerantut lay one hundred miles inland of the east coast, on the main line between Kota Bharu and Singapore. 'The Japs could be anywhere,' Quiller said.

'Mate, they're right in our pockets, and that's good enough for me.'

'The fuel dump,' said Quiller helplessly. 'We need to destroy it. And the bombs, the supplies, the landing strips.'

'All yours, cobber.'

Out on the road, the taxi drivers and the merchant had ganged up to ask for compensation. Their hands out, they shuffled through the dust to the edge of the crowd. The Australians shouted, 'Fucking wogs, piss off.' One man spun the Indian around, grasped his collar and the seat of his sarong, and propelled him down the road for several feet. 'Don't come asking me for money, you black bastard. I'm in this godforsaken place because of you.'

Quiller pushed through to the road, digging into his pockets for money. 'Come on, do the decent thing,' he said.

'Fuck off, you Pommy bastard.'

Quiller crammed some notes into the hands of the taxi drivers and the merchant. 'Take this and go. It's dangerous for you here.'

Ignoring the Australians at his back, he watched the three men retreat to a bus shelter opposite the main gate. He glanced both ways along the road, which was empty, then turned and began to count the men crowding the gate.

'Taking charge are you, you Limey bastard?'

Twenty-eight men. Quiller didn't know what to do with them. He walked along the road to the Sikh Bren-gun post at the corner of the aerodrome. The two gunners eyed him nervously. 'Sir, is it your wish that we abandon our post?'

'That's not up to me,' Quiller said. 'Where's your commanding officer?'

'Sir, he has taken five men into the jungle, sir, to kill the Japanese snipers.'

'Good man,' Quiller said.

'Is all lost, sir?'

'Of course not.'

'We have seen the Air Force pulling out, sir, and those men there, sir, are clearly evacuating.'

Their morale was low. 'Those men,' Quiller replied, 'were not given authority to evacuate. They have taken it upon themselves to do so.'

The gunners were shocked. 'How can this be? They are sahibs.'

'They're certainly not sahibs,' Quiller said with feeling.

A bullet slammed into a wooden rail above their heads. They ducked. 'Is this …? Have you …?'

'Every little while they shoot at us from the jungle, sir. One man, he is recovering from a minor flesh wound.'

The margins can't be expected to hold, Quiller thought, if the centre isn't holding. He waited to follow the lead of the Sikhs before raising his head. 'You're doing a fine job. Hold on. I expect you'll receive instructions soon.'

'Not if the captain is killed, sir.'

Quiller had no answer for that. He dropped down inside the perimeter fence and, as he headed across to the operations room, saw an Australian officer emerge from the barracks with a revolver on a lanyard. He shadowed the man around behind the barracks and across open ground to a garage with padlocked doors. The man shot off the lock and pulled at the doors. They were badly warped and he was forced to kick and tug at them. He saw Quiller and waved the revolver. 'You stay out of this, cobber.'

Quiller held up his hands placatingly. He could see an Alvis staff car inside the garage. The Australian went around the car, tugging at the handles. He fired again, into the lock on the driver's door, got in behind the wheel and ducked his head under the dash. A moment later, the engine turned over, caught with a belch of exhaust smoke, and the car drove heavily out of the shed.

Quiller stepped out of its path and watched it bear down on the gate, the horn blasting a way through the crowd of men. Then it was through, making a wide, clumsy turn onto the road, but the wheels lost traction suddenly and Quiller saw the rear of the car swing out and slide inexorably into a monsoon drain. The man got out and kicked the car. He stared about, still waving the gun, then froze. He'd seen something in the distance. It was a smoking, dirty white village bus, nosing its way out of a side road. The next stop was opposite the aerodrome, where the Indian merchant and the Chinese taxi drivers were waiting. Quiller took a few running steps, gave up, and simply watched. When the bus drew in, the Australian officer simply stood before the grille, holding his hand up warningly, before going around to the driver's window and shouting. The door opened. There was a pause. The first passenger to alight was an old woman holding a baby goat. She was followed by a man and a younger woman clutching a baby and leading four small, frightened children. As they edged away, the officer beckoned to the men at the gate. 'This is your lucky day, fellas.'

The men began to crowd onto the bus. Quiller felt hot and useless, and when another rain squall passed over the aerodrome he opened himself to it. He was lashed with rain, deafened by rain, and when it cleared as rapidly as it had begun there was further shouting at the gate. A pair of jeeps carrying an Australian Army captain and four soldiers had pulled in behind the bus. The captain was demanding, 'Where are you jokers going?'

'Singapore, eventually.'

'Do you have travel orders?'

'Mate, we don't need them.'

'Let me talk to your commanding officer.'

'Shot through, didn't he, in an aeroplane.'

'I want you please to leave the bus until we get this sorted out.'

'Try and stop us.'

'You bolshie bastards.'

The bus gave a long grinding clanging shudder as the driver searched for first gear. The captain pushed back his cap and put his hands on his hips. 'You make me ashamed to call myself an Australian. This is desertion, pure and simple.'

The bus inched painfully away from the stop and began to pick up speed. A faint voice called back to him, 'Not desertion, cob, just relocation.'

The captain turned to Quiller and eyed him bitterly. 'We had a report of snipers.'

Quiller pointed past the Sikh gun post at the plantation trees and said, 'They're in there.'

If He's in Some
Battle Slain

Given that the western flank of Haarlem Downs held against the ceaseless abrasions of the Indian Ocean for a distance of twenty miles, and the homestead itself was no more than one mile inland, it was little wonder that a Japanese reconnaissance seaplane would be visible to Jeannie and Crystal as it droned down the long beaches of the west Kimberley coast.

'Look, the rising sun, as clear as anything,' Crystal said, handing Leonard's Great War field glasses to Jeannie.

Jeannie watched the Japanese pilot fly on unconcernedly toward Port Hedland. 'We'd better finish the shelter today and dig a couple of slit trenches.'

But Crystal was marking time next to her with small, impotent steps. Then she stopped emphatically. 'No. I can't bear it any longer. We'll evacuate. We'll do it now while we can.'

A silence built between them. They turned back to the house.

'It's too soon, surely—'

'The war's not going our way,' Crystal said.

She meant the sinking of the *Repulse* and the *Prince of Wales* near the coast of Malaya, and the speed and extent of the Japanese offensive. She also meant the visit of Dulcie Pearce and the

Reverend Dr Sandilands on the pedal wireless last night, urging her to evacuate. 'It's early days yet,' Jeannie protested.

'Better safe than sorry. Ask the men to meet us in the kitchen, will you please?'

Jeannie found Harry Horsetalk asleep in his humpy but didn't find Wally until she thought to check the bulk store. He was counting saddles, bridles, stirrups and horseshoes, pausing to jot figures in a ledger and set aside worn and damaged items.

'Hello, gorgeous one.'

The blacksmith was about sixty but the years vanished when he snapped her his wink. He made her feel jaunty. 'Herself has sent me to fetch you for a conference.'

Wally wore a collarless khaki shirt, gappy boots and thick twill trousers that reached his ribcage and were cinched loosely around his thick waist with a greasy leather belt and supported by firemen's braces for good measure. He grasped the braces like a city councillor. 'Is she in a flap?'

'You could say that.'

'I thought she might be.'

He stopped to thumb tobacco into his pipe. He was powerful and barrelly, and sharp on the nose in the heat of his work in the airless storeroom.

'You were expecting it?' Jeannie asked.

'Oh yes.'

All of his attention was on the pipe. When he'd drawn deeply on the first coals he said, 'Just before young Cam went off to enlist they had me in for a natter. What to do. Where to go. This, that and the other.'

'They might have included me.'

He cocked his head, his smile crooked and disbelieving. 'Well, love.'

She knew what he meant. She was the little wife and had her head in the clouds. Once Crystal had been the little wife but Leonard had died and she'd taken on his colouring—coloured more intensely, in fact. Crystal was better at most things than Leonard had ever been. She'd built Haarlem Downs back up from the dust.

'What did they say?'

'She had it all worked out. You'll see.'

• • •

They sat mutely on the stiff chairs while Crystal made ticks on a pad of notepaper. Tea steamed gently in their cups and a fly explored the rock-buns arranged on a floral plate at the midpoint of the kitchen table. Harry Horsetalk looked ill at ease. He didn't belong here and his opinions had never been sought in just this way before.

'In effect we'll be putting the place in mothballs,' Crystal announced. 'We're not a large concern, so it is possible. Besides, it may not be for long.'

'How, mothballs?' Jeannie wanted to know.

'We close up the main house,' Crystal said. 'Clothing, books, valuables and other small items will be sealed in empty drums for burial in the bush. The same goes for excess petrol and kerosene. No sense in letting the Japs get their hands on it. The furniture can stay—but I want dustsheets over everything except the piano. Jeannie, I want you to sew up the piano in calico.'

Jeannie imagined these ghostly forms in the ghostly house and little men, with bayonets fixed, gazing about in the silent doorways.

'As for the sheep, approximately one-third will go to the meatworks, one-third to Eleanora Plains on agistment until things sort themselves out, and the remainder, the older, more rubbishy sheep can stay here to fend for themselves. No great loss.'

Jeannie had once spent two nights in the visitors' quarters at Eleanora Plains homestead, a guest at a wedding. Some of the facts flickered at the edges of her mind—one-and-a-half million acres on the Fitzroy River; leased by Vesteys in London—but one memory prevailed: her mosquito net had made her sneeze. She'd woken at dusk, swung her feet to the floor of her iron cot, and felt the net hard against her face. Mould, dust, cigarette smoke, gin and semen—the trace elements of the men from London who stayed there over the years and demanded their black velvet. She had clawed for the parting in the fabric and rushed to find clean air.

'Harry, I want you and Wally to round up a few stockmen and drive both mobs north. Jeannie and I'll finish up here.'

'It's all so sudden,' Jeannie said, looking around to the men for support. 'The tide might turn our way soon.'

Crystal ignored her. 'All of this will take some time, of course, so, starting today, we'll each pack a suitcase of essentials—clothing, toiletries and whatnot—and more or less live out of it. We need to be able to leave at a moment's notice. And we'll sleep in the cave at night to be on the safe side.'

The cave was a fissure in the wall of a gorge south-east of the big house, which led to a room-sized chamber of cool, dim air. It had been one of Jeannie and Cameron's places before they got married. Jeannie would circle the chamber with a candle held high and animate the painted dramas—hunters, kangaroos, dogs, caravels in full sail, and Wandjina rain-spirit figures—as Cameron ran his big gingery hands under her dress.

Harry raised and lowered his arms helplessly. 'I all about live here, Missus Dunn. Where I go after?'

'It's all right, Harry,' Crystal said gently. 'I want you and Wal to come back here and keep an eye on things for me. You probably won't get back until some time in the new year, but that's all right, the place will keep till then. If there's an invasion then get out.'

Wally took his pipe from his mouth. 'What about you and the girlie, Mrs D?'

'Perth for me. That's where my people come from. I expect Jeannie will want to stay with her mum and dad in Albany.'

The world and time were whirling past Jeannie, and her mother-in-law was well in the lead. She saw war's end, Crystal back on Haarlem Downs with Cameron, restoring the old order and leaving her out of it. 'Oh, I think Perth, too.'

'There's the matter of Cam's plane,' Wally said.

'Yes, indeed. That's another thing we don't want the Japs getting their hands on. Jeannie, I want you to fly it out. Do you think you can manage that? Otherwise I'll have to pay someone to do it.'

Jeannie bit her lip. 'Wally, can you give her a good going over first?'

'Of course, love.'

Jeannie knew that Crystal hated to fly. She watched Crystal keenly: 'Why don't you fly down with me, Mrs Dunn?'

'No sense in risking both our lives now, is there? Not with Cam away for God knows how long. No, it would be simplest if you were to drive me to Broome in the car and I'll sail on the *Koolama*. She docks later this week, so that can be our deadline.'

'Then I drive the car back here again?' Jeannie asked.

Crystal nodded. 'Lock it up in the garage, then fly down to Perth in the Gull. Wally, I don't expect you'll have a use for the car, but perhaps you could turn the motor over once in a while.'

'You'd make a good general, Mrs D.'

Crystal glanced at him irritably. 'If that's all, we have a lot to do.'

That evening Jeannie began to pack up the books. It was a terrible, stop-start task to expect of someone who liked to sink inside words and pictures the way she did, and she was stopped for good by a line from an old ballad: 'And if he's in some battle slain'.

And so at bedtime she had red eyes and trouble concentrating when Crystal came to her in the visitors' quarters. Crystal was carrying a heavy revolver and wearing a stern, this-isn't-a-game face, and without preamble said: 'This was Leonard's during the war. If you're alone, and capture is imminent, then you'll know what to do.'

A Dirty Squall

Hume had seen the Australians under his command vanish into the clouds and melt away at the gate like sand in an hourglass. Quiller found him standing disconsolately outside the operations room, combing his limp hair with his fingers, repeating the action for comfort. They stood together, taking stock. Only fifteen British pilots, gunners, navigators and ground staff remained. 'You and I bring that number to seventeen, Flight Lieutenant.'

Three of the Vildebeeste torpedo bombers were serviceable. Quiller had seen first-hand how fast and tricky combat was in the air—the Vildebeeste were simply too slow, too tame, too outworn for it. Range, ceiling and armaments were poor. But three Vildebeeste could carry nine men west to Butterworth, where many of the squadrons of the northern aerodromes were regrouping. Finally Hume straightened his back, selected his nine men, and ordered the remainder to stay behind and keep Sungei Dungun operational as an advanced rearming and refuelling base.

'Until you're recalled,' he said.

At mid-afternoon the three Vildebeeste took off as a dirty squall blew in from the South China Sea. They were buffeted and blinded by the winds and the curtaining rain, and lost hope of crossing the peninsula in formation. Quiller's pilot slipped to the height of the mountains, which lay saturated and dully green, and whenever the sky closed in he'd climb and trust that the clouds would offer him a way through. Quiller was seated behind the pilot but flew with him, inhabiting the man's skin, his own feet and hands and stomach guiding, nudging, recoiling.

Their route took them in a north-westerly arc over the airfield towns of Ipoh and Taiping, then directly north along the Strait of Malacca to Penang Island. They were banking east above the island when it became clear that something was wrong. The pilot shouted 'Bandits!' and slipped immediately down and to the west, heading for the hidden, seaward side of the island. Quiller saw a small wave of Japanese dive-bombers, old biplanes mostly, laying sticks of bombs along the landing strips of the Butterworth base on the mainland, delayed-action bombs that began to flash and smoke one after the other as he watched. It was barely four o'clock in the afternoon.

Quiller's Vildebeeste lurked out at sea for several minutes, the pilot waiting for an all-clear signal. When it came they approached from the west, low above the shallows where maintenance staff on Butterworth still waited chin-deep in the sea. Quiller felt edgy. 'Keep an eye out for bandits,' the pilot said, making a low, exploratory pass over the aerodrome, searching for an un-obstructed stretch of runway. Caught napping, Quiller thought, looking down. An Albacore torpedo bomber lay tilted on the ground, one wing blasted away. A Glenn Martin with Dutch markings had apparently swerved around a Blenheim with a broken back and tipped into a drain so that its tail poked at the sky like a stubby cross. Other bombers and fighters sat shot-up on the runways, halted in their tracks. Some of the buildings were alight. As the Vildebeeste came around again and levelled out for landing, a Buffalo fighter that had managed to take off after the Japanese raiders came in behind them, low and fast, as though the pilot's nerve was gone. Quiller watched it flash by and said, tugging on an imaginary stick, 'Pull up! Pull up!' He saw the Buffalo touch down too far and too late and power off the end of the strip and into a swamp, where sluggish water seemed to reach out and pull down violently on its nose, cartwheeling it onto its back.

'Godfather,' the Vildebeeste pilot said. He touched down

gently, sweetly, steering with great precision among the wrecks and the shallow craters.

The ground crew waved them into an empty pen behind the ammunition dump. Looking out at the chaos, Quiller saw how cramped Butterworth was, with its remnants of Australian, British and Dutch squadrons, its makeshift tents in careless rows on the sodden grass between the outer trenches and the perimeter fence. Several Australian Hudson bombers, and some Blenheims he recognised from Bandar Star, had escaped the bombing and were now rolling onto the main strip before lifting heavily into the sky, bearing north and east toward the invasion points, with no power to spare for evasive flight. Quiller watched them anxiously, willing them safely out over the mountains, scanning the grey sky through his scratched and salt-scummed window as his pilot braked and switched off.

Quiller felt naked and purposeless when he finally stood on the ground. He hadn't brought his aeroplane with him; he had no aeroplane to call his own. Then he heard his name called out.

'Quill! Blow me down!'

Quiller burst into a grin and half-ran to shake Taffy's hand.

'We thought you were a goner, squire.'

'I baled out,' Quiller said, 'and found my way to Sungei Dungun. When did you get here?'

'This morning. First light. Out of the frying pan and into the fire, you might say. What a lark. The Nips have been at us all day.'

'Did they take Bandar?'

Taffy shrugged. 'No Nips about when we left, but we didn't wait around for them. I drove Freddy and Janeway down in Freddy's car.'

Quiller said, 'Where's Janeway now?'

'Never around during a raid, that's for sure,' Taffy said, indicating a cluster of native huts between a monsoon drain and a stand of coconut palms at the edge of the sea. 'There's a shortage of beds, your grace, so Janeway and a couple of others are bunked down over there.'

Taffy paused, then became curiously formal with Quiller. 'Sir, how does a typewriter work?'

Quiller frowned, looking for the trap. He said cautiously, 'I don't follow you.'

'I took one of Freddy's situation reports to Captain Janeway for analysis and when I stepped inside his hut he started typing.'

Quiller pictured Janeway's portable typewriter. It was bulky, lacquered a high, glossy black and fitted into a battered black case. Janeway refused to let anyone use it, tapping his nose as if to say that only he knew what secrets it contained for the war effort.

'So, he started typing.'

'The thing is, I couldn't see any paper in the thingummy.'

Quiller searched the skies. 'When was this?'

'Less than an hour ago.'

'Keep this to yourself, Taff.'

'Right you are,' Taffy said. He was in high spirits, bouncing on his toes. 'It's grand that you're safe, squire.'

'You, too, Taff. He was typing with no paper, you say?'

'You need paper, don't you, skip?'

'Is Freddy about?'

'It's like Piccadilly Circus here,' Taffy said, 'so he's turned the staff car into a mobile recce office. He'll be there or in the mess or the lav.'

Quiller made for the officers' mess. There was no avoiding Janeway. The Intelligence Officer had positioned himself on a small bench behind the door, where he could watch, unseen, the men who entered and left the mess. 'Neil,' he said, startling Quiller. 'Don't tell me it's you.'

Quiller turned. 'Captain.'

Janeway stood, his hand outstretched. 'Sit down, for goodness' sake. Take the weight off your feet. When did you get here? How? We thought you were finished.'

Quiller told him. As he spoke he stared at Janeway's face, at the clever, fluid expressions of concern, pleasure and hunger that flickered across it.

'What was it like at Sungei Dungun?' Janeway demanded. 'You say the Australians pulled out? Where? Were they at full strength? Did the Japs bomb *and* strafe? How was the order to evacuate given? Seems a right mess to me. How sound would you say Hume is—off the record, mind? It's to be a refuelling base? How many men are left there? Are the ack-ack guns manned?'

Quiller answered, thinking that it couldn't matter now that his lost two days were consigned to history, and he was fascinated to see Janeway's quivering need to know. He tried to leave, half standing from time to time, but Janeway always called him back, his finger raised: 'Oh, Quill, just one other thing, old chap ...'

Finally the man's lack of plausibility was too much for Quiller. Working a derisive expression onto his face he asked, 'Mike, did you ever discover who sabotaged my plane?'

Just then the three Vildebeeste pilots entered the mess, pausing awkwardly in the doorway, spinning their caps on their forefingers. Quiller felt loud and buoyant now. He walked away from Janeway, calling back over his shoulder, 'Captain, these men were based at Sungei Dungun. They've got all the gen you'll need.'

Quiller searched the whole camp before learning that Freddy was spending the night at the fortress on Penang. Exhausted, disgruntled, he scrounged an iron cot and found an empty storeroom and by nine o'clock was stretched out, trying to sleep. He'd showered, but in the simple exertion of towelling himself dry in such humid conditions he had felt his skin exude the oily wastes of his body again. He got up, drank a dipperful of water and returned to the cot. As he lay there, all the facts of Janeway's existence and role in Malaya seemed to magnify and take on disturbing shapes. Quiller didn't trust the night and feared his blindness under the shroud of his mosquito net, and so he crawled out and, lighting a candle, stared for a while around the storeroom. Then, taking six feet of white cotton thread from his sewing kit, he set a simple line from the door knob to his shaving pannikin.

Finally he slept. At two o'clock the pannikin fell to the hardwood floor with a hollow tock. Quiller jerked upright. Silence, then running footsteps retreating into the night.

Footfalls at the dead of night. Quiller lay back, his heart hammering under the twisted sheet in the close, sticky, soulless air, and listened down the years to his own footslaps running scared outside a window at Haarlem Downs, Cameron Dunn and Jeannie Verco demanding to know who was out there, spying on them.

At dawn Quiller watched a flight of bombers take off, then found a shadowy corner and staked out the entrance to the officers' mess. As soon as Janeway had gone inside for breakfast he backed away, skirting behind the cookhouse and a row of makeshift tents. He wasn't convinced that he couldn't be observed from the mess, and so, for appearance's sake, he strolled into the latrine block. There were no partitions, only half-a-dozen maintenance and armament staff seated on a line of lidded buckets, their shorts and trousers around their ankles. The stench was stupefying. All six were talking around their cigarettes, squinting through the smoke at letters from home as though they'd had enough of the war all around and intended to sit it out. Quiller quickened to hear a Geordie say, 'Me Mam only saw a fookin' German submarine off the Shields, clear as day.'

As Quiller passed down the line, the man straightened, reached behind with a page of his mother's letter, and scooped himself clean.

'Oi, sir, the pilots generally use the officers' latrine.'

Quiller ignored him, making for the wall at the end, where he ducked through the ventilation gap between the earthen floor and the lower part of the wall.

'Lost his marbles.'

'Bomb happy.'

'Eating shit.'

Quiller scarcely heard them. Here on the other side he could not be seen by Janeway in the mess. He hurried in a straight line for the native huts and poked about from one to the other until a nervy, red-eyed Medical Corps captain irritably told him which was Janeway's.

Quiller went in. A haversack, a bedroll, a photograph of an elderly man and woman in front of a climbing rose, a creased uniform shirt on the back of a wooden chair and a warped, water-stained Somerset Maugham novel were all that accounted for Janeway's life.

And the typewriter, which Quiller could not spot on first glance. But there was a tea-chest next to Janeway's bedroll in which it could be hiding. Quiller removed the photograph in its silver frame, a scratched tin of malaria pills and a water glass, placed them on the bamboo floor slats, and carefully tipped the chest over.

The typewriter case sat glum and battered on the floor, almost cringing against the grey daylight. Quiller unlatched the lid, lifted it off, and saw the machine itself, gleaming up at him. There was a worn, gold manufacturer's name scrolled on the breastplate that concealed the ribcage of keys. But Quiller was most interested in the base. The lid formed the greater part of the carrying case, enclosing the entire machine and clipping onto a base almost three inches deep.

Why so deep?

He smacked the edge of the machine itself to free the four feet from their metal slots, lifted the lid off and saw a plywood second lid. It wasn't hinged but ran in grooves, and when he slid it out he found a codebook in the form of an owner's manual, copies of battle orders for the British army divisions in Malaya, and a two-way radio transmitter and receiver.

'I knew it, you bugger.'

He restored Janeway's hut and went to look for Freddy.

'A two-way radio?' Freddy said. 'For his liaison work, do you suppose?'

'Doubtful, sir,' Quiller said, and explained why. 'He's sold us out, right down the line.'

They were in the back seat of Freddy's car, doors and windows open. Freddy sat with a lapful of reports and signals, only half-attending to Quiller. Taffy was watching them side-on in the driver's seat.

'Think about it, sir,' Quiller said, and he began to tick off the evidence, starting with Janeway's meetings with a so-called Dutchman across the border, the photographs, the air-recognition codes and other information to which Janeway had access. 'The Japs have had complete mastery of the skies for the past two days,' he said, 'always hitting us when we were sitting ducks. That adds up to more than coincidence in my book.' He turned to Taffy. 'Taff, you've always thought there was something iffy about him, haven't you? I should have paid more attention the other night in the Lulu Club.'

'Taff?' queried Freddy.

'I didn't tell you, sir, it was *me* Janeway had drive him into Siam to see this Dutch geezer—only he told me there was no need to bother you about it.'

Freddy looked kindly at him. 'Too much brass in this man's air force, right, Taff?'

'Too right there is. Sir.'

Freddy swept the paperwork onto the seat. He looked out at the Strait as though the war had turned rotten in his mouth. 'So this blighter's been living among us for months, drinking with us, playing cards with us, generally pitching in, and all the time he's been selling us out? I'd better inform the General at the Fortress, see what he advises.'

Quiller shook his head. 'Can't we arrest Janeway first?'

Freddy rubbed his face with both hands. 'You're sure about the radio?'

'Positive.'

'All right, then, I'll whistle up some red caps to assist us.'

It was after eight o'clock now. Quiller was uneasy. He pointed: the Hudsons and Blenheims were returning in ragged formations. 'Sir.'

'I can see them.'

'As soon as they're on the ground, Janeway's going to whistle up the Japs. That's what he does. That's what he did at Bandar.'

'Then let's get our skates on and find him.'

While two patrols searched the aerodrome, Quiller, Freddy and a detachment of military policemen went by jeep to Janeway's hut. The police were armed with Tommy-guns and immediately posted themselves around the hut while Freddy and Quiller approached the entrance.

'Captain Janeway!'

They waited. There was no answer.

'Let's go in.'

They found that the tea-chest had been pushed over. The typewriter and the lid of the carrying case sat on Janeway's bedroll but the radio was gone. Janeway's haversack was open and his uniform lay crumpled on the floor. 'He must've got wind that we were on to him,' Freddy said. 'He's in civvies and taken the radio with him.'

Quiller went cold. A last Hudson bomber straggled in, but otherwise the skies were empty. Would they stay empty? Was Janeway calling up another strike now that the bombers were helpless on the ground again?

Freddy was beginning to take charge. He turned to the officer in charge of the red caps. 'Captain Janeway has a woman over there on the island. White Russian. Tania Something-or-other.'

The officer saluted. He was full of jerks and snaps like a mechanical toy. 'Leave it to us, sir.'

Freddy sighed. 'Good work, Quill. Now we sit tight and wait.'

At nine o'clock dive-bombers, in three formations of nine, dropped from the skies. Always nine, Quiller thought. In the ack-ack barrage a number of the bombers were forced to break away and turn over the Strait, but not before they'd released their bombs. Quiller ran to the shoreline and watched from the sea, in water that reached his collarbone, in a school of human heads craned to watch the dogfights. Two Buffalo fighters managed to take off and climb toward the bombers, but a formation of Zeros was following hard behind the dive-bombers and first one and then another broke formation to tackle the Buffaloes. Quiller was in the cockpit again, pulling hard on the stick and working the pedals. He knew exactly what his limits were. He saw one Buffalo flip over onto its back and come in behind a Zero. 'Oh, good flying!' he shouted. 'Fire. Fire.' All around him floating heads were shouting in the mild green water. But the Buffalo didn't fire, and Quiller knew. 'His guns are jammed.' Men groaned softly.

They watched the Buffalo dive away toward the aerodrome, drawing the Zero into the ack-ack barrage. Quiller shouted encouragement. The Buffalo was low and fast, too fast, and overshot the runway and was forced to come around for another approach. The Zero held off until the Buffalo was touching down, then followed hard on its tail, raking the ground with cannon fire. Quiller was jumping on the spot. It was like standing in honey. He saw the Buffalo pilot leap out and run headlong for a slit trench and tumble into it. Where was the second Buffalo? Quiller turned his head to seaward and saw it plough into the water, trailing smoke. The men were silent. Quiller looked up at the ramparts of the city and pictured Janeway's mobile lips and tongue lapping between the parted thighs of the woman with the White Russian name.

Do Her While She's Hot

Leonard's big Packard touring car strained against the pressure of Jeannie's foot on the brake, wanting the lope of the open road—but conditions were too choked and binding for that. Her legs, arms and shoulders ached with the battle, mediating between the impulses of the car and the traps that had been set by the Wet: red mud, minor floods, greasy logs and stone reefs laid bare in the washaways. She didn't want to lose the muffler, or hole the sump, or overheat the engine, or lose her way in grass now as high as the roofline where there had been plain, scrubby dirt a matter of weeks ago. Blisters were raised on her hands from the constant wrenching of the steering wheel. Crystal, next to her, was tense and wordless with the expectation that they might not reach Broome before the *Koolama* raised anchor for Fremantle. And they were suffocating in the airless tunnels of grass, yet if they opened their windows the grass seeds flew into their eyes, their mouths, their hair, down the necks of their dresses. Jeannie thought suddenly of the huge empty sky above them, of sailing down it in the Gull, one finger on the relevant page of Neil Quiller's pilots' guide, which would have dismissed all this as 'terrain obscured by tall grasses in the wet season'.

Six hours to travel one hundred and five miles. The next ten —a high, clean, fast, red, open road through grey scrubland—were perfect for the Packard, and so their spirits lifted. Soon they could smell the mudflats and the saltwater tides, a natural odour of decay and renewal overlaying the human traces of aviation fuel, greasy sweat encouraged by corrugated-iron walls and roofs, stale beer, smoky exhaust pipes and meat spitting in hot metal pans.

Jeannie began to feel alive again. She swung her head around, taking in the airy bungalows of the pearling masters—all hung with clumps of poinciana and frangipani—the humpies of the servants, the shellgrit paths along the lawns and between the traveller palms that faced the broad streets. They passed the official residence of the Inspector of Pearl Fisheries where she'd lived for most of the 1920s. The better side of town gave way to a scattering of tin shops, pubs and banks. She puttered along Carnarvon Street and into Chinatown; they had time to spare after all. The Japanese guesthouses were boarded up and one had been scorched by fire, but the billiard saloons, barbershops and gambling dens favoured by the Chinese and the contract labourers from the islands of the Flores, Banda and Arafura seas were still doing business.

The tide was on the rise in Roebuck Bay. The *Koolama* had sat in mud all day but now she was knocking gently against the wooden jetty, inching up the piles, and the steam train was carrying goods and passengers to the pierhead. The sea would be creeping across the mudflats, too, and among the mangroves, filling the crablairs and secret holes and channels with gentle plops and susurrations, and floating the luggers that had been laid up along Dampier Creek for the duration of the stormy months.

Jeannie parked under a palm tree and unloaded Crystal's trunk. There were other women, and women and children, waiting to board the *Koolama*.

'It's just as well you reserved a berth when you did, Mrs Dunn,' the agent said. 'This is the last boatload of women and kiddies from Darwin, so we're chock-a-block. If you don't mind sharing a cabin? We'll reach Fremantle on Boxing Day.'

It was then that Jeannie began to grasp the extent of Crystal's fear and the seriousness of the situation in the north. Her heart clenched and she glanced with concern first at Crystal's face and then at the little steam train rattling down the half-mile of jetty with a load of passengers. Their fear crept over her skin. It was as if the north were draining into the south and she'd be left exposed. She tried to picture Crystal in a small, hot, iron cabin, enduring the tears and conversations of other women, the leakiness and squabbling of the children.

Crystal grasped her by the upper arms. 'Will you be all right?'

They were both blinking away tears. 'Yes.'

'Drive straight back in the morning. Have plenty of water with you in case the radiator boils over. I wouldn't offer anyone a ride if I were you.'

Jeannie nodded.

'You have my address in Perth?'

'Yes.'

The little train was coming back. 'What will you do with yourself this evening?'

Jeannie dabbed at her eyes. 'It's ages since I went to the pictures.'

Crystal gave her a startled look. 'Are you sure that's wise? The town seems to be full of servicemen. A woman alone. They can be pretty rowdy.'

'I'll manage, Mrs Dunn.'

'Keep alert, dear. I don't just mean where men are concerned but your sketchbook. Don't get lost in it.'

'I won't.'

After watching the *Koolama* weigh anchor, pass through the horseshoe points of Roebuck Bay and change course for Fremantle, Jeannie returned to the Packard, her attention caught by a huddle of blacks in the shade of a traveller palm. They were wrapped in blankets, and then she saw the sores. Lepers. She looked about. Trooper Dalvean was talking to the harbourmaster, signing a form and pointing to a small coastal steamer, a rust-bucket, tied to the jetty. She climbed into the Packard and drove away. Dalvean never travelled overland during the Wet. If he had lepers for the leprosarium then he'd have no choice but to send them by sea.

As Jeannie searched for a room she realised how thoroughly a garrison town Broome had become. Few women were about; young men in uniforms strolled the streets and spilled out of the saloon bars. Sandbag defences, raw new trenches and trucks in camouflage colours altered the configurations of the town. And most of the hotels and guesthouses were occupied by air force officers waiting for mess accommodation to become available at the new aerodrome.

As evening settled beneath a cloud-stacked sky and spattering rain, she discovered a tiny boarding house in Sheba Lane and paid five shillings for a lumpy mattress on an iron frame at one end of the screened-in front porch. She heard half-a-dozen languages as she sponge-bathed the dust and perspiration from her body and combed the grass seeds out of her hair. Bare or sandalled feet slapped the baked dirt outside and someone was cooking spiced fish in a wok nearby. When she left later to find a cafe, islander men —many badly scarred from knife fights, coral and marine rope— watched as she passed, and softly hissed and clicked their tongues behind her.

She ate barramundi and mashed potatoes washed down with lemon squash, then set out for the cinema. She was directed along a back street that opened on to lanes and alleyways, and at one intersection, lit by a pair of pressure lamps that washed the tin and dust with yellow light, she came upon a swy school, fifteen men playing two-up on a threadbare carpet ten feet across. When the ringer, an army corporal, spotted her he called out: 'How about being our next spinner, sweetheart?' The others roared and Jeannie blushed and smiled and carried on past them, toward the cinema, as bets and side bets flashed in a kind of short-hand speech behind her and the new spinner flipped the coins into the air.

An English drawing-room comedy was playing with a Western. Both were years old, and she was the only woman in the place. The air filled with cigarette smoke. She expected 'God Save the King' but not 'The Star-Spangled Banner'. Perhaps no-one did, for there were shouts of 'What about old Joe Stalin?' When the lights went off she sank into her seat. She was invisible in a back corner; not many of the soldiers and airmen had seen her when they'd come in. Would they have been more circumspect if they'd known she was there? She preferred them like this, bawdy, ironical and given to inventing dialogue when the rain pelted hard on the iron roof and drowned out the sound. 'Do her while she's hot,' they shouted whenever there was a kiss or a clinch. Both films were bad and deserved the catcalling. It gave her a quite peculiar sensation of security and fellow-feeling to be sitting there like that, among those harmless, vigorous boys, and she felt free to picture Cameron, not as a corpse or visiting a Chinese brothel, but skylarking with his mates. The men gave her looks of mock dismay when she filed out with them at the end.

Jeannie awoke at daybreak, curiously buoyed by the town, the good humour of the servicemen and her freedom from Crystal. She packed her few things then made a circuit of the Packard. It was a lovely car. Her mind adjusting for the mud splashes and patina of dust, she took in the big chrome grille, headlamps, driving lights, running board, wheel arches, luggage box and mounted spare wheel. She had a full drum of petrol in the boot, plenty of air in the tyres and her own company to look forward to. She itched to be away.

The Packard fought her but she had a clearer route through the grass this time. There was more water about but not enough to wash above the floor pan or splash the electrics. She made better time and sailed into the yard at Haarlem Downs with a sense of relief and expansion, knowing that she was going to wait out the war there, not down south.

Part 2

BLOCKADE

10 December 1941–
15 February 1942

Taxi Girl

Toward the end of their long journey south on 10 December, the warm air flowing through the open windows of the staff car, Freddy stirred into wakefulness, sniffed once or twice and asked, 'What's that smell?'

'Singapore,' Quiller said. 'You always smell it before you see it.'

Even in an aeroplane, and certainly when approaching by road or sea. Two years ago, when he'd been Landy's spy, Quiller had been taken by car up into the cool reaches of the Cameron Highlands, returning from Port Swettenham four days later in one of Landy's coastal launches. Then, as now, he'd drawn the city in through his nostrils, and he'd tingled where others had recoiled.

The Causeway came into view, Singapore Island on the other side of the Strait of Johore. Quiller wondered how the natural light could be so clear, given such a deadlocked soup of odours. As quickly as he'd isolated sandalwood or urine, joss sticks or pork spitting on an iron grill, other smells would lick and eddy at his nose and flick away: rubber, wood smoke, kerosene, tidal debris, garbage, rotting vegetables, bullock droppings. And then there were the people themselves, who lived in hot, damp nests along the Singapore River and its tidal inlets, in outlying kampongs, and in the grand houses of Thompson Road and Mount Pleasant, trading, praying, cooking, eating, socialising, voiding their wastes.

They generated the Chinatown odours of Broome and Darwin magnified ten thousand times, and today, after all of his fear and hectic hours of war, Quiller began to relax.

There was a lot of military traffic, both rail and road. Quiller saw a troop train crammed with faces and was suddenly back in England, on leave in 1940, expecting his first movement orders soon and snatching a moment to go back to his roots. The army privates crowding his train window had been bound for a windy hillside in the Scottish Highlands, just as every southbound train they'd encountered had been full of weary privates leaving the Highlands. The carriage had creaked as the train lurched and stopped and lurched again intolerably, filling with cigarette smoke now that the passage of air past the window had ceased and the grey city clouds pressed down.

Quiller had alighted at Central Station in Newcastle. Five minutes later he was on a local train, and soon after that alighting at Jesmond, which was strangely shut down. There had never been many motor cars in Jesmond, but now there were none—no-one to drive them and no petrol to power them. He headed toward his street, expecting a certain amount of curtain-twitching at the blacked-out windows, but saw only a solitary child in grey gabardine short pants spinning a hoop with an inky school ruler, a couple of old codgers nursing brown ales inside the swing doors of the corner pub and, around the next corner, a queue of overcoated women waiting to buy bread with their coupon books, in a patient joshing mood to see him there on the other side of the street. "E can put 'is clodhoppers under my bed any time ... Eee, lud, 'ow many coupons for a quick one?'

He'd expected that time would have diminished the house in which he'd grown up, but it was exactly as he'd remembered it. He made to rattle the letter flap, but withdrew his hand. What would be the point? He stood there. The door had not been repainted in all that time. Seven years and several shades lighter, but the same pillbox red, the same paint bubbles leaking from the top hinge. Then, inside the bay window where his mother's bed had been, a woman coughed, and it had been more than Quiller could bear. His hand unconsciously at the gold band on the leather thong around his neck, he'd retreated from Jesmond and Newcastle without even making peace with the Dene and all of its scuttling shadows.

• • •

Now, as Taffy steered the Alvis over the Causeway and onto Singapore island, Freddy pointed out gangs of Indian coolies in shorts and singlets, who were hastily building sandbag defences and gun emplacements along the shoreline overlooking the Strait and the mainland. 'Finally, some sense,' he said.

Quiller nodded. Airmen knew how blinkered Singapore's defence planning had been, only a couple of big guns on Changi Beach against a seaward attack. He could see Bukit Timah hill and the water towers at Selarang and Roberts Barracks. There was only one main reservoir on the island; the others were across the Strait at Johore Baru.

Eventually the road became a funnel of odours and sounds. The banyan, palm and rain trees pressed in on either side of the car and a long roof of latticing fronds and leaves ran above their heads. Taffy slowed for hand- and bullock-carts, rickshaws and bicycles, occasionally brapping the wheezy horn. They had been travelling since ten that morning, setting out only when news had come of Janeway's arrest. Now dusk was falling, the light bluish in this tunnel of commerce. Quiller saw the weak, still pools of lamplight hanging in the sinuous arms of the banyans, squared and banded inside the kampong huts beyond them or pale behind the awnings of the roadside stalls. 'Anybody hungry?'

They were. Taffy pulled the big car next to an old Chinese woman standing at a bicycle-wheel cart. She wore clogs, black pantaloons and a straw coolie hat, and bobbed at the three men as they got out of the car and peered into her pots: beans, noodles, strips of red pork, and strong black tea. There was a small boy with her, squatting behind the cart, washing bowls in a bucket of water. He dip-rinsed three of the bowls in a second bucket and held them up to the old woman, who scooped food into them and held out her hand for money, baring teeth stained by tea and opium.

They ate standing next to the car, downed pannikins of heavily sweetened tea, and drove on. After a while, Taffy began to clear his throat and spit.

'What's the matter, Corp?'

'That cup of char was all right but I can't stomach the mucky food, sir.'

Then he peered at his watch, waggling his wrist irritably.

'Another problem, Corp?' Freddy asked.

'Blasted watch, sir. It's stopped.'

'I know just the place to repair it,' Quiller said. 'In Chinatown.'

Taffy shook his head. 'Oh I don't fancy letting these coloured people have a go at it, your grace.'

Quiller didn't respond; Freddy lapsed into sleep again. Then they were on an open stretch of road and Quiller looked west across to the sun as it settled behind Sumatra across the water. Lights winked on in the spiced darkness: houses, hotels, barracks, tents, ships, junks.

Eventually he leaned forward and tapped Taffy on the shoulder. 'There's Outram Road.'

With Freddy's blessing Quiller had telephoned ahead and reserved three rooms in a hotel, the Hangar, where the flying-boat captains had put up before the war. A long white colonial building with deep verandahs, a tiled roof and a cluster of bungalows, it sat well back from the road behind an iron railing fence and was shaded from the daylight by fan palms, banyan trees and jacarandas. An elderly Cantonese showed them to bungalows set among bougainvillea and flame-of-the-forest trees. The front doors were lacquered a glossy celestial blue; the interior doors, chair upholstery, curtains and bedside tables were the same colour.

'A fellow could bring his popsy here,' Freddy said, 'and feel cut off from prying eyes. If he had a popsy, that is. Goodnight.'

'Goodnight, sir,' Quiller and Taffy said.

Quiller lay on his bed and watched geckoes emerge from behind the ventilation slats in darting movements of their quicksilver grey, yellow and green bodies. The night settled around him. Thunder rolled somewhere far out to sea, and it seemed to shake the air minutely, rattling the seedpods in the trees. A bullock cart creaked by out on the road and there were cars now and then, and distant shouts and music. Some of the hotel's servants lived behind the bungalows. One was walking around in clogs, another hawked and spat, a third began to sing in Cantonese, high, sweet and apparently full of longing, which unsettled Quiller. Tomorrow he would be bounced from airfield to airfield around the island until Air Headquarters found an aeroplane for him to fly and a job for him to do, and he didn't want to think about that. Instead, he let the sense of longing grow. Freddy and his talk of popsies; the frank appraisal of the women in Jesmond Dene last year; the clubs and bars of Singapore, full of nurses, taxi girls and evacuees from Malaya. He might even fall in love.

After breakfast Freddy said, 'Sembawang, chaps. We'll take the long way round, have a look-see first.'

To Quiller, Singapore seemed enlivened by the onset of hostilities. The river was crammed with junks, barges and sampans, the harbour with merchant ships unloading military supplies and other goods into the godowns, or warehouses, along the docks. There was a troopship at Collyer Quay and several small warships in the navy yard at the north of the island. Twice during the morning the sky blackened with the rapid accumulation of monsoon clouds above the city and the harbour. Thunder crackled and whumped with the intensity of detonating bombs, and the rain blinded them in the Alvis and surged along the gutters and the monsoon drains. With the clearing of the sky and the vivid sunsplashes of light on flowers, chrome and painted shutters, Quiller was forced to wince and shade his eyes. Steam rose, water dripped, and then the lacerating light was gone and Singapore was muggy and dusty again.

Sembawang was the busiest of the airfields. Clearings had been cut into the surrounding rubber plantations for improved access to the bombers, fighters and reconnaissance aircraft, the stores and pilots' barracks. Conditions were hectic and the tension high, suggesting efficiency; but there were few spare parts, essential supplies had been abandoned to the Japanese on the northern airfields, and the pilots were obliged to scrounge for code lists and charts before every sortie and then return them when they got back.

By the end of the day, Freddy had been given command of a new photo-reconnaissance unit and Quiller a new Buffalo. The Buffalo was fitted with a vertically mounted, long-focal-length camera, and painted a pale blue-green—'Just like your old aeroplane,' Freddy said.

As though Quiller would be pleased. But he shook his head. Faulty undercarriage, fuel-pressure problems ... In Europe the RAF used the Mosquito for photo-reconnaissance—twin engines, four hundred and fifteen miles per hour, a ceiling of twenty-eight thousand feet and almost twice the Buffalo's range. And ironically, some were fitted with German Leica Reporters capable of taking two hundred and fifty exposures on a single roll of film.

'HQ want fast, high-altitude sorties over the east coast of the Peninsula and the islands off Mersing and Endau,' Freddy said. 'The Dutch will patrol the west coast.'

Despite the Buffalo, Quiller's life settled into a pattern. He'd make an early-morning reconnaissance flight, tackle some paperwork in the middle of the day, tramp around the unfamiliar regions of the island in the afternoon, and visit a club at night. From time to time he was expected to make a second, late-afternoon sortie, reaching the target area just before failing light. Most of his work involved high-altitude shots, resulting in a mapping mosaic, a series of overlapping photographs; but from time to time he was also asked to secure low-level obliques of bridge damage along roads and railway lines. He was often fired on from the ground and twice had to shake off Zero fighters, but felt that he had some constancy in his life. He'd had it and lost it in Newcastle, and again in the north-west of Australia and northern Malaya, and expected his world to be disassembled and scattered again one day, but for now his days had the order he craved.

His sourest moment came on Christmas Eve, when he helped Freddy and Taffy to distribute hampers from the Comfort Fund. Every man received one cake, one tin each of plum pudding, sliced peaches and Nugget shoe polish, a half-pound of chocolate, four ounces of cheese, cigarette papers and two ounces of tobacco, and a razor blade, toothpaste and a brush. Quiller let an ungrateful thought enter his head: Am I supposed to thank someone? This isn't a hamper from my loving family but from strangers. He'd seen these strangers photographed in the English newspapers, widows and spinsters in heavy woollen coats standing at sorting tables in drafty church halls, smiling inanely at the camera. What would they know of the Far East? Sometimes he hated England.

But he didn't hate Singapore, despite the worsening war news and the regular bombing raids. Friendships were forged rapidly and soon he belonged to a loose, freewheeling band of four or five fellow pilots. Furthermore, he was a veteran; he'd been shot at, shot down, bombed and betrayed by a spy, and lived to tell about it. Looking to attract love and desire, looking for a good time, he began to stride into cabarets as fine and flashing as the fighter pilots who were with him, and as brave—braver, given that his job was to fly into enemy sectors and out again unarmed. He liked his friends and they liked him. The sensation was new to Quiller. They'd pile into a staff car or a supply lorry and tour the clubs almost every night of the week. Nobody was serious. The girls weren't.

In the Flame Tree Club on Oxley Rise they fell in with a gang of nurses. Now they were eight, more or less, and roamed the city together in two or three borrowed cars. They kissed and sat on one another's laps and laughed, laughed through Christmas and New Year and into January. Quiller closed his eyes in the darkness sometimes and breathed in deeply the smell of the leather seats in Freddy's staff car, the Singapore air after bucketing monsoon rain, and the perfumed, sweaty skin and ironed cotton of the woman on his lap.

If he rested his cheek against her breast and listened, he'd hear her soft breathing, the crepitation of her underwear as she breathed and shifted with the motions of the car, and faint, intricate, liquid swirlings deep inside her body. Her name was Dorry Barrowman, she was from Brisbane; in the darkness she seemed to want his head against her breasts, for the surface tension of her body relaxed minutely and she let him sink into her a little more, and for a brief moment her chin knuckled his scalp and she wriggled to get comfortable. They were all smoking. Someone passed a bottle around. The car bumped over a kerb and now they were in the long bar of the Raffles Hotel, someone calling to the Chinese barman, 'Boy! Eight stengahs, long ones, plenty of ice!' And then they would dance, the women with their shoulders bare and flexing. Even if air-raid sirens could be heard through the dance band music they wouldn't stop, and when the band leader broke off to warn of an approaching raid on New Year's Eve, they had all stood their ground on the waxy dance floor and heckled him until he grinned and raised his baton to resume the music.

They were no more than friends. They didn't sleep together— or, rather, if now and then they did, the others didn't know about it. They were innocent, and no-one seemed to notice Quiller's greater innocence. He hid it well. He observed, absorbed, learnt what to say and do.

But one day in early January, after the Japanese had won the battle of Slim River and the loss of central Malaya seemed certain, Quiller pressed unmistakeably hard against Dorry on the dance floor of the Golden Orchid Club and said, 'I want to spend the night with you.' He'd been hot in the face and noisy. Even to himself he was unappealing. That day he'd flown two sorties, investigating barge movements on Bernam River and trains laden with British stores stranded on a Malaccan branch line, and even though he'd not been in any danger he'd come to believe that the war was lost. All day long, the Buffalo had jarred his spine. A kind of ugly temper had boiled up inside him. He said it more roughly, directly into Dorry's face: 'I want to be with you. We both want it.'

Dorothy Barrowman was large but neatly made, with slim, twirling legs beneath her cushiony trunk. She had long, shapely fingers and a clever, questing, ready-to-grin face, and seemed permanently amused and delighted by life, other people and her strong, healthy body. She let Quiller press against her thighs but tipped back her head in order to examine his face.

He said, 'Don't tell me I'm a sweet boy. I couldn't bear that.'

'I wasn't going to.' She spun him around and around, grinning at him. 'We have fun together, all of us, don't we?'

He said sourly, 'Now you're going to say you don't want to spoil that. Or I'm the brother you never had.'

She was rubbery and jolly with him. Perfume gusted from the bare upper slopes of her breasts as she tightened her arms around him and leaned in to take his sulky lower lip between her teeth. She had thick, short, curly dark hair and some of it brushed like little springs against his nose, chin and ears as she smothered him on the dance floor and the others around them cheered.

But no-one could hear them above the little orchestra. 'Do you feel as if you're a brother, Quill?'

Quiller shook his head. He saw how skilled she was. He felt better and wanted to sigh and fall asleep against her even as he wanted to peel her clothes away and sink into her.

'I have never made love with anyone,' Dorry said after a while.

'Neither have I.'

'I'm not saving myself.'

Quiller waited.

'Neil, I'm scared all the time now. Something bad's going to happen to us. All I want is to have fun. If I slept with you, everything would change, I would start to care too much all the time.'

Quiller hadn't given any consideration to the period after sleeping with her. She leaned back again, still accommodating him against the flexing tendons of her lower body, apparently watching the thoughts that passed across his face.

'Do you see?'

'Yes,' he admitted.

She said, 'Cheer up,' and took him breathlessly around the outer circle of the floor where they could fling out their elbows and feet and pitch and roll like cheerful painted rowboats in the wake of a big ship. At the end, tears glistened in Dorry's eyes. 'Watch how you go, Quill boy.'

So he had a friend, but that wasn't enough. He became convinced that the island was composed of lovers and people in love, and when Freddy took him aside and asked him to be a censor he tried not to let his alacrity show. He was hungry to read the letters and learn the secrets of the lonely, hot and careless men who serviced his aeroplane or swaggered skyward and came back badly shot up. He was hungry for news of love.

In the end, he was mostly disappointed. The men wrote to their mothers, wives or sweethearts, and sometimes—gravely, formally—to fathers, brothers and male friends, yet offered few insights into themselves, so that he rarely put down a letter to stare into space, thinking: *That's very true* or *I recognise that feeling*, or *I wish I'd loved that strongly*. Complaints were muted—'Bully beef is the order of the day here … The mozzies gave me what-ho last night … We had a bit of a flap on yesterday, the air-raid sirens blowing like anything'—and scarcely a threat to security. It was only with the newly arrived or newly enlisted men that he was obliged to delete a placename, a date, or a reference to a movement order, incident or general morale, and this he did perfunctorily.

But now and then he'd strike men who were mired in misunderstandings of epic proportions: 'It tears me apart, not being able to ring you and clear this matter up.' 'I suppose I'll just have to square this off with you some other way.' 'Didn't you get the letter where I explain …?' 'Looking at the dates, it seems I didn't receive a letter from you in the last week of October. Was there one?' Quiller was impressed by the pain these men felt. He wanted to be as powerfully in love, and be torn apart by it.

There were always letters, floods of letters. Pain, dislocation, clumsiness and boredom seemed to encourage the pen hand. And if not letters then daily notes in little blue or black diaries, which of course were not Quiller's to read. Quiller sometimes thought that his own desire to write had been stopped for good. It had been more than Jeannie Verco spotting the missing apostrophe in the title of his pilots' guide; it had also been the calm, untested, unearned assumption of confidence in the family that had taken him in after he was orphaned.

One morning in mid-January he returned to Singapore from a sortie over Tioman island, Mersing and Endau to find Sembawang aerodrome under heavy attack. He banked to avoid the bombers, counting twenty-seven of them in a V formation at sixteen thousand feet. He made a large circle inland toward the centre of the island, and when he came back he saw numbers of damaged and destroyed Buffaloes and Hudsons and large, irregular craters on the landing strips. Water was leaking from the mains, and the station headquarters, operations room, storerooms, barracks, messes and hangars had received direct hits. Men were darting about in the smoke, salvaging undamaged aircraft and fighting spot fires. Quiller made a pass over the aerodrome, looking for the red, green and white lights that marked the craters and the safe landing stretches of the runway, keeping low and slow so that the ack-ack gunners could see who he was through the smoke.

He touched down and parked the Buffalo. Seletar and Tengah aerodromes had all been bombed before, several times, but Sembawang only recently. Everybody cursed the lack of radio equipment and the unreliability of the island's radio-telecommunication system. There was never enough time to send fighters up to intercept the raiders and not enough ground staff for aerodrome repair work. Quiller ran across the main strip to join a party at work filling the bomb craters. Someone gave him a ramming pole and when each hole had been filled with dirt and the little hand roller drawn over it once or twice, he and two other men stood around the rim, ramming the dirt. 'Double, double, toil and trouble, fire burn and cauldron bubble,' the man who drove the dirt lorry said, but only Quiller laughed.

After his debriefing, Freddy told him to report to Kallang aerodrome. 'We're too congested here, Quill.'

Kallang was the island's civil airport, wedged between Singapore City and the sea, and constructed of marl laid out over salt marsh. It couldn't be extended and marsh waters would seep into the bomb craters. It was also the last point of south-easterly land before the open sea and that seemed significant to Quiller, an indication that they were being squeezed from the north and soon they'd all have their backs to the sea.

'When are we getting the Hurricanes?'

'Shortly.'

The Hurricane had made its mark in the air war over England. It was sleek and fast and up-to-the-minute. Over fifty Hurricanes were expected, and they would tip the balance. Everyone felt it.

On 21 January the Hurricanes snarled in like silver darts and all over the city spirits were hectic and restless as servicemen, nurses, planters, civil servants and women in evening gowns ordered long drinks and lost themselves in the arms of friends and strangers. Quiller joined them, wanting to absorb their elation, but during his long trawl of the night spots he began to think of Dorry Barrowman and the night declined into a pointless, exhausting tramp in search of her. 'Leave it,' he told himself finally, while all about him there was a jaunty, desperate refrain, 'The Hurricanes are here, the Hurricanes will sort the blighters out.'

But when the Hurricanes saw action the next day they came off badly, and every day after that they were shot down or damaged on the ground. Quiller's spirits dropped. He thought: Now what?

And he'd seen how crammed the island had become. Trains and cars from across the Causeway were arriving every hour, disgorging Chinese and Malay evacuees from the mainland, all in need of accommodation and food. Exhausted women dragged suitcases and small children from hotel to hotel and finally to emergency shelters in the schools. Prices escalated. Tent cities sprang up under the trees along the approach roads and in empty fields. And Allied troops were withdrawing from Malaya, thousands at a time, bringing with them tales of bitter rear-guard actions and desperate bravery. They wandered the streets and filled the bars, their heads still spinning to think that they'd been run out of Malaya in a matter of weeks. 'You bastards gave us no air support,' they said, noting Quiller's RAF uniform.

It did no good for Quiller to explain that the air forces were too reduced to support armies in retreat. There were daily bombing raids on Singapore now, supply convoys to protect, airfields on the mainland to deny. These were identifiable, locatable needs; there was not the time nor the resources to shadow and attack the Japanese advance parties landing on the beaches of Malaya and racing up the waterways *ahead* of the retreating allies even as the main force closed in on them from the north. Pilots who tried to explain these facts in the bars or on the street found themselves with chipped teeth and blooded noses.

Meanwhile Quiller had tried to put sexual longing to one side, but it stirred like a bear coming out of hibernation—not mean, but slow and hungry. He felt it when the Buffalo shuddered around him above the stretches of empty sea, when a nurse held him tightly on a dancefloor, and alone in his serviceman's cot at night, when the face attached to the warm, stretched-out, imagined limbs beside him was disturbingly revealed as Jeannie Verco's.

The solution came to him in the witness box.

'Flight Lieutenant Quiller, who were Captain Janeway's acquaintances off the aerodrome?'

'He had a Malay woman in the kampong on the river.'

'Were there others?'

'A woman in Penang, another in the Cameron Highlands.'

'Other than women.'

'He had Indian friends, army officers,' Quiller said, 'in the Hyderabad and Punjabi regiments.'

'Kindly tell us more about these officers.'

'He'd visit them, or they'd visit him.'

'In the mess?'

'And occasionally in the Lulu Club, a dance club in the town.'

Those nights swirled around in his head as he stood beneath a ceiling fan at military headquarters in Fort Canning, giving evidence against Janeway. The Lulu Club in Bandar Star had been a hard, shiny, artificially wrought place. You purchased a book of ten-cent tickets and when the music started you approached a hostess and asked her for a dance. The hostesses were Chinese and Eurasian, shy and pleasant company, paid by the club's manager according to the number of tickets they'd collected during the evening. Men like Janeway expected them to be knowing and glittering with their slimline Chinese dresses, their eyes screwed up against the smoke coiling from their lacquered black cigarette holders—but most feigned it. They were called taxi girls, and some of them took men like Janeway to their rooms when the club closed.

'Do you know what Captain Janeway and these Indian officers talked about?'

'Not specifically, sir.'

'Generally, then.'

Quiller replied, 'I understood that they wanted independence for India, sir.'

'Anything else?'

Quiller remembered Janeway's accounts of his childhood in Burma and schooling in England. The latter had been hateful, he'd said, full of braying louts, beatings and ostracism. Quiller said: 'I once heard Captain Janeway say that the Empire was rotten to the core.'

That night he went to the Pagoda Cabaret, and in the dark and brassy light paid for ten dances with a taxi girl named Lee Lin Koh. He was forthright about wanting her. By the fifth dance she was swinging her hand in his, and at midnight she took him to a stuccoed shophouse in Boat Quay. An old man sat on a box on the footpath outside the double doorway. He wore a singlet, sandals and baggy shorts, and began a rapid exchange with Lee Lin, breaking off regularly to bob and smile at Quiller, showing a mouthful of gaps and gold teeth. One of the doors behind him opened on to a shop crammed with woks, wooden clogs, boxed ivory chopsticks, bolts of cloth, kerosene lanterns, ricepaper screens, fans and umbrellas, wrapped soaps, china bowls, joss sticks, candles and tiger-tooth necklaces. The adjoining shop sold spices, herbs, medicines and tea, and a line of glazed roast ducks, dried fish and sharks' fins hung from a rail in the front window. The man finally said to Quiller, 'You go up now, be happy.'

On the first landing Lee Lin said, 'He own whole building.' At the top of the stairs she pressed her tiny hand against Quiller's chest. 'You wait, please.'

Quiller stood in the spicy dark. Boat Quay was a slow curve of tiled shophouses and godowns along the river, upstream of the wide harbour, and the scents of the day were trapped in the hallway: the stinking brown tide, marine engine exhausts, rotting food, sauces and hot oil, incense and mould. It was almost midnight but Boat Quay was wide awake. Quiller heard the scrape of bare feet, whispers, a distant gramophone, sudden shouts.

Lee Lin came back and took him into a small room lit by a lantern that cast a grainy yellow light over a cluster of cheap porcelain gods, a calligraphy scroll and fuming joss sticks. He stopped when he saw a woman and two girls in school tunics sitting on wooden chairs at a table next to a pair of pushed-together beds, but Lee Lin said 'Come,' and tugged him by the hand into a one-bed corner, partitioned from the room by a rice-paper screen. The colours swam in his head—rampant dragons breathing fire, palaces afloat on cloudtops, streams with humpback footbridges— and Quiller doubted that the thin paper could possibly mute his sighs and moist kisses and the liquid slap of his body against Lee Lin's. It was a narrow iron bed. The plastered walls were comforting in the light of a tiny scented candle but thoroughly water stained, and he wondered if he would ever spend time in this little space, staring at the stains until they shifted in his imagination and told him wonderful lies. That had been his trick in the damp house near Jesmond Dene, except those had been ceiling stains. He glanced at Lee Lin's ceiling; there was only darkness beyond the warm ball of candle flame. She took his hand and sat him next to her on the bed and gently, stopping often to place her hand against his cheek, unfastened the buttons of his shirt. She put her hand on his scorching stomach and he ejaculated.

'Oh, no.'

Lee Lin's arms could scarcely encircle him. 'No matter. You beautiful roundeye. We wait.'

In that way, helping him with the helpless impulses of his body—his skin would ripple; his nerve endings were too finely tuned; he splashed onto her bare stomach again; his hands were too impulsive—she taught him how to make love to her. Afterward he supposed that his body had betrayed him audibly to the woman and the children on the other side of the screen, but he didn't care. He also supposed that Lee Lin had brought servicemen home before. He didn't care about that, either. It was the world ticking over and he was a part of it at last.

In curious ways the war was a relaxant. Freddy let him stay away overnight sometimes, and so Quiller would pay the extra to Lee Lin and remain with her until the morning. The paying was necessary and they got it out of the way first, Lee Lin mysteriously turning the transaction into a part of the play before making love, as anticipatory and teasing as the disrobing, the bathing and the whispering of nonsense into his ears. In the mornings he'd awaken and prop himself on one elbow and feel tender for the way Lee Lin slept with her head supported in the crook of her arm; then he'd lie back and stare at the stains on the walls. Finally he'd get up, sluice water over himself from a bowl in the corner, dress, step through the louvred shutter doors onto the narrow balcony and stand for a while, breathing the humid air and watching other shutters open and brown hands draw in washing poles laden with sarongs, shorts and shirts. In the little courtyard sat a stone table beside a goldfish pond and before the day was fully alive he'd sometimes see a bond maid in the garden plot, tending to chillies, lemon grass and kaffir limes.

Then downstairs to eat noodles at an open-air restaurant, among the Indian and Chinese coolies who worked the waterfront. The Chinatown streets were hot and dense, with stocky Cantonese and skinny Indians moving restlessly against the sun-touched stucco shopfronts. Quiller would drink thick black coffee and stick his shoe out for a shoeshine boy, then wander down to the stone ferry steps on the river to watch bales of rubber being unloaded, drawn more to the painted eye on the bow of the flatboats than to the men or what they were doing. He wanted those eyes to watch over him and outstare the evil eyes. When he said this to Lee Lin one day she took him to a back-street temple, a jaunty place with its red railing, paper lanterns swinging and vivid dragons looping like sea serpents over the green roof. There she prayed for him, chanting and tapping wooden sticks together.

If sometimes the locals of Boat Quay muttered darkly to see Lee Lin with a roundeye, she offered relief and a kind of home life for Quiller. In her family's partitioned room in a building full of families in partitioned rooms, the war seemed to be very far away. Quiller said hello to Lee Lin's landlord in his shopfront, climbed the stairs into the torpid air, returned the bobs and smiles of the mother and the sisters, and let the war recede. He'd be taken by the sleeve and urged to sit and eat: Hokkien noodles, fried fish, chilli and shrimp paste, pork-and-white-carrot soup ladled from a large tureen, or snacks of roasted peanuts, depending upon the time of the day. His shirts and trousers were washed and pressed in the laundry where Lee Lin's mother worked. He taught the sisters how to count. He gave extra sums of money to Lee Lin. Lee Lin would say, 'You lucky roundeye,' fingering his identity tag and tracing the serial number stamped in the metal: no unlucky 4s, but three auspicious 9s, representing peace, prosperity, happiness, longevity.

And then he'd step outside and shake off his dreaminess. At irregular times during the hours of daylight the air-raid sirens would sound and the Japanese bombers, flying in tight formations from the captured aerodromes of northern Malaya, would pattern bomb the docks, airfields and oil and ammunition dumps of the island, unconcerned by the ack-ack fire or fighter resistance. Sometimes Quiller watched from Kallang aerodrome as godowns along the waterfront scored direct hits. The smoke when it drifted thick as cotton wool past his streaming eyes smelt of burning wood, oil, rubber, coffee, tar and human flesh.

One day in late January he wandered across to the quays, stepping over the tangled cables of toppled telegraph poles and firefighting hoses that coiled like fat, black, dreaming worms around bomb craters and rubble; the dockside felt warm and soft through the soles of his shoes. He helped a gang of coolies pull crates of tinned tomato soup from a gap in the side wall of a bomb-damaged godown. There was a sign further down the alley: *unexploded bomb*. Quiller feared for Lee Lin in Chinatown. He fingered the ring from the Canadian soldier and wondered why he didn't fear for himself.

When he wandered through Change Alley an hour later, heading for Lee Lin's house but intending to buy a bracelet for her first, and saw Cameron, his cousin, haggling with a tailor in the man's trading booth, Quiller's first thought was: Don't take her away from me.

The Good Plates

In the profound silences and satisfactions of her solitary life, Jeannie read, gardened, sewed and wrote to Cameron Dunn. She didn't send the letters, even though Dr Sandilands touched down at Haarlem Downs once a fortnight, ostensibly to ask after her but really to do Crystal's bidding. 'She's cross and worried. There's scarcely a woman or child left in the north, you know.' Jeannie didn't send the letters out with the pastor because they were conversations—with herself as much as with Cameron—and not intended for consumption. Now that time wasn't squeezed but spread out like a warm, still ocean, she put away her sketchbook. There was no urgency anymore, only a sense of the days slowly repeating themselves. The war news was worsening, the Japanese were burning across the map, but time outside of Jeannie was ordered differently.

She sealed the visitors' quarters and set up camp in Cam's boyhood room, the kitchen and the sitting room. She had no interest in the remainder of the big house and after one desultory exploration, in which she found a hoard of books about Malaya on Crystal's bedside cabinet, she shut the unwanted rooms away.

Her first task was to sew a calico shroud for the piano. Given that the pedal sewing machine—along with the wind-up gramophone, the vases, the knick-knacks, the clothing and most

126

of the books—had been sealed in fuel drums and buried in the bush, Jeannie sewed by hand. She had all the time in the world for it, all of the long afternoons when it was sticky outside, and the long evenings beside the mantel radio, listening to Tokyo Rose and the Department of Information's hate broadcasts. Once she heard Tokyo Rose name Cameron's battalion and some of the men in it. How had Tokyo Rose obtained their names? Possibly in a brothel, Jeannie thought, or a club. Her images of Malaya and Singapore were obtained not from Cameron's paltry letters but from Somerset Maugham. She pictured bored, idle, flapperish, faintly stupid, wealthy memsahibs flirting with whisky-swilling planters on the verandahs or under the ceiling fans of some social or sporting club, some haven where the strain of alien outlooks or of keeping face could evaporate for a few hours.

What was Cam making of it all? Brothels had always been at the back of Jeannie's mind, but the high spirits of the boys in the cinema in Broome had cured her of that kind of jealousy. Then, for a time, Maugham caused her to see Cameron in the company of a slender, languid heartbreaker and head-turner, who would let him buy her a gin sling or take him for a spin down a palm-tree boulevard in her open tourer, smoke trailing from the ivory cigarette holder held between her slender, careless fingers. But now, with territories falling rapidly to the Japanese and the Allies being squeezed down the Peninsula toward Singapore, and with no news from him, and encouraged by Crystal's throbbing mother-love, she began to see her husband as a hero. A lost hero? The pedal wireless would crackle into life at odd times and Crystal would say, 'If he's been taken from me, do you know how I'll remember him? As a cocky little boy on his favourite horse.' Or, 'I've been thinking: Dampier's Hill should be renamed Cameron's Hill.' And, 'Jeannie, what are you up to? I want you down here with me, missy.'

Jeannie supposed that she *would* go down south eventually—the fact that she was stitching the piano into a calico slip cover seemed to indicate her intention—but when the government advised that all clocks were soon to be advanced by one hour, the gift of extra light to the beat of her days made her blink and smile calmly like a woman in the unhurried middle stages of pregnancy. There was plenty of time.

It rained on Christmas Eve, and late on Christmas morning an extraordinary thing happened. She'd set a place at the table with the good plates and cutlery, prepared cold tinned meat with chutney and tomatoes, and taken a slice of the Christmas pudding that she'd found hanging in the pantry in a calico bag—why was there so much calico about the place? The things you can do with calico—when a dozen bush and station blacks came to the back door.

'Him Christmas, missus. Got any tucker?'

The stockmen wore shirts and trousers, the house-girls dresses, the bush blacks loin cloths or flour-bag trousers and dresses. Jeannie felt a small elation stirring within herself: she'd been rather lonely, she discovered.

'Let's see what we can find,' she said.

They followed her to the storeroom, a small shaded building next to the laundry. As Jeannie opened the door on stale warm air, dustlights danced before her eyes. 'Empty,' she said after a while, and realised that Harry Horsetalk and Wally Webb had probably buried everything somewhere in the bush. Why hadn't she paid attention? 'Sorry, we're fresh out,' she said, and suddenly remembered an old saying of Leonard's: 'If a mouse fell in the tuckerbox he'd break his flaming neck.'

'Come into the house,' she said.

An old man demurred, a little aghast. 'You bringem out, missus.'

And so she went to the pantry and scanned the shelves, making rapid calculations: she could spare a sack of flour, a sack of sugar, four packets of tea, all of the dried peas, the tobacco, some bars of soap, some boxes of matches, a few tins of beef, and boiled sweets for the little ones.

She carried everything out to them as a spatter of rain was borne on a gust of wind, darkening their dusty clothing and glistening on their faces and arms. 'Where are you camped?'

The old man indicated the country beyond the holding paddocks. 'All 'em creek run a banker, missus. All about lookin' for 'igh ground.'

'Camp here if you like.'

He demurred again. 'That's orright, missus. We got 'im tucker, got a good place now.' He gestured toward the distant ridges beyond the pindan scrub, then paused and lifted his trouser leg. 'Him plenty sore, missus.'

She peered at his leg, alarmed, but saw only a small, clean, healing injury. Not leprosy, thank God, or otherwise she'd have been obliged to notify Trooper Dalvean. 'What happened?'

'Wild goat, bloody bastard.'

'I'll get you some ointment.'

The old man pointed at the others. 'Him crook and him crook and him crook ...'

'All right, I'll give you what I can.'

She gathered a boxful of phenol, cough medicine and bandages, then changed her mind about the cough medicine. 'Here you are.'

'Ta missus.' He paused. 'Missus, how come the army shoot old blackfellas?'

'I beg your pardon?'

'This old fella plurry scared. God save the King. Them Japs come I run and hide.'

Jeannie didn't know what he was talking about. 'Good idea.'

'Not good you stay around here, missus.'

She flapped her wings. 'I'll fly down south soon.'

He nodded and turned to the others, and she watched them all slip away between the silent buildings and fencelines. She returned to her place at the table and poured herself a glass of sweet sherry, for there was nothing else. Desire flooded through her, Cam behind her chair, his hands slanting down the slopes of her breasts whenever Crystal's back was turned. She shivered and tingled. If he *was* there behind her, then he must be dead. In the corners of her childhood home, the residence of the Inspectorate of Fisheries in Broome, casual cruelties had breathed. There was her father's steel-tipped leather belt, for example, and her mother's visions of a ghost. The ghost was a beau lost to a German mortar bomb at Vimy Ridge in 1917. Jeannie's mother always felt him at her left shoulder, dressed in his khaki sapper's uniform, one hand floating tentatively above the crown of her head, attempting to say that he'd always love and look over her. The ghost was no secret, and Jeannie's father always stood sourly in the wings of this drama.

And so he had wielded his leather belt. Jeannie reached her hands to her breasts to clamp Cam's hands over them before he broke down to dust.

Disappointing New Toys

Quiller spied on Cameron for a couple of minutes, concealed by a crumbling shopfront archway that was grimy with the tides of Cantonese, Indians and Malays who brushed by it hour after hour. He'd never expected to see his cousin so altered, so degenerated and out of repair. Cameron looked thin and undernourished, the limpness of his uniform owing as much to his loss of body tone as to the humidity. His shorts gaped around his skinny legs, around the knobbly knees of an old man who stands through the summer days with a garden hose, and his shins were cratered with tropical ulcers. His eyes looked about wildly as he turned, his arm outstretched, for the tailor and his measuring tape, then narrowed as he registered Quiller's presence.

'I'll be blowed.'

'Hello, Cam.'

'So you did it, you bastard, went *hawm* and joined the RAF.'

To hear that voice, still faithful to the slights and intonations of the past, brought on a swamp of useless old emotions in Quiller. He came closer. Cameron's eyes were deep in their hollows, his cheeks shrunken, and he looked fatigued and vulnerable—apt, Quiller thought in surprise, to cry.

Cameron wiped a trace of scum from the corner of his

mouth, then rubbed it off on his baggy shorts. 'Damn fool medicine,' he said, wiping the other corner. 'This calls for a celebration, old son.'

He looked down at the tailor. 'Me come back, understand?'

At the end of the lane he whistled for rickshaws, telling the drivers, 'Raffles Hotel, chop chop.'

They jerked like toys through the streets. There were often traffic jams in Singapore now and, as his rickshaw crept along, Quiller stared out at the throngs of dispossessed people, who stared back at him. Some of them darted a hand under his chin and said, 'Give me money, Joe.' Soon his pockets were empty of coins.

'Too much brass here for my liking,' Cameron said when they were in the Long Bar of the Raffles Hotel, taking in the marks of rank: captains, majors, a general, Royal Navy commodores, a police superintendent, wing commanders, all with their legs outstretched in cane chairs. 'As if they own the flaming place.'

An elderly Cantonese waiter delivered their beer and peanuts on a tray. Cameron drank deeply and then talked. He didn't stop. He was a little wild, and even with the most innocuous expressions his voice would break with emotions barely held in check. 'Mate,' he said at last, 'I don't know if I'm coming or going.' He drank. 'I can talk to you like this, can't I, mate to mate, cousin to cousin?'

'Of course.'

'We've had it, mate, she's a goner.'

Cameron shuddered and drained his beer. When his eyes finished their darting they'd fasten on Quiller as though to implore him. To do what? Quiller wanted to ask. What do you want, Cam? What happened in the jungle? What did you see there?

'Sorry. Mustn't crack up. I'm still alive, aren't I?'

Barely. Quiller nodded.

'I tell you what, Quill, it's Christmas just having a bed to sleep in. For bloody weeks now I've slept on a fucking groundsheet and my cuddle has been a loaded rifle. Incidentally, what are the sheilas like around here?'

Quiller opened his mouth to reply.

'At least I'm here, eh?' Cameron went on, with corrosive savagery. 'My best mate, *he* got used for bayonet practice. They tied him to a tree and stuck him like a pig.'

To distract his cousin, Quiller asked, 'How's Auntie Crystal?'

The words sounded absurd given the setting, and ran together as ArnieCrystal, an automatic, incantatory name that made him feel as if he were fourteen years old again, displaced from his old life in England.

'Fine. Why don't you write to her?'

'I will. How about—' Quiller paused for the tiniest moment—'Jeannie Verco?'

He saw Cameron register the hesitation and its significance. If their years together had been a competition, then they'd returned to it again. Cameron showed his teeth. To an observer it was an open grin of pleasure, but Quiller knew how to read it.

'We got married.'

Quiller discovered that he'd prepared for this moment, and didn't allow himself to react. 'Good show.'

Cameron's mood shifted dangerously and his hand clamped hard over Quiller's forearm. There was a scar on the back of his wrist, like a sluggish, shiny worm, and as he leaned forward, his breath gusted rottenly over Quiller's face. 'Good show? Not if I never see her again.'

'No-one knows how the war's going to progress,' Quiller said.

'Mate, take it from me, Singapore's a goner. Finished.'

He whistled for another round, then rolled a cigarette as mean and pinched as a shrivelled vein. 'Quill, the Japs are going to come pouring over the Causeway in the next couple of weeks and there's not a flaming thing we can do about it. She'll be on for young and old. Look around you, the brass sitting on their fat arses like there's no tomorrow.'

'Cam, what went wrong?'

'I bloody told you what happened.' He whistled again. 'Boy, another couple of beers, chop chop. Now, how did you spend Christmas? We shot and ate duck, best meal I ever had.'

When they left the hotel two hours later, Cameron returned to his battalion, which had been posted to the north-west corner of the island, and Quiller made for Lee Lin's house. The sky was unnaturally dark. His eyes pricked; his head ached; oily black specks settled on him as softly as December snow on Hadrian's Wall. In the past couple of days Empire Dock had been bombed from the air and the oil storage tanks at Bukit Timah shelled from across the Strait, and both continued to burn, smothering the island in dense black smoke. When he'd returned from his dawn sortie that morning and flown through the blanketing cloud above the city itself he'd seen leaping orange flames in the area of the docks, which were increasingly congested with people, goods and shipping. Fort Canning, the military headquarters at the end of Orchard Road, was now under intensive bombardment throughout the day, and the Japanese were also block-bombing the Chinese residential areas. Quiller was forced to weave along roads that were badly cratered and littered with the shells of burnt-out motor cars and transport lorries. Bodies lay heaped untidily along the verges, awaiting collection.

At that moment a leaflet blew against his chest: *This fate befalls womans of Singapore if no immediate surrender to Nippon Army.* There were drawings, the lines smudged and spidery, and raw descriptions. Quiller threw the leaflet away. He'd seen other leaflets that warned the Chinese, the Malays and the Indians that the Allies were secretly abandoning them. In response, the surviving walls of city buildings were pasted with large captioned ears and the warning: *Don't listen to rumours!* There was also a sure-fire way to distinguish Japanese infiltrators dressed in civilian clothing, according to one of the local newspapers: 'If he says he's "Merayu" instead of "Melayu" then you know he's a Jap. There's no letter "l" in the Jap language.' When the fire goes out of the sun, Quiller thought, we'll still be flinging words with our stones and bullets.

In the corridor outside the flat in Boat Quay, Lee Lin wrinkled her nose. 'Pooh, you stink.'

He was overwhelmed by the sweetness of her face in the dim light. He held it between his big knuckly white hands and said, 'I love you, Lee Lin.'

'You silly boy. My cousin here.'

He followed her into the room. Lee Lin's mother and sisters smiled at him from the wooden chairs but in the centre of the room stood a Eurasian girl of about fifteen. She regarded Quiller solemnly with dark eyes, quite motionless, then hooked a wing of glossy black hair behind her ear. She wore a dirty torn school tunic, dusty black shoes and long, white, slipping-down socks.

'This Primrose.'

The sister of Lee Lin's mother had married an English

policeman stationed on the island of Penang. Quiller came into the room and sat with Lee Lin and her family and, as food and tea were brought in, listened to Primrose's story.

How was it, she wanted to know, that the garrison abandoned the island so early, leaving the people of Penang undefended? So much for the fine promises of the British. No guns, no soldiers, no air support. And who was evacuated? Why, the British and other Europeans, the wealthy Chinese, and a handful of Eurasians like herself, leaving behind thousands of loyal subjects to fall into the hands of the Japanese. She had witnessed many terrible sights—shops alight, the rotting dead in the gutters, children's bodies torn apart amid lath and plaster rubble, and her own father holding his spilling intestines as he fired his police revolver at the tailplane of the Zero that had machine-gunned him. She was very proud and stern.

Quiller had to look away. He'd been to Penang—with Janeway. Penang had beaches, the streets were always swept clean, the plasterwork was always white and clean in the sun. The blue sea was always still and now he pictured the little boats fleeing across it, carrying the garrison away from the hills with their rose bushes, the red and gold banners outside the Chinese shops, the tall masts like telegraph poles rocking at the quays, the Snake Temple and the terracotta tiles like icing on the white mansions of the merchants.

'Your mother?'

Primrose's English was clear and precise. 'My mother died when I was born. Now I have no-one.'

'Have us,' Lee Lin said.

'I have you,' Primrose agreed.

Cameron looked fine in his new white suit later that week, and the candles were kind to the ravaged planes of his face. As they sat beneath a paper lantern on a long verandah in Orchard Road, idly watching pedestrians backlit by distant orange flames, Quiller thought that he could introduce him to Dorry and her nurses, to pilots and planters. But not to Lee Lin yet.

They began to get drunk. After a while, Cameron cocked his head: 'Have you got a sort in town?'

'What do you mean?'

'Come on, Neil, are you dipping your wick or aren't you?'

Quiller started to reply but Cameron blinked and suddenly knuckled his eyes. 'Mate,' he gasped, 'my emotions are topsy-turvy at the moment.'

Quiller leaned forward. 'What is it?'

'I miss her like anything. I miss home like anything.'

It was curious; the word 'her' glowed in Quiller's head, a warm, sly, scented, soft word that stood for Jeannie Verco's skin and hair as heated by the sun. He could smell her and desired to touch her bare arms and see her smile. 'Her' stood for Jeannie Verco's skirt-swishing readiness to take on any challenge. He fell in love with 'her' and wondered how drunk he was.

Cameron picked at a loose piece of rattan and wouldn't meet his gaze. 'I said to her one day, "I know you're not a virgin." She said, "I am." I said, "Come off it, Jeannie, what about all those blokes down south, school socials and whatnot. If you can do it with them you can do it with me." I wore her down, Quill. I went on and on at her. It was cruel. I had a bee in my bonnet and couldn't rest. Finally she gives in, says, "All right, make love to me then," so I did. And she was a virgin after all. Blood everywhere and it was all my doing. What a cunt of a thing to do to a woman. How's she going to look back on that and say it was special to her?' Cameron slumped back in a wash of misery. 'I feel dirty. She deserves better. I might as well put a bullet in my brain.'

'Cam, don't. She's over the moon about you. She always was.'

'She'd be better off with some other bastard.'

Cameron began to cry. Quiller, moved to see his cousin so distressed, bumped his chair around and held him tightly about the shoulders, not caring what the complacent men and women around them might think. Cameron resisted briefly, then leaned against him, and Quiller held him like that for some time.

He remembered Uncle Leonard and the horse. Where Cameron lacked aeroplane sense, Leonard lacked horse sense. Leonard drove his horses hard over that hard country, often returning them dirty, thirsty and shuddering with fatigue, and neglecting to rub them down or check their hooves or murmur in their ears. Once, when Quiller was sixteen, he'd seen Leonard return from a muster on a mare with a badly gashed foreleg. Cam was already back, currying his own horse in the stable block, and had been outraged. 'Dad, what's the matter with you? Can't you see she's hurt?'

Leonard dismounted and glanced at the injury. 'The bitch stumbled on me, nearly tipped me onto a reef in the long grass.'

'She stumbled for a reason.'

Leonard shrugged. 'Par for the course, son. Plenty of good horses where she comes from. Can you do anything for her?'

'I'd like to do something for you, you bloody bastard.'

'Ah, shut up, Cam. Bloody sook.'

For Cam was crying, in fury, in pain for the horse. He'd turned away from Neil and his father, fetched a bucket of warm water and a rag and begun to sponge the blood, dirt and sweat away from the gash. The mare snickered, flicked her tail, and stretched her neck and widened her eyes at him as he worked. But she trusted him, as did all of the horses on Haarlem Downs, and he counted it a bitter failure when an infection caught her, creeping hotly through her leg. He'd shot her, and there was another blazing row.

Now Quiller felt Cameron shaking him off gently and so he slid his chair back to where it had been.

'Quill, you'll get me out, won't you?'

'Back to your barracks?'

'No, no, *home*,' Cameron said irritably. 'You'll get me out safely in one of your aeroplanes. I'm relying on you. All I've been through, my nerves are shot.' He held out his hands. They were quite still. He jerked them into his lap as if they didn't belong to him. 'All I'm asking is, when the time comes you get me on a plane out of here, okay? That's all I'm asking. Get me to Broome, even Darwin, even fucking Sumatra for all I care. Anywhere but this joint.'

'Look, you're wrung out, you need a good night's sleep. I—'

Cameron's face twisted and he leaned forward again and wrapped an arm around Quiller's shoulders. 'Oh, fuck it, Quill, just listen, all right? I'm bloody serious. Get me out.'

Feeling absurd, Quiller said, 'But I only fly single-seaters.'

'Forget the flaming rules. They're not going to mean anything after the next few days. Everything's going to break down, utter chaos, you mark my words. No-one's going to care if you fly a few mates out in a bigger plane. Just forget right and wrong, can't you, just for once in your life? I tell you what …'

He took out a small black notebook, looked around for something to write with, and snapped his fingers at the waiter. 'Pencil, fountain pen, Charlie, quick as you like.'

The waiter gave him the stub of a lead pencil. 'This is what I'm going to do, cousin of mine,' Cameron said, tearing out a page and dating it. He enunciated as he wrote, in thick sloping letters: 'I, Cameron Leonard Dunn, of Haarlem Downs homestead, via Broome, Western Australia, do solemnly swear that when I am safely delivered from Singapore and Japanese hands by my cousin, Neil—what's your middle name? Doesn't matter—Neil Quiller, I will repay his selflessness by signing over to him full and unconditional ownership of the Percival Gull aeroplane currently housed in a hanger at the said Haarlem Downs homestead.' He looked up. 'That should do it. What do you say? Happy? With the Gull you could start your own charter service. I don't want the frigging thing. You were the one who loved flying it.'

'Cam, no.'

'Go on, you'd be a fool not to take me up on it,' Cameron said, folding the promissory note into Quiller's shirt pocket. 'Blokes are doing this kind of thing left, right and centre. Get me home safely. Keep me alive if the Nips get us. That kind of thing.'

In a daze Quiller buttoned the flap of his pocket. Around them the night was full of shouts and laughter, bared teeth catching the lamplight and cotton garments as light as air. Four men suddenly surrounded their table. 'Dunn, you poor sad bastard.'

Quiller watched the sadness vanish from his cousin's face. Mad crooked happiness lit it from within and he saw Cameron stand and slap the backs of his mates and spin away with them. He thought they'd be back, but when he checked his watch again an hour had passed and he knew they were gone for the night.

Quiller flew a sortie the next morning, and the next. By now it was clear that the Hurricanes were losing the fight. More than a third had been destroyed. Meanwhile the Allied troops were abandoning the mainland, choking the Causeway as they retreated to the island, jamming the Strait with small boats like autumn leaves in a roadside ditch. It was a time of anxiety, false alarms and contradictory orders.

When he returned from a sortie over Mersing in the last week of January, Kallang was under heavy bombing. So he diverted to Sembawang, first circling over the army barracks, the Bofors gun defences around the aerodrome, and the cranes and workshops of the naval base on the Strait of Johore, and peering down through heavy rain at soldiers, sailors and ground crew angling into the heaving wind in their rain capes.

Cameron was stationed somewhere nearby. Quiller could not fly over the Australian positions now without feeling an invisible pull from the ground. The promissory note in his tunic pocket seemed to vibrate as if to remind him he'd become his cousin's guardian and nothing could reverse that.

He landed, parked in the shelter of a hangar and unloaded the film magazine. As he turned, he was struck by the configuration of cranes at the naval base, their stark silhouettes against the cloud- and rain-darkened sky, and tumbled back through the years and miles to the shipbuilding yards along the River Tyne on a grey day. He stood dreaming and didn't know if he owed the dampness in his eyes to the wind or his heart. Then, as he stood there, the air-raid siren sounded, a low wail that built to a high, wind-snatched pitch, and the men in their capes around him scattered for the slit trenches.

The raids lasted for most of the remainder of the day. In V formations, the bombers came over in waves and pattern-bombed the aerodrome and the naval base across from Quiller's trench. Gradually through the hours the base was blown apart. The fires raged and were so hot that Quiller could feel them on the wind and see steel girders melt and lean like dying flowers. When the power station finally blew, the base seemed to die. The only living things were the spewing flames in the fuel tanks, the oily smoke and the air-borne ash and debris.

Quiller borrowed a Triumph motorbike and searched the Australian camp for Cameron after the all-clear had sounded, but no-one had seen him. He left a message, returned the bike and flew the Buffalo down to Kallang.

He made another early sortie the next day and then made his way to the Australian camp in Freddy's staff car. Cameron was waiting for him in a mess tent near the Causeway, staring through the steam drifts from the tea in his enamel cup, dreamily agitating the surface with a tarnished teaspoon. He'd shaved carelessly, his eyes were red, his hair scraped in oiled clumps away from his forehead.

Quiller said, 'They'll put you on notice, dressed like that.'

Cameron's uniform was creased and dirty and his boots gaped, unlaced, around his bare ankles. He said nothing.

'You make me feel hot,' Quiller said. 'Roll up your sleeves.'

Cameron sniffed and straightened, and seemed to wince in pain.

'Heavy night?'

In reply, Cameron thumbed open the cuff buttons at each wrist and, holding out his left arm stiffly, began to fold back his sleeves, punctuating the movements with sharp intakes of breath. Then he rolled back the other sleeve, saying through his teeth, 'I was bushwacked.'

Quiller looked. His cousin's left forearm and right upper arm bore fresh tattoos, raw and barely encrusted, one delineating a dragon, the other a naked woman composed of curves that shifted and swelled with the unconscious motions of muscles and tendons.

'How?'

'My mates, that's how.'

'Why?'

'I was unconscious. They didn't need any more reason than that.'

Cameron slurped at his tea, then set the cup down, turning the chipped handle away from him until it pointed across the trestle table to the tarpaulin flap of the mess tent. 'How the hell am I going to explain this to Jeannie? Worse still, the old girl?'

Quiller recalled his aunt's relations with the rough working men on Haarlem Downs. Crystal seemed to stiffen and draw a cloak of aversion and distaste about her bony frame whenever they came to the back door. What would Jeannie think? Would she believe Cam's story? Explain it away as an indiscretion born of underlying fear and dislocation? Then, or later, would she freeze to think of the things Cameron had done and might have done, if that lewd image against her own skin was anything to go by?

Quiller pictured the reactions of the women and Cameron's face in the stone kitchen and felt himself standing back at a vast, sly distance from the actions of these mortals. 'You could go back to the tattooist,' he said, 'ask him to put a dress on the naked lady and call her "mother" or "Jeannie".'

Cameron snarled, 'That's not funny.'

'Sorry. You're quite right.'

'Butter wouldn't fucking melt in your mouth.'

Cameron's eyes were red and watery and a little of the tea had splashed onto his lapels. Quiller's twist of hate and laughter left him and he put an arm around his cousin's shoulders. 'I'll keep in touch.'

'Do better than that,' Cameron said. 'Keep your motor warm and your tank full.'

Quiller sat back. 'I was going to suggest screwing up your promissory note. There's a troopship of reinforcements due any day.'

Cameron shot out his hand and pinned Quiller's forearm to the rattan tabletop. He was as fast and spitting as a snake. 'We have a deal. You can't go back on it.'

'But the pressure's off.'

Cameron squeezed viciously. 'You lousy so and so, you lurk merchant, you no-mater, you're not worth a cuntful of cold water.'

Quiller tugged at the manacle of bony, war-torn, steel-hard fingers. 'Let me go, Cam.'

Cameron stared at him, then flung himself back, showing his empty hands to the world. 'Suit yourself. I thought you were my cousin.'

'I am your cousin.'

'Blood cousin. Blood to blood.'

'By that notion, you have to look out for my safety as much as I look out for yours.'

'But you have access to a plane, I don't.'

One day Cameron said, 'Going troppo, are you?'

'What are you talking about?'

'Last night I saw you with a Chinese sheila.'

Quiller gazed at him levelly, assessing him. Lee Lin continued to dance at the Pagoda Cabaret. She would assure Quiller, one hand on his chest, 'Me no love no-one else, only you,' and if the black feelings welled up in him sometimes he'd tell himself that he was only a sojourner in Singapore and Lee Lin's life and that Lee Lin and women like her had never factored in his dreams. Nevertheless, he'd always steered Cameron Dunn away from the Pagoda. He didn't want to hear what he'd sometimes hear in the mess, or muttered behind his back when he walked along the street with Lee Lin: 'These bints can't speak a word of English', or 'Your Asian twat is aligned horizontally, not vertically.'

'Come on, Quill, who is she?'

The words were heartfelt, tinged with shyness, loneliness and envy, so Quiller said, 'Would you like to meet her?'

Cameron's eyes were crusty with tiredness; a nerve jumped in the corner of his mouth. But he straightened and apparently pulled himself together to reply, 'That would be nice.'

They would take Lee Lin to see the *Lady Grey* disembarking the long-awaited Australian reinforcements the next afternoon, then take her to see *Blood and Sand* at the Odeon, and finish with a slap-up dinner at the Rex Hotel.

They met her in Change Alley. Lee Lin wore a short-sleeved printed cotton dress with a fabric belt, slim black shoes with low heels and ankle straps, and a narrow-brimmed hat at a jaunty angle over one ear. She'd painted her lips and carried a clutch bag under one arm. She looked as fine as anyone in Singapore, and when she took Quiller's arm proudly, he squeezed her hand against his ribs.

Primrose was with her, dressed in a plain skirt and silk blouse. She was silent, detached, but Cameron grew very still when he saw her. He wore a long-sleeved white shirt and the creamy white trousers of his new suit. His eyes were clear, his manner attentive as he shook first Lee Lin's hand and then Primrose's.

Lee Lin said apologetically, 'All right Primrose come too?'

'Of course,' Quiller said, uneasily watching as Cameron circled around to flank Primrose as though she might bolt as they walked four abreast down to the dockside.

Like most of the spectators, Quiller's eyes flickered from the *Lady Grey* to the sky above and back again as the tugs nudged the ship against the wharf. Troops lined the rails, staring down curiously. Cameron muttered, 'Christ, Quill, they're babies.'

That impression was reinforced when the Australians disembarked, mustered and marched to a line of lorries. They had newly shaven, sore-looking necks and cheeks, ill-fitting uniforms and an air of gauche intensity and self-consciousness. They were not carrying arms and seemed too poorly outfitted to make war or stand against invaders. Cameron was barely older than any of them, but he'd been blunted and haunted by the dripping jungles and long nights of Malaya, and he catcalled feelingly: 'Hope you jokers have got a note to be out of school,' and 'Soon you'll be shaving off that bum-fluff.'

Primrose stepped away from him, a severe, solitary figure. Lee Lin squeezed Quiller's arm and said sadly as the soldiers filed past her, 'Too young, like boys.'

Quiller turned away from the ship. 'Come on, the cinema awaits.'

Two days later the bombers were withdrawn from the Singapore bases to airfields on Sumatra. Apart from the Hurricanes, the only operable aircraft left on the island were three Swordfish, a Catalina and Quiller's surveillance Buffalo. According to Freddy, he was indispensable now. 'You and your kite will stay here, Quill. We need information quickly. You'd be too far away from the centre of things if we sent you to Sumatra.'

They'd expected him to balk at flying his daily sorties from the torn-up airfields of Singapore, through the waves of Japanese bombers and fighters, but Quiller was pleased. He needed to stay close to Lee Lin, Primrose and Cameron.

On 30 January he left the alert hut and watched a crippled Hudson take off for Palembang, on Sumatra. It had a badly crushed fuselage and warped ailerons. Quiller put himself in the pilot's seat, imagining the vibrations and the wallowing passage through the air, the early-morning Zeros behind the sun, and the light of the sun rendering the surface of the sea practically invisible, impossible to fix and tricky to the eye. Where was the water, exactly? Lower, or higher than apparent? The Hudson limped toward the horizon, one engine smoking slightly. Quiller supposed that it would be stripped at Palembang and patched together with other, less damaged Hudsons.

His sortie that morning took him out over the Anambas Islands, and then up the east coast of Malaya to Endau, where the Japanese had landed on 26 January. It was a fast, high-altitude sweep of the sea and the coast, his camera freezing images of enemy cruisers east of the islands and heavy troop movements on the coast and the inland roads.

When he touched down at Kallang, a slow, short-stopping landing to avoid the run-on that might have tipped him into the sea, he got word that a woman was waiting for him at the gate. It was Primrose.

'We could not allow her to enter, sir,' said the Sikh guard.

'I understand.'

Primrose stepped forward, all of her severity gone. 'Quickly. It's Lee Lin.'

The city had been bombed during the morning. Primrose held a scented handkerchief to her nose; she wore a smut of ash like a beauty spot at the edge of her mouth. Quiller began to cough, and he blinked to clear his eyes. 'Has she been hurt?'

'Her mother and sisters have.'

Quiller borrowed a motorcycle with a sidecar and drove them to Chinatown. It was an area smaller than an English hamlet, yet thousands of people lived there, jammed together in one-room apartments. He knew they had no air-raid shelters, only monsoon drains and cupboards under staircases. On the approach roads they passed Chinese firemen directing water over burning roofs and through smoking windows. The water pressure was weak; the firemen clung to the nozzles like children with disappointing new toys. Then a petrol station exploded with a slap of heated air and oily flames that tossed motorcars aside. Quiller wobbled, over-steered, and the bike and sidecar mounted the outer bricks of a caved-out wall, stalling the engine. He dismounted and helped Primrose to get out of the sidecar. She was dazed, compliant, her face streaked with plaster dust and ash. A segment of wall whumped at their feet, raising more dust, and then there were the rattles and pings of torn armoury smacking against the bike. Primrose said dazedly, 'Look.'

She lifted a jagged dart of shrapnel from the seat of the sidecar, looked at it in wonder, then clasped it to her chest. 'My lucky omen.'

Quiller's hand went unconsciously to the ring hanging with his dogtags. 'There could be more unexploded bombs,' he said, taking her hand as they picked their way across the fallen masonry, which seemed to have been peeled rather than blown away from the building. They tried to avoid the worst blood splashes and only looked once at the room left bare by the wall: a foot in a smoking shoe; a blinded face in a rictus of pain; a child sliced into two pieces; another patting at an adult torso to wake it up. Somewhere men and women were weeping.

Quiller looked for a short cut through to Boat Quay. Once or twice he caught himself hyperventilating, and his voice whimpered involuntarily to be in the midst of such massive, ungovernable destruction. They passed into foetid lanes where the overhanging buildings trapped heat and smoke and putre-fying flesh and fruit. The Communists had been released from gaol and the Chinese flag, slogans and posters of Chiang Kai Shek and Churchill had been pasted to the friable walls.

They came to Lee Lin's street. A squad of Chinese civil defence volunteers had cleared the road of debris to admit an ambulance, while rescue workers, joined by survivors, were swarming over the rubble. Quiller counted eighteen dead laid out on the road. They lay in their blood. The blood looked sticky and smelt warm, like the taste of iron. A couple of people were still dying, he realised, for the blood oozed from the tears in their flesh and they were calling out. He looked for Lee Lin there, not believing Primrose that she was all right. The flies were gathering like currants on the stomach wall of an old man. With a start, Quiller recognised the old man who always sat in the ground-floor doorway. His eyes stared back, sick and frightened. Quiller could see that he was going and tried to close the man's eyes, but the lids kept popping open and the old man's gaze in death was hurtful, reproachful.

Primrose tugged at Quiller's sleeve. 'Lee Lin,' she said, pointing into a corner.

Quiller let the old man go. Lee Lin was tugging on a window shutter that he recognised as the one from her little partitioned room. He realised irrelevantly that the rear wall had fallen into the courtyard where the bond maid had picked Chinese vegetables and Lee Lin's mother sometimes played mah-jong at the stone table, sharing bursts of laughing gossip with her friends as the tiles clacked and slid about. Lee Lin sat suddenly and put her hands to her head. The wooden laths had popped free of the window frame like splayed fingers or teeth. He hurried to help her. 'Lee Lin.'

'My mother. My sisters.'

She'd been cut and bruised and most of her clothing was torn away. Quiller gave her his shirt for the sake of her breasts, which were so small, pointy and blood-splashed that he wanted to cry. He could give her back some respect; he could not find her mother and sisters for her, not even if he tore off all of his nails and stripped the skin from his fingers in the attempt.

'Lee Lin, stop.'

She ignored him. Her strength was superhuman, the veins popping out in her forehead and temples.

'Let me help you.'

They turned over doors, door frames and bricks and plaster but the rubble seemed to slide down into the excavation like water finding its true level.

Someone shouted, 'Over here.'

Lee Lin darted over the mess like a rabbit. 'You find? You find?'

Lodestar

Wally Webb and Harry Horsetalk slipped back so unobtrusively that they might not have been away for six weeks. They were simply there one morning, whistling as they worked, and when Jeannie emerged into the damp heat with a tray of tea and scones for them, they removed their hats and forearmed away the perspiration with their old familiar motions. They'd bought her a late Christmas present of a carved emu egg. She gave them pipe tobacco that she'd bought in Broome.

The days passed and she monitored the news. Crystal's orders were that they should walk off the property if an invasion was imminent, but Jeannie wondered how they would ever know that. Then in February she was passing the wireless room just as the transceiver crackled into life with the Haarlem Downs call sign.

It was Dr Sandilands, the pastor, his voice clipped behind the pops and scratches of the atmosphere. 'Is that you, Jeannie?'

'It is.'

'Expect me directly with mail for you.'

And he signed off. Jeannie went outside to examine the landing strip. The surface was often poor during the Wet: corrugations, exposed stones, drifts of sand, twigs and leaves.

She fetched the wheelbarrow and a rake and worked swiftly, carting away rubbish and raking the sand, but had barely finished when the Desoutter appeared above the scrubline. Compared to the Gull it looked unfinished, a construction of mismatched plates, perspex window slabs at all angles, big toy-like wheels on struts under the wings, and a high, dainty propeller. The pastor made an exploratory run over the homestead then bounced down in a skittish sideslip against the wind, throwing up clouds of grit as he spun to a stop.

Dr Sandilands dropped to the ground. He was as thinly austere and buttoned together as an undertaker in Trollope, Jeannie thought. Leonard had despised him. 'I won't take up much of your time, Jeannie.'

'You'll stay for a cuppa? Lunch?'

'Perhaps a cup of tea. You must be very worried about Cameron. I thought perhaps we could talk about it.'

He glanced uneasily at the sky. A gusting wind had set up a shiver in the fuselage and the wings. 'I should tie her down,' he said, fishing behind his seat for rope and a number of metal stakes, which he began to hammer into the ground. Jeannie helped him to rope the wheels to the stakes and throw a steadying loop over each wing.

'Now, your mail.'

He handed her a sack and, as they walked across to the house, began to wring his hands. 'Hope I'm not intruding. I only wish I could be visiting under more propitious circumstances.'

He followed her into the kitchen and sat at the table. 'Jeannie, Crystal's been in touch with me.'

'Has she?'

Jeannie was undoing the strap of the mail sack. She tipped the contents onto the table: half a dozen newspapers, *Hansard*, late Christmas cards, business letters, several letters from Crystal. None from Cameron. She broke, turning her brimming face away from the pastor. 'White with two sugars, if I remember correctly.'

'She's worried about you.'

'I'm fine.'

'Broome's on a war footing. I've seen American warplanes on the ground there, American servicemen walking the streets.'

But Rabaul had fallen, Singapore was under seige and Java would probably fall, so Jeannie wasn't much comforted to hear about the Americans.

'This really isn't the place for a single woman, you know,' the pastor said.

Jeannie hunched over the table, caught in her thoughts. She wouldn't look at him. A word from—or about—Cameron would release her, but she couldn't tell the pastor that.

When he was gone she opened and scanned Crystal's letters:

'It's selfish what you're doing. The munitions factories are crying out for staff.'

'I'll thank you not to go poking about the house.'

'Do you remember how brave he was when the horse dragged him? He was more worried what I would say about his shirt than the cuts to his back. Things like that make me think he'll have acquitted himself well at the end.'

'Get out while you can, Jeannie dear. You're all I have left.'

All I have left. As she marked time through the long days, Jeannie began to concur with Crystal. The news from Singapore, Cam's silence, the sensation of his hands on Christmas Day—all were pushing her over the line, freeing her to be an ennobled widow. But now she was even less inclined to pack up and leave.

She began to make forays into the bush, rolling back drums of clothing and books, and she opened the house as she opened her heart. In Leonard's wardrobe, under new puttees in a dusty box, she found a copy of Neil Quiller's guide for pilots. *To Uncle Len, with thanks.*

It was a shock, remembering that tactless moment when she'd pointed out the missing apostrophe in the title. Why couldn't she have admired the book straight off and corrected him later—or not said anything at all? She took the book to the sitting room, where the spectral armchairs in their dustsheets faced the piano, or rather the slab of off-white, rough-weave calico in the shape of a piano. But she couldn't bear those silent witnesses and, turning the wooden rocking chair side-on to the window, settled there with the book, tea and stale rock-buns.

What was that? She stiffened in the rocking chair. A coughing motor, a chaffcutter rattle above the house and a deeper, faster snarl behind it. She put down Quiller's guidebook and hurried into the yard.

Wally and Harry were watching a small silver airliner bank and turn above the landing strip. The makes went through her mind. Some kind of Lockheed. Lodestar? Vega? The markings were unfamiliar to her, an orange triangle on the tail, wings and fuselage. Not Japanese, not American, British or Australian.

Probably Dutch.

Then the snarl, and a fighter plane came out of the sun. It seemed to drop a silvery fish into the scrub, but there was no explosion. Jeannie saw the Rising Sun on the fuselage then and ducked as the wing cannons opened up on the little airliner.

The Lockheed shuddered, turned its back on Haarlem Downs and flew low toward the ocean, trailing smoke. Gradually the sounds of hunter and prey died away. Jeannie listened intently. She thought that she heard another burst of gunfire, but her ears were ringing and her heart hammering, so she couldn't be sure. 'The shelter,' she shouted. 'He could come back for us.'

It was hot, moist and dense in the air-raid shelter and mosquitoes swarmed heavily, heedlessly. They stayed until they couldn't bear it any longer and made for the cave in the gorge. On the way they stumbled upon the object dropped by the Japanese fighter plane. It was light in weight, about the size of a dolphin, badly dented and smelt of petrol. Jeannie put the words together as if Neil were encouraging her to reach the answer for herself: long-range fuel tank.

There was no invasion, but four days later, as Jeannie was at the kitchen window slicing tomatoes for her supper, a young woman appeared from out of the dusty light. She was slender, dark and splashed with someone's old blood.

'I am Anneliese,' she said, as though that explained everything.

Fortress Complex

Dorry helped him. 'I can't stay long. We're getting hundreds of casualties a day now.'

'I understand,' Quiller said.

She'd driven to Boat Quay in a touring car that had belonged to a planter from Malacca. An irregular stitching of machine-gun bullet holes ran along the metal and the upholstery from the boot lid to the dashboard. 'Strafed from the air,' Dorry explained. 'Drove himself all the way down here with bullets in his shoulder and knee.' She pointed: 'Lost a lot of blood. Dead now.'

Then she straightened, her hands on her hips, watching as Lee Lin, lost somewhere inside of herself, was comforted by Primrose on a mound of rubble. 'A pretty little thing.'

Quiller said nothing. For all he knew, Dorry shared the prejudices of the men he worked with.

'Both of them. Like birds.'

'They've got nowhere to live,' Quiller said. 'They've only got each other.'

'They have you,' Dorry said.

Quiller waited, his face neutral.

'Well, let's get them loaded up. I've brought some dresses and underwear from the hospital.' She glanced at him apologetically. 'No longer needed, if you get my drift.'

'Thank you.'

With Quiller, Lee Lin and Primrose aboard, Dorry threaded the elegant wheel arches and big chrome headlamps among the alleys and lost souls of the city. Quiller had never seen so many Allied soldiers wandering the streets. At the Rex Hotel Dorry said, 'I won't come in.'

He leaned across and kissed her before getting out of the car. 'You've been marvellous.'

When they were all on the footpath Dorry said 'Toodle ooh' and trailed a hand carelessly as she drove away, her hair lifting in the passing air.

It was dimly lit inside the lobby of the Rex. Sandbags and mattresses had been stacked against the windows, and a number of men and women sat in the deep club chairs, smoking, talking, reading newspapers from London. Their gaiety was forced; they had the look of dispossessed planters from across the Causeway.

At that moment the air-raid siren started its long winding note and Quiller saw how everyone froze, listening, gauging the path of the bombers and the trajectory of their bombs. As the building began to shake he pulled Lee Lin and Primrose behind the registration desk and, when he peered out after the bombers had passed, he saw people emerging from cupboards and under tables. Others lay where they were, their feet showing, toes digging into carpet and floorboards. One or two took their hands from their ears and cocked their heads. Within seconds of the all-clear sounding, the lobby had returned to its old aplomb, as though nothing had ever punctuated the calm.

'We are full up, sir,' the desk clerk told Quiller.

Lee Lin was holding his arm. She was trembling with unfocused distress.

'My companions have just lost their home to a bomb.'

'I'm sorry, sir, but all of our rooms are taken.' The clerk waved an agitated hand at the lobby. 'Just look around you. Completely booked out.'

Primrose said firmly, 'Where do you suggest we go?'

The clerk scribbled on a sheet of hotel notepaper. 'The Jade Horse Mansions in Orchard Road,' he said. 'My landlady may have something for you.'

By mid-afternoon Quiller had settled Primrose and Lee Lin

into an upstairs room of a small, subdivided two-storey building. A shipping agent from Port Swettenham lived in one of the adjacent rooms, a planter and his wife and baby son in another, the landlady in the ground-floor rooms. They all shared the kitchen. There was a sandbagged shelter under the stairs, a piano in the hallway and a small courtyard.

The shipping clerk, who hovered in doorways, the hall and the stairs as they explored the building, was named Magill. He'd whisper, 'If you need anything ...' and had a habit of hunching his thin shoulders, hooding his soft, damp brown eyes and fixing Primrose with a stare of longing and reproach.

'Ugh,' she told Quiller, when Magill finally disappeared.

Lee Lin was getting her spirits back. 'Cousin, Mr Mag a good husband for you.'

Primrose punched her. 'Stop it.'

There was brownout paper on their window. 'Remember to use it tonight,' Quiller said, making a last tour of the room.

'You go now?'

'I'll look in again tomorrow.'

They kissed him and burrowed their heads against his chest. He wondered: Is this what it's like for husbands and fathers? Then he thought: We're orphans, that's what joins us.

Concern for Lee Lin settled in Quiller like a dull ache. He obtained permission from Freddy to live at the Jade Horse Mansions on the proviso that he report to Kallang every day for the dawn sortie, but felt incapable of helping her in ways that mattered. She might emerge from the shocked inner reaches of herself to say, 'You my rock,' but he knew that he wasn't, and was thankful that Primrose, whose own grieving was angry, practical and forthright, could be with her during the day.

He slept on a bedroll in the corner, and as the night bombardments intensified he liked to stand at the window and watch the muzzle-flash of the big guns in the north-west. They rumbled like distant thunder; the flashes were like lightning, illuminating the roofless city.

One evening a bullet smacked against the stucco wall near the windowsill. He ducked, hearing a voice cry, 'You there, on the first floor.'

He looked out. An air-raid warden wearing a steel hat stood below the window, his bony knees like washed potatoes below the hem of his shorts. He was waving a revolver up at Quiller. 'Turn off that light at once.'

We're all sick of being besieged, Quiller thought, grinning apologetically at the warden, who was probably just as sick of recalcitrant civilians as the civilians were of the chaos and the stream of regulations. 'Right you are.'

Suddenly Lee Lin was crouching beside him in the open window. 'What for you shoot at us, silly man?'

'By Jove,' the warden spluttered, 'I'll have you up on a charge, see if I don't.'

Quiller sighed and pushed away and turned off the light. The shipping clerk from Port Swettenham was in the doorway. Magill always seemed to arrive silently, becoming a presence at their elbows before they realised it. Quiller said, 'Not you again.'

Magill slipped by him into the room and made for Primrose, who backed up against a wardrobe and demanded, 'What do you want, Mr Mag?'

The man's voice cracked in the face of his ungovernable terrors. 'Would it help if I just held you a little?'

'No. Go away.'

He sulked. 'But I love you,' he said with baleful honesty.

'I don't love you.'

'You could learn to.'

He'd been drinking. When he took a few peevish, importunate, defeatist steps toward Primrose and made to pat her upper arms and aim a kiss at her cheek, she took her lucky slice of shrapnel from her pocket and waved it fiercely in his face.

Quiller stepped between them and took Magill by the arm. 'Come on, friend. Go to your room and sleep it off.'

The clerk sat on the floor and began to weep. His face worked wetly: 'I'm scared. I don't know where to go.'

Lee Lin grabbed him and hauled him to his feet. 'All scared here, Mr Mag,' she said as she led him out.

She returned and tugged on Quiller's hand. He looked closely at her. Bit by bit she pulled him to her little bed and scooted back to make room for him. They sat with their backs against the wall. She was making a brave effort and Quiller found himself telling her stories and encouraging her to talk. It was never fully dark in that room. They were forbidden to display any light to the outside world at night but the reverse didn't hold, for a permanent glow always leaked into the room, intensifying and fading as the flames and percussive flashes waxed and waned over the crippled city. Quiller could see Primrose in the adjacent bed, one arm flung over her eyes as she drowsily listened and contributed to the conversation. Presently she turned her back to the room and fell silent.

When they were certain that she was asleep, Quiller and Lee Lin made love. It should have been silent but Lee Lin had never been silent and tonight her exertions were tinged with her losses and desperation. Primrose awoke, saw them, and flopped irritably onto her side again, and so Quiller couldn't finish. He lay with Lee Lin's arms around him, his heart beating heavily. He remembered a line written to his mother by the Canadian soldier: 'I am terribly tired now. If I were to lie with you I might die in your arms, dearest one.'

Whenever Cameron had a half-day pass Quiller met him that evening in a temporary dancehall at Bukit Timah village, at the edge of the Australian Army's command area in the north-west sector of the island. More often than not Cameron would be fingering a roll of unused ten-cent dance tickets and staring dejectedly at the handful of listless taxi girls standing at one side of the little orchestra. 'Help yourself, Quill.'

Quiller would shake his head.

One evening Cameron sighed, pocketed the tickets and said, 'Things are pretty hot, mate.'

'In what way?'

'The Nips are shelling us now. They're just across the Strait. We can see them, thousands of the buggers digging in.'

Quiller shook his head. 'The gen is, they'll come across at the British sector.'

'You're talking out of your arse. We can see them massing. Besides, the Strait is only a few hundred yards across at our sector, so it makes sense.'

They sipped their stengahs. The orchestra began to saw and blow in tinny, wheezy notes.

'They've got artillery spotters in the tall buildings in Johore Bharu,' Cameron said. 'If we could lob some shells over we'd knock them off their perches, only the word's come down: Don't damage the Sultan's palace.' He struck an exaggerated attitude: 'The Sultan is a spiffing good chap, don't you know. Polo. Cricket. Mustn't hurt the old boy's palace.'

'Are you digging in?'

'Ah,' said Cameron, dismissing the notion with an offhand but faintly embittered curl of his lip, 'it's too fucking hot. Plus the ground's too swampy.'

Quiller stared at the gouges and scorch marks on the tabletop, thinking of the English defences, ninety degrees to the east of the Australian sector. He'd seen, when coming in low over the island, only a handful of tree-trunk blockhouses, sandbag defence lines and earthen gun emplacements. Apparently the generals believed that solid defences would be bad for morale, encouraging a fortress complex in everybody.

'Quill?'

He looked up.

Cameron was staring at his top pocket. 'Mate, you still got that promissory note?'

'Not on me, no.'

'But you've got it?'

'Yes.'

'You haven't lost it?'

'No.'

'It's not that I'm scared. We'll help each other.'

'We will,' Quiller said.

Cameron flung himself back in his chair aggrievedly. 'Though how the fuck you're going to fly me out in a one-seater, I don't know.'

'We'll manage something.'

'Mum and Dad and me, we took you in, Neil.'

'I know.'

Cameron flattened his hand in a scything motion. 'Don't get me wrong, I'm not retracting the offer. Get me out and the Gull is yours to keep.'

'I understand.'

Cameron swallowed and he looked shorn and vulnerable. 'Mate, those shells come screaming over like express trains.'

'Cam, I'll get you out.'

'She's going to blow any day now, Quill.'

On 2 February Quiller was suddenly scrambled to help fighters from Sumatra tend to a relief convoy that was steaming through the Durian Strait toward Singapore Harbour. While the fighters tackled the Japanese attack planes, Quiller flew in wide arcs, watching out for enemy ships and aircraft. He spotted the nine dive-bombers that attacked the *Empress of Asia*, setting her alight, but could do nothing but send his warning signal and hang back and watch. Before he was aware of it, a Zero appeared from out of the sun, flying directly at him, holding off and then firing a short burst at close range. Quiller had a moment to suppose that the pilot had all but exhausted his magazines—for otherwise he'd have fired a more intensive burst or at least banked and come in on his tail—when bits of the Buffalo fell away and holes appeared across the wings and nose cowling.

Quiller dropped altitude and sped back across the tops of the waves to Kallang. Most of the buildings were on fire and a number of Hurricanes lay broken-backed beside the hangars. The runway, less than half a mile in length, was badly cratered after weeks of bombing and, as he touched down, his motor throttled back and he ran into a poorly filled crater that seemed to grab the Buffalo by the wheels, wrench her around and tip her nose into the ground. He heard the propellers and one wing snap and then his forehead smacked against the controls.

He lay like that for a while, dazed and shaken. A voice said, 'I can smell petrol.'

'Get him out.'

Someone slid open the cockpit. A hand shook him. 'I say, can you hear me?'

Quiller pulled his head back. 'I'm blind. I'm blind.' The panic rose in him. 'I've been blinded.'

A handkerchief swiped roughly across his forehead and eyes. 'It's only blood, old chap. Let's get you out before she goes up.'

'She leaks fuel like buggery,' Quiller said agreeably as he climbed from the wreckage. He was thankful they'd saved his sight and his life, and eager to show that he had no intention of defending the Brewster Buffalo.

They stood back in the lowering smoke and gauged the damage, Quiller holding the handkerchief to the cut on his head. Pressure seemed to be building behind his eyes, threatening to split his skull. 'Sorry, but I think I should sit for a moment.'

He was led away as a tractor drove onto the runway and a chain was thrown around the Buffalo to drag it clear. Later a warrant officer took him into the city in a black Humber and dropped him by the statue of Raffles. When Quiller tried to stand he was forced to reach out his arm and lean against the base of the statue until the world stopped sawing. A passing Australian glanced at him keenly. 'There's a casualty clearing station in the Cathay Building,' he said, helping Quiller across the street.

Quiller went in, holding on to doors and pillars. The stench was overwhelming—death and blood and the wastes of dozens of people. He could see only one nurse on duty. 'Dorry, we have to stop meeting like this.'

'Quill?'

'It's just a cut.'

When she drew near and peered at him, he grinned. 'Got any peace news, love?'

'Idiot,' Dorry said, easing him onto the marble floor with his back against a marble column.

Quiller liked the Cathay Building. A lifetime ago, when he was spying for Landy, he would climb to its roof to fix the city in his mind. The Town Hall, the Supreme Court, the Fullerton Buildings, the high spire of St Andrew's Cathedral, and the rooftops of serried tiles marching back through the palm fronds, banyan elbows, spiky fruits and the fleshy red of tropical flowers. He closed his eyes while Dorry cleaned the injury. The bridges and the water traffic. Junks, launches, sampans, sometimes barges and coastal lighters. Dorry hadn't washed for some time. She reeked. Quiller opened his eyes, found her blood-splashed bodice at the level of his face, and wanted to take her to bed. Then he felt pity, and said:

'How long since you slept, love?'

A fly droned and set down on an uncovered body nearby. 'Don't make me laugh,' Dorry said. She sat back on her heels to gauge the effect of her nursing. 'There. You'll live.'

He tried to get up. She pushed him down. 'Stay until you feel stronger.'

'Nurse!' someone shouted.

'That blooming man,' she fumed, 'he never lets up.'

'Go,' Quiller said.

Then he was puzzled to see movement in a line of men, women and children who'd been lying, sitting or standing nearby. They crawled, shuffled and dragged themselves along for a few feet, then stopped resignedly. He pointed: 'What's up with that lot?'

'The surgeon's at the head of the queue. He's operating in what used to be the storeroom.' Dorry stood. 'Will you be all right?'

'Yes.'

'What about your popsies?'

'I don't know,' Quiller admitted. 'I haven't seen them for a few hours.'

'They should evacuate.' Dorry squatted again. Her voice was a tired murmur. 'Stay in touch, all right? I may be able to help them.' She touched her nose. 'Not a word, mind.'

'You're an angel.'

Dorry said sadly, 'I'd rather have a bit of the devil in me again.'

Quiller rested and at nightfall, under a barrage of shelling, made his way to the Jade Horse Mansions on Orchard Road. The lights were out, the hallway densely dark, and so he didn't see the man who stopped him with a hand hard against his chest.

'State your business.'

The accent was Glaswegian. 'I've come to see friends,' Quiller said shakily, stressing the Geordie tones in his voice.

His eyes adjusted to the darkness. The sentry was a corporal in a Scottish regiment. 'I've come to see how Lee Lin and Primrose are,' he went on.

The corporal stepped back. 'A word to the wise, sir. Whenever you go up and down the stairs, announce yourself: "RAF coming up, RAF coming down." '

'But who are you?'

'There are six of us. We've taken the ground-floor rooms.'

'Where's the landlady?'

'Packed up and gone. Got a berth on a ship.'

Quiller mounted the stairs and at the first landing sensed another man waiting in the darkness. Hearing a gasp of fright, he said quickly, 'RAF coming up.'

'Christ, sir, you almost got yourself shot, you did.'

The bombardment continued overhead, irregular, unceasing. Before Quiller could finish climbing to the first floor, a shell burst at roof level in the adjacent flat, shaking the Mansions and throwing him against the sentry, and both of them against the stone balustrade. Chunks of powdery plaster broke from the walls and ceiling. As Quiller gasped and coughed and tore at his throat for air, footsteps clattered down the stairs, and he heard Primrose call out, 'Civilians coming down.'

'Primrose, it's me,' he said. He could see her with Lee Lin and Magill, all holding handkerchiefs over their faces. 'Are you all right?'

Primrose grinned ironically. 'We're surrounded by brave Scottish lads.'

The corporal called up to them. 'Everyone to the shelter.'

In the space beneath the stairs, Quiller sat Lee Lin between his knees and against his chest and rested his chin on the crown of her head. Primrose settled next to him, and the two Scottish soldiers opposite, with Magill, who glowered at Primrose in petulance and misery. As the shelling continued and the walls trembled around them they found themselves looking up, waiting, listening.

Later the little door opened and the remaining Scottish soldiers crowded into the shelter, bringing flasks of tea and tins of bully beef. 'A wee bit friendly out there,' one man said.

As if released by the interruption, Lee Lin began to draw the Scotsmen out. 'Where you from?' 'How many in family?' 'You married?' 'Have a sweetheart?' 'How long been in Singapore?' 'You like?'

They'd been in continuous action since early December, the corporal told her, addressing her as 'hen'. After being cut off at the battle for Slim River they'd walked overland the four hundred miles to the Strait of Johore and across the Causeway, dodging potshots, eventually finding their way to Orchard Road. They talked in snatches, punctuated by the whistling of the shells, the tense silence as everyone tracked the trajectories, the crumples of the explosions.

At midnight on Sunday, 8 February, the Japanese slipped across the Strait of Johore in small boats. By Tuesday morning they held the Causeway, repairing it quickly for the tanks to move across in support of the ground troops. Even so, Quiller continued to report daily at Kallang aerodrome, where he'd hang about pointlessly before returning to Orchard Road again at nightfall. 'Stick around, old boy,' Freddy would say. 'We'll get you another kite as soon as we can.'

Late on the 10th, Quiller saw two new and distinct columns of smoke above the island. The Japanese had destroyed the fuel dumps near the Australian positions at Bukit Timah and near the naval base in the north-west. Then rain swept across, combining with the smoke to fall in oily black smuts that soon soaked his uniform and smudged his skin.

On Wednesday, 11 February, Freddy said, 'Quill, it's official. All remaining RAF personnel are to be evacuated to Sumatra. Get your kit ready.'

There was only a handful of RAF officers and men left now. Most were radar operators. The next day Quiller helped them to sledge-hammer radar and signals equipment, spike fuel tanks, burn documents, plough up the airfield and throw weapons into the water, and then he scrounged extra atabrine tablets for his kit and finally went to find Freddy, who was sitting in the passenger seat of one of the two unit lorries. Taffy was the driver. 'Hop aboard squire,' Taffy said, jerking his head.

Quiller climbed onto the tray with ten other men. As the lorries bumped through the main gate and toward the docks, he realised that he'd forgotten his revolver. He looked back. Kallang was dying behind him, the black mud oozing into the craters, an oily wind moaning around the splintered control tower, seagulls huddling withdrawn and reproachful on the broken black spines of the Hurricanes.

On the roads and streets outside the aerodrome the drivers were forced to stay in bottom gear as they steered around the bomb craters, gutted cars and shops, overturned electric trams and crazy twists of cables and firehoses. One or two of the ground staff rocked in distress. The others looked white and shocked. One by one they put handkerchiefs or the flaps of their shirts over their noses. 'I had no idea,' one man said.

Quiller looked out. By now he was accustomed to the stench, the gouts and pools of blood and human matter. Not numbed— he sometimes said to himself, 'There but for the grace of God' —but accustomed, unlike the Kallang radar operators, who had spent their days in darkened rooms, listening, watching, charting the unseen.

They reached the docks and stopped at a gate in a barbed-wire security fence, military policemen barring their way. Dozens of soldiers were milling about, each with a fag-end in one fist and a kitbag over one shoulder, trying to gain access to the dockside, and they eyed the RAF lorries hopefully. Then they scattered. A wave of bombers was approaching, and Quiller counted fifty-three of them. As the bombs erupted in a long line across the wharves and godowns, he clambered over the side of the lorry and squatted beside the rear wheels with Taffy and two other men. There was nowhere else to go. There were no air-raid shelters and the available doorways and sheltering walls were alive with a curious life form, a kind of sobbing rugby scrum of bowed backs and tucked-in heads and limbs.

Quiller peered around the knobs of the tyres. The dock felt warm and molten under his shoe-leather. He could see two small passenger ships tied up at the wharf, a huddle of private launches, junks and sampans further around toward Chinatown, and larger cargo ships and navy destroyers at anchor in the harbour. The dockside itself was congested with people—civilian men, women and children, and a handful of evacuating officers and nurses—all crouching behind bollards, gangways, steamer trunks, wooden crates and each other, while ships' officers checked passports and boarding cards and waved people aboard the waiting ships. Some of the men boarded; others stood miserably by, waving to their wives and children.

At that moment a stick of bombs straddled the fence and one landed in the harbour, sending up a geyser of greasy water. A nearby fuel dump exploded, heating and saturating the air and setting fire to the shantytown behind the godowns. Three men in thigh-length leather boots and old firemen's helmets ran toward a dribbling hose and began to tug on it. Quiller didn't know if they were European or Chinese. They were caked in a paste of plaster, brick dust, oil, blood and water, had eyes sunk deep in exhaustion and, in the tired mopping of their faces, had streaked themselves with oil smuts. He watched them play a weak stream of water onto the flames. With the damaged mains and weakened reservoir walls, the city's water was trickling away toward the harbour hour by hour, and it was a wonder the firemen had any pressure at all.

A minute later, the sky was clear. People began to stand shakily, in a cautious flinch against the darkening sky, but it was early evening and Quiller doubted that there'd be another raid so late in the day.

Then he realised that the fence had been breached. He heard a burst of machine-gun fire, followed by a desultory pop and crackle from rifles and revolvers. Some Australian soldiers had burst out from behind bales of rubber to storm through the break in the fence, stepping high over the wire strands and knocking the sentries aside with their gun butts. They smacked into the midst of the civilian evacuees, creating a path through to the gangways of the waiting ships, like a whirlwind through grass. The sentries chased them, beating away all but a handful, who boarded one of the ships, elbowing women and children aside, levelling their rifles and snarling at their pursuers. Those who'd been unsuccessful wandered away down the dock, firing their rifles into the air and forcing their way aboard the smaller craft.

Freddy appeared, his face tight with anger. 'Right, chaps, unlike our colonial cousins we are not deserters. Time to board, but I want volunteers to drive the lorries onto that patch of waste ground, drain the oil and run the motors till they seize. No sense leaving good vehicles behind for the Nips to use against us.'

Until that moment, Quiller hadn't known what he'd do about Lee Lin, Primrose and Cameron. He'd been operating automatically, obeying orders, as though he did intend to evacuate. Now he knew. 'I'll volunteer.'

'And me,' Taffy said.

Night was falling. Quiller and Taffy drove both trucks onto the waste ground and, working by flamelight, breathing an oily fog, disabled the first truck. A bonded warehouse of gin and whisky went up nearby, the flames a vivid blue. There were other, smaller explosions all the time, and the regular express-train rush of the heavy shells from the big guns on Pulau Blakang Mati, which had been turned around to fire back across the island to the Japanese positions.

Then Quiller gathered his kit, climbed into the second truck and started the engine. As he engaged first gear, a knowing look settled on Taffy's face. He stepped back. 'Don't pike on us, your grace.'

'Tell Freddy I'll be delayed,' Quiller said, accelerating away.

The streets leading away from the dockside were choked with cars and trucks, many abandoned with the keys in the ignition, others arriving, top-heavy with cases, tea-chests, lumpy pillowcases, kitbags and school satchels. A defensive perimeter around the city had been declared and no-one wanted to be outside it and all wanted to evacuate. Quiller saw some Chinese people but knew that most were still in Chinatown, while the homeless Chinese from the mainland, whose camp had been burnt out, were crouched or wandering dazed in the alleys and lanes. He saw them in the flamelight and the hooded light of his headlamps as he ground by in the RAF lorry. He guessed that, to them, this was Penang all over again—the Europeans running out on them, despite the Governor's promise of no differentiation between the King's subjects this time around.

He headed north-west toward the Australian lines. Smoke and the stench of ruptured sewers and decomposing carcasses were thick in the cabin of the lorry. Figures flicked by in the queer light and there was no end to the whistling shells and explosions.

Then, on a narrow street, he was forced to swerve as four Australian soldiers shepherded a Chinese woman past the nose of the lorry and into an alley. He saw two of them turn suddenly and club aside a young captain, who was waving his revolver and plucking uselessly at their shirts.

The captain wheeled around when he saw the truck, and stepped onto the road. Quiller braked. The captain shouted through blood and broken teeth, 'Where are you heading, Air Force?'

'The front, sir.'

The captain laughed crazily. 'Mate, it's close, and getting closer by the minute. The Japs are less than a mile away.' He looked wildly back into the alley. 'Are you going to do the decent thing?'

The woman was screaming now. Quiller nodded, switched off the engine, pocketed the key and got out, fishing for the starter handle under the seat.

The lookout at the entrance to the alleyway was watching the rape with his mouth open and one hand tweaking the front of his trousers. He didn't see them coming and dropped with a squeal when Quiller slammed the starter handle into his groin. The captain stepped past and fired, creasing the bunched, fleshless buttocks of the man who had the woman pinned against the alley wall. The man screamed and arched his back, forcing the breath from the woman's lungs, before pushing away and turning to face his attacker. Quiller stepped past him, gathered the woman and swiped at her splashed thighs with his handkerchief.

The captain had his revolver against another man's forehead. 'The rest of you—do you want to die?'

They began to edge away, eyeing him bitterly. He gestured to the wounded man. 'You're nothing but animals.'

'What do you care?'

'I'm going to find the rest of your unit—'

'More fool you!'

'—and I want you to accompany me. We're regrouping.'

'What for? It's a shambles.'

They slipped away into the night, the wounded man running in a stiff waddle. The young woman began to squirm in Quiller's arms. She pulled away from him, her face averted. He watched her go.

The captain swung around and trained his revolver at Quiller. 'You're taking me with you.'

'Put that bloody thing away.'

As they left the soldiers reappeared, stepping onto the road behind the lorry, firing a machine-gun. The bullets pinged and howled from the chassis.

'It's heartbreaking,' the captain said. 'In general our blokes have been putting up a good fight, but this morning a handful ran back through Tengah airfield, chucking their rifles in the nearest well.

That sort of thing can spread like dry rot, so I tried to plug the gap, but it was a waste of time. Since then I've been rounding up strays and stragglers. Look at that.'

They were entering a main road. An ambulance had been used to ram the doors of a liquor store, and Quiller counted fifteen Australian and British soldiers sitting shirtless with their feet in the gutter, singing 'It won't be long now' and toasting the flame-lick light on the underside of the monsoon clouds above the burning city with bottles of rum and brandy.

'I've seen pockets of them driving brand new Jaguars through showroom windows, hijacking food lorries, you name it. Discipline's gone all to pieces.'

'They've also been forcing their way aboard the evacuation ships,' Quiller said.

'They're very bolshie. Their attitude is, "Chum, to hell with the whole show. The navy let us down, the air force let us down, so why not let the boongs fight for their own bloody country." ' The captain sighed heavily. 'You can see their point. Poorly trained reinforcements, and the Japs have already taken half the island.'

As they left the city behind, the banyans and palm trees were close and dark around them. Shapes slipped across the road.

'Christ, were they Japs?'

'Who knows?' the captain said. He turned to Quiller in the dim light. 'I should warn you, there's been an order to fire on deserters. If you're challenged, sing out "Patrol" or "Looking for my unit". All right?'

Quiller nodded. Heading for the front lines had been instinctive, a habit of thought encouraged by Cameron's promissory note, but now he didn't know what he was trying to accomplish. Assuming that he found Cameron, what would he do with him? There were no serviceable aeroplanes left on Singapore, only the burnt-out shells of them.

The captain announced, 'Friday the thirteenth tomorrow. You superstitious?'

Quiller's hand went to the ring that rattled around with his dogtags. 'No more than the next man.'

The captain directed him to an area of abandoned mansions set in walled gardens about five miles north-west of the city centre. 'General Bennett's got his HQ just along here,' the captain said. He swung and pointed. 'The French Consul used to live there. Last night we were swilling Bordeaux by the tin pannikin. This is as far as we go.'

Quiller braked. They had come to an open lorry with a Lewis gun mounted on the tray and 'Tokio or bust' chalked on the dropboard. Two AIF sentries wearing tin hats approached carrying rifles. 'Rejoining our units,' the captain said.

'Carry on.'

The captain disappeared. Quiller named Cameron's unit.

'Fee fi fo fum, it's a bloody Englishman,' one sentry said.

Quiller waited.

'Things are tight—what do you want with them?'

'I'm looking for a pal.'

The sentry tapped the end of his cigarette against his thumbnail then rolled his tongue around it and gestured with his rifle at the enveloping night. 'Your funeral. Take this road, they're a mile or two up.'

Quiller looked back the way he'd come. The city skyline was a flicker of firelight under the absolute blackness of smoke. He was ready to abandon Cameron and hide under the bedclothes with Lee Lin, blocking everything out. That's what he wanted. He wanted to live in the cushioning darkness flank to flank with a warm body, warm arms around his neck, warm breath upon his cheek, soft, warm cotton blotting out the light.

He was halfway to the front line when a band of Australian deserters ran a bullock cart across the road. He swerved, braked, and then they were on him, dragging him out at gunpoint. Nothing was said by them, but Quiller found himself saying, 'You're worthless. You're full of piss and wind and always were.'

The Australians punched him wordlessly and left him alone on the road. He shrank away, feeling exposed. It occurred to him that advance parties of Japanese might be about. The shells from the big guns whistled above his head.

The front was a slippery notion. Here and there along the road to the northern half of the island Quiller found pockets of men from a ragtag army—gunners, drivers, signallers, cooks and infantrymen lumped together to fight a rearguard action. Most of them had been separated from their units or had run or straggled to safe positions, then been rounded up by senior officers into something called Z Force. They passed him down the line to a monsoon drain, where Cameron was crouching with a rifle, peering out at the darkness.

'Here I am, as promised.'

Startled, Cameron jerked back, then clicked his tongue in greeting and swung back immediately to his scrutiny of the moon shadows, full of tricks, that lay between the drain and a hill beyond.

His air of tension and concentration terrified Quiller. 'I'm supposed to be evacuating.'

'Then go.'

'But I came to get you. I did have a truck but it was hijacked.'

'It's all moot now, old son.'

They fell silent and the night crawled at the reaches of their eyes and ears. Men to the left and right of them made small settling motions or coughed and cleared their throats.

'What's happening?'

'Who knows?'

Quiller tried again. 'Have you seen much action?'

'Enough,' Cameron said.

He became less clipped suddenly, seeming to want to unburden himself. 'Starting Sunday night when we had shells lobbed on us, frigging shells creeping up the beach until we were knocked out of our trenches. Then about midnight the Japs came across in collapsible boats, sampans, anything they could lay their hands on. They'd land, fire off a blue rocket, and go back for another load. We had wave after wave of the bastards screaming up the beach at us.'

He fell into a moody rumination. 'Killed my first Jap two nights ago. We were pinned down by a sniper and I couldn't stand it anymore so I ran up to his tree and chucked a grenade at him. Blew the top of the tree right off.'

'Where's your unit?'

Cameron shrugged. 'In the last few days I've been separated from them twice. *Twice*. After the first time I was sent back up Bukit Timah Road, Poms streaming the other way, telling us we were mad. I got lost again, made it halfway back to headquarters, and the next thing I know I'm being rounded up with a lot of other poor bastards and told I'm part of Z Force. And here I am.'

Quiller peered out at the shapes, close and distant, that held his fear. 'What's happening now?' he asked, knowing it was an absurd question but wanting something specific to hold on to in the perilous shifting of the night.

'About two hours ago we sent three blokes out on a recce, but they haven't come back. So, who knows?'

Quiller trembled. He was too close to the ground and missed the security and perspective of his cockpit. And this was a Cameron different from the Cameron who'd wheedled promises after losing all of his faith and nerve in Malaya, maybe the Cameron who could regroup internally when he had nothing else to fall back on. Quiller was about to say, 'This time *I'm* relying on *you,*' when a flare shot up from the brow of the hill, paused at the lip of the sky, and settled slowly, casting a vivid light on the men in the monsoon drain.

Quiller burrowed into the crumbling cement, knowing that it was no good, his body was too large, a graceless target licked by flare light. He was like every European out here—too big, a clodhopper, an easy target.

First came a wave of grenades from the slopes of the hill, tumbling down, exploding, sending scraps of metal howling through the drain, indiscriminate and worse than bullets. Quiller felt the wet slap of another man's blood across his cheek and shook his head to clear it. Then, in the dying light of the flare, he heard and saw the Japanese separating from the other shapes and shadows on the slope of the hill in a bayonet charge. He sank, whimpering, into the bottom of the drain.

Cameron seized his arm. 'Quick. Get up.'

They vaulted out onto softer, boggy ground and ran for a roadside fruit stall. It had an *atap* roof, and paint dripped from a rotting sign suspended from the lintel: coconut, durian, mango. The fighting was hand-to-hand now—they could hear it—and they huddled together, waiting to put their backs to the bamboo walls of the shelter and feebly slap away the first of the bayonets. Cameron's arm was clamped around Quiller to keep him still. The minutes passed. Then, as they waited, the shouting and shooting gave way to snatches of Japanese words and metallic scrapes and punching sounds.

Cameron whispered, 'They're bayoneting the wounded.'

'What do we do?'
'Wait.'

When the Japanese moved on, the energy of the night diffused into distant, random rifle shots and occasional flickers of light, like a lurking storm on a far-off horizon, and Quiller felt overwhelmingly that misrule and mischance had overtaken the world. 'Now what?'

'Find our way to Orchard Road and dig in there,' Cameron said. 'Bugger Z Force.'

They walked for two hours and came to the edge of the burning city. Other men took them for fellow deserters or stragglers—which we are, Quiller thought—and offered them swigs of crème de menthe and sang 'Sod 'em all, sod 'em all' whenever an officer appeared. Later they were challenged by a lorry-load of officers and rounded-up stragglers, but Quiller kept walking, his head averted, one arm around Cameron as if to support a wounded man, saying stubbornly, 'Royal Air Force. I've orders to evacuate.'

'Lucky so and so.'

In the centre of the city they found themselves dodging, veering and ducking to avoid stragglers and looters. One gang was wheeling handcarts loaded with shirts and trousers through the shattered plate-glass window of a clothing shop, stripping off their uniforms and pulling on civilian shirts and trousers. There were men passed out in doorways or drinking in Raffles Square. Chinese families huddled outside the bricked entrance to the cinema in the Cathay Building, waiting for shelter, a soldier saying 'Give us a kiss, love' to a Chinese schoolgirl. Children were crying and, everywhere, soldiers and civilians were preparing to wait out the night. There was nothing else for them to do. Quiller and Cameron plodded on. Quiller wondered if they should be seeking shelter, too, and steered Cameron into a bank, their boots ringing out coldly on the marble; but, spotting people stretched out uncomfortably in the candlelight, he remembered Dorry and her promises, and steered Cameron out into the street again to head for the Jade Horse Mansions on Orchard Road.

They came to a British soldier kneading the breasts of an

Indian woman, who waited unresponsively, her body moving only as the man nudged and fumbled. Quiller stopped and said, 'Leave her alone.'

The soldier turned, snarling and pulling a Mills grenade from a clip on his webbing. 'Frigging ponce, I'll blow you to hell, see if I don't.'

Quiller backed away, but the soldier wandered off. Quiller nodded curtly at the woman and continued toward Orchard Road. Cameron was some distance ahead now, turning into Orchard Road. A bomb exploded. It seemed to set off another, and Quiller ran, thinking of the signs he'd seen in roped-off alleys: *unexploded bomb.*

As he rounded the corner a pair of tiny arms wrapped around his knees. It was a small Chinese boy. Quiller knelt, disentangling the child's grip, and pulled him tightly against his chest, holding him until the trembling stopped. The child's trunk was no thicker than a man's calf, and Quiller had never before felt this kind of tenderness. The boy was warm but coldly afraid and the fear registered in the thudding of his heart. When it seemed there would be no more explosions, the boy hugged and kissed Quiller, shook his hand and trotted away, turning once to grin and wave, so that Quiller felt a strange power and elation.

He went on. He couldn't see Cameron. There were no bodies along Orchard Road that he could see. Fort Canning was ablaze in the distance, the Japanese gunners lobbing shell after shell onto it. At the Jade Horse Mansions he made his way past the Scotsman on sentry duty to the flat on the first floor, and stopped short in the doorway. 'Cam? Thank Christ.'

Cameron was standing between Primrose and Lee Lin in the centre of the room, looking haggard, swiping at his leaking eyes and nose while Magill circled smirking behind him, ignored by the women. Lee Lin looked up, spotted Quiller and burst through in a flurry of little squeals and jumps. 'Neil!'

He wrapped her against his chest. She was scarcely more substantial than the child he'd comforted on Orchard Road.

'We go shelter now,' she said.

They settled beneath the stairs, and there, where the world was not laid wide open to him, Cameron began to relax and tell Lee Lin, Primrose, Magill and the curious Scotsmen of his days

and nights since the Japanese had taken the Causeway. Quiller
dozed, listening to Cameron spin a story full of humour and
chaos. He appreciated it, the more so with Lee Lin soft against his
chest. From time to time he opened his eyes and glanced around
the little shelter. Cameron's story was going badly for Magill.
Magill would grin crazily at Cameron and try to catch Primrose's
eye, but Primrose was pale and unreachable, and once when he
reached out his fingers to her ankles, she drew her feet under
her—but that pushed her closer to Cameron, and Quiller saw that
she felt hemmed in.

After a while, everyone slept. Quiller woke once and found
Primrose staring at him. She was upright against the wall, with
her lucky shrapnel blade in one hand, Cameron asleep on her
shoulder and Magill asleep across her ankles. Seeing his intention,
her gaze altered subtly and she murmured, 'No, let them sleep.'

In the morning they climbed upstairs to the flat. 'Girls, we have to
get you out,' Cameron said.

Primrose snorted. 'How, pray tell? Yesterday we went down to
P&O and they refused to issue tickets, me because I can't produce
a birth certificate to show that my father was British and Lee Lin,
well, she's Chinese, isn't she?'

'We'll find Dorry,' Quiller said. 'She's got some plan in mind.'

Magill had begun drinking at first light. As the two men
and the two women packed their belongings into kitbags and
pillowcases, and said goodbye to the Scots, he trailed after them
through the building, distraught and desperately smiling.
'Primrose, stay with me, dear. I'll look after you.'

'Come with us, Mr Mag,' said Primrose, gently pushing his
hands away.

'It's too dangerous out there, my dear.'

'Well, then.'

They felt his eyes at their backs as they walked out onto the
buckled street and into a desultory stream of men, women and
children. Quiller led the way to Raffles Square, where the hotel
seemed to cower away from the missiles of the past few days that
had chipped away at its face. They skirted the big monsoon drain,
which was flowing with brandy, champagne and globs of liqueur

as men and women from the liquor stores sat on the rim, smashing bottles, singing and bumping shoulders giddily in the sway of the fumes. Outside the bank in Raffles Place they flinched away from a pyre of burning banknotes. A brief air raid drove them into a doorway; across the square a shopfront fell out. With the all-clear they heard a Chinese woman scream, 'My husband, my children!' She began to claw at the rubble. They ran to help and after thirty minutes uncovered an air-raid shelter, its sides blown in. The woman bent to touch a dusty bare foot and Quiller turned Lee Lin away from bad memories. And so the four of them went on, over the hoses and masonry, past the drunks and the looters still shouting 'It won't be long now', to the casualty clearing station in the Cathay Building, where they were directed to St Andrew's Cathedral.

There they found Australian Army nurses in red capes and steel helmets waiting in the pews while others tended the rows of wounded on the far side of the main chamber. Quiller prowled up and down the main aisle, looking for Dorry. Finally he asked for her, and learnt that he was too late—she'd been evacuated.

'We're just waiting for our turn,' a nurse told him. 'Some of us don't want to go, but it's orders.' She was fiddling with the pocket of her uniform, drawing Quiller's gaze. 'We've been issued with morphine and syringes,' she explained, 'in case we're attacked or imprisoned.'

Just then a Royal Navy officer tapped Quiller on the shoulder. 'Look here, I'm taking names. Please move along.'

Quiller jerked away. He looked up into the vaulted ceiling as another wave of bombers droned overhead. He waited through the barking ack-ack barrage, the shudder of the cathedral dome and the eddies of dust, then rejoined the others with the bad news. 'Down to the docks,' he said, 'though they say the last ship has already gone.'

Down to disorder, where they were indistinguishable from the fearful and the brave. They were pushed and pulled by the tide of people banking up at the dockside, waving useless passes, arguing with officials, swerving in a wave as a fresh stick of bombs crumpled along the line of godowns. On the other side of the security fence, a merchant ship was waiting and lost children ran sobbing up and down the wire. Quiller felt that his feet were sticky, heavy, bound to the tarred surface of the wharf and realised he was treading in oil from cast-aside feeder pipes used to refuel the ships. His shoes, and thousands of others, had spread the oil in a sticky coat over the wharf and in a lapping tide against suitcases, coats, a birdcage, a kitten in a box, a score of lumpish pillowcases. More and more suitcases piled up as officers tossed them off the overcrowded gangways, and men with the look of servicemen dressed as civilians attempted to push aboard or swarm up the mooring ropes.

Another wave of bombers came in. The bomb doors opened and bombs tumbled out, scarcely straightening before they landed among the warehouses. Most people ducked and crouched, but a man and a woman, the man clutching a baby against his chest, didn't flinch but stood in the open, staring intently at the gangway of the ship. They were next in line and their passes were in order.

Quiller watched the sentries open the gate for them. Screaming and shouting were commonplace all around him. Life had become this, in the past few days. But then he distinguished the lone note of a Japanese Zero coming in low across the harbour and, when its wing cannons began to flash and stutter, it was a worse sound than any explosion or shout. Like an organism the crowd sighed and ducked, temporarily shocked into silence by the buzz of the shrapnel. At the end of it, just one voice broke out. It was the husband. His wife lay twitching on the wharf, her neck sliced open to the spine, her blood spurting in bright red arcs from the open stem of her neck. The husband broke to see her like that, his mouth wide in agony. A sailor at the gangway shouted, 'Hurry up, sir.' The man looked at his wife. Again the sailor shouted to him. The husband could not see for tears and tripped over a crate, landing awkwardly and rolling in the oil to protect the baby. They were the last ones allowed to board before the ship cast off.

Quiller felt a tug on his sleeve. Cameron, one arm still around Primrose, who was weeping, said, 'Mate, we've got Buckley's here.'

Quiller agreed. They'd seen the last of the 'big ship' evacuations; only yachts, sampans, launches and smaller cargo boats were left, as scarce as hens' teeth. They slipped through the congestion to the back streets and trudged parallel to the curve of burning godowns. They put one foot after the other automatically, and then it seemed apparent that Lee Lin was leading them. She drew ahead. She had energy.

'Where's she taking us, Quill?'

Lee Lin said over her shoulder, 'We go to river.'

'What good's that?'

Quiller shrugged despondently.

They trudged for thirty minutes in the smoky air, Lee Lin taking them to the mooring place of dozens of sampans and small junks. Quiller looked down from the top of the river bank and brightened, remembering his first visit with Lee Lin, weeks before the seige, when children had been jumping from deck to deck, ducking under the laundered pantaloons and blouses strung from the rigging, while old men and women sat on the hatches, smoking or spitting betel juice into the water. He'd met Lee Lin's grandparents, and they'd sat beaming at one another over little bowls of jasmine tea.

But then his spirits fell again. A detachment of British sailors had beaten them to it.

'Damn, too late,' Cameron said.

The sailors were armed and while some had already cast off into the river on commandeered sampans and junks, others were splintering doors and hatches with the butts of rifles, herding people off their decks or dumping cooking pots, clothing and bedding onto the river bank. The sailors were shouting, the Chinese were shouting, and none had words in common. Further along a young Chinese man was standing in the river, holing his sampan at the waterline with an axe. When Lee Lin shouted, 'You bad mens,' half-a-dozen sailors swung around, saw Quiller and Cameron, and raised their rifles. 'This is our show,' one man called.

Cameron shrugged at them and turned away, murmuring, 'What now?'

'Back to the docks.'

'You're sure you can't get us onto a plane?'

'Positive.'

'So what do we do?'

Quiller stopped. 'First things first. We get the girls off.'

Lee Lin clutched his arm and swung on it as if this were a walk in the park. 'Why we no go together?'

Quiller said helplessly, 'It depends on what we find.'

· · ·

For days the harbour waters had heaved slowly, tidally, under a permanent smoke haze, so that evening was banished; there was only oily blackness out upon the water and a bright ribbon of flamelight along the shoreline. That's why Quiller and the others, waiting, talking, snatching at sleep in a looted godown far from the gates and the sentries, were not aware of the MV *Delphinium* until she had let down her anchor. She carried no running lights and stood about one minute's row out from the wharf.

Quiller walked to the edge and shouted, 'We have four people here in need of a passage.'

There was no answer, but presently he heard the plash and creak of oars on the water. A Chinese seaman tied up and climbed the rusting ladder to the top of the wharf.

'Hey. Boy. Where's your boat going?' Cameron demanded.

The seaman bowed. 'I am Goh Ming Wong. You have brandy?'

'Mr Goh,' Quiller said, 'what is the destination of your ship?'

'We no open ship bar until tomorrow,' the seaman said. He grinned. 'Crew very thirsty.'

Lee Lin called out in Cantonese from the darkness, startling him. He replied, and Quiller made out the word 'Colombo'.

'Jesus Christ, Colombo,' Cameron said. 'We can do better than that, Quill.'

'The girls can't. Mr Goh, there's a crate of sherry back there. You can have it, but only if you help us. Can you smuggle two young women aboard?'

They guided him into the shadows, where he peered at Lee Lin and Primrose, then past them at a splintered case of sherry bottles, rejected by the looters. 'Is a deal. Womens come with me now. I Christian man, they hide in kitchen, show self tomorrow, Captain no turn back.'

'Thank you,' Quiller said.

'No room for more.'

'I understand.'

Quiller found an old signal from Air HQ in his pocket and scribbled the address of Haarlem Downs on the back of it. 'You can contact either of us here,' he told Primrose.

She kissed him, then did an odd thing—she rubbed the

blade of shrapnel against his chest. She held back from blessing Cameron, looking intently at him instead, as though to say she was free at last of all his pushing and pulling, but he stepped forward to embrace her and the expression vanished. She looked past his shoulder, wooden and unresponsive.

Lee Lin's face was wet against Quiller's shirt. He felt sad and irritable and wanted it over with. 'Go,' he said, directing her to the rusty ladder that led down to Mr Goh's rowboat.

The hours passed. Cameron slept on a bale of rubber but Quiller could not sleep while the MV *Delphinium* waited out there, lit dully by the burning city. He needed to know that Lee Lin and Primrose would not be sent back to him.

He was dozing when he heard a slow, burbling motor on the water. It was a police launch, running with lights—as a show of strength against looters and deserters looking for a boat to steal, Quiller supposed—and he saw it bump against the hull of the *Delphinium*.

The voice came clearly across the water. 'Ahoy, *Delphinium*.'

'State your business.'

'Major Sime and Sergeant Riggs and the prisoner Janeway, awaiting permission to come aboard.'

A rope ladder was dropped over the side. 'You coves took your sweet time.'

The Unwhitening
of the Indies

The distressed airliner had seemed to go down close to Haarlem Downs, but according to Anneliese it was two days' walk south-west of the homestead—if, indeed, it was still there, given the size of the swamping tides. The pilot had dropped altitude and skimmed above the breakers, she said, hoping the ribbon of spray might deter the Japanese fighter and even put out the flames, for the port engine was ablaze. But the Zero had stuck close behind them, firing short bursts and dodging when they dodged, finally chasing them around a headland to a stretch of sand that shelved steeply into the sea. The Dutch pilot had made a belly landing on the beach, slewing around at the last minute in the hope of extinguishing the flames in the surf. Jeannie's insides contracted as she pictured it: the sand, as sluggish as wet cement, seizes and smothers the nose of the airliner, snaps off the propellers and folds thickly over the leading edge of each wing, while the rear half of the plane heaves up in a kinetic rush that breaks its back. The Japanese pilot buzzed them, Anneliese said, then came round and emptied his guns into them when he saw movement inside the fuselage.

'Now they are all dead—my master, my mistress and their baby.'

'We should investigate.'

Anneliese shook her head violently. 'I could not go back there. They are all dead, madam.'

'At least give them a decent burial.'

'They are in the ocean, I think. The aeroplane is in many pieces by now; sucked down.'

Jeannie examined Anneliese for signs of heatstroke or dementia. Anneliese had arrived wearing a torn frock and sandals and carrying a briefcase, her exposed skin scratched, bruised and burnt by the sun. The hair at the back of her head had been scorched and frizzled by fire, and the rest stood up hectically, coarse, dark, tufted with twigs, dust and perspiration, a frame for her finely shaped face. She was young, delicately arranged, bewildered but glad to be alive. Seated in Crystal's bed now, wearing nothing but a silk slip that Crystal had left behind—bathed, rested, her eyes darkly smudged with exhaustion—she seemed to Jeannie to be combined of contrasting attributes: exotic but at home there; deferential but bold; ingenuous but one step ahead of everyone.

Jeannie patted her hand. 'I'll send someone.'

'No, madam, it is too late.'

A small band of bush blacks had found Anneliese. She'd spent two days and nights with them until, guided by them to a vantage point on Dampier's Hill, she'd seen the homestead, airstrip and sheds laid out before her on the plain.

'Poof! Those natives disappeared, so I walk down the hill and here I am.'

Anneliese hadn't let the briefcase out of her sight. She's carrying all she has left in the world, Jeannie thought.

The girl glanced about doubtfully at the massive dark bedroom furniture, the bare shelves and dressing table, and finally at Jeannie, as if to say that she, a coloured servant, hadn't the right. Then she hooded her eyes and uttered a brief, sly laugh, and eased contentedly into the bed until her head sank into Crystal's fine embroidered pillowcase.

'I will sleep now.'

Anneliese's story, as told to Jeannie throughout the afternoon, had begun in a car on the outskirts of Batavia, on the island of Java, with a leaflet floating through the open rear window and adhering to her cheek with a soft, warm slap. At first she'd thought a butterfly, one of those kampong butterflies with velvety wings a handspan across, had been caught up in the turbulence of the car, but one corner of the leaflet flapped and she peeled it away, just as her mistress said:

'Anneliese?'

'A scrap of paper, madam.'

They were in the back seat with Jeroen, who lay across their laps, dozing, his thumb in his mouth. The car braked sharply and the chauffeur muttered.

'Hasan, do be careful,' Mrs Rodenwalt said.

Hasan half turned his head. 'There is much paper in the sky, madam. From an aeroplane, look, see?'

They ducked to follow his pointing finger. Through the leaflets pasted to the windscreen Anneliese could see a little aeroplane ahead of them, spilling paper across the city. She returned her gaze to the leaflet in her hand.

Mrs Rodenwalt held out her palm. 'Anneliese, show me, please.'

Anneliese ignored her. The leaflet depicted overjoyed Indonesian soldiers rushing toward the kindly embrace of Japanese troops, who all held rising-sun flags. A caption at the bottom read: 'Soldiers of Java. The Nippon Army has come to liberate you and put out the Dutch.'

Mrs Rodenwalt said sharply, 'Anneliese, wicked girl.'

Anneliese passed her the leaflet. Lottie Rodenwalt read it without expression, then folded it into the pocket of her dress. 'I must show Edouard when we get home.'

Anneliese turned away and gazed out of her window. They were nearing the Shell Oil depot and the wharves at Tanjong Priok. Jeroen liked to see the ships, otherwise there would be no reason for them to pass this way. Hasan had taken them out to the cemetery at Ptamboeran, a few kilometres outside Batavia, to place flowers on Lottie's mother's grave, and now they were returning by a long route to Weltervreden, where the wealthiest Dutch merchants and government servants lived. Anneliese had somehow doubted that she'd find any of the leaflets on the footpaths of Weltervreden.

'Jeroen,' she said, poking his ribs to make him squirm. 'See the big ships.'

He stood on the seat beside her, then crawled across her to the window. He was two years old and often called her *moeder* by mistake. She'd looked after him from the moment he was born but at the same time was a reminder of what could happen to a blond Dutch boy—for she was an Indo, a *mengbloeden*, the daughter of a Dutch civil servant who had been posted to the Indies in 1919, and a Javanese woman, his *huishoudster*.

'I had strict orders not to let Jeroen mix with Javanese or Indo children,' Anneliese said, looking up at Jeannie from her pillow on Crystal's bed.

This was news from a faraway place for Jeannie. She realised how lonely she'd become on Haarlem Downs, and found herself hanging on to every word. Anneliese cocked her head lazily. 'Madam has servants?'

It's as if she's testing me, Jeannie thought. 'Please call me Jeannie.'

'Yes, madam.'

'You speak English well.'

Anneliese acknowledged the fact gravely. When her parents had been killed in a mudslide on a mountain road, all she'd had left was her schooling. She'd been to an elementary school, then junior and senior middle schools, and at the time of her parents' death had been about to complete her diploma in the Dutch-built city in the Priangan Highlands. It was 1934, the end of the Great Depression, and Java swelled with white and Indo paupers and abandoned Indo children. She'd been wandering the streets of the city, scrounging for food, when the authorities picked her up. She was the product of a union frowned upon by both the Netherlandshen Vrouwenbond and the Sarekat Islam, she told Jeannie. She blurred the colonial divide, and she was ambiguous, poor, unclaimed.

She gave Jeannie that look again. 'But my schooling impressed them. You see, I had not attended the type of Indies school that fails to instil a proper Dutch essence.'

'Then what happened?'

'I was sent to an abandoned hill station that had been taken over by the Red Cross.'

The hill station sat on a cool mountain slope and before the Great Depression it had been a little outpost of Holland.

The Dutch merchants and civil servants and their families would stay in bungalows, recuperate in the sanatorium and send their children to a school that emphasised Dutch customs, language and games. Leaving the layout of the buildings intact, the Red Cross used the hill station to rehabilitate the victims of the European crisis. Anneliese ate and slept well, sang the Dutch national anthem, could tell you in a flash where the Rhine enters Holland, learnt to type and cook, studied English and cared for the smaller children.

Then one day in 1936, Charlotte—Lottie—and her mother arrived in a big black Plymouth motor car, looked around, met her, and took her away with them.

'In a sense, I was rescued by my mistress.'

'You were lucky.'

'I expect so. Of course, Lottie was not a *trekker*.'

Jeannie raised her eyebrows inquiringly.

'Dutch, but not from Holland, madam.'

Anneliese explained that her mistress had been born in Java, and grown up in two houses, one in Batavia, the other—a holiday retreat—close to the hill station. Her *babu*, a Javanese woman, nominally Muslim but steeped in animist beliefs, had suckled and pampered her and taught her to speak Malay, so that she'd used that language more often than Dutch when she was a child and felt comfortable with Javanese dress, food and friendships. She was full of the ghost stories, myths and legends of her *babu*, and had never been to Holland.

But Lottie's husband, Edouard, was a *trekker*, a colonial civil servant from Holland. Anneliese laughed. 'Soon Lottie was dressing for dinner and eating roast meat with him.'

'And Edouard didn't want you to let his son mix with native children?' Jeannie asked.

Anneliese knuckled her eyes. 'That is so.'

Jeannie stroked the back of Anneliese's hand. 'Won't you let us look for their bodies?'

'No. They are in the water. You know, little Jeroen, he crawled from my lap into Lottie's just before we were attacked. If only he had not done that.'

• • •

Harry Horsetalk took a horse and was back by morning tea the next day to say that he'd found the wreckage of the downed plane but no bodies. 'Him shot up plurry bad,' he said. 'King tides there, missus. Wash everything away.'

In the days that followed, Anneliese regained her strength and began to shadow Jeannie like a younger sister or cousin, always ready to laugh and help out but wondering how far she could push the boundaries—or, Jeannie thought, like a bound servant who suddenly finds herself a free woman. Jeannie was careful not to order, or instruct, but suggest. She was cheered by Anneliese, who went about uncomplainingly and spoke English well enough to fill the days with stories of the Indies: harvest festival feasts, dragons, the image of the Dutch Queen on every classroom wall, the Japanese photographer who turned out to be a spy and, with a hand to her mouth, her master's big pink belly.

'Edouard took advantage of you?'

Anneliese gestured indifferently. 'Of course.'

Jeannie thought of the briefcase. 'What was his job?'

'A senior officer in the Treasury.'

Anneliese described a tall, soft, balding man with perspiration always dotted like clear oil on his temples and brow. He was fresh out from Holland and belonged to a new breed of colonial officers who saw themselves as closing ranks, shoring up and setting boundaries against slackness, moral decay and temptation.

'At first he would watch to see if I was shifty or lazy, so he could say my native blood was showing through.'

And then Anneliese registered a shift in his gaze, as though he saw the native strain as carrying not only delinquency but also the slow, sly pulse of the sensualist. His eyes would linger on her, grow glazed, and he'd moisten his lips. Once, Anneliese said, her hand comically over her mouth, he'd bent her forward over the desk in his study when the others had been out of the house, pulled down her underwear with a jolly slap, then shuffled up to her with a series of little shoves and pokes until he was well inside of her. He seemed to tread on the spot and walk himself into a whimpering ejaculation.

Afterward he'd been vicious and sulky with her. It was always the same: he hadn't expected to backslide so quickly or so easily in the tropics, and in his shame and guilt would often lash out at her, then take her again a day or two later.

'I think Edouard was angry with me for making him weak.'

Jeannie was reminded vividly of Cameron. She listened through the hours as Anneliese's story wove in and out of her position in the Rodenwalt household and the last, confused days before Edouard bundled them out of Java.

On the day of the leaflets and the visit to the dockyards for little Jeroen, gulls had cried and humid saltwater odours had drifted toward them on the harbour wall. Anneliese had watched Lottie swing Jeroen onto her shoulders. The dear little boy, he'd pointed at the cranes, the crated armaments and military vehicles, the Dutch Army officers shouting at the Javanese labourers—who were working hard and efficiently to Anneliese's eye. Another leaflet blew against her ankle. It was the second week of February and everyone knew that the Japanese were on Singapore island.

'I was certain we would be invaded, too. Java is very rich in tin, rubber and oil, you know.'

Finally Jeroen had tired of the ships. Lottie handed him to Anneliese and said, with a clap of her hands, 'Into the car, everybody. Father will be very worried about us.'

Hasan drove them from the harbour, the seafront slums giving way to prosperous suburbs. Soon it would be dusk and the devout would be called to evening prayers. They came to their street. Hasan slowed for the gate and sounded the horn for the gardener. The gate creaked. The tyres of the big car crushed the tiny white pebbles of the driveway, and there was Edouard at the door, wringing his hands, looking heated.

'I was worried about you. There was an aeroplane.'

Lottie stood on her toes to kiss his moist cheek. 'We saw it.' She gave him the leaflet from her pocket.

Edouard glanced at Anneliese standing there and jerked his head crossly. 'Your duties, Anneliese.'

Anneliese placed her hands on Jeroen's shoulders and steered him toward the bathroom, where she ran water into the bath and wriggled the child out of his little shorts and shirt. She supposed that Edouard would come to observe in a minute or so. Far from being a Dutch burgher who stood aloof from the ways of the household, Edouard liked to hover.

'You have to understand,' Anneliese explained to Jeannie, her voice taking on a solemn, masculine timbre, 'the Dutch essence is so fragile. A child is especially vulnerable to contamination, laziness, degeneration, dependence. A loss,' she thundered, a laugh beind her voice, 'of the white self.'

Jeannie laughed along with her. Then Anneliese lowered her voice conspiratorially and Jeannie could almost see and hear Edouard and his damp lips. 'A man has natural inclinations. In an innocent male child, unclean habits can easily be encouraged and then channelled in unhealthy directions.' And so Edouard would lean against the bathroom door and watch as Anneliese bathed his son. A quick wipe of the washcloth around Jeroen's little scrotum and penis was all she allowed herself. Edouard was like a hawk waiting to pounce. He'd say to Lottie, so that Anneliese could hear: 'It's the duty of the modern white mother to take more into her own hands. If everything is left to the servants then sloth and vanity are the result, and our child becomes more *inlander* than Dutch.'

The ideas were not his alone. He was a great one for books. He belonged to the Vaderlandse Club, which tackled the unwhitening of the Indies and provided him with housekeeping guides and medical manuals that advised on the dangers of contamination in the tropics and urged self-mastery and discipline.

If it hadn't been for Anneliese, he'd have thought himself on top of things. But Anneliese was always there, a woman, poor, of mixed blood. He would drift fatally if he were not careful. Anneliese knew all of these things about him. One look at the turmoil in his eyes and she knew.

He tried to be vigilant. 'One day he came to me with an old pamphlet published by the Netherlands Indies Eugenics Society and said, "Are you a true and fit compatriot, Anneliese? What do I really know of your parents and your upbringing?"—and he began to test me. "It is possible," he said, "to prevent degeneration and preserve our beloved *moedervolken*. Naturally in your case I must make certain allowances."'

He'd been obliged to stand close to her. He was sweaty, breathing audibly. She'd washed her hair and rubbed coconut oil into her skin that day. His hands went to her body. She'd tingled and swelled to see him so unhinged by her, so afraid of her and of himself. She was an affront to everything that mattered to him and it gave her a peculiar thrill to destabilise him. She was a threat to his self-control, to his family, nation and race. She straddled ruler and ruled, and he couldn't trust her even as he desired her.

But on the day of the leaflets in the sky he'd come to the bathroom door and said her name worriedly: 'Anneliese.'

Startled, she'd finished bathing Jeroen, gathered him from the bath and wrapped him in a towel, patting him dry before sprinkling his rubbery limbs with talcum powder. 'I was blushing,' she told Jeannie. 'He sounded so different. So I hurried Jeroen into his pyjamas and then looked around at the door. Lottie was there too. They were both looking at me. Edouard was full of pain. He said, "First thing tomorrow morning you will accompany my wife and son and the servants to the house in Bandoeng. It will be safer there. Then we must find an even safer place for all of us. If only we could return to Holland. Forests, lakes, snow, daffodils ..." He burst into tears.'

Anneliese glanced out over the stockyards, muddy red soil and scrubby trees of Haarlem Downs. '*This* would have given him a shock.'

Part 3

ESCAPE

February–April 1942

The Companionable
Noises of the War

Four armed Australians had apparently been watching the *Delphinium*, and when it finally sailed they ran out onto the edge of the stone wharf, firing rifles at it, but Cameron challenged them and they moved on. They were young and unhinged, and there were no more ships.

Quiller and Cameron slept a little and on Sunday morning ate army biscuits washed down with warm Tiger beer. They were deeply fatigued, their faces gaunt, their arms and hands grimy, their uniforms rent and gathered by the snags of war—nail heads, splintered doorframes, torn car bodies. All they had in the world were the clothes they stood in, their haversacks and Cameron's Lee-Enfield rifle, but Primrose had abandoned her school satchel and Quiller rummaged through it as they wandered back to Orchard Road. He kept her lead pencils, a primer of English verse and prose, and an item of treasure as far as he was concerned: her school atlas. These reminders that Primrose was a child stopped him. She'd seemed too poised, too grave, in the past weeks.

On the streets there was talk of a ceasefire. Quiller and Cameron skirted bomb craters and leapt over fallen masonry and firefighting hoses as limp as bootlaces, encountering Australians who seethed with anger at General Percival's call to surrender, and lost men with looted bottles spoked between their fingers who asked, 'Where are we supposed to fall in?', and Indian soldiers who'd stripped off their uniforms and wrapped themselves in sarongs, or tied strips of white cotton around their hats and sewn tiny Rising Suns to their breast pockets and upper sleeves.

Cameron was dazed, trembling, close to tears as they walked. 'I can't believe it. I didn't think it would get this far. I thought, this is just a temporary setback ...'

Quiller wanted to say, 'If you thought that, why were you so keen for me to get you out of here?' The promissory note was burning inside him. 'Have you got any cash?' he asked.

'What for?'

'Anything of value? Jewellery? Cigarette case? Wristwatch? Better hold on to the rifle.'

'Why?'

'We may need to buy our way out.'

Cameron brightened. 'I knew I could rely on you, Quill.'

They trod through the morning to Orchard Road, Quiller letting his mind sort through the implications of Janeway's evacuation. Was Janeway an embarrassment now, with the Japanese about to take the city? Was his life in danger? Did he still hold sensitive information that had to be denied the Japs—or sensitive information *about* the Japs? Was that why he hadn't yet been executed? In the Great War he'd have been summarily shot by now, Quiller thought.

They reached the Mansions, calling 'Allied servicemen coming up' as they mounted the stairs.

But the building had been abandoned. They tried to wash and shave, but there was no pressure in the taps and so they made do with water from a slimy bucket that had been wedged under a garden tap in the courtyard. Meanwhile the shells whined overhead and the bombers passed by, but with diminishing intensity.

Quiller took out Primrose's atlas, angry with himself for having burned rather than pocketed the RAF charts and maps at Kallang aerodrome. The atlas was on a scale of half-an-inch to one hundred miles. He found a writing pad and began to transcribe Singapore, Sumatra, Java and the islands of Berhala and Banka Straits on a series of blank pages at a scale of half-an-inch to ten miles.

Toward evening there were footsteps on the stairs, a voice calling 'Civilian coming up', and Magill appeared in the doorway. He'd been drinking, and wavered in a gin cloud. 'You!' he hissed, pointing at Cameron. 'Where is she? Where is my Primrose?'

Quiller slipped between the two men. 'Mag, have you got any money?'

The gin had loosened all of Magill's defences. Cunning and connivance passed across his features like sunlight and shadow. 'What if I do?'

'How much?'

Magill straightened and said, 'Five thousand Malay dollars.' His eyes narrowed. 'You can have it if you take me with you.'

At eight o'clock that evening the sirens signalled the all-clear and for the first time in weeks the city fell silent. The three men could not bear it at first; they were reluctant to shake off the habits of listening for the guns, the bombers and the windrush of the bombs, of waiting for the explosions. Without the companionable noises of the war they felt obscurely abandoned.

They made up packs of tinned food and bottled water in bed-sheets and set out, comforted by their bootsteps and the crackling of fires. They met bands of despondent troops who said, 'Surrender? Can't be true,' men too tired to escape, and others who hunted out food, clothing, needles, thread and spare boots, anything to give them the edge in a prisoner-of-war camp. Quiller wondered how close Cameron and Magill were to these men. Were their ambitions as local and contingent? He touched his breast pocket unconsciously, feeling for the promissory note, which rested there damp and soft from his sweaty skin. There were no Japanese in the city yet.

Near the docks they stole a Bren-gun carrier. Cameron said agitatedly, 'Where the hell are we going, Quill?'

Quiller snapped, 'Well, I don't know, but I used to see a few sampans tied up to the seawall at Kallang.'

An Indian sentry challenged them at a barbed-wire entanglement at the edge of the water. When Quiller told him of the surrender, the sentry touched his temples and said 'I go now' and slipped away, leaving his rifle.

Magill picked it up. 'More trouble than it's worth,' Quiller said, gently prising it out of the clerk's hands and tossing it into the water, where it broke the flat, reflected image of a burning petrol dump on Blakan Mati island. A smoky wind blew and the oily water rose and fell against the seawall.

Quiller unbolted the prismatic compass from the Bren-gun carrier and they carried their swag to the edge of the stone wall. There was only one sampan. It had a broad beam and was scarcely longer than the wing of a Buffalo. Quiller stepped down into it, found the oars and called Cameron and Magill to join him.

But Magill retreated a few steps, spun around and vomited. He wiped his mouth. 'Better out than in.'

'Get a move on, Mag,' Cameron said.

Magill looked in distaste at the sampan. 'I'm not a soldier. The Japs can't put me in a prison,' and he stumbled away toward the barbed-wire and darkness.

'Forget about him,' Quiller said, handing an oar to Cameron. 'These things are the devil to row.'

'But he had money, Quill.'

It was after midnight. Owing to the smoke from the fuel dumps and the seasonal cloud banks, they couldn't see far, and were fearful as they rowed through the minefield. When they were free of the harbour, a strengthening current took them further out, into a log jam of small boats: barges, launches, junks, a seaplane tender and other sampans. From time to time Quiller called into the gloom, 'Two men here. Any room to spare?'

'No.'

'Sorry, old chap, no can do.'

'Fuck off.'

Someone fired a round into the deck at his feet.

Then a black submarine glided past, its motors knocking badly.

They drifted past a sandbank near St John's Lighthouse, where a launch and a seaplane tender had run aground. Now and then Quiller thumbed his cigarette lighter, read the compass and made small directional adjustments with the oars.

'Mate, you got me off. I knew you would.'

Quiller rowed. 'It's early days yet.'

'No, mate,' Cameron said. 'I feel good about this.' Then: 'Quill, where are we going by the way?'

Quiller stared curiously at the dark form of his cousin. It occurred to him that Cameron had never read or depended upon a map. If his feet were on the ground then he was somewhere and there would always be someone to lead him to another place. Cameron was incurious about distances and directions, and the horizon never promised anything as far as he was concerned. When they'd flown about in the Gull, he'd not been interested in the ground or their tiny shadow racing across the savannah, basalt flats or dunes below but in Jeannie Verco, always tickling her, whispering in her ear.

'Rengat,' Quiller replied, 'on the Indragiri River.'

'Where in blazes is that?'

'Sumatra.'

'Fair enough. You can do it if anyone can, Quill.'

'Not in this punt we won't. We need something bigger.'

In his mind's eye Quiller could see his maps: islands, both inhabited and deserted; reefs; an archipelago; several narrow straits with fast-flowing currents; and the larger masses of Sumatra and Java. The mouth of the Indragiri was south of a narrow headland on the Durian Strait, west of the island of Singkep, and probably difficult to locate, even if they hugged the shoreline. He looked back over his shoulder. Singapore was burning, a band of crimson marking the line between the sea and the black sky. He realised that his nostrils had been scoured for days by the stench of burning rubber and oil. A large, darkened ship materialised from the oily smoke that rolled over the sea and washed by them, an Aldis lamp flashing. Quiller shouted; no-one replied.

Toward dawn they spotted a small, dense shape in the greater darkness. They stopped rowing and drifted silently until Quiller made out a large, twin-masted junk fastened to a series of bamboo poles which he recognised as part of a fish trap. He let the sampan bump softly against the stern before pulling it hand over hand around the hull, making for the lowest point. He swore once and sucked the fleshy web between his thumb and forefinger: a splinter. The hull had been punctured. His shirt caught on another splintered gash. He whispered to Cameron: 'She's been shot up.'

At the midpoint of the starboard bow, Quiller climbed aboard the junk then took their haversacks and the Lee-Enfield from

Cameron and helped him aboard. They began to prowl, Cameron poking into corners with the rifle. An awning of tarred tarpaulin, held at each corner by bamboo poles, was suspended over the open hold. Someone had collapsed the battened sails. There was no sound apart from the constant oily slap of the sea and cries of 'Help!' and 'Mummy!' from a dying man far away across the water and impossible to pinpoint.

Cameron found her with an unconscious Australian pilot in the darkest corner of the hold. She sat up and said, 'Are you the Japanese?'

They knelt to peer at her. 'No, sweetheart.'

She was about eight years old and sat with her tiny bowed spine against an ammunition box, clutching her knees hard against her chest, blinking at the spurt of flame as Cameron scraped his cigarette lighter into life.

'What's your name, love?' Quiller said.

It was a precise English voice. 'Maisie.'

He put his hand on the unconscious pilot. 'Is this your father?'

'No. We found him in the water yesterday.'

'Who else is here?'

'No-one,' the girl said. 'They're all dead.' She stood on her thin legs. 'There's a lamp. I didn't light it in case they shot at us again.'

'In case who shot at you?'

'The aeroplanes.'

Quiller lit the lamp and listened to Maisie's story. Her mother had bled to death on a stretcher in the cathedral. Her father had paid a man for the junk and they'd set sail—Maisie, her nanny, her father and a manager from her father's mine—two days earlier. They hadn't known which direction to take and often bobbed becalmed with the yachts of the Singapore yacht squadron while little motor boats buzzed past them for hour after hour. They saw a launch ripped open by a hidden reef, and sampans and rowboats just drifting by, empty. They beached on a sandbar the first night and when they floated free in the morning, found a packing case with the Australian pilot clinging to it.

'He was all sunburnt and had the cramps because he'd been swimming before he saw the packing case.'

Quiller knelt and in the lamplight could see the sun damage on the pilot's face. He touched the man's forehead: hot, feverish. Weak, dry, irregular breaths whistled through cracked, blackened lips.

'It was a huge packing case,' Maisie said. 'He said there'd been a Hurricane inside it, except the Hurricane had fallen out the bottom when the ship sunk. He said there were five other men but in the morning he was the only one still holding on.'

Quiller poured water onto his handkerchief and dabbed at the ravaged face. The pilot coughed once but remained unconscious.

'We didn't have a gun,' Maisie said. 'Some of the other boats did. My papa and my nanny got killed and fell in the water, then Mr Lucas jumped in but I think a shark got him. Alf saved me. He made me lie down and cuddled around me so he'd get hit first.'

She was lucky that the bullets hadn't gone through and through. Quiller made another examination of the pilot and found an entry point in Alf's pelvis and another in his thigh. The blood had probably spilled freely for a while but now there was little but an oozing into the stiff, caked trousers.

'Before he fainted he got the sails working and sailed till he found those poles in the water. Is he going to die?'

Quiller said, 'I think so, little one. Don't be sad.'

'But I am sad. I haven't got anyone. Am I going to die?'

'Not if I can help it.'

'I'm thirsty.'

Quiller gave her his water bottle and heard the very liquid and desperate workings of her tiny throat. 'You'd better take this, too,' he said, handing her an atabrine tablet.

When dawn broke Quiller untied the junk and Cameron raised the sails, a weak wind sending them into the channel. As they drifted among the stony atolls, people waved frantically at them, but Quiller could see reefs and wreckage, so he marked the positions on his map and didn't attempt to stop. He wondered if he were running out of pity for people. Late in the morning a flight of dive bombers attacked and sunk a freighter on the horizon and then a pair of Zeros came in low over the sea for sport among the little boats.

Later he found a seeping hole below the waterline. He carved a soap plug with his penknife, stopped the hole with it and tacked a tarpaulin patch over the repair. The junk was listing when the wind caught the battered sails and took them up to three knots along a narrow strait between small islands that ranged from rocky outcrops to green humps with fishing villages among the sea-level palm trees and mangrove fringe. A monsoon shower pursued and passed the junk, bringing down smuts from the burning city far behind them. The day was steamy and Quiller scarcely had the energy to help Cameron roll the Australian pilot into the water, say a prayer over the ripples and crouch with Maisie under the awning afterward to give her a bucking up.

They were sailing south-west, always between islands. If the sun appeared in the scudding sky it lit up the shallows in shades of green, and the fathomless trenches in deep, dark, blues. They rationed their water and caught rain squalls in a mackintosh. Quiller toted up their food with the supplies on the junk. They had six tins of bully beef and one of Irish stew, a Christmas pudding, a sack of rice and a box of rotting oranges, durians and mangoes. He tried to match his hand-drawn maps and Primrose's atlas to the specks on the horizon and the islands they were closer to, and judged that Sumatra was three days away, allowing for the calm spells between the three-knot breezes.

Late in the afternoon they saw aircraft and heard explosions. While Cameron hid in the hold with Maisie, Quiller swapped his uniform for black pantaloons and a coolie hat from a wooden trunk, and squatted on the deck. Presently a Zero made a low, desultory pass over the sea and droned away.

The wind picked up. At one point they passed a wall of cliffs rising straight out of the sea, and Maisie saw the tiny figure of a man on the cliff top, waving a shirt at them. They couldn't see where to stop for him or even how he'd got there.

At dusk Quiller cooked rice and stirred the Irish stew into it. The heat was intolerable and when the wind dropped again they made barely two knots against the tide.

By nightfall they were creeping uselessly between the islands of the Riau Archipelago when a tiny island, hard against a larger island, uncannily began to lose its cover of leafy branches and palm fronds, slowly transfiguring itself into a coastal steamer, with a rusty flank, portholes and superstructure. An effective job of camouflage, Quiller realised. A chain screeched as the anchor was wound in. Then the chain rattled out again, the anchor splashed down, and a man holding a megaphone called across the water: 'How many are you?'

Quiller hoped his voice would carry. The dusk was fading to full darkness now. 'Two men and a child.'

'Drop your anchor.'

He did. A small boat put out from the ship and when it was alongside the junk, he dropped the Jacob's ladder over the side. Their transfer to the ship was quick and wordless and, as soon as they were aboard, the captain ordered the anchor raised again and the ship began to nose through the jettisoned camouflage into a channel of deeper water.

'We only steam at night,' the captain explained. 'At dawn we anchor off an island, put a working party ashore to collect saplings for camouflage, and wait there until nightfall. Better than dodging Nips in daylight.'

Quiller peered in the half light at the name stencilled on a nearby lifeboat. They were on board the *Alma*. Dim figures crammed the upper deck: women, children, government officials, sailors, exhausted servicemen in scraps of clothing, and not one of them interested in Quiller or his cousin. These people are meeting new strangers every day, Quiller thought, and most of their hope is gone.

'Counting passengers and crew,' the captain said, 'there are three hundred and twenty of us. The old dear's never carried more than twenty in her life.' He seemed obscurely proud, and Quiller wondered if he'd continue to inch away from Singapore, picking up shipwreck survivors until the *Alma* sank under the weight of them.

'I'm afraid it's deck down where you can, chaps,' the captain said, kneeling to chuck Maisie under the chin.

When he was gone, Cameron snarled, 'If we'd gone with Primrose we would've saved ourselves a lot of bother.'

'You didn't want to go to Colombo,' Quiller pointed out. He sounded petulant. He didn't want to talk to Cameron. Theirs was a hateful, tugging relationship, as though they were brothers.

'Just get me out of this, like you promised,' Cameron said.

Quiller knelt and lifted Maisie into his arms. 'We need sleep, little one.'

As the *Alma* laboured through the night they explored the decks and corridors, stepping over sleeping bodies and around fuggy enclosed spaces, searching without luck for unoccupied corners and floorspace. Even as Maisie fell asleep in his arms and became a dead weight, and Cameron slipped away to curl up in a doorway, Quiller continued to search. He'd encounter members of the crew from time to time, and would ask, 'Is there somewhere I can doss down with the kiddie?' but they would shrug at him as if he'd lost his wits.

Presently he lifted Maisie into number 6 lifeboat and crawled in with her to sleep.

At dawn they climbed out to claim the first cups of tea of the morning and watch the captain make for deep water about three hundred yards out from a hump of jungle-capped volcanic rock. Cameron found them and they stared at the sun's reflections in the sea, flashing like blades of glass. There was a pleasant breeze and the taste of the tea, sweetened with condensed milk. Quiller stretched mightily and watched as lifeboats put out from the ship with axemen on board. The sun climbed and axes rang out on the tiny island; women washed their children, and if they had a change of clothing turned their bare backs on the tired men and shrugged into underclothes and dresses. Someone gave Maisie a plate of rice. By now the lifeboats were returning, the axemen rowing hard against a swift current, and when they were alongside they passed the cut saplings hand over hand from the lifeboats to the top deck. Quiller found himself lashing branches and palm fronds to the funnel, mast, davits, bridgehouse and side rails. He looked at the island through the salt-rimed window of the bridgehouse and thought: Why not put the women and children ashore for the day, for extra protection?

A sailor said then, 'Oh, Jesus Christ.'

Quiller shaded his eyes. About a mile off a large ship was drifting toward them. It had left its run for shelter too late, and looked to be wide open to any killers lurking behind the sun, which had been up for three hours now.

'She'll draw the Nips to us,' the sailor said, and he began to semaphore uselessly with his arms.

Quiller looked toward the island. It rose three hundred feet above the sea. No-one could live on it and survive—no fresh water that he could see, no cultivatable land. But people could hide there for a day or so.

He shrugged his haversack onto his back and glanced around the deck. People were stretched lazily in the middling shade of the saplings and palm fronds.

The spotter plane came from the east. It circled the other ship, then, driven away by Bren-gun and rifle fire, turned toward the *Alma*. It circled them, flying just above the sea, and Quiller knew their rusty steel flanks would be unmistakeable at that range and altitude. It made one more pass and then disappeared.

'We have about thirty minutes,' Quiller told the sailor. 'We should get the civilians onto the island.'

The sailor shrugged. 'Talk to the captain,' he said, then froze. 'Listen.'

Quiller heard the anchor chain rattle, and presently the engines began to throb and the *Alma* began to pull away from the island.

'I expect the old man hopes he can find another island first.'

The attack came forty minutes later. They were steaming south-west, closing in on another atoll, when twenty-seven silver bombers, in formations of nine, appeared from the east at an altitude of ten thousand feet. The alarm sounded and passengers were ordered below deck and, for a time, there was a tense silence. Quiller strained to listen, crouched with his arms around Maisie. Suddenly the ship turned hard to starboard, sending a complaining shudder down along the deck as a salvo of bombs burst in the sea so close that the water geysered and washed over the deck. People screamed and Maisie, rocking against Quiller's chest in the shelter of the bridge, began to sob and moan, her eyes screwed shut and her hands over her ears. This is like Singapore all over again, Quiller thought, and held her tighter. A man fell against him, his heels scrabbling. It was Cameron, and Cameron burrowed his head into the gap between Quiller's arms and Maisie's tiny body.

The ship veered again, a sharp turn to port and again the near misses sent water pluming over the deck. The ship twisted and turned, its rivets popping from the strain and the percussive force of explosions so hard against its hull.

The next salvo straddled the ship. Three bombs stuck the upper deck between the bridge and the bow and Quiller slid a little with Maisie and Cameron in the plunge and shudder that followed. The deck splintered and hot shards of metal whined and tore at the superstructure. Other bombs hit and ruptured the pipes and set off a depth charge with a lick of hot yellow flame. There was a layer of human pain and fear under the crackling, stuttering and rattling of wood and metal. Quiller heard fear in his own voice but he couldn't stop it or be brave for Maisie as the people around him scrambled for cover and pieces of the ship broke away and splashed into the water.

Then the ship began to burn and steam in circles. Shooting out a hand, Quiller grabbed a sailor who was scrabbling past. He couldn't control the sobbing of his voice or the panicky clamp of his fingers around the man's arm. 'What the hell's the captain doing!'

The sailor jerked viciously to free himself. 'The ship's stopped answering to the helm, all right? Now let go.'

When the attack had passed Quiller stood dazedly, one hand absently patting the tiny unprotected space between the wingbuds of Maisie's shoulder blades. Blood was running with sea water around his boots. The air was fumy and he felt the ship begin to list. Leaving Maisie with Cameron, he helped a woman to stand. She had lost a strip of flesh from her jaw. People were jumping overboard and sliding down ropes and ladders into the sea, where the swift currents caught them and swept them away. Few of them wore lifebelts. Quiller helped two sailors tear a dead man's shirt into strips, stuff them into the shrapnel holes of a lifeboat, and drop it over the side. Then he seized a raft and threw that into the sea, then a deckchair and a door that had been blown off its hinges. Anything that would float.

Then he heard Cameron shout, 'Planes!'

He looked up. Cameron was standing rockily on the pitching deck, firing his rifle. The bombers had circled around. They came in at mast height this time, machine-gunning the ship and the bobbing heads and lifeboats.

Quiller ran forward, knocking Cameron off his feet and dragging him to the rail, where Maisie had begun to shriek and claw the air and run on the spot. Quiller grabbed her, dealt her a sharp face slap, then clamped her close to his chest again. He was deafened now, trembling, and Cameron was forced to tug hard on his sleeve and shout in his ear: 'Quill, we have to get off. Now.'

The ship lurched abruptly and they slid to the rail. Cameron disentangled himself, helped Quiller and Maisie to their feet, and pointed. 'There.'

A Jacob's ladder had been thrown over the side. They edged toward it hand over hand along the rail. The sun was reflecting off the surface of the sea, broken by wreckage, water-slicked heads and bodies caught in the oily currents and eddies like blackened leaves in a river. Quiller glanced toward the island, where a lifeboat was beached and people ran from the machine-guns. He dropped into the sea and held by one hand to the rope ladder and the other to a dead man wearing a lifebelt. When Maisie came down into the water he rolled the dead man out of the lifebelt and tied it around her, then grasped a bobbing table by one leg and pushed her onto it.

Then Cameron was in the water with him, holding to a table leg. Maisie crouched and dared to kneel and grin at Quiller between solemnly watching dead people swirl by in the currents. Other people were shouting, kicking and swimming around them, gradually falling silent as they lost consciousness and drowned or the quick-licking sharks tore at their wounds and injuries.

Quiller kicked, steering the table until they were well clear of the *Alma*, which was burning to the waterline now. Faces were crammed together at a large, ragged hole amidships, beseeching the sailors in a lifeboat beneath them. One sailor stood to catch a thrashing child. A man swept past the table. He shrieked, over and over again, 'It hurts, shoot me, it hurts,' then rolled onto his face. Maisie glanced at Quiller and shrugged. She was getting older before his eyes, and he wondered if she'd ever feel what he'd felt when he'd lost his mother, an aching sense of emptiness and things unfinished. Then the *Alma* gave up, settling into the layers of the sea, showing only its funnel above a breaking fringe of camouflage saplings and palm fronds.

As the long hours passed in the beating sun, their arms and faces began to burn and their tongues to swell. They developed fierce headaches that gave way to sunstroke and a hazy dreaminess. The water was indistinguishable from the sky and one hour from the next. Whenever other people drifted toward them from out of the long slick of ships' rubbish, oil and bloated carcasses, and held on for a while to the rim of the table, Quiller was never quite sure that it had happened, but the pattern was always the same, a final sigh uttered before they slid away again, as though to say it had been exhausting to maintain so insubstantial a grip on a humble table, let alone life itself.

He remembered an old joke of his Uncle Leonard's. Leonard owned one-tenth of a fleet of luggers yet refused ever to sail, and liked to say: 'The sea's never been in my blood and I'm making damn sure my blood will never be in the sea.' Leonard in a chiacking mood, full of half-smiles and winks, as he sometimes could be.

But Leonard had died. Who deserves to die? Who decides?

Quiller, bobbing in a swift current and bumping against a seawrack of corpses, planks and upright bottles, dared to ask why it had been Leonard and not Crystal. As it happened he'd been visiting Haarlem Downs, en route for Derby with goods for the leprosarium, when the stockmen had brought Leonard in, slung over the spine of a horse. There was the floppy quality to his body, all of its tension lost, and then, when they pulled it down for a closer look, deep abrasions. The hooves of the maddened steer had done their work on the head, too. It had been a swollen, crooked face that looked back at them from the dirt.

Quiller hadn't known what to do. 'Do? You've done quite enough,' Crystal had said.

Merely by existing, Quiller supposed.

He glanced around the table now at Cameron and Maisie, and they were glancing at him and one another, as though to gauge nerve, stamina or luck. The more Quiller thought about death, the more confused and distressed he felt. Maisie, the youngest and most vulnerable, might be expected to go first, which was all the more reason why he couldn't let that happen. He'd found her and felt responsible for her, just as he'd felt responsible for Lee Lin and Primrose, and continued to feel responsible for Cameron. He didn't notice anyone returning the favour.

Who of them would die, then?

Was Primrose safe? Quiller thought of her quality of stillness and estimation, and knew that she wouldn't go readily, any more than she deserved to go.

Perhaps Lee Lin would fall, with her archness, her vanity, her pretensions. But she'd also had a heart of gold for him, and she was no longer arch and vain.

Cameron? Quiller was under contract to the fellow, had his promissory note safe and dry inside his tobacco tin.

That leaves me.

Quiller listened to the tick of his being and thought it unlikely that he'd be the one. Getting killed was always something that happened to someone else.

He shook his head violently. Mad. Macabre. Too much sun. Swallowed too much sea water. Seen too much, too quickly.

'Neil, are you all right?'

Quiller said, 'Do either of you know the words to "Whisky in the Jar"?'

And so he began to jolly them along. He made them talk, even sing through their dried-out lips. A mother and her baby son bumped against them. Maisie held out her arms to the baby, pulled it onto the table, and the mother smiled, closed her eyes and drifted away. They dreamed through the day, a tiny cluster of four now, sometimes passing other clusters, who held on to mattresses, painters' planks lashed together into makeshift rafts, shipping crates and lifeboats. 'The baby just died,' Maisie said, still crouching, looking down at the little bundle like a mother. 'Let him go,' Cameron said, and Quiller nodded, 'Yes, dump him into the water.'

The current bore them along. Their only expense of energy lay in holding on and later stripping two bodies of lifebelts. They drifted past island after island and the sea teased them, taking them close to little beaches then bearing them into open waters again. Whenever the sharks circled, Quiller and Cameron screamed, yelled and churned the water with their hands and feet. Once Cameron glanced at Quiller with his eyes and mouth wide open in shock. 'A shark just scraped against my leg. Like sandpaper.'

Dusk, then darkness fell across the water and there was a good flying moon to light their way. Quiller looked up at it and tried to read the stars. The water grew cold and he wanted to sleep. Then he did sleep and only the sensation of the table leg pulling from his hands woke him. He shouted, 'Wait! I fell asleep. Wait for me.'

Cameron heard him and thrashed his legs in the water to

bring the table around. Quiller heaved toward the table and grabbed hold, no energy left. 'Never ...' he gasped, 'fall ... asleep.' After that he thought: Please, God, just another short nap, I won't let go again, and managed that way to sleep a little, always waking before he let go of the table leg. He tried to wriggle the numbness out of his toes. Suddenly, warm water streamed about his thighs. It felt wonderfully warm, and promised land nearby. 'Can you feel it?' he cried. 'Warm water. We're nearing land, I think.'

Next to him, Cameron laughed quietly. 'Sorry, son, it was me. I just pissed in the water.'

Quiller laughed. Then Maisie laughed and that awoke their good spirits. For a short time Quiller felt fully awake although his arms ached, his lower limbs were numb and he craved rainwater for his parched mouth. They began to keep a check on one another: 'You were mad, firing at those bombers.' 'Maisie, would you like a story?' 'What was it like going back to Newcastle?'

At first light the current eddied near an island, casting them aside, and they seemed to dream of the firm sand under their feet, the sloping beach and shady palms, the knot of men and women wading out to help them over the last little distance. Then brackish but saltless water was dribbled past the cracks in their swollen black lips.

As Tight as a
Drum Around Her

One morning the barometric pressure began to plummet. Even Anneliese was subdued by the premonitory cast of the dawn light and was there, hard on Jeannie's heels, whenever Jeannie felt the compulsion to revisit Leonard's study and rap her knuckles against the face of the barometer. The obliging needle would drop a little further each time, calibrating the approaching storm front. An electric charge seemed to crackle on Jeannie's skin. The house was as tight as a drum around her. She couldn't control the ends of her hair.

At one point Wally Webb came to the back door, wringing his greasy felt hat in his big hands. 'I don't like it, love. There's a big blow on the way.'

Jeannie nodded. 'The barometer's been falling all day.'

'We need to batten down.'

The two women stepped out into a queer, expectant light and helped Wally and Harry to drag wire cables over the roof of the main house and stake each end to the ground. The wind began to build as they worked, shaking the poinciana trees, and as Jeannie and Anneliese hurried around the outside walls, unpinning the shutters and folding them across the windows, they were buffeted by wind gusts and stung by grit.

'Wal, it could be a long one,' Jeannie said. 'You and Harry come inside and wait it out with us.'

But Wally tugged the brim of his hat low over his brow and surveyed the house and outbuildings. 'Me and Harry'll stay in the air-raid shelter where we can keep an eye on things.'

Throughout the long day the wind began to build, and Jeannie and Anneliese shrank before it. It seemed to herd them into a spot in the centre of the sitting room and mutter, then howl, around the margins. By mid-afternoon it had reached cyclone strength, gusting heavily from the north-west, full of stamping contempt, sounding like an invasion of cannoneers and mallet beaters. The two women couldn't talk but sat with bowed heads as the dark rooms darkened. Here and there above them flaps of roofing iron had admitted the wind, pulling free of the beams to stutter like machine-guns. Jeannie heard a long scrape and rattle above the porch and knew that the gutter was gone, and waited for the roofs and walls of the sheds to smack against the house like second skins.

Then a bucketing rain came in on the wind and they ran about with saucepans to catch the drops that bled like slow wounds from the ceiling. If not for the howl of the wind they'd have heard a symphony of plinks and plonks. It was Anneliese who noted the mysterious sudden stream first; she clutched Jeannie's arm. Water was pouring across the linoleum from the base of the chimney. It began to broaden like a shallow lake, proof, thought Jeannie irrelevantly, that the floor was perfectly flat in this room. She turned to Anneliese and held her forearms together in the shape of a narrow channel, and was relieved to see under-standing in the other woman's face.

But what to use? They cast about desperately from room to room, unable to converse above the howl of the wind. They needed to build a dyke of some kind, but all they had were useless sticks of furniture, with not a straight edge on any one of them. Jeannie stopped rushing. She paused at the door of Leonard's study with Anneliese and pointed toward the bookshelf. Row upon row of *Hansard*, yearbooks and bound reports, deemed by Crystal of insufficient value to be buried in some drum in the bush.

They made many trips with the heavy books, dropping them with thick fat splats onto the wet floor until they had the crooked arms of a makeshift drain from the chimney to the verandah door. Jeannie opened the door to release the stream. Outside the rain was sheeting down and the poincianas were losing their branches. She shivered. The temperature had fallen with the barometric pressure.

Late in the afternoon the wind dropped to an occasional dying moan and the rain drew back into the lowering clouds and they could converse at last. Jeannie felt that she had little to offer Anneliese, apart from a violent cyclone, and Anneliese had had plenty of those, so she was mostly content to listen, for Anneliese made pictures in Jeannie's head, and all Jeannie had to do was place Cameron inside them and know, a little more clearly, where he was.

On the day they'd driven to the Rodenwalt's country house in central Java, Anneliese said, they'd been obliged by the movement of troops and convoys to detour through a region of markets and shanties along the banks of the Ciliwung, a slow, viscous, rotten-smelling sludge. Women stallholders predominated, selling satays, sticky rice, martabak omelettes, Chinese meatballs-and-noodle soup, gado gado and fried bananas to other women, many of whom stopped to gossip, a baby tied under one armpit. A *dukun*—a faith-healer or sorcerer—sat inside a small bamboo and rattan hutch next to the Paradise Hotel, where prostitutes waited.

'We should shop here, not in the mountains,' Lottie had said.

So Hasan pulled into the kerb and they got out. Lottie moved easily among the stalls, talking and smiling as the stallholders swooped to pat Jeroen on the head. Anneliese trailed behind, speculating about their diverse fates after the Japanese invasion— for they would invade, she was certain of that.

She watched Lottie negotiating with a woman who sold fried bananas. Lottie was turning bit by bit, casting off her 'brown' skin. The changes were subtle. Before Edouard came along Lottie would have scoffed and bantered with the market stallholders like a local, but lately, in Anneliese's eyes, the colonial wife was in the ascendancy. Lottie might sometimes joke with Anneliese about the *trekker* she'd married, but Anneliese was no longer invited to laugh along with her.

'Now we really must hurry,' Lottie said, bundling them all into the car.

They drove through the morning. The Bandoeng house was a large bungalow with a verandah, white walls and a red tiled roof sitting high above a valley on Oengaran Mountain, where the cooling breezes of the higher altitudes lured the Dutch away from the sweltering coastal flats of Batavia. They saw many other cars on the road that day, piled high, like theirs, with servants and luggage, and there was evidence on the mountain itself that other families had been spooked by the leaflets—shutters open, cars in driveways, Europeans in the marketplaces, food vendors cycling from house to house balancing their shoulder kitchens, the women of the kampongs hurrying about the *atap* houses bearing heavy jars and trays upon their heads.

They arrived at midday, and Anneliese walked with Jeroen to a vantage point on the sloping lawn. After the whine of the engine and gearbox, and the passage of the wind past her ears, she expected silence, but it was time for the devout to pray and the valleys echoed with the calls of the holy men. And the birds— she'd forgotten their endless cries and whistles. All nature loved Bandoeng: huge rice terraces descended to the plains, the plants shot through with crackling green light; dragonflies fizzed and popped in staticky flashes; ducks stirred the paddy water, fracturing the immense reflected sky; and hunting birds hung in the trembling electric air between the ground and the clouds, which reached in stamping high towers and promised afternoon storms. The sun at that time of the day came through in bronze lances and lit up the golden straw hats of the paddy workers.

Jeroen had swung abstractedly on her hand, quiet after the journey. He would point suddenly, wordlessly, and let his hand drop again. 'Malabar,' Anneliese said, naming mountains and volcanos for him. 'The mountain of the arrow. The ship turned upside down.'

Suddenly lightning forked from a darkening cloud mass and Jeroen jumped. The rain came just as suddenly, sheeting past, and through it the lightning seemed blue and mauve and purple. Jeroen uttered a slow, throaty chuckle of appreciation and pleasure, until Lottie emerged from the house and clapped her hands, saying, 'Are you mad, you two? Anneliese, he'll catch his death of cold. Come inside at once.'

Three tiny lizards clung to the upper walls of Jeroen's room and watched companionably as Anneliese unpacked his toys, short pants, shirts and underwear. On a shelf next to the window, painted puppets, dragons and dolls of the rice harvest festival, gifts from the kampong people, also watched silently as she moved about the room. So strong was her sense of her mother at that moment, and of her mother's kampong far away, 'that I had to sit on the edge of Jeroen's bed with my hand over my heart to keep it still. In Batavia I always felt a little bit Dutch, but not there on the mountain. Do you understand what I am saying?'

Jeannie nodded.

Then Lottie had ordered Anneliese to answer a knock on the back door. 'I went, grumbling under my breath. She was more and more like a *trekker*.'

A Chinese man in black had bobbed at her and silently opened a box of embroidered linen. He'd tried to look past her into the house. She took a guilder from her pocket, selected a pillowcase, and waved him away.

He was the first vendor. Another man arrived, offering tamarillos from baskets swinging from a heavy yoke across his shoulders, followed by two children wheeling a little cart of flavoured ice-water. Anneliese bought a drink for Jeroen, and Wilhelmina, the cook, bought some tamarillos for the kitchen.

'Jeroen was slow to settle at bedtime, so I took him outside for a little while.'

At night the frogs would start up, the toads jump for insects and the fireflies hover by the irrigation ditch; the nightwatchman, an ancient villager with missing teeth, would beat upon a hollow bamboo gong that all was well, the other kampongs responding up and down the valleys. 'Then back to bed but still I had to sit with him for almost one hour, stroking his temples and singing "Nina Bobok". My mouth was so dry. I wonder if he sensed something, the war. Afterward I collapsed into a cane chair to sew a frayed collar.'

'Where was Lottie?'

Anneliese looked away. 'She was in another room, waiting to say things to me.'

A silence gathered, awkward because Anneliese had stopped to muse, and eerie because they were in the eye of the cyclone and could expect it to turn on its axis, somewhere out on the basalt plain, and come batter at the walls again for another six hours. 'Let's eat,' Jeannie said finally.

She went out to the air-raid shelter and found Wally and Harry perched on a wooden crate lapped by floodwaters. 'The bloody thing might be proof against an air raid but not a good old blow,' Wally said.

Jeannie waded across the floor of the shelter and helped them down. 'Come inside, both of you. We're going to eat now.'

'S'orright, missus,' Harry said, shaking his head.

Jeannie didn't push it. 'Wally?'

'Ta, gorgeous. I'm starving. How's the coloured lass holding up?'

'Like a trooper.'

Jeannie glanced about as they returned to the house. The roof from the shearers' kitchen sat in the middle of the drive like a buried house and the poincianas had been uprooted or torn back to the central stem. The wireless mast was bent at the middle and touched the ground like a skinny man poised to dive. They'd already had twenty-four inches of rain for the season. The mosquitoes and sandflies were bad and the ground crawled with frogs. The swamp was churning and a chain of waist-deep lakes stretched across the flats. They certainly didn't need more rain. There would be mills out of action and drowned and stranded sheep to recover. Jeannie and Wally talked about these things as they circled the house and inspected the shutters and roof.

'Look at this,' Wally said, putting his face to a knothole in the sitting-room shutter.

The shutter looked damp and scratched. Jeannie peered through the hole and there on the other side the glass was frosted. 'Sand did that,' Wally said.

She nodded. 'The windows up at the hut are just the same.'

They went indoors and stopped dead, their jaws agape. Anneliese was standing in the middle of the dining-room floor, wearing a beaded, pearlshell-pink dress. She'd pushed the table back against the wall and beamed when she saw them standing in the doorway, beamed and flung out her arms and made a graceful pirouette.

Bread, cold sliced meat, tomatoes, a jar of chutney, a jug of milk and plates and cutlery were on the table. 'Dear lady and gentleman, you are please to eat now.'

With a sense of disconnection, Jeannie allowed herself to be seated with Wally at the long table. They had an hour's grace before the cyclone returned, a little gap in which nothing was right outside and anything could happen inside, and she realised she didn't care that Anneliese had been snooping and found Crystal's old dresses, for they were beautiful, slim-fitting, out-of-date dresses from the 1920s, when Crystal had been a young woman in another, better place than this. Jeannie sat with Wally at the table while Anneliese modelled one dress after another, slinking in and out of the dining room in tight, knee-length sheath dresses, ball gowns, jackets and pillbox hats, in white patterned stockings and court shoes, in stoles and silken slips. Her teeth were dazzling and she filled the shut-down, timorous house with colour. Jeannie needed it, after the drab days and months. The house needed it, and she thought of the two sisters, Crystal and Hazel, before they fell out and never saw one another again.

She glanced at Wally. He was watching Anneliese with shy longing.

Then the wind rose and shook the windows and drove them together into a dark huddle again.

They stepped outside the next morning into a clearing sky and examined the damage. It was as if an army of giants had marched through, snapping off branches and scattering rubbish. Wally and Harry took three days to chop away the fallen trees. After several days of pumping, water continued to seep from the ground and fill the air-raid shelter. The linoleum had lifted in the sitting room and Anneliese helped Jeannie to roll it up and hang it outside to dry. When Jeannie and Harry rode out to count sheep carcasses and check on the mills, the floodwaters reached their saddle pads. Five hundred dead sheep—she stopped counting eventually. A dozen mills out of action. And the wind had wrenched away the doors of the hangar and borne branches, lengths of guttering and a sheet of roofing iron in upon the lonely Gull, slashing one of the wings to ribbons and holing the fuselage. That hurt more than anything, bringing her brave man to mind when she wanted him the most and couldn't have him.

You Cannot Expect
the Savoy Hotel

They rested through the day in the shade of the palms, half-delirious and prone to testing their senses to pull themselves out of their dreaming state. When Quiller had the strength to prop himself against a palm tree, he saw that a nurse had swept clear a patch of sand to make a dressing station under the trees. Men and women with shrapnel wounds and coral lesions sat or lay in a row, sharp-faced with pain. Those who'd been dragged naked from the water wore over- and under-sized soldiers' tunics and sailcloth capes. Using salvaged medical packs and strips torn from cotton shirts, the nurse crouched beside one patient and then another, applying gauze plugs, clearing away dribbles of blood, offering water, murmuring encouragement.

Then she saw that he was awake and came across the sand toward him. 'Who are you?'

He told her. 'And you?'

'Eleven of us came in a lifeboat,' she said. 'It was badly holed so we scuttled it. The others have drifted here one by one, like you and your friends.'

There were twenty-eight altogether, she said. 'And I hope we don't get any more.' They were down to a daily ration of one ships' biscuit, one slice of bully beef, and a tin cup of water from the spring—which was no more that a shrinking seepage from a rock at the base of the only hill on the island. 'And no more medical supplies.'

Quiller gazed around the clearing. There was a Chinese woman with three small children, an English naval officer, two English pilots, four Australian soldiers, and a handful of men and women in civilian dress. Quiller had no wish to speak to the pilots. He felt no sense of community with anyone but Maisie and Cameron.

When the tide-line receded, he set out to explore the sandy fringe of the island. Many corpses had washed ashore, badly cut by coral or eaten to the bone by sharks and other fishes, and naked or badly bloated inside scraps of clothing. Saying 'There but for the grace of God go I' over and over again, Quiller stripped several of the corpses, then wandered back to the clearing with a large bundle of serviceable shirts, dresses and trousers. A ragged cheer went up.

Although his air force shirt was intact his trousers had been reduced to scraps, so he scrounged in the pile and claimed a pair of gabardine trousers. He noticed blood on his leg as he drew them on. He'd cut his shin on a vine or an edge of coral. It would need watching.

Late in the afternoon a sea-going junk passed close to the island and Cameron ran into the shallows to shout and wave his shirt over his head. Quiller joined him, watching as the junk dropped anchor and lowered a sampan over the side. The man who rowed across was Malay, and he'd loaded the sampan with coconuts, durians and rambutans. He beamed at Quiller, ignoring him when he asked, 'Can you take us to Sumatra?'

'You eat first.'

The others crowded on to the little beach and the nurse and the pilots began to slice the fruit and cut open the coconuts. They ate standing up, the juice running down from their mouths, listening as Quiller tackled the man again.

'Where are you from?'

'Senanjang.'

'Where are you going?'

'The Amir, he say is very bad, so many peoples on the islands, must find and bring them in.'

Quiller indicated the people behind him. 'Have you got room for us?'

'Much room. Three hundred dollar.'

The Royal Navy officer stepped forward, full of hectoring dignity. 'You blighter. Do the decent thing.'

The Malay shrugged. 'I go now. Bye-bye.'

'Wait,' the nurse said.

'Three hundred dollar.'

'For all of us? Some of us are wounded.'

'Three hundred dollar.'

She looked around, searching their faces. 'Anybody? Any money at all?'

They shook their heads. Most of them barely had the shirts on their backs. 'We'll get money to you later,' Quiller said.

'Pay now.'

The naval officer glanced around, taking in Cameron and the other Australian soldiers. 'Any of you chappies got a rifle?'

Cameron gazed at him in his lazy way, a cigarette as narrow as a twig glued to his lower lip, and said, squinting in offhand, deadly casualness, 'Come off it, sport. What's that there under your flaming shirt?'

The officer stepped back. 'I don't know what you're talking about.'

Another soldier said, 'The game's up, Admiral.'

The navy man retreated further. 'I say, steady on.'

'The bastard's got a money belt,' Cameron said. 'I saw it on him when he took a bog this morning.'

The navy man went red and tight-faced. 'And you were intending to rob me, I suppose.'

Cameron spat a fleck of tobacco angrily at the man's feet.

The nurse said, 'Commander, do you have three hundred dollars?'

'Might do. But I object to giving it to a wog.'

'We have no choice. I'm sure you'll be reimbursed one way or another when this is all over.'

The man was fretful and stamped across the sand and behind a rock. He came out waving a fistful of money and slapped it into the Malay captain's hand. 'You should be shot.'

'We go now.'

They were ferried out to the junk and found shelter under a bamboo and *atap* lean-to on the deck. The captain hauled in the anchor and the sails caught the wind. As they passed down the Tjombol Strait, the captain pointed out and named the islands. Quiller pulled out his sodden maps and tried to chart their progress. The islands of the archipelago lay to the east, and Sumatra, thinly populated owing to mountains and jungle, lay to the west, across thirty miles of open sea. But one by one the maps disintegrated and he rolled them into pellets and flicked them into the water.

They sailed through the night, making no more than three or four knots, and at daybreak Quiller saw land on the port bow. 'Singkep,' the captain said. Quiller remembered it from his maps, a large island, but Sumatra and the Indragiri River mouth still lay to starboard, across open sea.

'We buy food,' the captain explained.

The nurse had joined them. 'No, *you* buy the food, out of your fee.'

The captain spat betel juice onto the deck, cocked his head at her, then shrugged. 'No matter.'

As they drew nearer to the island a village took shape, bamboo huts crowding the shore and extending out over the sea on stakes. Villagers began to mill on the jetty, shouting instructions to the captain to guide him toward the markers of a deep-water channel. The captain swung the junk around and edged along it, darting from one side of the deck to the other, gauging the width. Quiller was too absorbed with their progress to pay attention to the villagers until voices, faint across the water, called his name. He glanced up. Cameron was at the rail, pointing, urging him to look.

'Primrose and Lee Lin.'

Quiller gaped. 'Where?'

He sought to locate the voices, which were no longer faint but full of Lee Lin's noise now that the junk was hard against the jetty. Then he and Cameron were scrambling out behind the captain and thin arms were hard around them and he was blinking, full of emotion.

'We've been here since Monday,' Primrose said, stepping back.

'It's a kind of way station. People arrive, if they're lucky they're taken across to Sumatra, then more people arrive. Today we got lucky—doubly lucky,' she added shyly, grinning at him.

'What happened to your ship?'

Lee Lin shivered. 'Aeroplanes come.'

Both women were shoeless, bare-legged, dressed only in underwear and torn, over-sized shirts. Their thighs, arms and stomachs were streaked with smoke and blood that had been poorly sluiced away. Primrose caught Quiller's glance and said, 'We'd stripped off to sleep, it was so hot. Then we were bombed.' She looked down at herself. 'It looks worse than it is. The shirts aren't ours.'

'We'll scrounge something for you.'

'There are five more of us.'

'Bring them aboard.'

Primrose darted away and returned with an elderly man and four women, whom Quiller concealed, together with Lee Lin and Primrose, in a knot of the original passengers, and they all settled in to wait for the captain. When Primrose said, 'Who would have thought we'd meet up again?' Quiller shrugged, for he no longer believed in coincidence. The war had done away with chance. It had tossed them all into a funnel, which they were passing through at varying rates, bumping against one another from time to time on their way to the pit at the end. He said carefully, 'I saw a prisoner go aboard your ship, an army captain. Did you see what happened to him?'

Primrose waved at the water. 'They took him across two days ago.'

An hour later the captain returned with sun-dried fish, coconuts, duck eggs and a jerrycan of water. If he noticed the extra passengers he made no comment.

Late in the morning they began the crossing to Sumatra, some of the passengers falling ill, holding their stomachs and propping their skinny, straining shanks over the side until the junk was streaked with the thin gruel of their waste. It was the eggs. They were the flavour of oily, mud-dwelling fish, and repeated painfully in Quiller's stomach. He was obliged to hold Lee Lin's hands, then Primrose's, as they squatted over the side. They were too tired to say 'Don't look,' and too much had happened between them anyway. Cameron lay immobile on the deck with other men and women. Only Maisie seemed unaffected by the eggs and the general misery.

Some time in the afternoon they reached the mouth of the Indragiri River. It was deceptive, a broad tidal estuary of tiny islands and narrow channels before they were upon the river itself, which was broad, fast-flowing and lined with mangrove swamps. Eventually the swamps gave way to dense jungle. Monkeys screeched down at them, swivelling and baring their teeth, and birds the colour of rainbow splashes snapped across the water and between the trees. Quiller spotted wild pigs on the river banks, and crocodiles, disturbed by the junk, slid from the mud-flats and vanished into water carpeted with lilies. He asked to see the captain's charts. The first town was Tembilahan. According to the captain it was a stage in an escape route. After Rengat, the highest navigable point of the river, it was overland to Sawahlunto, in the mountains, then down to Padang, where the Dutch had ships waiting. Quiller thought that he'd take Cam and the others as far as Padang and then make his way south-east across the island and rejoin Freddy on the RAF base at Palembang. The jungle slipped by. He glanced across at the bank. Two men, bare-chested, wearing sarongs and standing upright in a canoe, were watching the junk from a narrow inlet overhung by bright swatches of leaves and creepers. They ducked away shyly when Quiller waved.

Tembilahan took shape as wooden warehouses along a quay, a market square, colonial buildings and huts spread against jungle and mountain greenery. The captain tied up at a scoured and weathered wooden jetty and stood back smoking and nodding encouragement as the wounded were lifted onto the quay, where a squad of native policemen in green uniforms took charge and whistled for rickshaws and drays.

When it was time for the able-bodied to climb out of the junk, the naval officer said, 'Has anybody seen my kit?'

He was ignored. Quiller hoisted Maisie and the Chinese children out of the junk, then helped an elderly planter carrying a small, warped cardboard suitcase.

'I said, has anybody seen my kit? You there, stop what you're doing and answer me.'

Quiller turned. 'Shut your cake hole,' he said levelly. 'Thank your lucky stars you're alive.'

The officer drew himself up. Waves of rum wafted from him and Quiller wondered what else the man had concealed under his shirt.

'I'm putting you on notice for insubordination.'

Quiller turned away to help Lee Lin onto the quay. The naval officer elbowed her aside as he scrambled out, and once on the quay he lashed truculently at the old planter's suitcase with his foot, sending it into the water. Then he was gone, pushing through food vendors and the listless survivors from other wrecks toward the market. The old man leaned over the rail and peered at his sinking suitcase. 'My wife's things,' he said.

Lee Lin collapsed onto a crate. She looked stunned, as though staring back down the months to the old happy ways of her life. 'We stick together,' she said after a while. 'We fine. We like family.'

They gathered with her, watching a European man in a white suit and sola topee threading through the crowd. He stopped when he reached them, and said, in Dutch-accented English, 'I am the District Controlleur. You are how many?'

Quiller looked around. Most of the other passengers from the junk had drifted away. 'Thirty-five.'

The Dutchman was shy and tentative, his eyes drooping with exhaustion. 'Hello, little one,' he said, stooping to lift Maisie's chin. Then he straightened and swung around to point toward the far edge of the town. 'We have set aside a guesthouse for the womens and a warehouse for the men. Naturally you cannot expect the Savoy Hotel.'

He showed his teeth; Quiller tried to smile, but was too fatigued to care for the man's feelings.

'There is not so much food available. So many mouths to feed. You have forced up the prices in the market and the villagers they are unhappy about it. Please you will not cause the problems with the local people. No shooting of guns, looting or molesting the womens.' He shook his head, crabbed and querulous. 'Very bad.' He beckoned. 'You come with me now.'

The Controlleur led them around the shoreline to a

run-down guesthouse with deep verandahs screened by bamboo blinds and a garden that was richly scented, damp and in vivid shades of red, yellow and green. But the women already gathered there had no colour beyond their grimy pale arms, legs and faces, their torn, bleached, salt-scummed dresses. One woman unwrapped her sarong and fastened it over her breasts when she saw the Controlleur. Other women wore scraps of underwear and two were fanning their bare, sticky bodies with thin bedsheets clutched high at the neck. They all stiffened to see Primrose and Lee Lin, and one woman stood, her fists clenched, hostility taking the place of the hopelessness that had been in her eyes. 'I can't imagine who you think you are or where you think you're going.'

'Madam, please,' the Controlleur said.

'This is Lee Lin,' Quiller said pleasantly, 'this is Maisie, and this is Primrose. They are badly in need of rest.'

The woman stared at Maisie. 'Your servants may bunk down with their own kind, my dear.'

'They are not my servants,' Maisie said. 'They're my friends.'

'Then you're bound to want to find a place together. I'm afraid there's no more room here.'

Cameron mounted the steps, jutting his jaw at the woman. 'You stuck-up cow, you fucking tight-arsed fucking bitch, can't you give them a fair go?'

The Controlleur coughed and began to back away. 'Another boat has docked.' He pointed to a warehouse further around the shoreline. 'Men please to stay there.'

'Off you go, Wilhelm,' Cameron said.

Then Lee Lin stepped onto the verandah, pulling Primrose and Maisie along with her. 'We sleep there,' she said, pointing along the verandah to a dark region of dead ferns in huge stained pots.

'We don't want any of your praying nonsense or filthy ways, no male callers,' the woman said, and she screwed up her face and began to utter a series of high, nasally *hoys* and *yings* that Quiller took to be a parody of Cantonese prayer.

Primrose stepped very close to her, communicating calm menace, holding her scrap of shrapnel at the woman's throat. 'The British left us to the Japanese in Penang, and they did it again in Singapore. You do not get a third opportunity.'

The woman retreated. 'Well, of all the nerve. What preposterous ...'

Primrose had forgotten her already. She leaned over the rail to wave at Quiller. 'Don't worry about us.'

Promising to look out for food and a boat heading upriver, Quiller and Cameron made for the warehouse. Inside the door they found hard, dry earthen floors littered with bedrolls, blankets and bamboo mats that had been supplied by the Red Cross. Otherwise the building was empty, the evacuees milling at the market, wandering around the town or squatting along the river-bank hoping for someone to take them upriver.

'I'm fagged out,' Cameron said. 'I need some shut-eye.'

'Go ahead. I'll look around for a boat and some food.'

Cameron's face narrowed. 'Don't leave me behind, Quill.'

'Grow up,' Quiller said angrily, and went out into the steamy heat.

He headed for the market square, where he paused to watch. He doubted that it had ever done such good business. A squad of Hyderabads was bartering a wristwatch for tinned peaches and two AIF privates were pooling Malay dollars from their pockets for tobacco, while a third exchanged his rifle for a pound of chocolate. The storekeepers were shouting and the evacuees, in their scraps of native, civilian and military dress, were haggling, sometimes turning to snarl at, or being menaced by, those who were still armed. A British corporal stuck a bayonet against the throat of a Chinese fruiterer and reached around him for a bunch of bananas; a Eurasian woman wriggled away from the arms of a surly British sailor.

Quiller walked through the market, stopping now and then to inquire about passages upriver. He didn't meet a man who hadn't been in Tembilahan for several days, waiting for a way out, and most had scarcely the energy or goodwill to answer him.

Meanwhile a wood-burning steam launch was coming in, towing an open barge crammed with servicemen and civilians, who stared dully at the town and the jungle that encroached upon it. They were naked, or dressed in rags and bloodied bandages, and some screamed in pain when the barge butted home against the wooden uprights of the jetty. Ropes were tossed and thrown around the stanchions. Then the wounded were slid onto the jetty, and Quiller sighed, threaded through the listless men and women who were watching, and grabbed the end of a stretcher.

An Australian Army captain was on the other end. 'Know where the hospital is, Air Force?'

'No.'

'Then I'll lead the way.'

They followed the river to a small building at the edge of the town. It had been the dispensary for a nearby tin mine, the metal roof and brick walls holding the heat of the sun all year round. When Quiller followed the officer in with the stretcher, he was stupefied by the screams of a man being held down on the operating table and the stench of blood, faeces, urine, gas, gangrene, perspiration and vomit in the superheated air. An Australian Army surgeon was leaning over the screaming man. The surgeon was shoeless and wore only blood-splashed shorts, with more blood on his face, chest and arms, fine arterial sprays of it laying across thicker, darker, intestinal gouts. He was sweating, more sweat breaking out as he tried to saw through flesh and bone with a kitchen knife. In the end he tossed the knife aside, took up a hatchet and began to chop. Four nurses struggled against the patient's bucking, and one of them was Dorry. Quiller was unsurprised to see her. All the world was washing up with him as he moved through time and places.

He helped for an hour in the foetid room, dispensing aspirin, bathing septic wounds and abscesses, sponging away squirts of diarrhoea, holding patients down for the surgeon's axe and kitchen knife before Dorry could spare a few minutes to be with him, out in the steaming but cleaner air beneath the coconut palms that lined the river. She stood close, peering at his face while she puffed on her cigarette.

'You're badly sunburnt.'

'I was in the water for twenty-four hours.'

She took a small round tin from her thigh pocket. 'Put some of this on.'

It was an ointment as thick and pungent as axle grease; a warm, smothering sensation on his fingers. 'The others are in a bad way, too.'

Dorry jerked and squinted as cigarette smoke licked her eyes. 'Keep it then. What others?'

'Primrose, Lee Lin, Cameron and a child we met called Maisie.'

Dorry drew smoke deeply into her lungs, observing him down the length of her nose. Her cheeks were baggy with fatigue, her spirits flagging, her cushiony weight worn away, and Quiller, suddenly moved, pulled her hard against him. She rested her head on his chest for a second and murmured, 'You're skin and bone, Quill.'

He indicated the soldiers and destitute civilians lying on stretchers or sprawled with their backs to the palm trees, waiting for surgery or recovering from it. No-one had the spirit to complain or entertain hope or curiosity. 'We're all skin and bone, love.'

'I'll miss your voice calling me "loov". It's nice. Do you have somewhere to stay?'

He told her about the guesthouse and the empty godown. 'What about you?'

'Down there,' Dorry said, indicating a launch moored at the end of a small wooden pier. It was badly shot up and partly scorched by fire. Two nurses were asleep on army cots on the deck, sheltered by a square of tarpaulin, and a New Zealand pilot whom Quiller recognised from Singapore, now shoeless and wearing only torn shorts and a cap and cradling a Bren-gun, was dealing out a round of patience on the blackened deck.

Quiller felt obscurely jealous. 'You've taken up with Doug?'

With an air of morose contempt, Dorry said, 'If you must know, Quill, he's there for protection. Some army types climbed aboard last night and tried to root one of the girls.' She hurled the butt of her cigarette away and gave a mighty stretch. 'Well, no rest for the wicked.'

A nurse had appeared at the dispensary door. She was drooping with exhaustion, and Quiller realised, from her hobbling progress down the steps and along the path to the launch, that she'd been injured or shot in the leg.

'I'll stop and help for a while,' Quiller said.

'Oh, would you, Quill? That'd be marvellous. You can start by scrounging some food.'

Quiller made his way back to the market. He felt the weight of hungry, idle and calculating eyes on his back as he went. People seemed to be speculating: Does he have food in his haversack? Does he have a boat in mind? Does he have stolen money or jewels worth stealing again? Is he armed?

Another junk was edging against the jetty. Quiller hurried, spending most of his few Malay dollars buying fruit, tinned meat and coconut milk, and returned to the dispensary. Dorry wasn't there. 'Asleep,' the surgeon said, so he deposited the bulk of the food in a corner and headed back toward the town. As he passed the nurses' launch he saw that the New Zealand pilot was asleep and extra cots and mattresses lay under the tarpaulin shelter. One of the lumps on one of the mattresses was Dorry. Quiller leaned over the gunwale, stacked the remainder of the fruit and tinned meat next to her feet, waved at a nurse who'd opened her eyes at the movement, and walked on.

He reached the quayside as a knot of armed men wearing scraps of military and native dress crossed silently in front of him to stand looking at the newly docked junk. He was unnerved by their grim purpose, their raptors' eyes, as they watched and waited to take advantage of opportunities and weaknesses.

This time he helped a wounded Australian Army major hobble to the dispensary. As they passed the market, the major stopped. 'Look, cobber, I'd go for a smoke and a tin of peaches.'

'I'm flat broke, sir.'

The major dug into his uniform shirt pocket. He was thin, with a caved-in chest, like a man fifty years Quiller's senior. As he pulled out a fistful of Malayan dollars, Quiller quickly turned him away from the hungry eyes all around. 'Watch where you flash your money, sir.'

The major thrust it at him. 'Take it, take it all. Get me some grub and keep the rest. Fucked if I want the burden.'

Quiller made several trips through the afternoon, carrying wounded evacuees to the dispensary. By five o'clock he'd had enough and used the major's dollars to buy two over-ripe mangoes and five small tins of Irish stew.

Primrose, Lee Lin and Maisie were resting in their spot in the darkest corner of the guesthouse verandah. Primrose stood to greet him. 'Oh, well done, sir.'

She grinned and he saw how clever and ironical she was. He liked her air of mockery and wondered if she'd ever taunted her father, the English policeman sent to serve in a hot country far from England. He sawed open the cans with his knife and they ate, tipping the glutinous mess into their mouths, careless of the jagged rims. Then Primrose opened the mangoes, removed the stones and, with Quiller's knife, sliced off broad petals of skin, the attached flesh scored into juicy cubes for eating. They slavered, their teeth shearing off the flesh, juice smearing their chins.

Then a twin-engined bomber came up the river, flying low, and dropped a stick of bombs that plumed in the water and tore off a corner of the jetty. The women waiting listlessly on the verandah of the guesthouse moaned and turned away, folding up as if to die, and Lee Lin wailed, 'Same like Singapore? No, no.'

Quiller watched the plane make a banking climb away from the river and disappear over the mountains that lay south-east of the town. He wondered if Freddy and Taffy were still at Palembang or if the field had been evacuated or captured. He wiped his mouth with the back of his hand. 'You'll be safe if you stay here. I'd better check on Cam.'

He found his cousin trembling inside the doorway of the warehouse, eyes skittering in all directions, from the darkness inside to the panic at the jetty to the river and the lowering sky. 'I can't stand much more of this, Quill.'

Quiller sawed open the last tin of Irish stew. 'Eat. You'll feel better.'

Cameron dug desultorily into the tin with a *kris*, a Malay dagger with a wavy blade. As Quiller watched him, further changes became apparent in the gloomy light: his cousin wore new trousers, shiny boots and a crisply ironed shirt in place of the torn and bleached AIF uniform. A peaked cap sat next to his bedroll. He also smelt of soap and was beardless for the first time in days. Finally, he'd been drinking. There was an empty bottle in the beaten dust beside the open door.

'Where did you get all of this stuff?'

Cameron's eyes jerked from the threat of the sky to Quiller's face and the earthen floor behind him. 'I didn't forget you, mate. Look.'

He pointed at Quiller's bedroll. A clean, pressed shirt sat on it like an offering.

'Whose is it?'

Cameron came closer and enveloped Quiller in a fug of brandy and fear. 'Me and some mates found this house.'

'What house? What mates?'

'Fucking Wilhelm's house, for all I know.'

'The Controlleur's?'

'How the hell should I know? Just some house.'

'You can't … things are bad enough without upsetting the locals, Cam.'

In reply, Cameron waggled the tin of stew. 'Want it? I'm not hungry.'

'You took food as well?'

'Don't you come over high and mighty with me, Neil. If it wasn't for us you'd of ended up in the poor house.'

Quiller took the can and scooped the stew into his mouth with his forefinger. 'Any more booze?'

Cameron's face lightened. 'That's my boy,' he said in tipsy high spirits, and fished a half-bottle of rum from his trousers.

It burned pleasantly in Quiller, washing down the stew and the bad feelings. Cameron watched him alertly, one hand itching to save the rum from extinction. Quiller handed it back. The sensation on his tongue and in his gullet was enough. He was very tired.

'Let's hope old Wilhelm doesn't come looking for his stuff.'

Cameron waved blearily at the town beyond the door. 'You've got civilians, you've got uniforms from all over the place. He wouldn't know where to start, poor bastard.'

'He'd start with the first clean shirt he saw,' Quiller said.

Cameron was shaking again, and Quiller realised how chronic and deeply rooted his fear was. He drew Cameron close and murmured, 'Shhh,' and rocked him gently. The simplest human warmth worked after a while and Cameron returned to his refrain. 'I mean it. Get me out of this and the Gull is yours.'

'Thanks,' Quiller said lamely.

'I'm not normally like this, you know.'

Quiller nodded. 'You got me out of that monsoon drain in Singapore.'

'I've just, I've just got the shakes bloody terrible.'

'I don't blame you.'

'Get me home and I'll be right as rain again.'

'I know.'

'The whole show's been a debacle. Not my flaming fault.'

'No,' Quiller said.

'Tell you what, mate—' pushing Quiller away '—you're a comfort but a darn sight worse smelling than Jeannie.'

Quiller stiffened. It was always there, that challenge and sense of triumph, and the reminder that he was the outsider in Cameron's family, his state provisional. He began to pull away but Cameron clutched him, saying, 'The old man was pretty darn hard on me, Neil.'

'Hard on all of us.'

'Harder on me than you.'

Quiller said nothing.

'Always expecting that little bit more. Bastard.'

Then, spooking Quiller, Cameron took on Leonard's tones: 'You great bawling calf. You sook. You great big girl.'

'He was hard on you all right,' Quiller said.

'He was a bastard.' Then: 'He always preferred you to me. You reminded him of the sister he should have married. He never wanted me, he wanted you.'

'Rubbish.'

'I don't think so.'

After a while, Cameron's grip tightened on Quiller's arm. 'You won't let me down.'

It was a statement, not a question. 'No.'

'You'll get me out.'

'Yes.'

'I mean, I'm not helpless, Quill, we'll get each other out. Strength in numbers.'

'Yes. Look, I badly need to sleep.'

Cameron released him. 'Go ahead.'

'There won't be any more bombers this late in the day,' Quiller said gently. 'It would mean flying back in the dark, and they don't want to do that. You should get some rest too and we'll scrounge a ride out of here in the morning.'

'I'll just smoke for a bit,' Cameron said. He took a mahogany pipe inlaid with silver licks and swirls from his pocket and tamped the bowl with tobacco from a Douwe Egbert's tin.

'Looks like you cleaned the poor bastard out.'

Cameron was full of winks and grins and rolling eyes. 'Just about.' He nodded at the spare shirt. 'You should slip into that. Make you feel cleaner.'

'I think I will,' Quiller said, taking off his air force tunic. The Dutchman's shirt felt cool and fresh against his bone-tired back, ribs and arms, and smelt of new cotton treated by sunlight and a scented wooden wardrobe. He really didn't want to crease it, but yawns racked him and he arranged his body on his bedroll and rested his head on his haversack. He closed his eyes. The floor and walls were redolent of rubber, fish and rotted food, old colonial odours caught forever and baked every day in airless heat.

He awoke with the evening call for prayer. Finding himself alone, he shouldered the haversack and headed for the guesthouse. It was in darkness, and a melancholy sense of the losses in his life crept through him. Here on the sloping hillside above the town he could see that something was happening at the jetty. He hurried down to the dockside, past lanterns in the trees around the market square, past light pooling on the dirt road from the doorways of the cafes, until he was overtaking nurses and doctors who were helping the walking and stretchered wounded toward waiting boats. A large crowd was gathering. He couldn't see and was squeezed out of the lighted places, forced to climb onto a loading ramp above the flagstones, where he stood watching as women boarded the junks, and the wounded the barges and launches. There was a scudding moon and the threat of a monsoon squall. The masts of the junks jerked like arthritic trees as the wind picked up across the water, and the wounded and injured whimpered and cried out, wanting the world to be still.

Then it dawned on Quiller that he was also in pain. Now that he'd placed his weight on his legs again after resting, he could feel a hot throbbing in his shin. He pulled up the leg of his trousers. The vine or coral scratch had turned septic. He needed sulfanilamide.

Meanwhile the Dutch Controlleur, his native police and a ragged line of armed British and Australian officers were at each of the embarkation points, keeping the able-bodied away from the boats. Quiller couldn't see as far as the decks of the waiting vessels in all of that darkness. He could not see Dorry or Lee Lin or Primrose or …

'Quill!'

He looked down. It was Maisie. He reached for her and hauled her up onto the ramp, where she swayed against him, panting, then gasped, 'I looked everywhere for you. You've got a new shirt on.'

'Why aren't you with the others?'

'I went to find you,' Maisie said.

They peered into the play of darkness and shifting moonglow broken by the ghosts who trod on one another's heels as they climbed down into the dark holds of the waiting boats. It made sense to Quiller. That bomber would be back in the morning and the town was crammed to breaking point.

'Someone came to the guesthouse to tell you there was a boat?'

'Yes.'

'I hope the others allowed Lee Lin and Primrose to go with them.'

'Primrose gave them what for.'

Quiller laughed. 'I bet she did. Sweetheart, I think you'd better go down there and join them.'

Her hand slipped into his. 'I went to find you,' she said. 'No-one told you.'

'Wouldn't have mattered,' Quiller said, pointing to those, like him, who would have to wait for another time.

Maisie shuffled close until she bumped against his sore leg. 'Ouch,' Quiller said, easing away from her. 'Look, we can get you aboard, it's not too late.'

'But I want to be with you. The others are too full of their own problems to care about me.'

Quiller himself had veered between fondness and dislike for the others in the unnavigatable turmoil of the past weeks. He wondered if he were losing his desire for Lee Lin, and Cameron kept him feeling wrong-footed. Primrose was another matter. It was complicated. He released Maisie's hand and placed his arm across her thin shoulder bones. 'I know what you mean.'

'Was Cam hurt when those bombs went off today?'

Quiller blinked. 'I beg your pardon?'

Maisie pointed toward the boats. 'I saw him.'

'I don't understand.'

'He was on crutches.'

Quiller knelt, stretching his hot shin, and held and questioned Maisie so intently that she recoiled in tears and bewilderment, but not before he discovered this: that Cameron had been wearing bloody, days' old bandages around his leg and scalp, and had been among the first of the walking wounded allowed aboard the junks.

Slaps and
Peevish Complaint

It was after dawn and the house was very still, but something was wrong, somewhere, somehow, and Jeannie lay motionless under her net, allowing her senses to open to the world. An aeroplane, that was it. Twin engines: she knew that by the substance and counterbeat of the droning sound. As she listened, one engine coughed and then cut out, and before she could drag on her dress and shoes, the other one cut out.

Anneliese was already there on the verandah steps, looking up. It was a Lockheed Orion, a small airliner bearing the orange triangle of the Netherlands on its fuselage and wings, aimed in a steep, tilted, powerless landing approach over the airstrip. Jeannie clenched her hands and said involuntarily, 'Straighten up, straighten up.'

She tracked the Lockheed's graceless descent below the treeline and when it was gone she hugged herself and bent over, anticipating the impact. There was a crack and a drawn-out sound of shearing and torment, then silence. Jeannie half expected smoke. There was no dust, not in these days of rain from the sea. No explosions. No screaming.

She began to run, Anneliese beside her, and discovered that Wally and Harry Horsetalk were already hurrying down the airstrip to the far band of trees, where the Lockheed had come to rest. It was facing the wrong way, exhausted and belly down in the red mud, looking as lost and incongruous as a memorial in an overlooked country town. The starboard wing had been torn away, and Jeannie put it together as she ran: he came in too steeply, the undercarriage snapped, one wing dipped into the mud, the fuselage spun around and settled.

The door above the intact wing opened. A woman stepped out, turned and began to help small children onto the wing. They gathered there uncertainly until Jeannie and Wally took them by the hand and helped them to jump to the ground. Six other women emerged, followed by the pilot and co-pilot, and when they were all out they gazed around dazedly, one or two clutching bruised ribs. Suddenly they broke into speech and laughter.

The pilot was courtly and fastidious. He snapped to attention before Wally. 'I am Captain van Haselen. What is this place, please?'

Wally turned to Jeannie, as if uncertain of his ability to converse with a foreigner. Jeannie explained what and where Haarlem Downs was, and introduced Wally, Anneliese and Harry. The pilot went to shake hands with Anneliese and Harry—and thought better of it. Jeannie heard Anneliese mutter sharply, scowl and turn her back on the aeroplane.

'We are leaving Tjilatjap on Java at midnight and getting lost in the darkness. Then there is no more fuel in the tanks and we must find a place to come down.'

'We have fuel,' Jeannie said, 'but I don't think your aeroplane will fly again.'

'I agree. We must be proceeding to Perth by train.'

Harry slapped his thigh and bent over, laughing wheezily. Wally smirked. Jeannie said, 'There is no train service out here, and the roads are impassable, owing to a cyclone.'

The pilot slumped a little, looking stunned and hollow-eyed with fatigue, as if he recognised finally what it meant to be stuck there with the empty sea on one side and the desert wastes on the other. Then he gathered himself, cocking his head interrogatively. 'You are having a wireless set?'

Jeannie nodded. 'We'll ask the air force to come and fetch you.'

The co-pilot had clambered back into the little airliner and was throwing suitcases and canvas sacks out onto the wing.

Jeannie and the others turned to watch as the women gathered below him and reached for their belongings. 'I am being with KNILM,' the pilot said conversationally, 'but in December I am joining the Royal Netherlands Air Force in Malaya. Very bad,' he said, shaking his head. 'Then Singapore is falling and I am sent to Java, then Java is falling and I am to take the womens and childrens to Australia before the Japanese can catch them.' His passengers were the wives and children of colonial officials, he said. They'd been inconsolable through the long night. Then, just after dawn, they'd seen a Japanese reconnaissance flying boat off the starboard wing. It had tracked them for some time.

'Are you sure?'

'Oh yes.'

Wally Webb seemed to understand Jeannie's tremor of unease. 'If they come back and see this ...'

'Precisely,' she said. 'We'll be seen as a legitimate target. Your plane will have to be concealed for now,' she told the pilots, 'then before it gets dark we can tow it somewhere and set fire to it.'

Wally and Harry went off to collect fallen branches and armfuls of high grass and desert scrub. Jeannie and Anneliese led the others in a straggly line across the airstrip and between the outbuildings to the main house. The women were petulant, the children listless, and one woman snapped at Anneliese for offering to carry her fretting child. A fast exchange in Dutch followed, the woman stiffening suddenly and slapping Anneliese's cheek.

Anneliese snarled at her and joined Jeannie. 'I am not their servant anymore. These people are finished, I think. See them run!'

The pilots and the women and children gathered in the dining room and looked expectantly at Jeannie. She addressed van Haselen: 'Will you translate?'

'Yes.'

'Or I can try German.'

'Oh no,' he said, horrified, 'they are all having mothers and fathers suffering in the Nazi occupation of Holland.'

'All right, ask them if they'd like something to eat and drink first, or would they prefer to wash and change?'

The pilot translated, listened and said, 'Please, they wish to bathe first.'

'Very well, I'll direct them to the bathrooms. Please advise them to use the water sparingly. Meanwhile Anneliese and I will get food ready and contact the air force in Broome.'

The pilot translated but the women stood waiting helplessly and those with fretting children seemed unable or unwilling to console them. Jeannie felt a curious irritation growing inside her. In the kitchen later, Anneliese smiled humourlessly. 'I understand these women. They are lost without a poor native girl to do the work.'

When the evacuees had bathed and eaten, Jeannie gathered mattresses, cushions and bedding together and encouraged them to rest. With so many corners taken up by sleeping forms, she felt trapped in the house and went outside to examine the wreckage of the Lockheed. Wally and Harry had covered the wings and fuselage with cuttings and deadfall, and were shovelling sand and mud onto the remaining patches of bright silver paintwork.

'When you're finished, Wal, could you butcher a couple of goats for tonight?'

'Of course.'

'You'll eat with us?'

He shook his head. There was no arguing with him.

Jeannie wandered away. She found Anneliese watching over two small boys who were clambering over the air-raid shelter and throwing stones into the muddy water. After a while she realised that it was cruel, aggressive play, a war game, and they were the killers.

Who were they killing?

Anneliese began to cry. Jeannie stood beside her, put an arm around her waist and drew her close. 'Hush. It's all right now.'

'If only Jeroen had remained in my lap.'

Late in the afternoon Jeannie and Anneliese began to cook: soup, roast goat and potatoes, and boiled eggs and bread and jam for the children. The kitchen grew stifling and the house was full of lost women and children and a sustained note of complaint, which seemed to kindle a rage in Anneliese.

'So my last memory of Bandoeng is an unhappy one,' she said later, when she and Jeannie were alone. 'Lottie was ... very difficult.'

Lottie had wandered from room to room with an abstracted,

provisional air, the loose floor tiles clacking under her sandals, the gaslights casting troubled shadows as she passed through the rooms where Anneliese sewed or read. She'd stop and finger an ornament, straighten a kink in a floor rug, examine a photograph in a pewter frame. Anneliese had tried to ignore her. Through the open window she could smell charcoal fires and satay, mosquito coils and the hot, dense, blowsy odours of fruits and flowers. Gamelan music somewhere nearby, cicadas and crickets, and the tiny bells of the satay vendor approaching someone's back door. Meanwhile Wilhelmina was in the kitchen, grinding chillies and cummin in a mortar with stony scrapes, rolls and thumps.

Finally Lottie had unburdened herself. 'You have been servicing my husband. Please do not deny it.'

There was a heartsick catch in her voice. She seemed to be trembling.

In the ensuing silence Anneliese had put her hands in her lap, stared at the ornamental tiles, and had the absurd notion that this conversation would be better conducted by way of one of the hinged message slates that were used before there were telephones. Lottie could scratch her questions on the left-hand slate, she her replies on the right. They were not meeting one another's gaze anyway, and their poor hands itched to be occupied.

'So I said to her, "Madam, he took me." '

Jeannie had stopped peeling and slicing, the knife arrested in her hand. 'What did she say?'

'She gave a mad laugh and said, "Oh yes?" '

'What did you do?'

Anneliese and her mistress had gazed at each other finally. At that moment, Lottie seemed fully to spite her lifetime in the tropics. No longer as languid as a local, her skin seemed to suffer from insects, heat and prickly rashes, as though she'd only recently stepped off the boat.

'I said to her, "Does madam wish me to seek other employment?" '

Lottie had suddenly let her guard down. Opening her hands in a gesture of bafflement she'd wailed, 'What is his game?'

Anneliese had listened to the silence beat like a heart between them. Presently Lottie snarled 'Kampong tramp', clacked away across the room and along the long central hallway, and slammed her bedroom door. Anneliese wrapped her arms around herself, convinced that she'd be cast away again.

It became a household of tiptoeing and apprehension. Something was bound to happen, and they waited, and couldn't talk about it. Anneliese's only solace was the dawn light, which she would race to beat each morning by rising before six o'clock and perching on the well behind the house. Dawn spread rapidly through the immense reaches of the mountains. It touched in red and orange strokes on the terraces, the hanging mists, the undersides of the clouds. Palm fronds started as gold fans, the coconuts as glowing orbs, before the greens emerged and the checkerboard lowlands appeared through the retreating mist. The coconut squirrels made antic furry leaps in the trees and scolded her.

Scolded and scolded, up and down the land.

But when Edouard Rodenwalt summoned the family back to Batavia, and sold the Plymouth and shut up the house and dismissed the servants, Anneliese found that she was not cast aside yet. Batavia was in chaos. At midnight a couple of days later, Edouard took them in a government saloon car to the airfield at Tjilatjap, explaining that he'd been ordered to help Dr van Mook set up an interim administration in Australia. He beamed: 'So, we all are saved. Anneliese, my wife and son need you in this very difficult time.'

He was carrying a briefcase. She felt it knock against her thigh when he shoved her gently ahead of him up the ramp of the waiting airliner, his hand lingering as she climbed and her haunches flexed at him. She took a last sniff of the spicy island. Ten hours to Broome, their first stop, on the north-west coast of Australia.

'And here you are,' Jeannie said.

'Here I am.'

At nightfall Jeannie heard the tractor and later smelt smoke: Wally and Harry were burning the Lockheed. With Anneliese's help she pushed a couple of tables together and scrounged all of the chairs she could find and called the evacuees to eat. The women were sulky to see Anneliese there and half expected her to serve them. It was a joyless meal and seemed to promise long, bad hours before the daylight.

And, with darkness, horrors set in. The women and children

were reluctant to be separated from one another so Jeannie and Anneliese dragged all of the temporary beds into the sitting room, where only the windows held back the wide, headlong rush of the world. There were no nets for these beds and with all of the comings and goings of the idle, undirected children, the house had filled with mosquitoes. Everyone danced a frenzied dance of slaps and peevish complaint until Jeannie set a fire on a sheet of iron in the middle of Crystal's rain-buckled linoleum floor and burned dung on it. Thanks weren't offered and she wondered sourly if anyone was out there bravely dying for these people.

His Days in
Cracked-Brain Hope

The Controlleur had placed Maisie into the care of his wife, the last Dutchwoman remaining in the town, but was back with her the next morning, looking rattled, his eyes bagged with sleeplessness. 'This is a very naughty child.'

Maisie stopped struggling and grinned at Quiller through the bars of his cell. 'Hello.'

Quiller climbed to his feet from the rattan mat on the earthen floor, putting his weight onto his good leg, and waited for the gaoler to push Maisie through to him. He crouched to hug her. Maisie squirmed eventually, rounding on the controlleur and retorting, 'I told you last night I wanted to be with my father.'

The Controlleur sniffed and tucked in his shirt in fuming silence, his face full of defensive and retaliatory expressions.

'How long will you keep us here?' Quiller asked.

'You are a thief, sir. You are answering the charges against you.'

Quiller explained again that another man was the thief. He could hear stallkeepers setting up in the market and smell fish and noodles frying in the kitchens of the town. The morning sun was latticed by a solitary gaolyard palm tree and not yet heat-addled and sticky. 'It's in your best interests to keep us moving upriver with the others,' he said.

Then Janeway stirred in the adjoining cell. 'Dr Tesselaar, they are not father and daughter.'

Along with the fleas, the mosquitoes and the pain of his ulcerous leg, Quiller had been kept awake during the night by Janeway, who had alternated between taunting him and attempting to turn him against the Allies.

'He is too my father,' Maisie retorted.

'I should warn you, Dr Tesselaar, they have a very unhealthy attachment.'

The Controlleur turned away with the look of a man who had more than enough on his plate. 'I have not had my breakfast.'

He left with the gaoler. Janeway said, 'Very clever, Quill. Is she your ticket out? So much for the moral fibre of the Royal Air Force.'

Quiller ignored him. Maisie was stepping in place unconsciously. 'I'm afraid you'll have to use the bucket,' he said gently. 'I'll block his view.'

Maisie regarded the bucket and its scabby seat with a long oooh of distaste, but hoisted her skirt, hovered above the seat and as her piss gushed in a hot rush her face cleared of strain.

'Is that better? Where are your underpants?'

These were the questions of a father, delivered with practical concern. Quiller tipped a half-pannikin of water over her hands and swilled away the urine splashes on her legs.

'Very touching, Quill.'

'Shut up.'

The outer door clanged and the gaoler came through to the cells, followed by a British soldier wearing the remnants of a sergeant's uniform and carrying a tray of noodles and black tea in a chipped cup. He could scarcely bring himself to look at Janeway but slid the tray onto the floor of his cell and went out again. He paid no attention to Quiller and Maisie.

Janeway smirked. 'I wonder how long my escorts intend to maintain their charade.'

'What charade?'

'Keeping me alive like this. Wouldn't it be easier simply to shoot me and have done with?'

Quiller clicked his tongue, sharing the humour. 'It's what I'd do.'

'I'm a burden. There's no point dragging me along. They should save their own skins, wouldn't you say?'

'I would. You were convicted, after all.'

Janeway said musingly, 'Unless they imagine I'll be their go-between when the Japanese arrive.'

'That's probably it.'

'Of course, my head is also full of secrets, most of which I am yet to share with anybody, so perhaps they're keeping me alive for a more, shall we say, intensive interrogation.'

'I'd like to give you an intensive interrogation,' Quiller said.

Janeway was delighted. 'I *knew* you were going to say that, Neil.'

Quiller didn't mind talking to Janeway now. Janeway couldn't touch him and it amused him to see his mental negotiations.

Janeway kept the tea but pushed the noodles away. 'I can't eat this muck.'

Maisie crossed to the bars. 'We'll eat it.'

'I think I'll put it with the slops,' Janeway said, with dark, measured, faintly contemptuous tones, and he tipped the noodles with a glug into his bucket of waste. Maisie turned to Quiller and back again, outraged.

'That wasn't necessary,' Quiller said.

He felt hollow now, and saw the hunger gnawing at Maisie.

'Oh, I rather think it was,' Janeway said.

'You're horrible and mean,' Maisie said.

There was a ripping snarl across the town and they stopped to listen, waiting for the bombs to explode. The air seemed to shudder briefly and fall still again, and Janeway grinned.

'An irony,' Quiller said, 'if a stick of bombs fell across this gaol right now.'

Janeway shrugged.

At mid-morning the gaoler entered with the Controlleur and a squad of three native policemen, who were guarding a local man dressed in a sarong, open-necked white shirt, sandals and black, brimless cap. Quiller and Maisie stood back as their cell door was opened for the new prisoner.

Janeway stood hooked to the bars. Like Quiller, he welcomed the distraction. 'Who is your prisoner, Dr Tesselaar?'

The Controlleur shrugged. 'An agitator.'

There was a spark of interest in Janeway. 'An agitator?'

The Controlleur said irritably, 'His name is Arief Sutedjo. He has been inciting the estate labourers in the south and must be prevented from collaborating with the enemy.'

'Why don't you put him in with me?'

The Controlleur shook his head emphatically. 'I know who you are and what you have done,' he said. 'If I had more cells or a second prison I would put this man as far away from you as possible.'

'Hear that, Mike?' Quiller said. He was enjoying himself.

'Shut up, Quiller. What will happen to Sutedjo, Dr Tesselaar?'

'He will be taken under guard to Padang and then into exile.'

As the Controlleur began to leave with the gaoler and the policemen, Quiller called him back. 'We're hungry,' he said.

'You will be on a boat shortly, you and the child.'

'What about the charges?'

The Controlleur threw up his hands. 'Do you think I have the time to prosecute you when the town is full of troublemakers and the bombs fall on us? I do not think so.'

When the Controlleur was gone, Janeway crossed to the adjoining bars and addressed the new prisoner. 'Do you speak English, Arief?'

Sutedjo sat crosslegged on the floor with ineradicable dignity and ignored him. Quiller grinned. 'Why should he talk to you, Mike?'

Janeway gave him a look of intimate contempt. 'Shared aims, Quill, old man, shared aims.'

He turned to Sutedjo again. 'Did you ever imagine, in your wildest dreams, that you'd see your colonial masters running away with their tails between their legs? Not only that but also disgracing themselves, looting, cheating and betraying their miserable ways across your country?'

Sutedjo closed his eyes.

'Freedom. Independence. There's no going back now.'

'Is that why you sold us out, Mike?' Quiller said. 'Lofty aims?'

Janeway snarled, 'I grew up in the Far East. Then I was sent to school in England, so I've seen both sides. I know which I prefer.'

Maisie quivered at him, 'Go away. You're horrible.'

'Hush,' Quiller said, pulling her against his legs, then stretching out on his palliasse with her and closing his eyes. Eventually he heard her breathing deepen as she drifted into sleep.

Quiller dozed. He wanted to shut everything out—everything but the actions of his cousin. He felt almost sick to think that he'd been betrayed like that. His first thought on the wharf last evening was that he'd fulfilled his part of the bargain and he was damn well going to turn up at Haarlem Downs and flash them the promissory note and demand the Gull. Hurt and angry, that's what he'd been feeling at first.

Then his heart had stopped.

The promissory note.

He'd tapped futilely at the breast pocket of the Dutchman's shirt.

'Quick,' he said, 'come with me.'

With Maisie in tow he'd pushed through the soured, dangerous air and away from the dockside. Threaded among the bare market stalls. Traced the waterline to the warehouse doorway and the darkness inside.

There he'd crouched and patted the floor. After a while, Maisie joined him. 'What are we looking for?'

'What was Cam wearing?'

He could see her face if he got close to her. 'It looked like your old shirt,' she said.

Cameron was a shape-slipper. He was a hurt RAF pilot now, on his way upriver and over the mountains to the safer seas, where he might turn into a Dutch colonial officer and demand a passage out. Somewhere along the way he'd tear up the scrap of paper that Quiller had been carrying all these weeks.

Maisie's hot dry hands had held Quiller's head where she could look into his face. 'Don't worry, Neil,' she said, although she couldn't have known what it was that so worried him.

Quiller had thought that two could play at Cameron's game. He'd stroked the front of his stolen shirt and imagined his way into the skin of a Dutchman with a poor, motherless daughter in tow.

That thinking had almost got them aboard the final junk. The Controlleur, recognising his shirt on Quiller's back, had thrown Quiller behind bars and taken Maisie home to his wife.

Now Quiller dozed. Maisie began to snore softly. The controlleur had said something about a boat to take them upriver. Would a boat let him close the distance on Cam? Quiller churned. He wasn't going to let this go. Vengeance could be as powerful as love in galvanising action. The Gull stood for love and hate, and to hell with the promissory note.

On 1 March, St David's Day, Quiller and Maisie boarded an open barge crammed with civilians and servicemen. Most were shipwreck survivors who'd been plucked from the water and the islands of the archipelago days before and dulled almost to catatonia by their helplessness and slow progress through the way stations across Sumatra. A small motor launch, under the control of an Australian tin miner from Malaya, towed the barge and, although they made no more than three knots, the barge jostled in the wake of the launch and the stretcher cases screamed out in pain. Children cried or tried to run about but there was little space for play and those adults who sought sleep, lying stretched out or propped against the rail with their heads on their knees, would curse and lash out at them, while others bickered in venomous undertones. There was no love lost. Maisie stayed close to Quiller, and they were close to the bow, which had been claimed by a band of glowering infantrymen armed with rifles, who had nothing else to claim. The river banks were lined with trees on either side and the bends always gave on to more trees and slow river water.

Rengat was the highest navigatable point of the river for the launch and the barge, a small town marked by lines of rubber trees instead of jungle. They docked in the gathering dusk at a quay constructed of axe-trimmed logs, and Quiller could see other ragtail soldiers and civilians milling about the entrances of the rubber warehouses. At the town end of the quay a pair of Dutch Red Cross ambulances waited and, at the other, adjacent to the launch and the barge, makeshift tables laden with rice, fish, coffee and tea had been set up.

A Royal Navy commodore loomed above them on the quay and announced: 'The arrangements are as follows. After a meal kindly supplied by the Red Cross you'll be taken to billets in the warehouses and coolie huts. Some time in the next couple of days you'll be taken by lorry to Sawahlunto, then by train down the mountains to Padang. There are five hundred people ahead of you and the system is first in, first out. Is that understood?'

The infantrymen in the bow began to murmur, then call abuse. Quiller heard the oiled snicker of one or two rifle bolts and one man fired into the air, but the commodore snapped his fingers and a dozen Australian and British officers armed with Bren-guns moved silently alongside him.

'Again, is that clear?'

The infantrymen lowered their rifles. They were the last to disembark, climbing out hard on the heels of Quiller and Maisie. Quiller half expected a welcoming party in Rengat, a Dutch policeman or British red cap with foreknowledge of his imprisonment for theft in Tembilahan, but he passed through to the tables of food unnoticed and unchallenged.

Twenty minutes later the commodore spoke again. 'I ask you to be patient. There are no local vehicles available, so please stay in your billets and stick together. The Dutch are doing all they can. Meanwhile, conditions in the countryside are risky. The native people are edgy. Planters in the south have been massacred and we don't want to spark off an uprising. All right? Dismissed.'

Quiller stopped the commodore as he left the wharf. Niggling in a corner of his mind was a need to give himself permission to remain absent without leave, as the charge against him might read, and so he said, 'Sir, do you have any word on the RAF base at Palembang? I'm trying to rejoin my squadron.'

The commodore's jaw dropped. 'You must be mad. That region's occupied. Sumatra's had it, chum. Take my advice, head for Padang and hope for the best.'

Quiller took Maisie to a rubber warehouse, a close, muggy place of low, soured expectations. Primrose and Lee Lin were there. They were next in line for the journey to Sawahlunto, they told him. He couldn't say that he was pleased to see them, or that he was displeased. But they were familiar to him and made a fuss of Maisie, and when he returned from a tour of the town he found that they'd scrounged a clean dress for her and washed her dirty one.

'Take her with you tomorrow,' he said.

Maisie immediately clutched his ulcerous leg. 'No. I want to be with you.'

Quiller winced. 'All right. Come on. But first I need some medicine.'

In a back street pharmacy he bartered his excess atabrine tablets, still dry in their tin, for sulfanilamide powder and a strip of plaster. Then, under a palm tree in the market, Maisie watched wide-eyed as he sterilised his knife blade over a candle, lanced the ulcer on his shin, sluiced away the poisons and applied the sulfanilamide. She was crouching on her haunches by now, and helped him to seal the oozing wound with the plaster.

She followed him with her eyes when he stood. Every little thing seemed to bind her closer to him.

Quiller didn't think that he could bear to wait in Rengat for a ride out. When it was fully dark he wandered through to the edge of the town with Maisie, and concealed in a clump of trees next to the main road he found a lorry with a bale of rubber on the tray. He knelt and tapped the petrol tank, rapping his knuckles from the cap at the top down to the underside. It was empty. He stood with his hands on his hips, thinking.

'Where now?' Maisie asked.

'Back to the dockside.'

'Why?'

'You'll see.'

The quay was deserted. Quiller stepped down onto the launch that had towed them to Rengat, checked that it was unoccupied, and began to open cupboards and drawers. Five minutes later he emerged carrying rice, a small carton of American cigarettes, a bottle of beer and tins of bully beef in a sack.

They took the dirt track through the rubber plantation. It was a night of clouds ploughing across the face of the moon, leaving them in absolute darkness for long stages, a rattling wind in the rubber trees, fireflies, and the scratch and frozen stillness of animals in the undergrowth.

Walking was easier once they had entered the metalled road, but the pain drummed through Quiller's bad leg, and as soon as Maisie began to stumble and complain, they stopped. They'd been walking past another plantation for some time and Quiller carried her down a side track until he found a deserted bungalow. They slept on straw mattresses and in the morning ate the bully beef washed down with tap water in a rubber tapper's porcelain cup, which was sticky with latex and tainted the water.

They made for the road again and several times during the morning were forced to stand back as bus loads of native troops passed, heading in the opposite direction. The soldiers had their wives and children with them and all gazed and waved at Quiller and Maisie.

Late in the afternoon they came to a village. Quiller said, 'Keep close to me,' and eyed the villagers warily, exchanging smiles with them and stopping to shake hands now and then. An old man gestured, offering Chinese biscuits from a tin. They took one each but were more thirsty than hungry and when Quiller pointed to the coconuts bunched in a palm tree the man climbed it and sliced off a couple, ignoring the protests of some younger men, who were armed with Lee-Enfield rifles. Quiller guessed that some Australians had passed through, bartering their way across Sumatra. He took two packets of cigarettes from the sack and gave one to the old man and one to the young men.

As they were leaving the next morning, a taxi rattled into the village. Quiller limped calmly into the centre of the road with Maisie and raised his hand to stop it. 'Sawahlunto?'

The driver shook his head.

Quiller fished cigarettes from the sack. The driver watched unresponsively. Quiller took out another packet, then another. The driver, irritated now, snatched at the sack, tipped the contents onto the passenger seat and sorted through them. He looked up, pointed at Quiller's pockets.

Quiller shook his head sadly.

'Me,' Maisie said.

She had a chamois pouch under the bodice of her dress. Quiller had seen the strap around her neck but thought nothing of it. Now he saw her take out a fistful of banknotes and shake them at the driver. 'More, more,' the driver indicated.

Maisie shook her head emphatically, tucked the money away, and took Quiller by the hand to tug him down the road and away from the town.

Gears protested; the taxi accelerated until it drew alongside them. 'Sawahlunto,' the driver said resignedly, reaching back to unlatch a door for them, then holding out his hand for payment.

'You kept that quiet,' Quiller said lightly when they were mobile.

'Money from my mother before she died,' Maisie explained.

'Have you given him all of it?'

'No. There's lots left.'

'Good.'

They were on the road for two days. In Bashira and other towns they overtook evacuees from Rengat and camped overnight with civilians in a school in Taluk. In the morning they saw Primrose and Lee Lin waiting for a lorry and exchanged glances devoid of feeling with them.

There had been monsoon rains in the mountains. The road dwindled to a muddy track across a flood plain then climbed through devil's elbows to peaks and deep ravines. Quiller could see the floods below, tumbling boulders and trees along the rivers and streams, and knew what it meant for those still downriver. From time to time they stopped to wade across running water while the taxi driver crept through to the other side, his mind on Maisie's chamois pouch. Once or twice they simply stopped and waited for the water levels to drop.

At dusk on the second day they passed through tobacco plantations in a misty rain and into Sawahlunto, where their headlights and the lights of the open-fronted shops and cafes splashed brightly across the wet streets.

This was the final stage before Padang, and they slept in a converted tobacco warehouse on groundsheets and blankets provided by Dutch women of the town. In the morning they bathed in a shed at the rear of the warehouse, faces upturned to water flowing weakly from perforated buckets. Quiller caught Maisie staring at him and diverted her with a series of soapy underarm belches and hair-lathering songs until she was singing along with him.

After a Dutch nurse had renewed the dressing on Quiller's leg, a boy scout in uniform took them to the railway station. He was learning to speak English at school and plied them with questions in a high, precise, singsong voice. Other scouts were guiding other bands of soldiers and civilians along the narrow streets, past Dutch men and women breakfasting in the cafes, and Quiller felt out of step with time. Didn't they realise the Japanese were only hours away?

A mist hung over the trees below the town. An old steam train and a line of carriages, some marked with red crosses and crescents, waited at the siding. It left an hour later, once an ambulance had completed transferring the wounded, and crept down through the layers of mist, sometimes inching by way of narrow log bridges over steep ravines and sometimes climbing again, helped by a system of ratcheted chains and trackside sprockets, while new waterfalls like long white ropes cascaded from the overhangs above them.

It must have been the conjunction of their cautious pace, the carriage rattles and the water far beneath them, for Quiller was in England again, crossing the River Tyne, creeping into Central Station. By rapid degrees he became his mother looking out and deciding that she will alight in Newcastle and stop her running. He's a kernel growing inside her, a knot of discomfort but surely loved, and a reminder that there are two of them now. After five years of the ceaseless tides of the world and her own motion— into welcome danger? away from obligations?—his mother is exhausted. The city and the river, so finger-latticed with cranes and riddled with history, will give her the illusion of headlong movement and allow her to rest. She misses her Canadian soldier. Was he slain before the Armistice or did he return to Canada ignorant of the fact that he'd left her with child?

Late in the day the mountainous slopes gave way to hills and terraced paddyfields, then small decorated huts among palm oil plantations and banana groves. Bullock carts plodded beside the track, one driver waving to Maisie when she shouted to him from her open window.

When they drew into the station for Padang there were ambulances, lorries and a handful of motor cars waiting, but Maisie wanted to ride in a gharry, a high-wheeled pony trap. The driver tocked his tongue, the cart jerked, and the wheels began to roll, scraping the surface of the road. By now Cameron had a head start of one week, but Quiller glanced about keenly on the short journey into the town from the station, hoping that no matter the disguise, he'd spot some unmistakeable flicker of Cameron in the crowd of escapees, deserters and evacuees, some aspect of his carriage, a certain angle of nose or chin. He saw that he wouldn't be out of place in his stolen Dutch shirt, for most of the European men walking or idling along the streets wore the remnants of their old uniforms along with crisp new Dutch Army shirts or trousers. Others wore black Chinese pantaloons or sarongs, and little else.

The gharry rolled along wide, tree-lined streets, past airy, shaded bungalows set in lawns and gardens. These were the homes of the Dutch; the local people lived in the old town, a tight fist of tiny crooked streets and houses. Quiller could see ships in the distant harbour and rows of bomb-damaged warehouses along the waterfront. The masts of sunken ships poked through the harbour water. But the Dutch had placed a boom across the harbour exit and Quiller felt a chill when he saw it. Beyond the town and the harbour were long stretches of sandy beachland fringed with palm trees. It was a good place to await capture.

The gharry pulled up outside the Oranje Hotel, which overlooked the waterfront. A British Army lieutenant called out, 'Full up, sport. Try the Enderaach Club.'

The driver, hearing the name, clacked his tongue at his horse. But the Enderaach Club was also full. Quiller could understand it. He'd seen hundreds of exhausted, listless people in the town.

'Try the school,' a navy officer called from the verandah.

'I thought we'd be taken out to those ships,' Quiller called back.

'Not a hope, old boy. The Dutch won't release them. It's a no-go area for us. Machine-gun posts all around it.'

The gharry moved off. As it passed the town hall, Quiller saw evacuee women on the steps, buying second-hand clothing from a stall, grooming their children or passing in and out of the doors. Then he saw Primrose and Lee Lin. Lee Lin was pulling native grassbags apart while Primrose wove the fibre into straw hats. They had set up a paper sign: *Hats, 1 guilder*. He turned to Maisie. 'Why don't you find a bed with the women tonight?'

'No.'

They skirted a park, where clumps of soldiers, dangerously bored, played cards or eyed the women on the steps of the town hall. One private carried a Bren-gun; Dutch soldiers were attempting to confiscate it and Quiller half expected to hear gunfire as the gharry drew away, passing coffee houses and cafes with their wrought-iron tables under canopies in the open air.

There was room at the school, but no beds and no women, only men who were unstable, restless or bitter to be trapped at the edge of the open sea with no way out. A sailor told Quiller, 'This is no place for a little tacker.'

'You're right,' Quiller said. He gazed at the man. 'Is it true the Dutch aren't releasing their ships to us?'

The sailor nodded. 'Bastards.'

'Are any of our ships due?'

'Your guess is as good as mine.'

'But there have been ships.'

'Taking off the wounded.'

Quiller nodded. He was certain now that Cameron had left Sumatra. 'There must be small craft in the villages along the coast.'

'Tried that, for my pains,' the sailor said. 'I was stoned and spat on. One fellow sounded halfway interested in selling me his fishing boat until his cousin intervened and threatened to report him to the Japs.'

'What's the going rate for a boat?'

The sailor eyed Quiller up and down. 'More than you can afford, matey, unless you've got plenty of Dutch guilders in your pocket.'

'So we're stuck here?'

'Looks like it.'

Quiller turned to look over his shoulder. The gharry was parked under a banyan tree at the school gate. Maisie was gazing at him trustingly. He turned back to the sailor. 'Are there any books in the classrooms?'

The man stood back and flipped his hand over like a courtier. 'Be my guest.'

Quiller found atlases, primers, textbooks and stationery in a cupboard next to a blackboard chalked with copulating shapes and insults against the Dutch and the Japanese. He tore the hard covers from a Dutch-language atlas and a copy of Grimm in English for Maisie, rolled them into a tube with pencils and blank paper, and walked out.

Maisie said, 'I gave the driver some money.'

Quiller felt bad about Maisie and her money. 'Good idea.'

Then: 'Look, Maisie, I'm taking you to the women's hostel in the town hall. I'll stay here. It's no good you staying here. But it's only for the nights. I'll spend the days with you.'

She gazed ahead stonily. The driver had clacked his tongue and the hard wheels were scraping and striking sparks beneath them.

Quiller went on gently, 'And things aren't looking very good for us. There may not be any ships to take us out. We may have to face capture.'

A shadow seemed to crawl through Maisie. She hugged herself and went very still. 'I don't want to go on a ship.'

'Why?'

'For the past two nights I've had a bad dream.'

'You're a restless sleeper, all right.'

'People in the sea,' she said. 'The sea was all burning. The lifeboats were on fire. There were sharks, everything.' She shuddered.

Quiller put his arm around her shoulders. 'It's just a bad dream.'

'The *same* dream. Two nights in a row.'

Quiller knew by now that uncertainty made people so edgy that coincidence ceased to be a factor in their lives and everything became a sign or symbol for something else. He cuddled Maisie against his chest and thought: For all I know, they're right to feel that.

As the gharry drew alongside a strip of cafes, Quiller glanced in, glanced away, then swung his head sharply to look again. The man called Sutedjo sat at an iron table, drinking coffee. He wasn't handcuffed or shackled or even under guard that Quiller could see. Everything was breaking down for the Allies. The nationalists were buying rifles from the ragtag Europeans, and he supposed that the native police were switching sides. If Sutedjo wanted to hold a rally, who could stop him? The Dutch were too busy keeping the evacuees in order.

That night he changed the dressing on his leg and turned the pages of his atlas. Ceylon was closer than the north-west of

Australia, west and slightly north across a vast open sea. Australia lay south-east, beyond a long string of islands, all possibly in the hands of the Japanese. There were sea currents and prevailing winds to consider, fuel, food and water, and raiders on the sea and in the air. The open sea frightened him. He liked to think that he could stay close to land, close to the islands that lay like dribbled paint across the pages of his atlas. He took out a pencil and blank paper, traced a set of island-hopping maps at a scale of 1:25,000,000 and marked a number of passages south-east and north-east of Sumatra, and one to Ceylon.

But he didn't think he'd find Cameron in Ceylon.

In the morning he walked to the town hall, encountering Primrose, Dorry and Lee Lin sitting on the steps of the town hall with Maisie. Dorry grinned to see him. 'Hello, Tiger.'

'The world's contracting,' Quiller said lightly. He noticed that they had sacks and cane baskets at their feet. 'Going somewhere?'

'Big ship come,' Lee Lin said. 'We have order wait here for lorry.'

'Maisie says she's not coming with us,' Primrose said. 'Can you talk some sense into her, Quill?'

'I had that dream again,' Maisie said. 'Three nights in a row now.'

Lee Lin was very superstitious. Quiller knew that. He saw her gnaw her lip and stare at Maisie. 'You have bad dream?'

'The Japanese are going to sink the ship,' Maisie said flatly.

Lee Lin began to rock on her haunches and mutter a prayer in Cantonese.

Quiller said, 'I think we should take the ship. It could be the last one.'

'It no take gentlemans,' Lee Lin said. 'Women, children first.'

Maisie stood and backed away, saying, 'I'm not going on that boat!'

Lee Lin moaned, 'What we do, what we do?'

The first of the lorries pulled in to the kerb. An Australian Army captain called out, 'Hurry up, ladies. Quick as you can. She sails in an hour.'

Women were standing. They were beaming and chattering, and the relief was infectious. Quiller saw the doubt drop away from

Lee Lin and she pushed through to the roadside with Primrose and Dorry, pausing once to twinkle her fingers at him. There was no love and not very much affection in the gesture. He might have been a man who'd proved to be a disappointment to her.

'I'm not going,' Maisie said again.

There were no more ships and the harbour boom was dropped for good. In the passing days Quiller found a compass, mapped out routes to Burma by way of the Andaman Islands, Australia by a route south of Christmas Island and the Java Trench, and New Guinea by way of the island clusters north of Java. During the week he heard that Java had surrendered on 8 March and was shown communiqués confirming that Darwin had been bombed on 19 February and Broome on 3 March. Sumatra itself was about to fall: the Japanese were only hours from Padang, and the Dutch expected them some time on 17 March. Quiller found new escape routes on his maps, made sorties by foot along the coast in search of a boat, and asked to join the escape parties that were forming.

'Not with a kiddie, you don't.'

Padang is as bad as Singapore was, he thought. The same time-wasting and incompetence, bluster and poor leadership, conflicting aims, groundless rumours and hot air. He was confiding in Maisie by now; her age was irrelevant. She'd been billeted with the nuns, nurses and remaining civilian women in the convent, and he would pick her up after breakfast and spend part of the day with her. There were always Chinese and Sumatran men gathered at the double wooden gates, one man busily trading the women's jewellery for bags of rice, tins of coffee, coconuts and fruit. The men believed that the women would eventually be sold to them by the Japanese and were sizing them up first.

'When will the Japs be here?' Maisie asked on 17 March.

'Tonight, tomorrow.'

She snorted, indicating the women inside the convent as she walked with Quiller out through the gates. 'The poor dears still think the Royal Navy will come for them.'

Quiller shook his head. 'We're as good as in the bag, Maze.'

She looked up at him. 'I like it when you call me that.'

They wandered through the narrow streets, stepping around the pungent, steaming pats of cow dung, past the shuttered shops. Above them windows opened briefly, wet washing jerked out on poles, the windows clanged shut and bolts were shot home. Some residents of the old town had pinned Japanese flags to their doors. The streets were deserted. A Dutch tobacconist lay open to the street, glass and shutters torn away and the shelves looted. Quiller tried to imagine what the next day would be like. The civilians would probably be allowed to wander about unchallenged for a day or so. Invasions were never instantaneous and absolute.

They turned corners and came to a park, where an elderly man walked with a Persian cat, saying, 'A little bit further, a little bit further, just over the mountains and down to the sea.' Quiller had met the man before and engaged him in conversation from time to time, learning that he'd been separated from his wife in Singapore and now spent his days in cracked-brain hope.

'You'd be better off indoors,' Quiller said.

'Over the mountains and down to the sea,' the man said, lost in the tormented deeps of himself.

They wandered on. Maisie said, 'Are you going to leave me again today?'

'I have things to do.'

'What things?'

'Today I intend to buy a boat.'

'You haven't got any money.'

'Steal a boat, then.'

Maisie gazed at him. It seemed unlikely that she disapproved. Finally he saw her slim brown hand creep down the front of her dress, past her thin, grimy, narrow, vulnerable throat, and pull out her chamois pouch. Watching him solemnly she hunched and twisted to release the leather thong from the clots of unwashed hair that sprang free of her head.

'You need a haircut and a good wash,' Quiller said.

'Look inside.'

The pouch was still crammed with cash: Sterling pounds, Straits dollars, Dutch guilders.

'Maisie, you might need this.'

'I need it now. We need it now. Take me with you and we'll buy a boat.'

Quiller gazed north along the coast to where the mountain jungle and shoreline palms were lost in the haze of the morning sun striking the residue of the night's monsoon falls. There were numerous ocean-going junks in Sasok, a hundred miles away. He had his kit with him; only a fool left his stuff at the school by day. 'All right.'

But at the edge of the town they were turned back by the British Consul, wearing a white tropical suit, a Dutch policeman and a Royal Navy officer. The Dutchman said, 'Please to go indoors now.'

The British Consul was a man whose anxieties and pretensions were always on display. 'The Governor doesn't want any of you coves to jeopardise the handover,' he said, sniffing at Quiller.

Then the Royal Navy officer peered at Quiller and at his beard and Dutch colonial officer's shirt, and at Maisie standing next to him, holding his hand. 'Who the hell are you, anyway? Are you in the services? If so, military discipline applies.'

'I mined tin in Malaya,' Quiller said.

The officer stared angrily, saying nothing, then shrugged. 'If you say so.'

Quiller and Maisie headed back to the old town, climbed through the tobacconist's broken window and settled into the deserted flat above the shop. Quiller's leg was hot and the ulcer leaky. There was no more sulfanilamide and only rags for bandages. He swallowed an atabrine tablet and gave one to Maisie, who crawled into his lap and did what she did from time to time—hooked his dogtags out of the throat of his shirt and played with them as Lee Lin had done. She liked the ring from the Canadian soldier. 'Tell me again about when you were a little boy and you lived with your mother and ...'

The air was fragrant with tobacco leaf, cigars and perfumed cigarettes. Later they went to the hawker at the convent gates and bought food for the remainder of the day and for their journey north. They slept then and at midnight set out again, onto the broad colonial streets, and were passing the Governor's office when the headlights of a motorised column forced them into the shrubbery at the side of the road.

The lead vehicle was a muddy touring car driven by a Dutch policeman. A Japanese officer sat next to him, a Japanese guard in the back seat. More cars and lorries were grinding in behind the touring car. While the Japanese officer and the Dutch policeman went into the Governor's office, leaving the guard lolling in the back seat, other Japanese officers and enlisted men got out to stretch the kinks in their spines, wipe their faces and shaved heads with grimy neckerchiefs, and light cigarettes. Some wore muddy yellow riding boots and curved swords, some beards and glasses, and their odour washed over Quiller and Maisie: perspiration, mud, jungle leaf mould and exhaustion. Their uniforms were torn and dirty. Here are men who've driven hard and fast through South-East Asia, Quiller thought.

Maisie hissed, 'Are they the Japs?'

'Yes.'

'I thought they'd be little.'

'Hush.'

After a while he whispered, 'Let's get away from here.'

They began to slither back on their bellies across the damp lawns of a silent bungalow. There was a movement at the head of the column. It was Janeway. He'd been held in the town, Quiller realised, and now he was out. Janeway stepped into the light with his hands up, wreathed in smiles, trying a greeting in Japanese and stepped onto the running board of the touring car, apparently believing that the guard was a senior man. He died with a bayonet thrust to the chest. It was a punching sound that Quiller heard. The guard was obliged to jam his canvas boot against Janeway's chest to retrieve his bayonet.

Pull a Long Face
and Carry On

When no aeroplane had come for the evacuees by mid-afternoon on 3 March, Jeannie went into the wireless room, shutting herself away from the wretched Dutch women and their hot, teary children and the two pilots with their air of having kept their end of the bargain, and contacted Broome again.

The reply was tense and rushed. 'You haven't heard? The Japs bombed us this morning, over.'

'Bombed you?'

'Shot us up, to be more precise. The military airfield and the harbour. Dozens killed, planes destroyed. There were fourteen flying boats in the harbour, waiting to refuel, been there since yesterday, chock-a-block with Dutchmen. Poor devils, they were killed like rats in a trap, over.'

'God.'

'Everything's upside down here, love. Half the townspeople have headed for the bush. I don't know when you'll get your plane, over.'

'I'll try Hedland.'

'Try them, but they're pretty nervous themselves, expecting a raid. Every spare plane is in the air, trying to get rid of the backlog of refugees. You can't get a bed here or in Hedland for love nor money.'

Hearing Jeannie sigh he murmured, 'Sit tight, love.'

'I'm being driven bonkers, quite frankly. I can't help them and they won't help themselves. They're terribly apathetic.'

The radio operator let that pass. 'Are you alone with them? Over.'

'Not quite.'

'Any injuries? Over.'

'No, over.'

'Grin and bear it, we'll have a plane to you as soon as one's available.' He paused. 'I'm surprised you're still there. There's not a white woman left in Hedland. You should have evacuated weeks ago, over.'

There was nothing to say to that. Encouraged by her silence he went on, 'You should think about hopping on that plane as well, while the going's good. We're full of invasion talk here, over.'

'Invasion,' she said weakly.

'Look, I'll do what I can for you. How many of you are there again? Over.'

'Six women, five children, two pilots, over.'

'And yourself. Any others? Over.'

She wondered if Harry or Wally would want to come with her. They were men for whom the world was wide and treacherous beyond the fenceline of Haarlem Downs.

'Maybe two others.'

'I'll do what I can, even if it means ferrying half of you now and half later. Chin up, lovey. Over and out.'

Chin up. There was Cameron in her head again. It was only an expression but it occurred to her that her chin was never really down. Voicing her concerns was not the same thing as having a whinge or losing control of the situation.

She signed off and went in search of Captain van Haselen.

'He is going for a walk,' Anneliese said.

'Perhaps you could translate for me. I need you to tell the women that—'

'I will not speak to my oppressors.'

There was a tone in Anneliese's voice that Jeannie hadn't heard before and didn't like. Frustrated, she went to the women, who were fanning themselves on the verandah while their children stripped leaves from the vine, and tried her Intermediate German. 'The aeroplane that will take you to safety has been delayed.'

One woman shrank from her, another wailed and rocked her baby and a third snarled, in German, 'Where are your good feelings? In Holland the Germans are committing unspeakable things to our people. Please to use our language,' she concluded, poking a chewed fingernail against her breastbone.

'Oh, I give up,' Jeannie said, and stamped from the house.

She had no destination in mind but wasn't surprised to find herself at the hangar doors, contemplating Cameron's poor, torn Gull.

'Dear lady.'

It was van Haselen, with the co-pilot, sprawled where the hard-packed earthen floor was cool. They were smoking pipes, surrounded by matches, dottle streaks on the underside of the fuselage where they'd emptied the bowls of their pipes. She felt a deep revulsion for all their helpless ways and wrung out the words: 'There was an air raid on Broome this morning. There may not be an aeroplane for some time.'

Van Haselen sucked briefly, sending up a cloud of fragrant smoke, then bit down on the stem of his pipe. 'Dear lady. You make us very welcome.'

Jeannie padded through the sun again, feeling a tightening band of heat and fury around her skull. She found Harry Horsetalk with Wally Webb in the blacksmith's shop. They had made a catapult for the oldest Dutch boy and were jumping in the dirt as he fired washers at their feet. It was a game that was beginning to tip out of control as she came through the double doors, into a kind of grinning hateful lust in the boy and anger in the men. 'Enough,' Wally said. 'Stop that.' His old stiff body twisted and turned as the strip of tyre rubber snapped between the forks and the tin washers thudded into the oily dirt.

Jeannie immediately crossed to the boy and bent and slapped his bare legs. His eyes widened and filled with tears. He stamped his feet, then ran crying into the sunlight.

Wally was embarrassed. 'Sorry, love, shouldn't have let it get out of hand like that.'

'They've been through a lot,' Jeannie said, 'but honestly …'

She went on to tell them about the raid on Broome.

'Godfather, eh?'

'So it could be days before a plane gets here.'

'Days? Pull a long face and carry on,' Wally said.

Days spent in listening and watching the sky, until it was late March and still the pedal wireless was silent and no planes came. Only one thing saved the evenings, as they sat wreathed in dung smoke and the mothers rocked the little ones to sleep: the co-pilot was a pianist. For hour after hour he played popular Dutch songs, fragments of symphonies and operas, and Dixieland jazz. 'You're a life saver,' Jeannie told him.

Anneliese kept to her room but encounters with the Dutch women were unavoidable and Jeannie saw the spitting anger on both sides. She didn't mediate. In her mind this was Anneliese's home and Anneliese had rights, and so she'd comfort her later, saying, 'Not long now, I hope.'

One day Anneliese looked at her sharply. 'I won't go with those women, you know.'

'Then you're welcome to stay here.'

Anneliese bent her head. 'I miss my people.'

Jeannie perched on the end of the bed to listen. 'Jeroen and—'

'No. Yes. No, I mean my mother's people. The native people.'

On the day of the leaflet, as Jeroen had watched the loading and unloading of the ships, Anneliese had become aware of the scrutiny of a Javanese foreman. When she caught his eye, he glanced away, and in that instant she remembered where she'd seen him before, and she tried futilely, by stepping to one side, to disavow any connection between herself and the Dutch woman and child.

The man's name was Tjak, from a village near the base of a volcano called Djaja-Sempoer, the mountain of the arrow. She wouldn't otherwise have remembered a detail like that but once, a year earlier, when the Rodenwalts and all of the servants had driven to the house in the mountains, she'd seen the ragged battlements of Djaja-Sempoer blazing red in the setting sun. That, and the fact that Tjak convened secret meetings of the nationalists and had banned her from attending any of them. As a mixed-blood her nationality was tied, in law, to her father's.

'I was very frustrated. Tjak would not let me claim ties to my mother's people. In his eyes I was Dutch, yet in the eyes of those *trekkers* I was less than Dutch.'

And so she always felt as if she were afloat, and would never dock or beach herself. All she'd wanted was to listen to a nationalist leader speak about *merdeka*, freedom.

'Did you speak to Tjak?' Jeannie asked.

Anneliese shook her head. She'd glared at him, she said. She'd wanted to stamp her foot and thrust her face into his and shout, 'I believe in *merdeka*, too, you know.'

The Wind and His Imagination

The Chevrolet had been abandoned by the road's edge with its headlamps burning, driver's door open and ignition key fob rocking gently as though the world had come to a stop and its inhabitants spirited away. Quiller put his palm against the long bonnet; no residual engine heat, only the dampness of the night. There was a small gold shield on the door and Dutch lettering which indicated that the car belonged to a trading company. Quiller supposed that he, too, would have fled if his lights had illuminated a Japanese column advancing from the opposite direction. The rocking key? That was the wind and his imagination.

Maisie climbed into the rear seat and was asleep within minutes. Quiller drove north without lights, hoping that the Japanese wouldn't send further parties before daylight. Even so, he took the first inland road he could find and wound through the reaches of the coastal mountains, climbing and dropping along switchbacks cut deep into the jungled slopes and creeping across creaky bridges high over plunging floodwaters, until by morning the same road began a slow descent to the flatlands of the coast again. Maisie awoke, hot, hungry and fretful, her damp skin peeling away from the upholstery. She climbed into the front seat and stared out. An hour later they arrived at a river mouth, a fishing village and a welcoming party of armed Europeans.

A New Zealand corporal yanked Quiller's door open. 'Who the hell are you?'

Quiller swung his legs to the ground, looked up at the man and told him who he was.

'And the kiddie?'

'Her name is Maisie.'

The New Zealander stepped back from the door, letting Quiller out. Maisie slid across the seat after him. They stood, regarding the four men ranged behind the New Zealander. One was the Royal Navy officer who'd kicked the old man's case off the wharf at Tembilahan. The others were a British major, a volunteer reserve civilian from Penang, and an Australian Army cook. They all wore the scraps of their uniforms, supplemented by sarongs, women's blouses and hats fashioned from straw and cotton. Quiller wondered if his own face looked as drawn, exhausted and unpredictable.

'We arrived yesterday,' the New Zealander said. 'We're an official escape party.'

Quiller watched them, anticipating the negotiations that were about to begin. He could see that the navy officer had recognised him. 'What supplies do you have?' he asked carefully.

'A book of nautical tables, a first-aid kit, some food, a rifle.'

'A boat?'

They glanced uneasily at each other. 'We don't have the money to buy one.'

Quiller said, 'I have maps and a compass. We want to join you.'

'Not the kiddie, not by any stretch of the imagination.'

'Yes, the kiddie.'

The navy officer gestured unheedingly. 'She'll be a burden. And you, sir, I don't much like.'

'She has money,' Quiller said, stepping protectively in front of Maisie. 'It's her money and it's her decision,' he added hastily, to forestall accusations that he was using her. He tucked her behind his legs, squared off against the men and said, 'That's the deal, take it or leave it.'

'Can you sail?'

Quiller was uncompromising. 'I can learn.'

Bit by bit the men relaxed. They began to move about and murmur, and eventually the major said, 'We've started negotiations through the local Controlleur.' He indicated a traditional island prau, tied up at the river mouth. 'She's ours for fifteen hundred guilders. We've scrounged together four hundred.'

'We'll make up the rest,' Quiller said.

They went to examine the prau. The *Pagai Selatan*, named for an island to the south, looked broad and wallowy in the water. The rigging consisted of main, jib, stay and missen sails, and the bamboo and palm-frond deckhouse, running the length of the deck, resembled a hut. There were no bunks, cockroaches ran from the light, and the sails were as thin as old bedsheets. 'But her hull's sound,' the navy officer said. 'Sheathed in copper.'

They paid for the boat and began to lay in stores. The navy officer had been an estuary sailor in England, and he bought sailcloth, rope, twine, sewing needles and a long dugout canoe, while the major returned with a wagonload of water in half-a-dozen large steel oil drums. The other two men guarded the boat and the stores, overhauled the rigging and made minor repairs. Quiller and Maisie haggled, with the remaining guilders, over limes, eggs, yams, tinned food, dried fish and sacks of rice that had been laid out on the river bank for them by the local traders. It seemed to Quiller that the economies of the villages passed through by the Allies had been changed forever, if not by the sudden injections of wealth then by the expectations of it.

Finally he asked their destination.

'Colombo,' the major said.

'Why not Australia?'

'Too risky. The Japs have overrun most of the islands east and north of here. Imagine creeping up on each one, waiting to see what flag they're flying, if any.'

He seemed adamant. Quiller could see that they all were. He shrugged: Cameron could wait.

At dawn the following day they had a practice run with the original crew, sailing over the bar at the river mouth and out to sea, where their speed reached seven knots and the paper-thin sails bellied and strained in the wind. Finally they returned the crew to the village and headed out for good, west toward a chain of islands that would be their last sign of land before the long crossing to

Colombo. They knew they'd miss being close to land once they were on the open sea, yet the islands were also repressive in their minds. There were no coral reefs or depth variations marked on Quiller's hand-drawn charts, no beach shelvings or gradients, and for all they knew the Japanese lurked everywhere.

They made fast progress in a brisk easterly wind. A sense of calm overtook them, and one by one they stretched out and slept. When Quiller was called to share the midnight watch he stared up at the stars behind the cloud drifts, listening to the pleasant slap of the water against the hull. Behind him the sea foam glowed and he thought: This is it, we're free.

He'd once before sat on a deck in just this fashion, at peace, the starry sky spread hugely above the unhurried sea. Or rather, the night sea and sky had seemed benign, but he'd been tangle-footed and afraid, for Jeannie Verco had been aboard and chosen that moment to sit with and talk to him.

They were on a lugger offshore from the Eighty Mile Beach —Jeannie, her parents, Cameron and Quiller, together with a scratch crew of raucous pearling masters who had arranged this jaunt to farewell Jeannie's father, the pearling inspector, before he went down south. Most of the men had drunk themselves to sleep. One old teetotal lugger captain was in the wheelhouse, whistling as he steered. Quiller could see him there, under lamplight, a rope- and coral-abraded fellow with a knobbly skull and grey whiskers. Mrs Verco had snapped at her husband and gone below. Now Jeannie had come to perch in the bow with Quiller, while Cameron skulked somewhere out of the range of the light that spilled from the wheelhouse.

So there hadn't been peace at all. Quiller was recasting the night because Jeannie Verco had come to sit with him. She looked to be angry or distressed or disappointed: it was difficult for Quiller to tell when he so distrusted his instincts. She hugged her knees. She spoke kindly and softly and looked right at him, not minding his juddery voice and failing vocabulary. If she bowed her head her hair fell forward concealingly. Her shins glowed. She had slender bare feet with longish, curved big toes. He watched one hand slip down and pick at a toenail. That's all. But he'd fallen for every bit of her and he wished now that he were sailing home to her.

• • •

Their position could never be reckoned precisely. The navy officer relied on guesswork backed up by the nautical tables, the stars and Quiller's compass. Islands passed by to starboard from time to time, the waves washing with a clearly audible rumble, sometimes boiling over sunken reefs and whirling in contra-directional pools at the entrance to tiny lagoons.

Then, on the second afternoon, the wind began to drop to nothing, only to return as brief, brisk slaps from every direction of the compass, bringing short bitter squalls of monsoonal rain. They'd sit becalmed, the sea tossing, then eye the flimsy sails anxiously when the wind gusted. Their meals through the long day were rice and fruit, rice and tinned beef, washed down with water from the oil drums. It was tainted water, barely potable, and the major had discovered leaks in four of the containers. He set out some coconut husk bowls to catch rainwater from the squalling sky.

Late in the day the wind grew hard and even. The main-sail filled, then split down the middle, a sound so sharp and familiar to Quiller that he was back in the house in Jesmond Dene, his mother tearing up old bedsheets to hem as handker-chiefs or fashion as short-sleeved shirts for summer. He was frozen by the image and wondered where he was, and why. When he glanced at the miserable scrap of sail on the mast, the navy officer shouldered him out of the way in an effort to rip it down and hoist a spare jig. 'Pull your weight there,' the navy man told him.

Now they were slower and wallowy in the water, heaving like a top-heavy wagon on a potholed country lane. The men sat on the deck and sewed, piecing together scraps of sailcloth into a patchwork mainsail, which they raised at sunset. It caught the wind and they picked up speed again, listening anxiously to the strain-ing seams.

At dawn they made for a lagoon enclosed by a reef and a tiny island of palms and white beaches, and dropped anchor a short distance out from a fishing village. They made two trips ashore, three men and all of the sails, then Quiller, Maisie, the major and the navy officer. 'We don't want you and the child sailing off without us, now do we?' the navy man said.

The village headman greeted them, the villagers gathered behind him. Quiller supposed they'd not yet been cheated or antagonised by armed stragglers, for they were wreathed in smiles, shaking hands and beckoning the party toward a palm-frond shelter, where bananas, fried chicken and glasses of coffee had been set out on a bamboo mat.

Quiller and the others ate on their haunches in the shade and at the end of the meal the New Zealand corporal passed his cache of cigarettes to the headman, who appropriated most of the packets and distributed single cigarettes to the people of the village. Everyone lit a cigarette, then stretched out to sleep. There was no urgency.

The preliminary rattle of a monsoon shower woke Quiller. He saw the headman and half-a-dozen fishermen sitting in a ring beneath the shelter, fashioning a new mainsail from the prau's supply of sailcloth. Quiller woke the others. 'Look.'

'Oh, good show,' the major said.

When the sail was ready the people came with packets of food for them and gourds full of water. 'Aren't they kind?' Maisie said, taking out her chamois pouch. 'I don't have much left,' she continued, peering into the mouth of it, automatically clawing her hair away from her eyes.

'Give it all to the chief,' Quiller said.

'Bugger that,' the army cook said. 'We need it more than these wogs.'

But Maisie was cramming the remainder of her Dutch guilders into the headman's hands.

'Christ almighty,' the cook said.

They rowed out to the prau, weighed anchor and waited for the new sail to belly in the wind. The sky lightened, bringing shafts of pure sunlight that penetrated the water, touching crisp red, yellow, blue and green lights, which materialised as schools of fish, and shelves and cathedrals of coral. Slowly they moved through the mouth of the lagoon and into open water, passing more island shores fringed with coconut palms that promised to stay cut off from the war and everything contentious. Maisie's hand slipped into Quiller's. 'I want you to be my dad.'

Quiller opened and closed his mouth. 'For the time being,' he said finally.

'No, always.'

He realised that he knew nothing of her extended family. There had been no point in asking her before this; no point in thinking beyond the next hour, or day. 'Haven't you a favourite aunt or uncle somewhere?'

'There's only me.'

'Grandparents?'

'There's only me.'

She has less than I do, he thought.

As the islands dropped away behind them, to smudges, then specks, and the grey line of the horizon was uninterrupted all around them, only a dark rain curtain prowling in the northern sector furnished the emptiness. They all felt a little fearful and diminished, wanting land again.

They weren't surprised when a Japanese aircraft carrier emerged from the folds of rain. They all ducked behind the water drums, leaving the Australian Army cook to squat at the tiller in the local fashion. With his olive skin, conical Chinese hat and long-sleeved shirt, he might pass as an islander. They waited, heads down, while the cook reported: 'She's on a south-easterly bearing ... Oh, bugger, there's more of them, destroyers, a couple of tankers ... No change ... No change ... I think we're in the clear.'

As the wind continued to bear them to the west, and the Japanese convoy powered south-east toward Java, the world grew open and empty again, and Quiller said, 'I thank my lucky stars we decided on Colombo.'

The major stared at him. 'We're not clear yet. Someone's bound to want to know what a prau is doing heading for the open sea.'

Thirty minutes later a Japanese torpedo bomber appeared from the east, flying low, and before it could circle them the major ordered everyone beneath the *atap* shelters. Meanwhile their tillerman squatted again, his coolie hat low over the hard angles of his face. The Japanese plane throttled back and, as Quiller tracked its slow, wide circles around them, he could see the goggles and helmets of the pilot and the gunner. He listened. The plane climbed steeply, made a banking curve, locked on their position in the water and dropped from the sky. The cannons clattered; the prau rocked with the dusty slap of bullets against the deck and hull; the sea hissed and spat on either side.

Quiller watched the plane climb away toward the south-eastern horizon, then realised that Maisie was no longer with him. He climbed to his feet. She was crouched beside the army cook, who was on his back beside the tiller. He'd been struck in the groin and fallen to the deck in shock as the blood arced from his femoral artery, powered by his heart. Quiller sank beside Maisie just as she lifted the man's head into her lap and placed her small hands against his temples to watch his eyes roll back and lose their lights.

'He's dead,' Maisie said.

It had seemed too rapid to Quiller. He opened the cook's blood-splattered shirt. There. Another wound in the centre of the chest.

They all stood while the major recited the Lord's Prayer, then tipped the cook into the sea and washed his blood away. From time to time Quiller would catch the other men glancing worriedly at Maisie, until finally the New Zealand corporal placed his hands on her shoulders to steer her away from the body bobbing in their wake. Quiller wanted to say: She's saving her nightmares for later. Let her be.

There was a gale before dusk. The navy officer was at the tiller now and he struggled to ride waves as high as their mainmast, directing the prau into the face of each wave and trying to anticipate the angle of the following wave. Meanwhile the prau took in water and the others bailed with their coconut bowls and a cut-down palm-oil drum. When Maisie slid like a weightless doll toward nothingness, Quiller seized her and lashed her to the mast, where she glared at him through the hours until the wind dropped and the prau ceased to pitch in the water like a cork.

After twelve days at sea they were down to one cup of water and rice a day. The last tin of Irish stew was teaspooned out to each of them in turn over the course of an afternoon until it was scraped bare, and when the water and condensed milk were dangerously low they tried their urine and gagged on it, it was so warm and intimate. They all thought they could catch fish and seagulls with their hands but when they looked between their palms they had hot air. Dreams and after-images flickered inside their eyelids.

There were always two glaring suns, one in the air and one in the water, and so their eyes grew weaker, and Quiller grew to mistrust everything he saw: the clouds, the distant ships, the land masses. They were illusions, imagined specks, and he'd hold his hands over his face and peer down at his feet. His toenails had turned yellow-brown and as hooked as talons. His leg continued to weep. For some reason—the constant rush of the elements in their ears?—they all suffered from deafness. The planter from Penang disappeared overboard one night; they didn't turn back to find him. The navy officer fashioned sailcloth sunhats for everyone and said, 'Try not to look out. Look only at each other and things on board.'The major taught them the words to music-hall songs, and the New Zealander, wanting to be useful, regularly washed their clothing by trailing it over the side. Maisie was incurious about their bodies. Quiller would read to her until eye-tiredness shut him down. His time was the night, when he had the watch and the starlight couldn't burn away his vision. The prau seemed light and fast in the water then, and the moon softened everything. Apparently they were leaving the monsoon regions behind them.The dawns would rise in pink and red bands behind the storm banks far away in the east and Quiller would watch the light changing, intensifying until his eyes were raw and played tricks on him again.

Could he fly again with eyes this bad?

'What's a whale doing in this neck of the woods?' he asked.

There was silence, then someone said, 'That's no whale.'

Quiller closed his eyes to rest them. He hadn't much energy left for hope.

'She's flying the British ensign,' the navy man said in a jittery old man's croak. He paused, then said, 'Oh dear, she's tacking away.'

Quiller felt the prau shift direction beneath his haunches.

'She's tacking again,' the major said. 'Not sure how to read us. Right, everybody, stand where they can see you, hats off to show your faces.'

The prau bobbed in the water. The voices of the others were far away. Quiller dreamed. Then he was being hauled aboard a larger vessel and could feel heavy vibrations deep within the steel shell. He could smell fuel, brilliantined hair and a galley stew on the hot air generated by twin funnels, and hear Maisie saying, 'Quill, we're safe now.'

He spoke. It may have been the first time for days. He didn't trust his eyes yet. They wore a crust of soreness. 'Maisie? Is that you?'

'It's me.'

'Where are we?'

'A British destroyer. It's taking us to Darwin.'

That unhinged Quiller and he slid onto his back and cackled. Maisie patted her little hands against his cheeks. 'What? What?'

When the bandages came off two days later, Quiller saw how gaunt Maisie was. She'd been reduced from a healthy child to a street vagrant with no tone in her skin or lights in her hair, and she searched his face just as anxiously, as if to read the changes he saw in her, as if he might not like or want her now.

The sea was calm. They'd passed from the ocean to the southern region of the Timor Sea, sighting land at Cape Levêque then turning north-west for Bathurst Island and Darwin, expecting, but not meeting, Japanese ships or planes. The air no longer smelt of the spicy islands where they'd been for so long but of a hot and dusty place, and in his mind's eye Quiller saw Cameron, Jeannie and Haarlem Downs. They sailed past Point Charles lighthouse, then were through the harbour boom and into the bay, where the black wedges in the water were ships that had been sunk at about the time Quiller was sunk in the waters off Sumatra, a dream or more away from there.

A Subtly Altered Map

The aeroplane that came for the refugees was a de Havilland 86A with the words Qantas Empire Airways Ltd persisting faintly through the new Royal Australian Air Force markings. Jeannie watched it touch down in a spray of red mud and taxi around to where the women and children lined the white rock perimeter. The first figure to emerge—bounding out, in fact, before the aeroplane had come to a full stop, so that his head was almost sliced open by a propeller, for he had no aeroplane sense at all—was Cameron Dunn.

Jeannie felt her jaw drop.

Then she thought, even as she began to run across the airstrip toward him: Things are going to change now.

They all made for the kitchen when the plane was gone and sat themselves at one end of the big table, where they hunched over cups of tea and half-stale cakes, hanging on to Cam's story as it poured out of him. He was exhilarated, his gaunt cheeks and exhausted eyes lit from within by familiar lights. Jeannie had never hung on to his words in quite this way before. He'd been honed and sculpted during his separation from her, the old untried formlessness worn away, but the look suited him and she felt a peculiar thrill, almost as if she'd taken an older, more exciting lover yet hadn't betrayed the boy she'd married.

He hadn't called to say he was coming, he explained, because he'd wanted to surprise her. His voice and face softened. Jeannie's insides tumbled.

'Show us on the map,' Wally said.

Leonard's atlas was kept permanently in the kitchen these days. Jeannie opened it to a map of Java and they leaned forward. Anneliese spoke first. 'I am coming from here and here,' she said shyly, tapping a slender finger on the page.

Cameron stared at her. Jeannie had explained who she was and what she was doing there and why she hadn't accompanied the other refugees, but it had been lost in the general excitement. He'd shrugged and smiled in an old, accept-everything way. Now his eyes flicked over her warmly. Jeannie wanted to say, 'Just a minute, I found her first.' Then he was indicating a large island north-west of Java. Jeannie peered: Sumatra.

'When I got to Padang, everything was a complete shambles. Not a boat to be had. So I said to myself, don't give up the ghost like everyone else, do something. So I met up with some other blokes of like mind and we headed out to the aerodrome.'

He looked at them one by one. 'The flaming Dutch, they'd only gone and driven a steamroller into every plane on the ground, and punctured all the fuel drums. The old scorched-earth policy. So, what to do?'

His teeth were yellow, Jeannie noticed. With penetrating clarity she began to pinpoint other differences, poring over his face, hands and neck as he talked, reading him as if he were a subtly altered map. Wasn't he hot with his sleeves down? She longed to roll them back and lay out his forearms and watch the tendons flexing inside his skin. Perhaps they were ulcerated. He had the scars of tropical ulcers on his legs, she'd noticed, as he'd banged through the screen door ahead of her just now.

'Never say die to a bloke from the bush. We'll scrounge, I told the others, and that's what we did—a tailplane here, an aileron there, a piece of rope here, a length of wire there, half a cupful of fuel drained from this old kite, two gallons from that one—till we had a halfway decent Lockheed bomber. No screwdrivers to speak of. I used the pocketknife Dad gave me one Christmas, another bloke the edge of a coin. Wally, you'd have been proud of me.'

Wally Webb was sitting quietly, his eyes half-closed, and he glanced up now, a tired, pleasant, non-committal expression on his face. Cameron continued:

'None of the others could fly, so it was up to me. We had full tanks but needed a lot more fuel than that, so we scrounged more fuel in a few small drums and cans and stacked them inside the plane. Next we cut a hole in the fuselage,' he said, his eyes alight, 'and led a hose from there to the wing tanks so we could refuel in the air. Clever, eh?'

Wally smiled and nodded his creased face. 'Go on.'

'After that we mounted one machine-gun in the nose and another in the top turret, and we were ready to go.'

Jeannie took her cup from her lip. 'This was a Lockheed bomber? Twin engined?'

Cameron faltered as if to listen to a distant part of himself. He considered her for a moment. 'That's right,' he said stiffly. 'Why?'

'Oh, sweetheart, nothing. I'm just trying to picture it, that's all.'

'You don't think I could fly a twin-engined job?'

'Darling, I'm just—'

'Well, that's what I did. I was the only one who'd flown before and it was up to me.' He settled back in his chair. 'But first we had to fill in the craters the Dutch had put all over the landing strip.' His smile took in Anneliese, who smiled back. 'We used every-thing but it was still bumpy as hell and we had to knock in stakes with rags tied to them to guide me. As it was I had to twist and turn like buggery and we were more or less bumped into the air when I hit the edge of the last crater.'

He put his head on one side and glanced at Jeannie. 'It put me in mind of those trips we used to make with Neil.'

'Yes.'

She didn't know what else to say. His eyes were red-rimmed and he'd shaved badly. He seemed to flicker in and out of a kind of partial madness and she had to blink to regain her longing and desire for him.

'We flew down along the coast, then across the water to the tip of Java. By this time the Japs were overrunning Java but mainly in the north and we'd heard we could pick up a boat at Tjilatjap.'

Anneliese straightened in her chair with a little sound of delight. 'I, too, escaped from Tjilatjap, but in an aeroplane.'

Cameron grinned at her, reached across the table and closed his bony hand around hers—in fellow-feeling or to shut her up, Jeannie didn't know, perhaps both, but the thing was, his sleeve rose to the limit of the cuff button and she saw the smudged, greenish black corner of a tattoo among the bleached hairs on his forearm before he withdrew his hand and nursed it in his lap. He went on:

'We could only do about a hundred miles an hour. Just about all our fuel was gone. Then when we get there the strip looks like it's been set up for a hurdle race, barricades all over it. Can't land, can't go on, so I put the wheels down and circle the field, hoping some bastard will come out, take a good look at us and clear the strip.'

Anneliese nodded. 'I remember the wooden apparatus there.'

'Yes. Any rate, eventually some joker clears the strip and we land. I tell you, Jeannie, that was the hard part. I tried to remember what you and Quill used to say, visualise the aeroplane as a part of your body.' He grinned. 'Easier said than done. I came in too steeply and snapped the undercarriage. The red tape, you wouldn't believe. This Dutchman comes out, starts yabbering away, shoves forms in triplicate in my face.'

My husband has something for all of us, Jeannie thought, gazing at him. Wally, his mechanical sense; me, his flying sense; Anneliese, her nationalism. Where was *he*, under all of that? Who was he? He kept advancing and receding and when he advanced she wanted to grab him and hold on for dear life.

She'd hate to have to fly a twin-engined bomber, let alone a cobbled-together one from a potholed landing strip.

'The Dutch,' Anneliese said, shaking her lovely head over the traits of her colonial masters. 'They are born to be clerks and shopkeepers.'

'You're not wrong,' Cameron said, gulping his tea. 'This joker got on all our goats so we told him where to get off and headed for the harbour. I mean, that Lockheed wasn't going an inch further. I reckon we got one of the last ships out.'

Jeannie had been examining the map. Cameron had flown east into almost certain danger instead of north-west to Colombo.

Still, what did she know about the condition of the Lockheed and the availability of fuel? And east brought him closer to her. She was weaving in and out of desire for him as he was transfigured by the tricky light.

'The *Shun Wo*,' Cameron said, 'a five hundred tonner, full of RAF aircrew and technicians from Singapore, some civilians, and us. Ten days to Fremantle, dodging enemy convoys and bombers.' He shivered, and to Jeannie that was his first convincing reaction. 'Like being in a floating coffin.'

She'd set out a cold leg of lamb and was slicing it as he talked. He was transfixed by the meat and the motions of the knife and she saw real starvation and privation in him and wanted to make it all better. He swallowed, faltered in his story. 'I saw Mum in Fremantle, Jeannie. She didn't want me to come up here but I knew I had to before the Japs got here.'

Jeannie was scraping the fatty scraps into a bucket she kept under the sink. Traces of mutton like dark veins and shavings were attached to the fat and Cam looked up at her in amazement and dismay. 'You're going to chuck that out, sweetheart? That's good meat you're throwing away there.'

Jeannie gestured helplessly at the huge slab of meat that was still intact. 'Cam,' she said gently, 'there's plenty left.'

'Still ...'

He looked ravenous. He'd gone without for weeks and months, she realised.

It was curious. She'd been encouraged by Crystal to see him as a brave man lost, probably dead, and therefore to be honoured. She pictured his reunion with Crystal. Was it inconvenient, his turning up again? He'd still have to be honoured as a brave man, but his version of that bravery, and hers, and Crystal's, were bound to mesh poorly. I bet he knocked the wind from Crystal's sails, she thought.

Oh, why were they sitting there like that? She should take him straight to bed, tattoos and all, and not give the doubts an even chance.

A Communication Between
Hurt and Doubting Souls

Air as hot and muggy as this sapped Quiller's energy. It was smothering, had weight and substance, like a damp sheet from a sleepless bed. The bricks stored the day's heat and released it by night, defeating the evening breezes, which were warm and sluggish anyway. Mosquitoes found the holes in the net above his bunk and the Chinese cookboy, tossing on an army cot in a room along the corridor from Quiller's cell, would call out in his sleep: 'You all right, Wes?' The only other prisoners in the police lockup were AIF privates on a looting charge. They had no time for Quiller; looting an abandoned house was nothing compared to spying, desertion and the carnal knowledge of youngsters.

'Rubbish, of course,' Sergeant Weston had said, 'but until we get it sorted you'll have to stay in the lockup.'

The Darwin policeman looked dessicated, his skin the colour of the dirt and his dusty uniform. It was only after Quiller had crouched shoulder to shoulder with him in a slit trench on the first day, trembling away the minutes until the Japanese bombers had finished their raid, that he began to identify the lines of character in Weston's face and voice. Weston was genial, unhurried, practical and beset by minor irritations, his sad eyes and large frame exuding diffidence and weariness. He'd never had to wear a tin helmet before, and now he had a skin rash. There were no clear lines of civilian and military authority in Darwin and so he and his little band of Northern Territory policemen were expected to be everywhere and pick up all the pieces. The main police station had been destroyed and so he was obliged to police the city from a suburban station and live in a nearby house on stilts abandoned by a schoolteacher after the big raid on 19 February. He spent his time arresting soldiers for looting, and whenever the air-raid sirens bleated he had to run for the cells, usher his prisoners into the slit trenches, and lock them up again when the all-clear sounded. 'It's always at flaming lunch-time,' he'd complain, 'before I've had time to dig into my dessert. Jimmy opens a tin of peaches, I pour on the custard, and the sirens start up.'

'What's Jimmy's story?' Quiller asked. 'He talks in his sleep, shouts, "You all right, Wes?" '

Weston nodded. 'There were two waves that first time. Jimmy and I were stuck in adjacent trenches. Every time a bomb went off he'd call, "You all right, Wes?" or I'd call "You all right, Jimmy?" He shot through that afternoon, camped out at the Ten Mile for a few weeks. Only turned up here again last week.'

Another day passed. The looters were tried and sent to Fannie Bay gaol.

'I've seen the best and the worst,' Weston said the next afternoon, settling into a canvas chair outside Quiller's cell door. 'One Saturday last August the Pioneers ran amok, smashing plate glass windows, looting pubs and shops, attacking civilians, provosts, my own constables. Hundreds of pounds worth of damage to the centre of Darwin. Blokes in hospital with con-cussion, cuts, broken bones. Sure, they were bored, said they wanted to join the fighting in Europe, but that same mob had earlier run riot in Tennant Creek and Alice Springs. If the Japs do land here those heroes would be the first to bolt. I take a few constables with me out to the camps sometimes and you wouldn't believe the wireless sets, cane chairs, lamps, gramophones, fridges —all looted when the civilians evacuated. And after that first big raid in mid-February, hundreds of RAAF blokes headed for the bush because someone said an order had come through, every man for himself. No such order. Four days later, three hundred of them are still AWL. One made it as far as Melbourne.'

'In Singapore they rushed the sampans,' Quiller said, and described his last days on the island. The contempt he'd felt for the Australians then had been like a dull ache; now, as he spoke to a sympathetic listener, and as Cameron's treachery clarified, the ache became a fever. After a while he grew self-conscious, and began to hear an Englishman's whine in his accent, and see that Weston was looking uncomfortable, as if he regretted encouraging Quiller, so he let his voice trail away. But the fever burned.

'By the same token,' Weston said, 'I've seen instances of great bravery.'

'Of course.'

'The ack-ack gunners, what a thankless task. The firemen, the ambulance drivers. And the pilots, sitting ducks half the time.'

'Yes.'

Weston lit cigarettes and handed one to Quiller. It was late morning; they had half an ear to the sky and the drone of bombers. A coolish breeze came through and Weston said, 'A great day for spine-bashing.' A kitten appeared, wound its way around the sergeant's legs then stepped between the bars, into the cell and onto Quiller's lap.

Weston went on, his face pursed in thought. 'The older bloke copes better. He can see the humorous side.'

'Like you.'

Weston said wryly, 'If you like. Some of the younger blokes under me, they're prone to self-pity, sometimes boredom. They can't keep themselves occupied after hours. Cut off from women and a normal social life, living in fear of the Japs, arresting army types who've been looting or shooting the headlights out of civilian motor cars, the same army types who're supposed to be there to protect everyone—no wonder they're discontented.'

Quiller stroked the kitten. He'd wanted to say more about the deserters and stragglers in Singapore and Sumatra but Weston's mild voice and long view were working changes in him, checking his anger. After all, how do you distinguish a deserter from a man cut off from his unit? Or cowardice from bitterness and poor alternatives? Those men were prisoners of war now and many of them were English. If the war went the way of the Allies and the prisoners survived the Japanese camps, some cachet would attach to them, and why not?

He listened to Weston. Weston was lonely, and as much as he wanted to talk about specifics, he also liked to theorise and speculate. He was a man who liked to think rather than merely yarn or complain, and seemed to see that quality in Quiller. Theirs was a gentle, two-way interrogation—yet also more a communication between hurt and doubting souls than an interrogation.

'It's the waiting,' Quiller said. 'I saw it in Malaya and then in Singapore. You're waiting and watching, it's hot, you're a long way from home, you're lucky if you're allowed two bottles of beer a week. You get tetchy with one another. It's worse for the married ones. They think about home and the wife and get morose. You tiptoe around hoping no-one's going to take anything you say the wrong way.'

Weston nodded, then glanced at his watch, went to the door and bellowed toward the house, 'Jimmy, lunch!'

'Coming, boss.'

The humour twinkled in Weston's eyes. 'Thought I'd eat with you today. That way when the buggers come over and interrupt my peaches and custard I can just reach over and let you out of your cell.'

'Let me out anyway,' Quiller said.

Weston nodded. 'I've a mind to.'

'Maisie will vouch for me.'

Weston patted the skin rash on his scalp. 'She already has. Most vigorously.'

'Well, then.'

Some aeroplanes sounded above their heads, quite low, the engine notes beating against the underside of the clouds. Quiller listened: Kittyhawks. The Americans were flying them, tackling the bombers and the Zero escorts to good effect. He knew the Japanese by now. They always came in at high altitudes then low for the clean-up that followed. But Weston was doubtful, and reached around for his tin helmet, which was hanging from the back of his chair.

'They're ours, Sergeant.'

'Oh.'

Weston was jittery. There had been a reconnaissance plane at dawn, and that often presaged a bombing raid. 'Where were we? Right. Maisie.'

She was staying with army nurses at a makeshift hospital at the Ten Mile. Quiller tried to fix the Ten Mile on his mental map. He saw rings of concentric circles surrounding the city, with settlements clustered at every mile post along the road to Adelaide River. He hoped that Maisie was safe there. Weston intended to send her to Perth or Adelaide as soon as her refugee status had been determined and he'd been able to work through the allegations against Quiller.

'I must say her story sounds credible.'

'Of course it's credible.'

'But see it from my point of view. She's a child, after all. And we've had all sorts trickling through here: Dutchmen who could be Germans, blokes like you wearing bits and pieces of uniform and native clobber. We found hand-drawn maps in your pocket. We heard that the youngster was carrying money. Who is she, anyway? What's the exact nature of your relationship with her? The Royal Navy bloke said you seemed pretty close. It bothered him. He said you weren't much of a mixer, like you were hiding something. He thought you were probably a deserter. The major reckoned you were held in a gaol on Sumatra for a few days. Mate, they all had an uncomfortable feeling about you.'

'I'd like to talk to them.'

'Impossible, I'm afraid. They made statements and they've scattered to the four corners. It all boils down to this: Who are you?'

Weston looked embarrassed and apologetic and touched his skin rash in a curious, self-anointing gesture, as though to confirm his existence. 'I've still to follow up those contacts you gave me.'

Haarlem Downs, where surely someone would vouch for him, and Freddy, care of the RAF in England, though England was far away and Freddy might have him up on some charge—assuming he'd got out of Sumatra ahead of the Japs. Quiller looked up as footsteps approached. It was Jimmy with lunch on a tray, canned stew and peaches that he'd spooned into chipped china bowls, mugs of black tea, sugar and wedges of bread and butter. There was no fresh food in Darwin. It was all canned and unpalatable to Quiller. A sharp longing for fresh tropical fruit, rice and spicy fish washed through him.

Weston swung Quiller's door open and set a wooden stool for him in the corridor, and they began to eat. Quiller picked desultorily at the food. He'd gained strength on the British destroyer but his weight and body tone were still down and his eyes tired quickly. The heat was worse here, too. He sweated more, which irritated his skin, he was spotted with sandfly and mosquito bites, his tropical ulcer was still weeping, and he wondered what he might pick up from his imprisonment: dengue fever? tinea? ringworm? He kicked the kitten aside.

'And paperwork, Godfather,' Weston said, as though continuing a previous conversation. 'If I want petrol for the police vehicles I'm supposed to fill up at one of the army camps—all the private garages and Public Works depots are closed. But that means signing forms in triplicate. So now I fill up at the American base. Their attitude is: We're in this together, buddy, forget about the paperwork.'

He forked a grey sludge into his mouth, chewed and went on: 'We've got an incendiary.'

Quiller looked alert.

'Six fires in the past month. These are not the fires that follow a bombing raid. Someone's setting fire to Chinese shops. Of course they'd been thoroughly looted first.' Weston looked shyly at Quiller and said, 'It's history repeating itself.'

Darwin was a repeat of Quiller's past few weeks in Malaya, Singapore and Sumatra, but he suspected that Weston meant something else. 'Is it?'

'When the Russians abandoned Moscow in Napoleon's time, a series of mysterious fires broke out.'

'You're a reader?' Quiller asked obligingly.

Weston patted his lips with a clean, pressed khaki handkerchief. 'When there's time.'

An air-raid siren started up nearby, winding into an unnerving howl. How often had Quiller heard it in his short life? What was the saturation point? He stood involuntarily, knocking his bowl to the floor for the cat, and stared at the tremor in his hands.

'Come on, son,' Weston said.

He grasped Quiller's elbow and pulled him into the slit trench that ran between the lockup and the house on stilts. Jimmy was already there, shaking badly. The air was superheated in the trench, close and muggy outside of it, with banks of dark clouds passing across the sun.

'The buggers prefer a day like this,' Weston muttered. 'Plenty of cover. You all right, Jimmy?'

'You all right, Wes?'

Weston lowered his voice. 'Poor beggar. In the big raid he was blown through two doorways, about thirty feet. No wonder his nerve is shot.'

They waited. The usual interval between a warning and a raid was about seven minutes, but time in Darwin was measured by false alarms, so the waiting was painful.

The ack-ack guns started then, and Quiller heard the bombs whistling and hissing down. There was always a pause. The detonations shook him, percussive crunch-crunches transmitted by the red earth and by the air. He heard a Kittyhawk, low and fast, and two close explosions which sent stones and shrapnel in howling trajectories above their heads and rattling down on nearby rooftops.

Weston looked shaken. 'Damn close,' he shouted. 'Hundred yards? Maybe less?'

'Less,' Quiller said, sticking his head over the lip of the trench. He could see black smoke boiling up. But there were no military targets out this way, which suggested that the gunners and the Kittyhawks had the measure of the raiders, dispersing them before they reached the docks, the camps or the aerodrome.

The all-clear sounded. Weston cocked his head sceptically. 'It's like the peaches. As soon as I climb out of the trench the warning sounds again.'

They waited for ten minutes, drawing deeply on cigarettes, Weston holding Jimmy around the shoulders. 'I think that's it, boys.'

They trudged back to the lockup. Suddenly Weston doubled over and vomited, the grey tinned food splashing violently between his boots. 'Ah, Christ, I hope my nerve's not going.'

Quiller supported the sergeant's elbow until he stopped shaking. The air was acrid with burning rubber and oil, spent incendiary explosive and Weston's sour void. Dust and smoke blotted out the cloudy sun and he could see that the power and telegraph lines were down. His first thought was: Now how will Weston send a transmission to Haarlem Downs?

A police car pulled into the kerb and four of Weston's constables got out. Eyeing Quiller warily they said, 'All right here, Sarge?'

'She's jake,' Weston said.

'Want the prisoner returned to the lockup?'

Weston straightened his back, frowned consideringly and replied, 'Actually, no. I could do with another pair of hands. You lads go and look for unexploded bombs. Mr Quiller's coming with me.'

Five minutes later, Quiller was in Weston's black Ford, heading across the city and south to the military camps in the scrubland beyond the outskirts. He tried to picture Darwin from his time before the war, but two things defeated memory: the altered outline of the city, and the lessons of his intervening years. Before the war Darwin had been a sleepy civil service town on a frontier, prone to rigid stratifications and therefore petty social bickering. Now it was an edgy garrison town, wearing bomb damage, gun emplacements, banks of searchlights, new paved roads, barbed-wire entanglements and sandbag defences. Most of the buildings were damaged, their windows broken, roofs gaping and walls pocked or crumbling. Weston drove him past places he'd once visited: the post office, a clothing emporium, a pilots' club, the Qantas manager's house.

Qantas. Were they still flying in and out of Darwin?

They reached the outskirts of the city. 'She was on for young and old that first time,' Weston said, driving on from an army checkpoint. 'There was a mad scramble south on bikes, cars, trucks, even the odd sanitary cart and road grader. Anything that moved. Went on for two weeks. Can't say I blame them. The papers said only a handful were killed on the nineteenth, but it was closer to two hundred and fifty. We don't even know who some of them were.'

Quiller looked out at the drab scrubland. 'Where are we going?'

'Army camp.'

'Why do you need me?'

The sky was low. Thunder had lurked and muttered throughout the morning but now it cracked openly above their heads and Weston, crying out, steered into a ditch. The engine stalled. They were both trembling. Weston looked across at Quiller: 'This is why. You take the wheel for a while, sport.'

'You'll be glad when the army takes over the policing around here,' Quiller said, changing places with him.

'You can say that again.'

Theirs was a curious relationship. In Singapore and Sumatra Quiller had shared the worst of things with other men and women, in pitiless proximity to them, but he had no shared history with Weston. It was rare to meet a man who let his feelings show. Weston apparently trusted him. What mattered—that Weston trusted another man, or that Weston had chosen *him*?

He started the engine and steered back onto the road. Just then, in the sparse, tussocky scrub, he glimpsed an Aboriginal man, standing utterly still with a spear and ochre dashes on his face and torso. He thought of the Sakai in Malaya. Now that he was on Australian soil, all of his memories and experiences were playing out again, strangely reconfigured but familiar. The world was upside down and inside out. Perhaps he'd died some days or weeks past and this was a station to heaven or hell. He blinked but the hunter had vanished into the scrub.

Quiller accelerated away, Weston directing him to a settlement of army tents strung among low, scrubby trees. The ground bore the disturbances of the wet season but was essentially baked into a hard, dusty, life-denying surface, speckled here and there with twigs and dead leaves. There was no wind and the storm had passed. Half-a-dozen men were reading, sleeping or playing cards, shirtless, cigarettes in the corners of their mouths in the old lazy careless way that Quiller knew from Singapore, before the panic had set in. Other men were digging a latrine and about thirty were on parade, sweating in the muggy air while a sergeant-major bawled at them. What a life, Quiller thought. Heat rash, tinea, sandflies, dengue fever, let alone the false alarms, the waiting and the uncertainty.

'Go around to the other side of the rise,' Weston said.

They came to a stand of larger, better equipped tents. 'Officers' quarters,' Weston muttered. 'Stop outside the one that says "Military Police".'

They went in. The world turned on its head again. Four military policemen were standing guard over a Japanese pilot.

Quiller felt his insides clench and wanted to back away but was also curious. Weston gave him a gentle shove.

The other prisoner was an Aboriginal man wearing cast-off army boots, trousers and shirt. One eye was blackened, his cheeks, forehead and lips cut and swollen. He tried to grin, revealing a broken tooth. 'Mr Weston.'

'Jackie, what have they done to you?'

'They reckon I been cabratin', boss.'

There was a captain behind the desk. 'Collaborating with the enemy, to be precise.'

'But he's my tracker.'

'A patrol found him wandering in the bush with that there Jap. If he's your tracker, what's he doing out here?'

Weston scratched his head. 'He shot through after the big raid. It's not the crime of the century.'

'He was helping the Jap, taking him into hiding.'

'I doubt it somehow.'

'I want him shot.'

'Don't be absurd.'

The captain gathered some papers together dismissively. 'I'm speaking about an ideal world. Gaol is the next best thing, but still too good for this so-and-so.'

In the half light inside the tent Quiller noticed another man, a civilian in quasi-military dress. Weston turned to him. 'Are you a party to this, Geoff?'

The man shrugged. The words Department of Native Affairs were sewn into a strip of cloth above his shirt pocket, a shirt that bagged over his small frame. He had the pinched, disappointed air of a government servant trapped in a thankless posting. 'Your man Jackie was caught in unlawful possession of a bag of flour, too. As an official Protector of Aborigines I'll be pleading guilty on his behalf when the matter is brought before the Supreme Court. Meanwhile I'd be obliged if you'd escort him to Fannie Bay gaol.'

'That's preposterous.'

'You'll be the prosecutor, Westie.'

'The whole thing's a concoction.'

'He was found with the Jap,' the captain said. 'I'd have shot the bastard on the spot.'

'He was probably bringing the Jap in,' Weston said.

They bundled Jackie into the Ford and Weston drove, threading among the tents and latrines toward the main road. When the camp was well behind them, he stopped the car and removed Jackie's wrist and ankle cuffs. 'Tell me the truth, Jackie. What were you doing with the Jap?'

'I took him prisoner, boss. It was all double-Dutch to him.'

Weston guffawed. 'I can just picture it.'

On the outskirts of Darwin he made a detour into bushland. 'Your people live out here, is that right, Jackie?'

'Too right, boss.'

'Off you go, then. I'll say you escaped during a raid. I'll make the paperwork disappear.'

'You're a good bloke, boss.'

When they were moving again, Quiller said, 'Can't you make my paperwork disappear, too?'

An Atmosphere of
Little Disturbances

As the days passed into early April, the winds and rains of the wet season began to dwindle. It was easier to get about, so Wally and Harry were often out repairing a bore or checking the sheep. The bush and station blacks were expected to return from their ceremonial grounds soon but Harry had his doubts, for the blacks of Broome and other towns had been trucked to the Beagle Bay mission station, and the Haarlem Downs stockmen and gins would know that and want to avoid it. 'No plurry rounden up blackfellas here about, no fear,' Harry said.

Jeannie had only slept with Cam once since he'd returned. It was on his first evening back, and they'd stood becalmed at the front door, afraid to cross the yard to their bed in the visitors' quarters—but afraid of different things, it seemed to Jeannie. The hallway stretched behind them full of calming shadows and silences. Then Anneliese had emerged from the bathroom at the end of the hall and drifted toward the main bedroom, where she paused, her hand on the doorknob, and with a glint of light on her eyes and teeth had murmured 'Good night' and disappeared.

Cameron had stiffened. 'She's sleeping in Mum's room?'

Jeannie tried to explain.

Anneliese had heard them and returned to the hallway. In that brief interval she'd kicked off her sandals, pulled her blouse free of the waistband of her skirt and shaken loose her hair. She looked tousled, relaxed, ready for bed, one slender hand already loosening the button at her throat. 'I will go to another room if you wish,' she said.

Cameron pulled free of Jeannie's fingers and strode toward Anneliese. 'Let me see.'

At the last moment he was obliged to edge past Anneliese, face to face in an atmosphere of little disturbances, and vanished into his mother's bedroom. Jeannie followed. She found him at the foot of the grand bed, staring down at the smooth counterpane, his arms loose at his sides. Then he registered her there and placed his hands on his hips and stared at the cleared walls and surfaces.

'Where is everything?'

Jeannie explained that most of the valuables were still buried in the bush. He nodded and poked his head back into the hallway. 'Come in, Anneliese. It's all yours.'

She returned shyly, refastening her top button as though she'd offered herself and been turned down. What got Jeannie's goat was that Cam wanted to hover, invent things to talk about or do for Anneliese: That window sticks—I'll free it in the morning. Would you like a glass of water beside the bed? Mosquitoes not bothering you, I hope?

Then: 'I'm terribly sorry about your country.'

Anneliese had cocked her head to watch and listen. In the filtered light of the wet-season moon she seemed to Jeannie to be composed of warm browns, shapely swells and skin that hungered for skin. Was it unconscious? But on Anneliese's face was a clear expression of disbelief, as though she couldn't believe how dazzling and adept she'd become now that she was a free woman and men like Cameron were coming her way. Jeannie relaxed to see it. She tugged Cameron, saying, 'Come along, old sleepy head.'

Outside as they crossed the yard he'd said, 'She's a corker, isn't she?'

'She is indeed.'

'In Malaya you'd see them all over the joint, bright as buttons, not a flaw, not a care in the world. Full of grace and beauty. Always smiling. I shudder to think what the Nips would have done to her.'

In the visitors' quarters she went around opening shutters and windows. 'The old marital quarters, eh?' Cameron said.

He sat on the bed, she stood by the dressing table, and suddenly Jeannie had felt twin and uncomplementary sensations: long-married wife and reluctant lover. 'If you need time …'

Cameron looked hard at her, glittered in his new thin ravaged corrupted way. 'Come here,' he growled.

There was the shirt, which he unbuttoned but chose to wear throughout, so that when he reared back on his locked arms above her she was tented by flaps of khaki cotton. And when he butted at her and found her dry he partly wilted. And she saw fury and self-loathing in the way he grimaced and screwed up his eyes to will back the hardness. It was as if the wrong man had come home to her. She gently spat onto her fingers to oil his cockhead, fed him into her and for both of them it was a concentrated, brain-bursting, localised little clinical root, happening far off to someone else. Cameron rolled onto his side away from her afterward, panting, while her skin crawled when his hand landed politely on her bare flank.

He turned over and presently she had felt a tremor that ran through the bed and she was dismayed to hear wretched sobs in his wracked frame, through his cracked voice: 'I'm no good for anything, Jeannie.'

She snaked an arm around his bony trunk and said what one always said: 'Of course you are.'

'I'm not.'

It was an automatic, responsive role and you played it out with family and friends without much thought sometimes. 'You've had a hard time of it but you're home now.'

He seemed to be offended and his body grew prohibitive against hers. 'You don't know the first thing about me.'

'I've known you all my life.'

'You know bugger all,' her husband had said, recoiling from her touch and their history together. 'I'm hungry and thirsty.'

He'd been snacking all day, ravenous, nothing would fill the corners. Jeannie gazed at him, sad to see him so driven and incomplete against the window's moonglow, picturing with sudden clarity the fear he'd felt these past few weeks, his empty insides hungering for nourishment while he ran from the guns. 'Let me fix you a snack.'

'Can't you tell, eh? Can't you? Stop—'

He made as though to claw cobwebs away from his face, 'Stop squashing me.'

'I've never squashed you.'

He went out and didn't return, and in the morning Jeannie had found him in the kitchen with Anneliese, who gazed at her levelly but otherwise was unchanged, while Cam had undergone another metamorphosis, into the sleepy sensualist wreathed in wisps of sunlit tea-steam, lazy and heavy-lidded to see her and pleased enough to smack her rump with slow affection. 'Give us a kiss.'

She had obliged in a friendly way. She'd felt that she'd been freed by him in the night and they could be friends, she the one who understood and tolerated his many faces without necessarily approving of them. She'd become his deeply patient best friend in the night, and thought that Anneliese might even be good for him.

And so a pillow and a roughly folded sheet now sat permanently on the leather couch in Leonard's study, and Cameron was always first in the kitchen in the mornings. If he had fears anymore they were night fears and not Jeannie's responsibility. In fact, a kind of remoteness came over her. Whenever a Japanese reconnaissance aeroplane droned by in the distance, hugging the coastline, she'd watch Cameron watching it, the way he drew nervily on his cigarette. She supposed that his leave would be up soon.

She also found herself speculating about the course of her life with him, chasing the notions to their logical ends. He'd be like poor Dulcie Pearce's husband, she decided. She could hear a man like Frank Pearce explaining to his new wife exactly what would be expected of her: 'You'll be tactful. Never interfere in the work or living quarters of the men, and never visit a mustering camp unless you're invited to or unless I'm with you. Your job is to make the house a haven from worry, provide good food and clean surroundings, treat the gins and yard boys fairly but firmly, and generally be a good mother, sister, nurse and mate.'

And this wife might insist that her house gins wear a uniform. She'd draw back from the edge of the table with a smothered sniff whenever a black arm reached in front of her to collect an empty plate. In running her big house she'd eventually become sharp and unkind, stressing civilised notions, strict control and everyone in his place. But no-one would see what was underneath, a kind of desiccation and despair owing to a life that offered nothing but service to her husband and their children.

As the unvoiced questions accumulated, it occurred to Jeannie that Cameron might not have been granted leave after all—a suspicion that was reinforced late one morning when he suddenly rode off into the scrub just as a Stinson Reliant with RAAF markings landed on the airstrip.

She gave the pilot tea on the verandah. He was delivering a wall chart of Japanese and Allied aircraft silhouettes to each of the inland and coastal stations. He was a joker, this RAAF man. 'Of course, if you know he's a Jap by the rising sun on the fuselage then he's too flaming close.'

They laughed without much humour and sipped their tea as Anneliese idled along the hedgeline tossing kitchen scraps to the hens. The RAAF officer leaned forward a little in his chair. Jeannie weighed it up rapidly: Do the authorities know that I have a part-Javanese woman staying with me? If so, should she be registered with them? Or is the fellow merely taken with her, his brains in his pants like all of them?

'That's Anna, the housegirl.'

'Part Malay, is she? Do you find your Malay half-caste a better worker than your Abo half-caste?'

'Oh, much,' Jeannie said in her new way of slipping in and out of different skins and remaining unremarked by everyone.

Cameron reappeared when the Stinson left. But the visit was prescient, for an hour later a Japanese seaplane made two low passes over the homestead, and Cameron was convinced that the RAAF plane had been spotted landing there. 'That makes us a legitimate target in the eyes of the Japs,' he said. He was badly frightened and twitchy.

It was Anneliese who took his arm. She stood very close to him and tucked her scalp under his jaw, Jeannie tingling to imagine the warm scraping sensation, and feeling bereft for a short, lonely moment. 'We are hiding in the cave,' Anneliese said, gazing at Jeannie from the corner of her eye.

They hurried on bicycle and horseback in a ragged caravan to the gorge, where Cameron said in disbelief, 'Fancy, this old place. Neil would sneak down here after us when we were kids, remember?'

He crawled in, the fear vanishing, and they all followed him into the close animal fug of the main chamber, breathing shallowly and hesitating to touch anything or rest in the dirt. Cameron sneered, 'I never knew what made him tick, did you, Jeannie? Neil, I mean?'

Jeannie gazed around at the figures on the walls and wondered about Neil Quiller's charts with their meticulously captioned fences, sheds, escarpments and washaways, realising that in Neil's mind every map had a secret layer. She felt the need to begin sketching again, and tried to pin it down. Why had she stopped? Because she'd been alone, with no-one hovering, no-one spelling out their expectations of her, that's why. I draw when I'm rubbed against the grain, she thought, rather than for the simple love of drawing.

The hours passed and they grew cramped and irritable. They'd need water soon, and food. Cameron began to chip around a Wandjina figure with his pocketknife. Jeannie hadn't the energy to tell him to stop.

Wally saved them. He suddenly asked Anneliese, 'Tell us about where you come from, love.'

Her big warm eyes brightened and she began to conjure up Java for them, a village, a parish school, volcanoes, and endless greenness and cool green mistiness in the mountains of the interior. They were parched for her stories. Even Cameron listened—surely she was describing a place he knew well even if it had been torn up and had crawled with movement like an itchy scalp.

'The Japs always send in the bombers an hour or two later,' the RAAF officer had said, and so when by mid-afternoon it was apparent that there'd be no raid, they returned to the big house.

Jeannie radioed the incident to the RAAF base in Broome. She'd barely finished and was outside on the path, hunting for a snake she'd spotted through the wireless room window, when she heard their call sign. She went to the back door and shouted into the house, 'Answer that, will you, Cam?'

Presently she heard his murmured voice in the wireless room. The snake had flicked away toward the wood heap and she was about to follow when she was stopped by Cameron saying clearly, 'The man's a spy.'

Jeannie gave up her search and returned to the wireless room, where Cameron was standing with his back to her, drawing the palms of his hands down his cheeks. 'Who was that?' she asked.

He didn't turn around. 'Oh, a policeman wanting information about a bloke I came across in Singapore.'

The Only Light
in the World

Toward the end of the week the wind rose and heavy rain lashed the town. Weston had gone out with his constables for the afternoon, leaving Quiller in the lock-up, but now it was late evening and Quiller was free again, on a stool in the corridor outside his cell, his leg freshly bandaged and a morse code buzzer in his lap. Weston sat across from him with another buzzer, tapping out agonised replies to Quiller's messages.

'SOS, three short, three long, three short, that's about all I'm good for.'

'You'll get the hang of it,' Quiller said.

'I'm tempted to keep you here just so I'll have someone to practice with.'

Through the main door they could see the slanting rain, and then a set of lights, like fearful, watery eyes, began to circle in the storm, low over the city. 'Poor bastard,' Weston said, 'fancy trying to land in this.'

As Quiller watched, a searchlight from the ack-ack battery at the Naval Victualling Yard was turned on, bathing the plane in a slick of light, catching it like a tiny animal of the night. In a storm as dense as this, the searchlight was the only light in the world, and the pilot hugged it for all he was worth. Quiller would have done the same thing, in his shoes. He held his breath, joined in the ordinary, everyday, understandable hazards of flying. For far too long now the only flying he'd seen had been the death-dealing kind, and he'd felt no connection to it. But this—this was a lumbering Qantas Short Empire flying boat, of the old Fremantle–Darwin–Singapore run, and Quiller was flying by the seat of his pants again in those years before the war. He almost loved being back here.

'She's going down!' Weston said.

They waited. The flying boat rose again timorously and came about, low over their heads this time, picking a route across the empty, looted, unlit city to a safe stretch of invisible harbour water. Then it dropped out of sight and the searchlight was extinguished. Quiller and Weston heard nothing above the rushing wind, saw no flame bursts where the flying boat had last been seen, and returned to their morse buzzing.

'One of your constables told me seven Jap bombers were shot down today.'

'A furphy,' Weston said. 'Was it Anderson? He's a notorious furphy spreader. Pay no attention to a thing he says.'

Weston's fingers were jittery on the buzzer. He stopped transmitting and held his hands out, looking curiously at their small ticks and tremors, as though they were unattached objects. 'I'm bomb happy, mate, there's no other word for it.'

'Ask to go on leave.'

'That's a joke. I'm likely to die in the saddle.'

Weston sighed and placed the buzzer on the floor. 'Look, mate, I can't beat about the bush—I finally made contact with your in-laws this afternoon.'

Quiller blinked. 'You did?'

'Courtesy of the Yanks.'

'And?'

Weston wouldn't look at him. 'Your cousin answered. Described you to a T, so I know you're not an imposter.'

Quiller swallowed and his voice cracked. 'Cameron? He was there?'

Weston glanced sidelong at Quiller's cell and raised his voice above the moaning wind. 'He said I should hand you over to the provosts and send you back to England. Said you were a spy, you fed reconnaissance information to the Japs.'

'Oh, for God's sake.'

'Do you see? I can't ignore it. That other business, your relations with Maisie, I'm satisfied it's all nonsense.'

'Well, that's all right then.'

'Don't get narky. I'm sure you're not a spy. If I thought that I'd never have let you out tonight.'

'My cousin's a liar. I held his hand all the way from Singapore to halfway across Sumatra, when he just shot through one night and left me there. Ask Maisie. She'll tell you.'

Weston shifted awkwardly. 'Can't do that just at the moment, old son. We managed to get her on a convoy to Alice Springs this afternoon. She'll be in Adelaide in a couple of days.'

'Bloody hell,' Quiller said. An acute sense of loss settled in him. 'Why would your cousin accuse you of spying?'

'There *was* a spy, in Malaya, a British Army officer attached to air liaison. I told Cameron all about it. He's just using the details.'

'What happened to this spy?'

'He was arrested and court-martialled. I gave evidence against him. He was escorted as far as Padang, where he somehow got away and tried to contact the Japs, who promptly killed him.'

'Will the British authorities here have knowledge of this man?'

Quiller stared bitterly at the needles of rain slanting across the open door to the lockup. 'I wouldn't bet on it. Let me speak to my cousin.'

Weston was in agony, his kind face red, his temple rash standing out painfully on the redness. 'It's official channels from now on, old son, sorry.'

The storm washed the sky clean during the night and the dawn was clear and mild—a good sortie dawn, Quiller thought. Weston left in the Ford to scrounge petrol from the Americans, leaving Quiller a handful of books he'd saved from a torched school. When the air-raid sirens bipped at ten o'clock Quiller thought: They're early today. Twenty minutes later, as Weston parked his Ford on the driveway between the lockup and the house, the all-clear sounded.

Weston appeared red-faced and puffing at the door to Quiller's cell. 'Everything all right? False alarm, I needn't have rushed.'

'What do you care anymore?' Quiller said, and immediately regretted it.

Weston was wounded. 'I'll not have a prisoner locked in a cell during an air raid.'

'I know. Forget I said it.'

Suddenly the sirens wailed again and the ack-ack guns started up. 'Let's have you in the trench, son.'

First there was the howling downrush of bombs, then a moment of silence, and finally the detonations. The first stick landed close, in the next street; their trench seemed to toss with it, and smoke and dust blacked out the sun. After the zips and howls of a second stick of bombs, Weston said 'Daisy cutters', meaning the anti-personnel bombs with their freight of sharp metal scraps. He huddled close to Quiller, and the involuntary twinges of his body distorted the rhythms of his speech. 'Last week two sailors new to Darwin stood out in the open to watch the Kittyhawks go up against the Zeros. A daisycutter cut them to pieces, poor stupid beggars.'

'*You all right, Wes?*' called Jimmy.

Weston stiffened. 'I'd better see to him,' and he disappeared around a distant bend in the trench, calling, '*You all right, Jimmy?*'

Through the crackle of the ack-ack and the howl of aero engines straining to chase and weave in the tight corridors of the sky, Quiller heard the chattering of wing cannons, and looked up. A Kittyhawk had a Zero pinned, sticking to its tail, firing long bursts that seemed to stop the Zero in its tracks. It hung in the sky. Part of a wing broke away, then the rudder, the tip of the tailplane. Finally the crippled fuselage caught fire, turned on its back and fell in a clumsy tumble toward the sea. Quiller blinked. His eyes seemed unable to adjust to shape or size or variations in focal lengths, for he could swear that the smaller pieces of the Zero were following it into the sea, but one piece sliced down like a discus, on an opposed trajectory, coming straight for the trench, and he saw that it was the tail wheel before it hit the ground.

'You all right, Wes? You all right, Jimmy?'

He strained, but heard only some pinging and rattling as tiny stones and air rubbish settled on tin roofs, on last night's mud, on Weston's black Ford.

The Cannibalism
Stopped Her

In his unguarded moments, if he felt himself unobserved, Cam often looked hunted to Jeannie. There was no other word to describe that conjunction of hollowness, dark fatigue and burdened air. But when he sensed her presence, or when she spoke to or worked beside him, he'd veer from being sly and sidling to callous and then abruptly apathetic. If he said that he was no good for anyone or anything, and she demurred, then he'd say that she was too good for him. Or he'd infer that, owing to the terrible things he'd seen and been through, he had carte blanche to trample on everyone's love and goodwill. What's more, the war news had worsened, they were all going to die, so why be constrained by the scruples of an ordered life? He'd sneer and flick an invisible duster when Jeannie cleaned the kitchen, place his hands on Anneliese's haunches in their thin cotton, and harangue Harry Horsetalk around the yard. But underneath it all he was running scared, and ever since the wireless transmission from the policeman he'd had a bee in his bonnet about the Gull.

'She can be repaired, Wally. You've got the tools, the wood, the wire, the scrap metal.'

'Yes.'

'And fuel.'

'Yes, but buried in drums,' Wally said.

'Piece of cake.'

'But she's badly holed,' Jeannie objected. 'The wings and fuselage were torn in the cyclone.'

'So what? We can fix her. I'll show you.'

He took them to the sitting room, to the piano. 'There.'

The calico slip cover on which she'd spent hours with a needle and cotton thread. 'But your mother—'

'Hang my mother.'

Jeannie made him look at her. 'What are you doing, Cam? Are you intending to fly somewhere?'

He shrugged her away. 'I'm bored. And I hate to see something of my father's falling to rack and ruin.'

Which was nonsense. Jeannie watched as he knelt beside the piano and with a violent wrench tore apart one of her carefully sewn seams. He rose, still tearing, following each seam until the calico lay in three irregular sheets on the floor. 'It's not aeroplane fabric,' she said.

Cameron ignored her. 'Wally?'

'It might do. But it won't be tight.'

'Try varnish,' said Cameron carelessly.

The days passed. Wally would come to her, shaking his head. 'Look, gorgeous, Cam doesn't know his arse from his elbow. Can't you keep him occupied for me?'

Wally didn't know that she and Cameron no longer shared a bed. He had no knowledge of how deeply altered her husband was. 'The rudder needs a new leading edge, right?' Wally might say. 'I had the perfect length of timber in the vise, marked up for the spokeshave, and he hacks at it with a chisel.'

Or: 'He just put his foot through the starboard wing.'

And: 'I caught him refuelling this morning.'

Jeannie cocked her head at that. 'I hope he used a filter.'

'Nope.'

Finally: 'He's in a hell of a hurry. Is there something I don't know?'

'Your guess is as good as mine,' Jeannie said. 'Perhaps he wants to ferry us down to Perth.'

Wally pushed back his greasy hat. 'Not me. I'm not going up in the flaming thing.'

• • •

With the ebbing of the wet season the delivery of the mail also improved, and one day there was a letter addressed to Neil Quiller. The envelope bore a Brisbane postmark; a mature and confident hand had written the name and Haarlem Downs' address. Jeannie supposed that she could send it on care of the RAF in England, but who was writing to Neil, and why here, and why now? Something made her hold back from telling Cameron about the letter. She slipped it beneath the unused drawing tablets in her bedside cabinet where it sat for a couple of days and agitated her senses. She felt as drawn to that letter as to the clasp on a treasure chest, and one day opened the flap of the envelope with the steam from the iron kettle.

'Dear Quill,' read the letter. The same firm hand went on to speak of heartsickness, longing and terrible ordeals, Jeannie saw, as she skimmed the first page. She flipped immediately to the last page and read, 'With love, Dorry Barrowman.'

Jeannie returned to the beginning and read more closely, asking herself who Dorry, Primrose and Lee Lin were, and which one Neil was attached to, and whether or not it mattered. And how did this Dorry know Cam? She seemed to be faintly disparaging of him.

And why hadn't Cam mentioned any of these people? Or that he'd escaped with Neil?

She read on:

'We stopped several times to pick up people drifting in lifeboats—troops, civilians, some with shocking burns and wounds. According to the captain we had six hundred on board.

'We were torpedoed before we reached Colombo and sank very quickly. Luckily I was on the upper deck caring for some stretcher cases, and because the other women hadn't let Lee Lin and Primrose have a cabin, they were there too, so the three of us were able to board a raft quite easily. We drifted for a while, then a lifeboat stopped for us. There were more than a hundred people standing in it shoulder to shoulder like sardines, dozens more clinging to the sides.

'Someone threw us a tow line, which angered the people in the lifeboat. We drifted like that for a couple of days, but people were dying or floating away all the time so eventually we were taken from the raft and onto the lifeboat. We didn't have much food or water, and the sun was beating down all the time. I honestly didn't feel much like nursing people, not that I had any medicine or bandages.'

Jeannie turned the page. The cannibalism stopped her: 'To make matters worse, some soldiers took over the bow and started killing people and throwing them overboard. I saw them eat someone. The lifeboat was divided across the middle with the gang in the bow and the rest of us in the stern.

'Soon it was down to about fifteen of us and eight of them. But they were armed and we weren't. God, they were looking at us in a crazy way. One day we just had enough. Primrose was awfully brave. She led us in a rush on them when they were half-asleep and we caught them completely by surprise and disarmed them and pushed a couple of them overboard. The others were quiet after that.

'We were down to twelve when a convoy spotted us. And here I am, in Brisbane! I keep expecting to run into you, given our past history. Primrose is in hospital, but recovering well. I don't know when or if you'll get this letter but she needs help. The immigration people have registered her as an alien under the security regulations, and she'll be allowed to stay as a temporary refugee on humanitarian grounds, but when it's all over she'll be sent back. In a roundabout way what I'm trying to say is, could your family take her in?

'Neil, I've saved the hardest part till last. You will be sad to hear that Lee Lin didn't make it. One morning I counted heads on the lifeboat and she wasn't there. She must have drifted away during the night. She would have gone peacefully, but I suspect she was suffering all along and wanted it to end. Do I sound too remote to you? In fact I'm writing this with tears streaming down my face.'

Jeannie resealed the letter and wondered not so much about whether or not God or fate determined who should live and who should die but about how that decision should be evaluated afterward. Had the right man come back to her? Had Quiller lost the wrong woman? She supposed that wars come down to those sorts of evaluations but who had the right to make them she really couldn't say.

When the Yellow Frog
Released the Waters
of the World

All along the incisions, knobs and scribbles of the Kimberley coast the south-easterlies were blowing. At each stop the Qantas pilot would make a broad sweep out to sea and come in on a north-westerly bearing, into the wind, finally touching the belly of the flying boat onto still water close to shore. Early April, the beginning of the dry season, the monsoon cloudstacks a memory, the Bonaparte Archipelago and the Lacepede Islands sharp against the sun-glistening sea. Quiller knew where he was at last: the well-watered mountains inland of the coast, then the hard, hot basalt; the long, empty beaches that shelved into the oyster beds beneath the Indian Ocean; the mangroves and mudflats of the coastal settlements; the forty-foot tides; the scrubland and stony inland along the Dampier Peninsula. He trembled with anticipation to see the horseshoe cup of Roebuck Bay at last, the long jetty on its wooden piles and the tin roofs of Broome.

But something was wrong. Black shapes were humped here and there in the bay like the carcasses of giant seabirds and whales. As the flying boat broke the oil-filmed water and aquaplaned and settled into a furious wallow, Quiller realised that he was looking at the graveyard of the Catalinas and Dorniers trapped by the

Japanese raiders on 3 March. He looked beyond the waterline at the town. It was still intact.

The tide was high. The pilot coasted toward the jetty and tied up for refuelling. 'Make sure you're back here in thirty minutes,' he said.

A handful of American airmen got out with their kit, followed by Quiller and a couple of civilians. The Americans were staying on in Broome; Quiller had travel documents that would take him as far as Fremantle. He'd found the blank forms in Weston's desk and the rubber stamp to make it official. He'd driven Weston's spot-dented Ford to the harbour, where he tracked down the flying boat pilot and begged a ride.

He wandered now down the jetty toward the strip of flat tin buildings and pearlers' bungalows that described the seaward edge of the town. There were no women about, only a few sailors, airmen and locals too old for military service, but even a few men can put up a wall of suspicion. Quiller looked reasonably fit. He wasn't in uniform. He might have been another Dutchman taking them all for granted.

When the two civilian passengers turned around and headed back along the jetty to the flying boat, Quiller stayed where he was. Haarlem Downs was so close now. He shaded his eyes and peered toward the flying boat, hoping there'd be no hullabaloo. The pilot looked anxious to claw back into the sky. He'd know he was a sitting duck there on the water. The other passengers boarded. The pilot cast off and the flying boat began to drift away from the jetty into deeper water. That's when Quiller shrugged Weston's haversack onto his back and set off on the start of the final stage.

Broome had been reduced to a village on a war footing and he was a stranger in it. He wouldn't be stealing a vehicle, not that he'd find any fuel for one if he did. Everything was rationed and he had no coupons. And he learnt that the Wet had been vicious this time around, filled with cyclonic winds and bucketing rains that had washed roads away and left boggy lakes on the flats. He knew all about the washaways and the mud, how weeks could go by before you'd venture out in a car.

He walked to the humpies on the southern outskirts of

Broome. Most of the people had been trucked away to the missions, leaving a few desert blacks and islanders who'd slipped the net and were generally tolerated by the authorities because they asked for nothing and kept the pubs and military messes supplied with fish. A few old men and women watched him materialise from out of the heat haze, his face dark and narrow under a slouch hat, his boots raising puffs of dust.

'You a crazy fella,' they called after him.

Quiller stopped when he reached a circle of old men under a boab tree. 'I want to buy a bicycle.'

They cocked their heads at him. He could see a few wrecked bikes among the humpies: spokes bent, tyre rubber perished, saddles worn through and crooked, chains broken. The men conferred in murmurs. One said finally, 'You mean a two-wheeler, boss? Pushbike?'

'That's right. How much?'

'How much you got?'

'Three quid.'

That was a huge joke, either because it was too little or far too much. Quiller cut them off. 'Add some tinned food, waterbags, tea, sugar, matches and a billy-can and I'll make it *five* quid.'

He had seven guineas in his pocket.

One man got up. 'Orright, boss.'

The others fell back to talking. Quiller was led to a substantial huddle of corrugated-iron roofs and walls, as though one simple shelter had spread in fits and starts over the years. The dirt was swept clean. Shirts and trousers flapped stiffly on a railing fence. One opening of the main structure was sheeted with a bolt of tarpaulin and, twitching it aside, the old man beckoned. 'How about this one here, boss?'

Quiller snorted. It was a Japanese machine, untidy but rugged and intact. Before the war it was said that anything Japanese would fall apart, but now the world knew how wrong that was.

'Him no good, boss?'

Quiller wheeled the bicycle up and down experimentally, then swung into the saddle. The tyres needed air, there was no tool kit, but it free-wheeled satisfactorily, the brakes worked and the spokes and forks were straight. 'Pump up the tyres and find me a couple of spanners and patches and it's a deal.'

'Orright, boss. Where you goin', boss?'

Quiller pointed. 'Down the coast.'

The old man nodded, then grinned. 'Hubert Opperman, eh?'

Quiller grinned back. He'd been at Haarlem Downs the year that Hubert Opperman had ridden from Albany to Perth, 251 miles, in twelve hours and thirty-eight minutes. 'Just about,' he said.

He examined the tyres. They were Dunlop Olympics; he'd had them at Haarlem Downs. They were suited to heavy conditions.

'Need anything else, boss?'

'The other things I mentioned. Also a tarp, big enough to sleep on or shelter under, and some tarpaulin scraps to tie around my legs.'

'That be another ten shillings, boss.'

'All right.'

Thirty minutes later, Quiller was wrapping broad strips of tarpaulin around his lower legs to protect them from thorns and snakebite. Some of his old lost vocabulary came back to him. One of the first things Wally Webb had said to him was, 'You want to protect them lily-white legs of yours from double-gee, son.' According to a reference book in Uncle Leonard's study, the Latin name was *Emex australis*. There were other thorns: prickly jacks, three-cornered jacks, bindy-eye. The blacksmith had also once helped rig up a burr scraper for the tyres, but that wasn't an option today.

Quiller packed the food into his haversack and hung the waterbags, billy and groundsheet from the saddle and the frame. There should be water along the track; otherwise evaporation and thirst would exhaust his supply before nightfall.

'The boss want something for the missus?'

Quiller straightened his back. The old man's manner had turned sly and confidential. 'Not married.'

'Fiancée? Girlfriend? Sister, maybe?'

Quiller was intrigued. 'Possibly. What about it?'

The old man fished a tobacco tin from his gappy trousers. 'Here, look.' His fingernails—split, worn and yellowed like talons—prised open the lid. 'See?'

A tumble of unset diamonds in a bed of petticoat lace caught the light in brilliant red and blue refractions. Quiller gaped. 'Are they real?'

The old man shrugged. 'They scratch glass, boss, too bloody right about that.'

'Where did you get them?'

'An old blackfella. Wanted smokes for 'em.'

'Where did he get them?'

The old man waved imprecisely toward the south. 'This is an old blackfella come walking out of the bush with a couple of gins. Don't speak much English, boss.'

'He gave you no explanation?'

'Said a lady came out of the sea and he took her to a whitefella's house.'

Quiller was bewitched. 'I'm almost flat broke.'

The old man inclined his head at Quiller's neck. 'You got a nice looking ring there.'

Quiller's hand flew involuntarily to his neck. 'My mother's ring. I couldn't possibly—'

The old man shrugged, snapped the lid and the tin disappeared into his pocket.

Quiller looked at him. 'You be careful who you show those to.'

The old man winked. 'I'm not in a hurry, boss.'

Quiller laughed and mounted the bicycle. 'Not in a hurry now that you've skinned me.'

He set out. There were no signposts; they'd all been taken down to fool the enemy. Where the track was clean, Quiller coasted, enjoying dry heat and the pumping of his legs, and where it was chopped about by washaways, hardened mud ruts, bulldust and bone-jarring corrugations and stones, he used the sheep and cattle pads that wound blindly through the scrub on either side. He remembered his first year on Haarlem Downs: the silence in his ears, his passage through the air, his steady panting and the tyres biting.

Other things came back to him. By the time he was fourteen he'd formulated a defence of the bicycle, a private argument designed to knock Cameron off his perch. So the horseman hates the pushbike man? But the pushbike can do what a horse can do—mustering, checking windmills, bore maintenance, hunting, prospecting, getting from A to B—*without* needing food, water or rest. Pushbikes are not wearied by heat or by drought. They don't shy away from shadows. They're low and silent. Any blacksmith can weld or straighten a damaged fork but he can't mend bones, the gripe or sand blindness. You can hoist a pushbike over your shoulder but you can't carry a horse.

The pushbike helped open up the interior. Your travelling dentist, tinker, shearer, seed man, insurance salesman, bush lawyer and union man all travelled by pushbike.

Quiller added now: And, from all that I have seen, I can say that the pushbike is winning the war.

He dismounted to drink from one of the waterbags, the water tasting of metal, dust and jute. Perhaps he should rest and ride at night; but then he remembered that he had no lights. Without lights he'd never distinguish the tip of a stump, root or boulder from a moon shadow. He could easily collapse his forks and die of a blow to the head, riding at night.

During the afternoon a set of raspy squeaks, of metal rubbing dryly against metal, settled in Quiller's bicycle. He began swivel-necking across the stony ridges and thorny flats for a glimpse of the silvery vanes of a windmill. The sun was low in the west, probably sizzling in the Indian Ocean, when he finally saw a flash of silver to his left. This was as good a time as any to set camp.

He woke often in the night, shivering violently, densely cold. The fire had gone out and at dawn his fingers could scarcely put another fire together. He boiled the billy, crouching over the coals, letting sugary tea heat his insides, his hands tight around his tin cup. Another cupful washed down a tin of bully beef. Now he had the strength to climb the windmill tower, scrape the excess grease from the bearings and grease nipples, and pack it around the chain and hubs of his bicycle. A few minutes later, he vomited. He touched his forehead. The sun? His blood? He was hot, anyway.

He filled the waterbags. He'd come far, as he gauged it. He had far to go.

Quiller rode on, passing in and out of dreams. He was hot and cold; steel bands tightened around his skull. He wanted only to dream, but the desert intruded: two snakes copulating in a tight dazed coil; a buried stump that spilled him into a thornbush; two punctures.

The second puncture shredded the inner tube. He pulled it out, saw that he couldn't mend it, and tossed it aside, then changed his mind. Anything was valuable, anything at all. That was an important lesson of his past few weeks. If he encountered Japs he could fashion the rubber into a catapult—'shanghai', another old word—and crack their winking spectacles with stones. He crammed the inner tube into his haversack, the rubber as plump, pliant, warm and lively as a human organ.

The grass here was wiry new growth, impossible to tear, so he used the lid of a soup tin as a blade, slashing at the tussocks until he'd gathered an armful of stalks. The action exhausted him. He drank, vomited again and sat, dazed, willing his senses to return.

He packed each tyre casing with the grass, his fingers coming away torn and bloody. He mounted, wobbled down along a cattle pad. The tyre seemed to hold, so he fell into dreaming again, and lost his faith ...

His pilots' guide was a lie, a failure of language and spirit. He should have stressed to everyone that the desert which slipped by beneath the cockpit can exact a penalty. That size is not liberating but claustrophobic. That when you put down on a deserted road or beach ahead of a darkening sky, evening comes on rapidly, bringing whispers and rustling and deep, moonshot shadows. That an escarpment is more than an escarpment: it's ancient; there are secrets locked inside it; it's full of malign intent.

Dunes fold into dunes in the north-west, savannah into savannah, in meaningless, hypnotic multiples. Nothing is particular. All you can see are the merging shades of a continuous terrain, like the rust on an old ploughshare varying between pitting and mere discolouration. But Quiller had made the wastes particular, grafting vital features onto empty tracts of land: 'creek bed', 'stony plateau' and 'stand of acacias'. In fact, some of that land was so empty that you'd write it into mythology as the final resting place of all the things that vanish in life.

And sometimes he'd simply looked over the side of the cockpit and read other people's memories. Surveyors and settlers had been there before him. He'd had the advantage—where they'd strained to find reference points, he'd had plenty of man-made objects, such as fences, iron roofs and roads—but he'd also been stuck with their frustrations, disappointments and lickspittling. How could he rename Mistake Creek, Point Torment or Prince Regent River when they were already marked on the maps? And what did Warrawagine mean? Beautiful river? Good tucker? The place where the serpent coils asleep? The first cattleman's approximation of the local expression for 'We don't want you here'?

What Quiller wanted to do now was reshape and re-imagine. Here Cameron and Jeannie quarrelled. There Cam and Jeannie bellowed songs from Gilbert and Sullivan while I repaired the magneto.

But there were other memories layered beneath his. Take that bay near Cape Levêque. One day in 1938 he'd put down on the last narrow strip of sand left by a king tide. A decade earlier, Japanese pearlers had raped and murdered four black women there. Before that a French sea captain had named it for his patron in Versailles. A Dutch merchant ship anchored there in 1634, a Portuguese caravel in 1540. Sailors from Timor had always fished it for trepang and traded with the local tribes. Down, down the centuries, to the beginning, when the Yellow Frog released the waters of the world from its belly ...

The sun beat down and Quiller's straw tyre shredded. The bands tightened around his skull. He'd been imagining the north-west even as he'd lived in it. The imagined coast, desert and savannah constituted the better place but, in being imagined, it shapeslipped and dissolved. He'd never been able to reach it, yet it was where he lived. He'd been bound to the earth—he'd never soared—and the world was flat, without curvature.

Now there was a trooper on horseback peering down at him, and black men in chains, shimmering, shimmering, filling in the gaps in his dreaming.

The Whip, the Boot
and the Hunting Rifle

When the Aborigines of Broome were evacuated to the Beagle Bay Mission station, one had been discovered suffering from the early stages of leprosy and three of the gins had the venereal disease, granuloma. Granuloma resembles leprosy in the early stages and so a mild flap ensued. Even if the gins had caught the disease from Asians in the pearling industry and not from white men, as was argued by Trooper Dalvean's sergeant in the Northwest Mounted Police, no-one wanted the granuloma to pass the other way, from infected gins to lonely, depraved or crack-brained pastoralists, lugger captains, beachcombers, soldiers and airmen. And no-one wanted an outbreak of leprosy.

'And another thing, Dal,' Sergeant Clark said. 'When you're around Abos, sound them out about the Japs. Do they seem pro-Jap? Been meeting Jap infiltrators or scouting parties? Likely to roll out the welcome map for them? One option being mentioned is rounding them all up and putting down the troublemakers.'

Dalvean nodded.

'Finally, see if there's anything in this diamond story,' his sergeant said.

All this under the cover of a routine leper patrol.

And so Dalvean plotted a zigzagging route that took in the coastal and inland sheep and cattle properties, missions, camps and one or two islands—over two thousand miles in all. At thirty-odd miles a day, give or take, with time to rest, chase escapees, refit and hunt down those other leads for Sergeant Clark, he should be back in three or four months' time. Just as well the Dry had started.

Then he put his police plant together: four horses, ten pack mules and plenty of stores, including manacles and chains. His horse was the big grey. Biscuit, Christmas and Slinger, the native police trackers, rode the smaller bays.

They pushed inland and then south for two days, covering seventy miles, and reached Lorna Plains homestead in time for the blacksmith to reshoe one of the mules. Rather than camp at the homestead and eat with the manager, Dalvean took his team to a watercourse near one of the mustering camps. The manager of Lorna Plains was always hospitable, even good company, but had once offered Dalvean some black velvet for the night and had a tendency to invent charges against his cheekier hands, just to be rid of them, knowing that Dalvean would be obliged to arrest them and remove them from the property. This was a leper patrol and Dalvean hadn't the time or energy to move a chain of fit, cheeky Abos around the countryside. Invariably they were wily and resentful, tried to escape, were distressed to be leaving their tribal country, or found themselves shackled to a man from a hostile country.

Most of the stations were mustering now, checking on stock numbers and condition after the long shut-down of the wet season. Wherever the stockmen went bush blacks would follow, always camping a mile or two from the mustering camp. Some of the bush blacks were related to the stockmen and all relied on them for food scraps.

According to the manager, his head stockman had reported seeing one leprous gin in the blacks' camp, and Dalvean, Christmas, Biscuit and Slinger surrounded and raided it at dawn. There were a dozen men, women and children lying in the dust around a dead camp fire like crooked radial spokes around a wheel hub. They looked wretched, ill, half-starved, mucousy, frightened and lethargic—and no wonder, for a stockman's diet consisted of bulk and starch, low in goodness, and the camp followers had the leavings of it. A young man cheeky enough and in his prime could kill a cow or sheep and eat well on it, first disguising the carcass as a dingo kill, or hook vegetables, tinned soup or bags of flour out through the cat door of the station store—but the youngsters in this camp were not in their prime.

'All about be still now,' Dalvean ordered, and he went from one to the other, looking for symptoms of leprosy and granuloma. Sure enough, one of the gins was leprous, fairly advanced too, but fit enough to travel. And the gin's son had the early stages of the disease. Their names in English were Sally and Mick, and Dalvean chained them together at the neck. They could walk for a while, ride a pack mule for a while—he'd ensure they got plenty of rest.

That left the dogs, at least twenty of them, half wild, half dingo, all ribs and prick, but treasured by these blacks who had nothing else to treasure. Dalvean shut out the wails as he began to cull the pack with his .22 rifle, starting with the oldest and mangiest, until there were a dozen left, about one per Abo, which was about right. He always did this as a favour to a station manager, for the natives' dogs were under-fed and liable to kill calves and lambs and breed with the dingoes.

Another wail went up when he led Sally and Mick away in chains. Dalvean had his doubts about rounding up lepers. True, it protected the healthy Abos by isolating the sick ones in the Derby leprosarium, where they were cared for by a doctor and nurses, and it cut down on the chances of the disease crossing the colour bar, but Jesus, what a fate. They were shoved together regardless of tribe or country, some transported hundreds of miles to a place where they were washed, dressed, poked, prodded, injected, bandaged and smothered with ointments day after day. As far as they were concerned they'd been taken to Derby to die. Some escaped, and it was Dalvean's job to track them down again, but many simply let themselves wither away into eventual death. Dalvean had heard them crying listlessly and monotonously as the disease intensified and fear and loneliness got them, while others stood at the fence and looked out to where their countries and ancestors lay. At night there would be makeshift corroborees and camp-fire dances, often with only one or two people left alive to represent a particular tribe or district, often with most people swaying on their hands and beating the dirt with a bunch of leaves because they were too weak and wasted away to stand. Dalvean did what he could, delivering message sticks, distributing surplus supplies and taking good care of his prisoners—if they were close to death he didn't bring them in; if they were too ill to travel he arranged for them to be trucked to Derby—but sometimes he thought it would be best to let the wretches breed themselves out.

They made dawn raids at another three camps that week and now Dalvean had four bush blacks in chains, all lepers. He also examined and approved the new airstrip at Jerusalem Hill and wasted a day tracking three myalls who had been harassing the station blacks and the bush blacks at Manna Gap. He was in terrible country now, mostly treeless, the sun beating back from the red rocks and hard-baked ground, country where half-wild men raised half-wild stock and lived by the whip, the boot and the hunting rifle. There were no proper homesteads out there, no women to put a homely touch to the canvas and corrugated-iron shacks or insist on decent houses and standards. The stockmen Dalvean saw were never paid and were issued only one set of clothing at a time, which meant they were always dirty and thought to be no better than scavenging dogs. They ate with their hands and drank from rusty tins.

He'd been on the track for some time now and word had got out, the bush blacks making themselves scarce. It was easy to out-think them—Dalvean simply went back a few days later, by which time they'd emerged from the secret gullies, not expecting a follow-up raid. One evening a gin named Eliza complained of stomach ache and Christmas unchained her—justifying it to Dalvean later as 'Him pretty crook gin, boss'—and she ran off. Dalvean smacked Christmas about the legs with his riding crop then rode after Eliza, capturing her before nightfall could blanket the desert and shift everything around and play tricks on his eyes. Once, a few years earlier, he'd had to track an escapee across hundreds of miles of open country and finally offshore to a tiny island—but Eliza's toes were mostly gone and she had no speed in her.

It was a relief to get back to the stations along the coast. Even if they were separated by huge distances there was the ocean on which to rest his eyes and ears and often there was a healing wind. As they filed along a sheep pad in view of the Eighty Mile Beach, it occurred to Dalvean that he hadn't been monitoring the Abos for Jap sentiments. Well, he wasn't about to start. The bush blacks were too ignorant or frightened to welcome infiltrators or saboteurs, and the station blacks were flat out with the mustering, every station short-handed now, owing to the war.

Dalvean's next stop was Somme Brae. The Pearces had a history of lepers. The absentee leaseholder was an English aristocrat who expected his managers to thrash the guts out of his estates in Argentina and northern Australia. If lepers appeared, no attempt was made to report or care for them. 'That's the job of the mounted police,' was Frank Pearce's attitude.

Dalvean had friends on the Derby waterfront and in the Australian Workers' Union. They were turning him bit by bit to their views and he'd sent half of his last pay to the people of Stalingrad.

The sea was dead calm today, almost milky, with a few big, half-hearted, late wet-season clouds well to the north-west. Now that he was on the coast he thought that he'd better look into the story of the reappearing diamonds. A Koepanger deckhand had paid for a drink in the Roebuck Arms in Broome with a diamond as big as a threepenny bit. A Chinese tailor had tried to pay a fine at the courthouse in Port Hedland with two diamonds in a matchbox. More diamonds were found in a pill bottle in his bathroom cabinet. The tailor said that he'd been paid in diamonds by an Aboriginal man who wanted a wedding suit, of all things. Neither the Abo nor the Koepanger could be found. Then a gin had been discovered in the drunks' cell in Derby wearing a massive diamond in a twist of electrical wire around her neck. She claimed that her man had given it to her. He'd been wandering in the bush and come upon a woman who was lost. He'd seen an aeroplane crash on the beach earlier, and assumed the woman had been a survivor. In return for taking her to a white man's house somewhere along the coast, she'd given him a few pretty bits of glass wrapped in tissue paper.

The CIB was called, the crashed plane located, and the providence of the diamonds was investigated. Apparently they'd originated in Amsterdam but were flown to the Indies on the eve on the German occupation of Holland in May 1940. Dozens of stones, £300 000 worth. Then, just before the invasion of Java a few weeks ago, the stones were despatched with a Dutch Treasury official to Australia for safekeeping by the Commonwealth Bank. The CIB detectives had been told to look for a briefcase concealing a package the size of a cigar box, wrapped innocuously in paper but sealed with string and wax. They'd searched the wreckage and found the paper, the string and the torn wax seals, but not the diamonds or the briefcase. It was impossible to tell, from the general state of the crippled airliner, whether or not the package had broken or been torn open. Some larger items of luggage were strewn about the fuselage. There were no signs of life.

But then the detectives had been obliged to hand the investigation over to the local police, their hands full with more pressing matters, including the security problem posed by the refugees and the formation of a Western Australian branch of the fascist Australia First Movement. Dalvean shrugged inwardly as his horse picked its way along the stock pads. If the mysterious woman had existed, and had taken the diamonds with her, was she still somewhere along the coast? More to the point, was she still alive? Perhaps there was no woman and the wandering Abo—or some beachcomber and his lugger crew—had come upon the wreckage and stripped it of everything. Whatever the truth, the diamonds were being passed from man to man and man to woman all along the Kimberley coast like snippets of gossip.

Just then Slinger, at the head of the shuffling column, came riding back, saying, 'Boss, boss, bin findem dead whitefella on the track.'

A Starveling Creature

Jeannie let the implications of Dorry Barrowman's letter settle in her for a couple of days, then began to niggle and probe. In the act of passing Cameron the sugar at morning tea she might ask about the night life in Singapore, or chatter about Neil Quiller while helping to repair the Gull.

'I wonder if he's still in England?'

But Cameron would only shrug or mutter, a man with other things on his mind.

One morning, about a week later, Jeannie was freshening the VH-U registration number on the fuselage with black paint when she glanced through the hangar doors and thought: It's one apparition after another. The first had been Anneliese staggering across the yard, then the Dutch women and children emerging from their crashed Lockheed, then Cameron, and now this. The others had seen it, too. Anneliese, dressed in shorts and a shirt tied up beneath her breasts, was chewing an apple and sticking, in her lazy, sleepy way, close to Cameron. Cam was treating a calico wing patch with varnish. Wally was adjusting an aileron cable. He straightened wearily and joined Jeannie at the door. 'Leper patrol.'

317

'We haven't got any lepers,' Cameron said. He'd grown withholding and still, and Anneliese, reading his mood, stepped into the shadows at the rear of the hangar.

Jeannie watched as the patrol stepped in pain and weariness from the belt of acacias, onto and along the airstrip, finally drawing adjacent to the hangar but failing, in their dogged way, to notice them there. Trooper Dalvean and a native policeman on horseback were at the head of the column, leading four Aborigines in neck chains, one of whom hobbled as though on burning coals. Two native policemen took up the rear, leading pack mules. The saddle leather creaked, bundled loads heaved, hooves puffed in the dirt, bridle rings tinkled and tails swished away the flies, but otherwise the patrol was soundless and measured, as though it might walk on forever.

Then it was clear that one of the pack mules was carrying a man, and that he'd been roped on.

'Hello,' Jeannie shouted. 'Over here.'

Dalvean glanced around, saw her and raised his hand to alert the others. Then he tugged the reins and slowly the animals and the policemen and their prisoners wheeled about and trailed behind him, uncoiling like a long rope in the dirt, until he called a halt at the doors of the hangar. He dismounted, wiping his face with a neckerchief.

'We found a man back there. He needs a doctor. Biscuit!'

A native policeman brought the mule forward. The man tied to it was skin and bone, ravaged by the sun, unshaven, grimy. But Jeannie, rushing to help the trooper undo the straps that bound him to the pack saddle, mentally cleared away the beard, put flesh on the bony face and took away the years, and said, 'It's Neil Quiller.'

They carried him to the big house, where Jeannie spread half-a-dozen towels across Crystal's bed and sponged him clean, noting the condition of his body. His legs were cratered with tropical ulcers—one of them still weeping—he'd been bitten by insects and he had the hollow, bowed look of a starveling creature. She moistened his swollen tongue with water from a rubber teat until he coughed and tossed his head from side to side. 'The Gull,' he said, his eyes fluttering.

Jeannie leaned over him. 'Neil? It's all right. You're home.'

Dalvean was looking on. 'Gull? He'd written Gull in the dirt.'

'It's the name of our aeroplane,' Jeannie said, 'but God knows why he's saying it.'

When Neil was settled she went to the wireless room with Dalvean. Through the window she could see the native policemen and the four lepers resting under the laundry trellis vine. They had water and food but looked bone tired, occasionally clawing the flies from the sockets of their eyes. She contacted the doctor, who said he'd come before nightfall, but if he was late she was to light flares to guide him in. Then while Dalvean reported to his sergeant, she returned to Crystal's room, Neil's condition uppermost in her mind now, a singular imperative driving all of the clutter from her head.

Anneliese was there, fanning him with a hand towel.

'Let me do that.'

Anneliese bobbed shyly and headed out of the room, colliding with Dalvean in the corridor. 'Sorry,' she said, ducking around him.

He watched her go, then entered the room. 'How's our patient?'

'He'll make it,' Jeannie said. 'What did your sergeant say?'

'I'm to continue with the patrol. I'll soon be out of your hair.'

With great reluctance, Jeannie offered him tea and took him through to the kitchen, where the kettle was shunting softly on the range. 'Let's take it outside,' she said, leading him to the deckchairs on the verandah.

She asked Dalvean about his work, the fate of his prisoners, and finding Quiller on the track. Apparently Quiller had been riding a bicycle, probably from Broome. Jeannie reeled. Memories and emotions were piling up in her today, all of them vivid and taking her breath away. Neil on his bicycle. It was an effort for her to pay attention to Dalvean.

And then she could hear Cameron in her head—Cameron in the radio room several days ago, saying: 'The man's a spy.'

She gathered herself and told Dalvean that Quiller had been serving with the RAF in Malaya and Singapore. 'He must have escaped before the surrender.'

Dalvean nodded slowly. 'But where and when did he arrive, how did he arrive, and why did he come all the way out here?'

Jeannie grew very still. If Dalvean pursued these questions, he would find that Cameron's hand had been at work somewhere in the background—she was certain of it. She was anxious for the policeman to leave. 'Neil grew up here,' she replied.

Dalvean watched her. Then he said: 'A few weeks ago a Dutch plane crashed along the coast. Apparently there was one survivor, a woman. You wouldn't know anything about that, I suppose?'

He's after Anneliese as well? Jeannie wanted to draw shutters around herself and the ones she loved. 'I'm afraid not.'

'That young woman I saw just now.'

'Yes?'

'Who is she?'

Jeannie swallowed her tea. 'She's a refugee from Java. She was on a Dutch plane that crash landed here last month. Right there, on the airstrip.'

Dalvean looked. 'Where is the plane now?'

'We towed it into the bush and destroyed it, just in case.'

'Who else was on board?'

'The pilot and co-pilot and several women and children. The Air Force evacuated them a couple of weeks later.'

'Your young woman didn't go with them?'

'She was too ill at the time.'

I'm making a poor fist of this, Jeannie thought, hating the way that Dalvean gazed at her, a pure sceptic.

'Perhaps I could have a word with her,' he said. 'There's the matter of her immigration status if nothing else.'

Jeannie had heard Anneliese just now, somewhere nearby, perhaps at a door or window. The house was always bone-creaking along the roof beams as the heat built up, but there had been a suggestion of a footfall, a bare sole flexing, and of fingernails scratching in consternation. Was Anneliese haunting the corners, listening, her thighs brushing the wall plaster? Jeannie glanced over the verandah rail at the airstrip. Cameron was pushing the Gull out into the sun. Why? Everyone around her wanted answers or reassurance, she thought, but why were they relying on *her*?

She faced Dalvean mildly and sipped her tea. 'As soon as she's ready to travel we'll arrange for the Air Force to come and pick her up.'

'Nevertheless, if I could have a word with her?'

'I'm afraid she doesn't speak English.'

'She spoke it just now.'

'Not very well, I mean.'

Dalvean said nothing. He watched and waited. 'Please don't tire her,' Jeannie said, a little desperately.

He shook his head.

Hoping that Anneliese had her wits about her, Jeannie went through the French doors into Leonard's study and across to the hallway door, calling, 'Anneliese? May I have a moment?'

When there was no answer she searched the rest of the house. She returned to Dalvean. 'I'm afraid—'

Dalvean was standing at the edge of the verandah. He tossed the dregs of his tea over the railing and said, 'Wait here, please.'

Jeannie leaned out. The door of the Gull was open, Cam reaching an arm out to Anneliese, who had clambered onto the wing with her briefcase. The door closed on them. Jeannie saw a puff of exhaust smoke. A moment later she heard the motor belch into life.

EPILOGUE

Haarlem Downs, Christmas 1947

A Kind of
Melancholy Sense

'**H**ere are the wild woods. Look. *You're not looking.*'

Quiller glances briefly away from the greasy track. 'I see.'

'You can't go in them. It's too dangerous. You have to stay on the road. Here you turn left and here you turn right.'

'Is there a railway line?'

'No railway line.'

'A lake?'

'No lake.'

'A bridge? All maps should have a bridge in them.'

The child contemplates the notebook in her lap, the intricate pencilled shapes reproducing one another like contour lines, and with blithe flicks of the lead tip indicates a waterway and a path across it. She is almost five and likes to be helpful and accommodating. She is also a chatterbox, but an antidote to the sour stranger in the back of the car.

Quiller's third passenger is Wally Webb, seated on the front seat on the other side of the child and apparently asleep, his old, seamed, wattled head against the window. It's understood that he's there to protect Quiller—and protect the child, who'd staged a tantrum and insisted on coming too, just as they were leaving

Haarlem Downs. Quiller glances out of his side window at the treeless basalt flats, saltpans and far-off escarpments swimming above mirage lakes, imagining his murder at the hands of the man in the back seat, the scouring winds one day unearthing his bones, his knife-knicked ribcage attracting the interest of the troopers, the Packard long gone and far away, sold for a few quid in Sydney.

But not with Wally Webb along for protection, Jeannie's idea, expressed *sotto voce* at lunchtime, as soon as the decision to pay off the stranger and get rid of him had been made. The fellow had wanted Quiller to take him all the way to Broome or Hedland, he wasn't fussy, but Jeannie had turned her scarifying tongue on him, telling him not to push his luck. She'd rung around; the cook and the storeman on Anna Plains were making a run into Hedland for Christmas supplies and he could jolly well hitch a ride with them.

'Quill!' the child says. 'Look, are you looking!'

'Yes, love.'

She has Jeannie's olive colouring and Cameron's long boniness, but now, confined between Wally and Quiller on the airless front seat, she seems soft, limp, hot-cheeked. Her flank and arm are pressed warmly, judderingly against Quiller's, and she's starting to give in to deep, racking yawns.

'You have to stay on this side of the mountains,' she says, yawning then blinking her eyes.

'I will.'

'There are things on the other side. Scary things. Nobody must go there.'

'I understand.'

'Are we to Anna Plains yet?'

'Another hour or so.'

'Want me to draw our Christmas tree?'

'Yes, please.'

Presently she topples sideways, her head landing like thistledown on Wally's lap, as though in unconsciousness she'd known it was there. He, equally unconsciously, places his big slab-like palm on her hip, and she draws her legs up onto the seat, soon digging her hot bare feet into Quiller's thigh.

Behind them the stranger has scarcely moved. Whenever Quiller glances at the mirror, the narrow, contentious face is always there, contemplating the horizon and who knows what dreams and grievances down the years of his life.

He'd walked in off the road that morning, so he'd probably spent the night under the stars. No-one saw him arrive. Maisie, home from her boarding school, was helping Jeannie's daughter to decorate the Christmas tree; Wally and Harry were in the storeroom; and Quiller and Jeannie were in Leonard's old study, drafting a letter of appeal to the Department of Immigration, which had issued Primrose with a deportation notice. 'Her father was British,' Quiller was writing, 'her family's dead, she has no roots in Singapore, she's become a useful member of the community, she's a qualified nurse ...' He was about to add that Primrose had a good job at the hospital in Broome when Maisie had shouted, 'Quill, Jeannie, quick!'

They found her at the sitting-room window, her finger quivering. The precise nature of her jitters made sense to Quiller. The man standing in the yard had the flat, estimating eyes, wasted frame and ragged partial army dress of the deserters on Sumatra.

They'd had the occasional stray wander in from the road in the past two years, harmless men who couldn't adjust to civilian life, but this fellow hadn't lost his way or his luck. There was nothing cap-in-hand about him. He stood there with his hands on his hips and his slouch hat pushed back as though he were weighing the merits of a property he wanted to buy.

They grouped at the verandah rail and looked down at him. Coldly, disparagingly, he returned their gaze. There was no reason to feel any motion of welcome for him.

Finally he'd muttered,' I don't intend to stand here looking up at you.'

So Quiller took the steps down to the yard and faced him off, saying, 'What do you want?'

'Where is he?'

'Who?'

'Cameron Dunn.'

Quiller glanced back at Jeannie. 'Not here.'

'Can you get him for me?'.

'Not possible.'

The man had cocked his head assessingly. It was a cunning face, calculating and ready for tricks, the survival traits of a man who'd suffered from years of privation. 'Where is the bastard?' he demanded. 'I know he got out safely. Who are you? His brother? Is the sheila there his wife? Sister?'

The man moved to pass Quiller and make for the house, but Quiller stayed him, registering how meagre the man's ribs were beneath his greasy coat. There was no physical tone left in him, only memories burning. 'First, why don't you tell me your name.'

'Anderson.'

'What do you want?'

'I want someone to honour this.'

Anderson fished inside the coat and came out with an envelope from the war years, brownish, small, printed with the words CARELESS TALK COSTS LIVES, and inside it was a stained, many-times opened and refolded scrap of paper. Quiller made to take it but Anderson jerked away like a griping child and said, 'No you don't, I'm not letting go of this.' And so Quiller read it standing hard up against Anderson's left arm, reproducing the man, even to the bowed head and shoulders, as though they were mates huddled around a match in a gusting wind.

It was an IOU:

'To Whom It May Concern: Let in be Known that I will Pay Corporal Clifford Anderson the Sum of One Thousand Pounds if he gets me Safely Home to Australia. Dated and Signed: Cameron Dunn, 1 March 1942.'

There was an address at the top, somewhere in Sydney.

'The cunt got out safely, I know he did. I got him from Sumatra to Java on a boat, but then he gave me the slip, got on another boat without telling me. I spent the rest of the war in Changi because of that bastard, while he made it home.'

Anderson flicked at the false address. 'Even then he was trying to put one over on me. Two years I've been tracking him.'

Jeannie had joined them unnoticed, perhaps encouraged by the agitation that had taken the place of rage in Anderson. She put her head on one side and said dryly, 'It's our understanding that he salvaged a plane on Sumatra and flew it to Java.'

Anderson snorted. 'Did he tell you that? No. I got him onto a boat. There were a couple of RAF jokers aboard, that was the closest he came to flying.'

'Just confirming,' Jeannie said. 'Now, what do you want?'

He showed her the letter. 'I want this honoured. If he's not here or if he's kicked the bucket, someone had better pay up, because buggered if I'm leaving here empty-handed.'

Quiller had glanced over Anderson's shoulder to the corner of the air-raid shelter. Wally was there with a rifle. He had a clear field of fire from that position, and he wasn't aiming exactly but he was ready and waiting. 'Anderson, look behind you.'

When Anderson spotted Wally, his contemptuousness came back. 'You can't scare me. You can't get rid of me that easy. I'm not going to fold, or bloody well hurt anyone. I just want what's mine.'

Then his eyes rolled back and he collapsed like a bundle of bones at their feet. Maisie said, 'Oh,' deeply affected and full of pain for him now. She'd been holding Jeannie's child against her, idly bumping her knees against her little spine in big-sister fashion, but the bad old memories overcame her and she turned away. Jeannie bent to touch his forehead and the pulse in his neck. 'No fever. He just needs a few days' rest and some solid meals. Let's get this coat off him.'

Anderson hadn't wanted a few days. He hadn't necessarily wanted a thousand pounds. He'd woken an hour later and eaten a sandwich brought to him in the shade, and when Jeannie handed him a cheque for five hundred pounds he said, 'What's a life worth?'

They had no answer for that.

'How do I know this won't bounce?'

'Because you'd be back here, that's how we know, and we don't want you to come back here.'

'And you deserve it,' Quiller said.

Anderson had seemed satisfied with that, and Quiller, watching him now in the rear-view mirror, knows they won't be hearing from him again. It's just as well that Crystal hadn't been there to hear her boy slandered. She likes to sail up from Perth from time to time to see her grand daughter, but the heat, the empty hangar and the ambiguities of the household are too much for her to contemplate long visits—not to mention Quiller's presence there like the wrong son come home, Quiller who'd recuperated, gained a secondment to the RAAF and come back again at the end of the war. She's abdicating control, and soon it will slip from her entirely because last week a surveyor, out in the desert country, found a Percival Gull lying broken-backed on a windless claypan. A perfectly preserved corpse was at the controls, another in the adjacent seat, and a handful of diamonds rattled around in a tobacco tin on the cockpit floor. A Gull, two corpses, a tin of diamonds. An elegant conjunction of facts, Quiller had thought, when he heard it on the news. And the location made a kind of melancholy sense—an untravelled region of the Gibson Desert between Windy Corner and Lake Disappointment on the Tropic of Capricorn. CIB detectives are bound to look into it, but Quiller's not bothered by the CIB. All that matters is that there had been a time when Cameron Dunn had washed about in his and Jeannie's lives with his unsupportable needs, undoing the sufficiency they'd found for themselves, and now it can be put to rest.

A Note on the Sources

Although *Past the Headlands* is a work of fiction, aspects of it have been inspired by real people and actual events.

The spy, Janeway, is based in part on Captain Patrick Heenan, who provided the Japanese with intelligence on Allied airfields and aircraft in northern Malaya in late 1941. He was later court-martialled, and summarily executed on 13 February 1942, two days before Singapore surrendered to the Japanese. Heenan's story is told in Peter Elphick and Michael Smith, *Odd Man Out* (London, 1993).

The airfields of Bandar Star and Sungei Dungun never existed but are composites of actual wartime airfields in northern Malaya. The precipitous evacuation of Sungei Dungun is based on events at Kota Bharu and Kuantan airfields on 8 and 9 December 1941, as described in Douglas Gillison, *Royal Australian Air Force, 1939–1942* (Canberra, 1962) and Peter Elphick, *Singapore: The Pregnable Fortress. A Study in Deception, Discord and Desertion* (London, 1995).

Elphick's subtitle points to another aspect of the story: the breakdown of military discipline and civilian order in Singapore, and the panicky dockside scenes and escape attempts.

These matters are well documented and may be found in many sources.

For an account of the fate of the 'little ships' that managed to clear Singapore, and of the escape routes across Sumatra ahead of the Japanese occupying forces, see Richard Gough, *The Escape From Singapore* (London, 1987). Hank Nelson's *Prisoners of War: Australians Under Nippon* (Melbourne, 1984) also describes escape attempts in the region.

I drew upon a number of sources for aspects of life in 1930s and wartime Malaya, Singapore, Java and Sumatra, including: Sheila Allan, *Diary of a Girl in Changi, 1941–1945* (Sydney, 1994); H. Gordon Bennett, *Why Singapore Fell* (Sydney, 1944); Albert Coates and Newman Rosenthal, *The Albert Coates Story* (Melbourne, 1977); Ernest Gordon, *Miracle on the River Kwai* (Sydney, 1963); Ann Laura Stoler, *Race and the Education of Desire* (Durham, NC, 1995); Laurens Van Der Post, *The Night of the New Moon* (London, 1971), and Albert Coates, diary, MS 10345, La Trobe Library, Melbourne.

The following published and unpublished sources provided information about life in north-western Australia in the 1930s and early 1940s: Frank Clune, *Roaming Around Australia* (Melbourne, 1947); Ion Idriess, *Forty Fathoms Deep* (Sydney, 1938); Richard Broome, *Aboriginal Australians* (Sydney, 1982); Garry Disher, '"Before the Age of Hurry-up": Australian Landscape Writing, 1925–1950', MA thesis, Monash University, 1978; and Grace Lacey, letter, MS 10114, La Trobe Library, Melbourne.

For aspects of civilian and military aviation of the period, see Douglas Gillison (above) and Edward P. Wixted, *The North-West Aerial Frontier, 1919–1934* (Brisbane, 1985).

The story of the Dutch diamonds is based very loosely on actual events as described in W. H. Tyler, *Flight of Diamonds: The Story of Broome's War and the Carnot Bay Diamonds* (Perth, 1987).

Many books have been written about the bombing of Darwin on 19 February 1942. It's less well known that Darwin endured 64 air-raids between February 1942 and November 1943. For information about life in Darwin in the weeks following the big raid, and the lot of the Darwin police, I am indebted to the unpublished letters of Gordon R. Birt, a police sergeant stationed in Darwin in 1942.